MW00760778

## A NOVEL

*Ashley ShaRee Hathaway*

Amy –
Hope you
love the story as
much as I do. :)
Ashley Hathaway

WHAT ONCE WAS LOST


A. ShaRee Books Publishing



Printed in the United States of America

Cover design by Ashley ShaRee Hathaway

Book edited by Kim Hathaway

1e.6v.20s.7.28.10
ISBN:978-0-578-06422-2

# Acknowledgements

*Back in the day when I was a nerd in high school, I wrote a short story for my English class with delirious excitement. My teacher commended me on my writing, telling me that I should definitely keep it up and that I had potential. Since that day, her words have always stayed with me. No matter what I write or how I do it, I will always know that it was my teacher's belief that got me to do it. So, I want to thank Ms. Baron—the teacher who always wore scarves—for her words of encouragement and for helping me to see that my mind could produce stuff that was actually worth something.*

*I would also like to thank my husband for being so patient with me while I've been reclusively writing, and my mother for helping me fix the words that were "too strong." I appreciate everyone's excitement and enthusiasm in my work and couldn't have done it without your encouragement. I love you all.*

*I hope that you, my dear readers, will enjoy reading my story as much as I enjoyed writing and researching it. The process is truly an amazing one.*

# Chapter One

"OF COURSE SHE DID," GREGORY SAID, roughly slamming his fist on the platform.

The stationmaster jumped back in surprise. "Take it easy there, son," he chuckled. "You could punch a hole clean through my platform with those hands of yours."

Ignoring the man, Gregory turned to his younger brother. "Why didn't we think of this in the first place, Dan? That little vixen is always getting herself into trouble. She must thrive on it. So, while we have been searching for her these many hours, Gwendolyn's just been traveling further and further away."

"At least we know she's alive."

Gregory grunted in frustration as he pinched the bridge of his nose.

What in heaven's name was that woman thinking, he wondered. What would make her just up and leave like that? Didn't she realize how dangerous it was to be traveling alone?

"Did she tell you where she was going, Marshall?" Dan asked.

The stationmaster lifted his oil-streaked cap and scratched at his graying head, appearing puzzled. "She said she was going to Leadville to visit family."

"She's never done that before," Gregory mused aloud before turning his attention back to his brother. "Rebecca's always been the one to come and visit. She was just here. Why would Gwendolyn be going there now?"

Dan shrugged. "It doesn't make much sense to me. I think it's highly possible she's not going there at all."

Although Dan was one year his junior, Gregory could see the wisdom in his words. He hung his head. The price of one train ticket to Leadville would take over a month for a young schoolteacher to earn, and Gwendolyn's sister Rebecca had just visited not two months ago. No, she probably wasn't going to Leadville, but where then? Gwendolyn was a smart young woman, smarter than all the girls her age, and even most of the women in town, for that matter. It was just not like her to do anything without giving it considerable thought first. She had to have some plan, some reason for leaving so hastily.

"Well, what do you think we should do then?" Dan asked.

"I'm going to go looking for her. I won't be getting anything done around here worrying over whether she's all right or not. Damn woman."

"Do you reckon that's a good idea, Greg?" he shifted nervously. "Seems to me she doesn't want to be found."

It didn't matter whether Gwendolyn wanted to be found or not, in his opinion. Everybody in town was worried about her, scouring every house, barn, and building. The people of Grovetown damn well had a right to know what had happened to her!

Gregory growled in protest and seriously considered punching his brother right in the nose.

"Hey, take it easy," Dan said, putting his work-worn hands up in surrender. "All I'm saying is she obviously left without a word or note. She intentionally left town with an unlikely cover story, which she had to have known we'd find out when we came looking for her. She gave no hint of her real whereabouts or any indication of ever returning. She obviously doesn't want anyone to come after her. You'd spend your entire savings trying to find her, especially if she transferred onto another train. Perhaps she wants us to think she's dead…maybe."

Gregory fumed indignantly. He didn't want to openly admit he'd been thinking along the same lines, but it just didn't seem right that Gwendolyn would do such an outrageous thing. She had never been so irrational. Something definitely did not smell right.

He roughly grabbed a schedule from the platform before exiting the men's waiting area with his brother in tow. "We will have Mrs. Mathewson send Rebecca a letter to either confirm or deny Gwendolyn's claim, if she hasn't already done so. Until we hear back from Rebecca, not one word to anyone. Understand?" Greg towered over his brother in superiority, daring him to refuse with his penetrating gaze.

Grabbing the reins, he mounted his horse in one swift motion. "If that little imp wants everyone to think she's dead, then so be it!"

Gregory and Dan sat atop their horses as Mrs. Marguerite Mathewson, Gwendolyn's aunt and guardian, came running out of her townhouse to meet them. Her swollen eyes and fruit-stained apron did nothing to hide her graceful beauty. She grabbed Gregory's hand tenderly.

"Anything?" she pleaded.

Gregory looked down at her and could see the tears threatening to fall from her eyes, like the bittersweet dew from the honeysuckle at dawn.

He'd imagined that moment at least a hundred times during the eight-mile ride back to town. What would Mrs. Mathewson think when he told her that Gwendolyn had purposely left to who knows where and for God knows how long? Without any note, no doubt the poor woman would blame herself, thinking she hadn't been enough of a real mother to Gwendolyn or given her the same attention and encouragement as her own daughter Daisy. Damn Gwendolyn for putting her family through such misery! he cursed silently.

With a heart full of regret, he shook his head in the negative, ready for the onslaught of the poor woman's tears. Out of the corner of his eyes, he could see Dan's thinly veiled confusion but knew his brother would understand soon enough. Gregory just prayed he was making the right decision.

Reluctantly, he urged his horse onward and left the woman to grieve on her own.

A band of men would be gathered next, most likely, and a search for Gwendolyn would ensue, but Gregory had no intention of joining it. He wasn't going to scour the town looking for her when he knew she was hundreds of miles away. Everyone would think he'd gone daft. The entire town would brand him as an outcast, but he didn't care. Besides, he wasn't going to dig himself deeper into the pit of deception he'd made for himself. He'd lied once, to a woman he greatly admired and respected, and he wasn't about to make it worse by verbally continuing the farce. He wasn't even sure he'd made the right decision. All he could do was sit back and wait for everything to unravel.

Dan suddenly galloped to his side, flicking up pieces of dirt as he slowed his chestnut mare to match the casual gait of Gregory's stallion.

"What have you done?" his brother accused, slightly breathless.

"I'm not quite sure, Dan." Gregory listened to the calm rush of wind through the trees, the chirping crickets, the clomping of the horses' hooves against the dirt and was suddenly hit with a big dose of reality. What good was there in life besides the backbreaking labor in the fields, the tedious tending of the mercantile, the splinters and accidental hammering of fingers while building barns and houses? he wondered. What good was there in any of it without Gwendolyn? Wasn't it just yesterday that she'd told him about Susie fighting with the goose while he'd been mucking out Pa's stalls?

He groaned inwardly, wishing she were back telling him more of her humorous stories. He didn't know how to live without her. They'd done everything together—just him, Dan, Gwendolyn, and Daisy. They were inseparable. Well, they had been inseparable.

He could feel his throat start to burn with the need to cry like some lost pup, but he ignored it. No one was allowed to see how much Gwendolyn had hurt him, no matter what. It was more important to focus on the Mathewsons' pain…on his own mother and sister's pain. While the rest of his family searched for Gwendolyn, he would keep himself occupied elsewhere. He would make sure his father's crop got the care it needed during the upcoming weeks so they could sell come harvest time, he could repair the leak in Mr. Gallagher's boat—anything to keep his mind off the current situation.

"I'm not going to question you," Dan stated slowly, "because I know you would never intentionally hurt anyone. I just want to know why I am to be bound in silence."

"This is how I see it," Gregory started wearily, stumbling over every word. "Everyone will be feeling guilt, confusion, heartache over her betrayal, or a sense that they somehow have not measured up in Gwendolyn's eyes, and be wondering every minute of their lives if she'll just show up on their doorstep one day. Either that, or they'll believe she got lost in the woods, was eaten by a bear, drowned in the river, or fell and broke every bone in her body. What is better," he said, hoping his brother didn't sense the quivering in his voice, "for them to forever blame themselves and her, or to have no one to blame?"

"What happens when she comes back?"

"You mean *if* she comes back."

The two of them turned their horses down the lane to Orchard Cottage. A small white picket fence lined the path on both sides, and Gregory suddenly remembered that Gwendolyn and his younger sister had helped him paint it. He growled inwardly, and then focused his attention on the towering oak trees with leaves just beginning to blush with autumn's color.

Dan cleared his throat.

"Uh," Gregory stumbled. "I suppose if she comes back, she'll prove me to be the liar that I am and I'll be even more of an outcast than I already predict I will be. But don't you worry, I'll make sure you're cleared from all the blame."

Dan scoffed. "Gee thanks…I think."

"And after giving our little Gwendolyn a well-deserved throttle from yours truly, I suppose the sheriff will hang me. It would give him something to do."

The dull throbbing pain radiating from somewhere in her head awakened the young woman. All was quiet except for the throbbing. It felt like thunder as its reverberating pulses cascaded through the darkened clouds of her mind.

Slowly, she raised a weakened limb to her head and was immediately surprised. Beneath her fingers she could feel several layers of gauze wound around her head, securing a wad of dampened cloth to her crown. She was sorely tempted to pry the bandages off for they felt tight and itchy, but she thought better of it. They were there for a reason.

She paused. How had she hurt her head, she wondered. Scrunching up her face, she tried to recall the moment prior to her injury but there were no images that made sense to her. They were nothing more than fragments.

With a grimace, she changed her position and pried her eyes open, hoping to get some idea of her current circumstance. She was startled to realize she was lying on a firm mattress with cotton sheets and was surrounded by a series of white screens with metal frames. A beam of light was shining through, reminding her of dawn breaking through the trees on a cool summer morning. She half expected to be found lying in the road having been trampled by a frightened stallion or lying at the base of a particularly hard set of mahogany stairs after making an unfortunate step.

What lay beyond the screens was a complete mystery to her and she couldn't decide whether she was more irritated or frightened by not knowing. She hated being confined and alone. If only she could just be out in the woods somewhere with the birds chirping in the trees and the wind caressing her with the fragrance of apple blossoms and fresh soil.

Unexpectedly, a severe pain pierced through her head. She shot up in bed and focused all her energy on getting through the pain and trying to breathe. It took no more than a few seconds for it to lessen a great deal, but the young woman was absolutely terrified of it ever happening again. She decided her questions would have to wait until a later time. For at that moment, she didn't really care to know.

Using great care, she lay back against her pillow and immediately fell into a deep sleep.

The sound of footsteps clattering atop a hard floor brought the young woman awake suddenly. A man with white hair and a pair of spectacles walked up to her bedside and was writing some notes on a palm-sized tablet.

"Good morning, Miss Mitchell," he said a little too cheerily for her mood. "I'm Doctor O'Reilly. I was a bit worried about you there, but you seem to have pulled through. How are you feeling?"

"Terrible," she croaked before closing her eyes to the incessant throbbing in her head.

Mitchell, she thought. That wasn't her name, was it? She thought about it for a few seconds before realizing she didn't actually know what her name was, and after a few more seconds she realized she didn't really care.

She moved her legs a bit to adjust her position, but the moment she did she experienced an unfamiliar bubble-like pain in her left foot.

"What's wrong with my foot?"

"You seem to have fractured a bone in your foot when you fell from the coach. But don't worry," he assured after seeing the look on her face. "Your foot should heal in no time at all. What you should be focusing on is your head injury. It will still take a week or two for the skin to heal properly, and after that, you'll likely have headaches for a long while."

She was terribly confused. She couldn't remember hurting her head, let alone falling from a coach and fracturing her foot. It all seemed too ridiculous, even in her imagination.

"Why can't I remember anything from my injury?"

Doctor O'Reilly began laying out bits of fresh gauze and sticking long strips of tape to the iron headboard on her bed. "It's common among most of my patients who have had head injuries," he answered casually. "But you should be feeling as good as new eventually. It takes time. I know it's hard but just try to be patient. There isn't much else you can do."

"How long will it take?" she asked. The doctor was being exasperatingly vague.

"It's different with everyone. With some, it's a matter of a couple months. Others, it can take several years."

He removed the bandages from around her head and, with a careful eye, began to examine the injury. "The swelling started going down yesterday and looks really good today."

With the bandages gone and her sweat-dampened hair free from its bonds, she quickly grew chilly. Reaching outward, she pulled the sheet and blanket up to her chin to cover the growing goose bumps.

In the next instant, she could feel the doctor's fingers beginning to poke and prod the naked flesh of her crown, and she felt a desperate need to distract herself somehow. "How long have I been here?" she nearly squeaked.

"Oh, it's been nearly a week. You had a terrible fever at first but you're over the worst of it now." He dropped his hands and carefully began applying the new bandage. "Your accident has caused some damage," he said much more gently. "Your life is going to be much different for the next while. You're going to have to make some major lifestyle changes—ones you may not like—but you've got friends who are willing and happy to help you." He smiled at her with something akin to pity, but she wasn't convinced. After all, from the sound of things he was a doctor that dealt with dozens of patients a day.

She couldn't imagine what he'd meant by 'lifestyle changes.' With every new piece of information he gave, she grew more and more uncomfortable. She closed her eyes and took a deep breath. Her questions hadn't really been answered, just her suspicions confirmed. When would she get some real answers?

"There's really nothing more we can do for you here in the hospital. Your fever is gone and you're healing well. So, I'm going to let you go today. I'd wager that you're anxious to be getting out of here."

Indeed she was. Her whole body was sore from lying in bed so long. Looking at the dreary white screens surrounding her, she decided it was definitely a good thing she'd been asleep most of the time or she'd have gone crazy.

"Your friend should be here any minute," he continued, "to help you change into your clothes and take you home. I'll be back once you're both finished, so you just sit tight, Miss Mitchell, until I return and we can go over your care instructions, all right?"

She nodded. All right, that was easy. If only all of her questions could be answered so simply.

Her mind was reeling. Serious head injury, fractured foot, major lifestyle changes, and memory loss—she couldn't get use to it. It was too much information to process all at once and it seemed to be coming in droves. Where had she been going in a coach? she wondered. Who were the friends the doctor kept referring to? And why couldn't she remember her name? Something was definitely wrong and she wished she knew when she would remember more, or anything.

She felt the sudden build up of tears behind her eyes, and her head started pounding even worse than before. In irritation, she commanded herself to relax. Crying would definitely not get her anywhere. But oh, how she wished to vent somehow. She was so confused and felt incredibly lonely.

No more than a minute had passed before a slim woman with graying hair flounced into the makeshift room holding a large carpetbag.

"Oh, Gwendolyn! I've been beside myself with worry. I was afraid you would never wake up." The older woman was wearing a high collared, white blouse with long sleeves and a plain slate blue skirt that fluttered as she approached the side of the bed. "May I call you 'Gwendolyn?' Or would you prefer I call you 'Miss Mitchell?'"

Gwendolyn. The young woman thought of the name. It seemed vaguely familiar and much more suitable than 'Miss Mitchell.' She supposed it had to be her name since the woman seemed so confident, but she still couldn't be sure.

"Could you tell me who you are?" she asked, ignoring the woman's question.

"Oh, bless you, child," she waved. "My name is Ellen Maynard. I'm with the Board of Education for the city, and you were to meet with me the day of your accident."

She set the carpetbag on the ground and, after hitching up her skirts, picked an empty place on the bed to sit on. "The coachman told me all about it…how you threw the door of the coach open and fell onto the street even before he'd gotten off his perch and had a chance to help you down the steps. It was a nasty fall it was—'blood everywhere,' he said." She shook her head in wonder.

Gwendolyn loved the woman instantly although the graphic description of her accident made her shudder. Although Mrs. Maynard's words came out at a speed that made Gwendolyn's mind whirl in confusion, she had an honest, almost playful quality about her that Gwendolyn greatly appreciated. She hoped they would become great friends.

"How did I fall?"

"Oh, the coachman said you were a spirited one. Knew it from the first moment he set eyes on you at the train station. Don't know how he noticed this, but he said the hem of your skirt was ripped and figured you must have tripped in your haste to exit the coach. I don't know any men that would notice something as little as that, but never mind. And I can't say I blame you for wanting to get out. Them coaches are too crammed and stuffy for the likes of me." She used one hand to fluff her hair as her eyes wandered a bit in idle concentration.

A few seconds went by before she shook herself from her reverie.

"Anyway," she continued, looking at Gwendolyn once again with her misty blue eyes, "the coachman brought you straight here then came and fetched me. I must say it was certainly a frightening way of being informed that my new teacher had finally arrived. But," she said, heaving a theatrical sigh, "I've gotten over it." She grinned wickedly, causing Gwendolyn to chuckle in spite of herself.

Teacher, she thought. Yes, the idea seemed right since she was able to recall certain math formulas and books she'd read with pleasure, but how would she be able to teach in her condition? She couldn't even remember her own name, and what kind of parent would allow her to teach their children if they knew that? She wasn't even sure she could trust herself to fill such a position. Sure, she knew some math formulas and books, but that wasn't enough to actually teach an entire class of real, breathing children.

Gwendolyn was baffled. How was it possible that she could remember certain algebraic expressions but not her birthday, or where she came from, or the faces of her family members? She paused and a feeling of horror came over her. Perhaps she didn't have a family, she thought. As hard as she tried, she couldn't recall any names or faces, just an endless void of blurry bodies. Surely she had to have a family, she reasoned before quickly brushing the disturbing thought aside.

She knew she couldn't tell Mrs. Maynard about her memory loss. The woman would think her incompetent as a teacher and send her back where she'd come from. And where was that? She imagined herself stranded along a road without food or money, having absolutely no idea who she was or where she could go. The image made her sick.

"When do I need to start teaching?" she asked, almost dreading the answer.

Mrs. Maynard put her hands on her hips and looked at Gwendolyn in awe. "For mercy sake, child! Don't be silly. I've found someone else to take your post for the term. You, my dear, need to relax and recover."

Gwendolyn sighed in relief. She could really use some time to herself, not just to recover but to get her thoughts together. If she was eventually going to do this job, she would have to use all of her recovery time doing research and making lesson plans. Otherwise,

Mrs. Maynard would terminate her contract and send her packing. She had no idea how she was going to pay for her lodging and food if she wasn't going to be teaching. She most likely hadn't planned on being in this situation, and she obviously didn't have any family to support her. She highly doubted she'd brought very much of her own money, if any.

"Now," Mrs. Maynard said, getting up and grabbing the bag from off the floor. "Let's get you dressed so you can get to the Jennys' and relax. I brought a few of my own things for you to wear since the stage driver took your bags back to the station, and you didn't seem to have anything suitable in your bag, anyhow. They're a little larger since you're such a skinny thing, but they should be all right in the meantime, I think."

"Who are the Jennys?"

The woman gently raised Gwendolyn to a sitting position before diving into the bag for some underclothes. "Elizabeth Jenny was a former schoolmate of mine and is now on the school board with me. I just can't seem to get rid of her." She smiled jokingly then continued. "Her daughter is actually the one you are replacing. Her name is Samantha and she's getting married in less than two weeks. She and her husband want children right away, so that leaves no time for teaching."

Gwendolyn put her arms through the blouse that was handed to her as she listened carefully to Mrs. Maynard's words. She didn't want to miss anything, but she was feeling overwhelmed with all of the information and additional questions that were coming up.

"Elizabeth and her husband David have a large country house just outside the borders of the city. It sits right beside the most darling brook, and their cat just had kittens. I simply knew it would be the best place for you the moment Elizabeth suggested it, you coming from the country and everything. They only have the two girls and their youngest is almost sixteen, so you'll have plenty of peace and quiet while you're recovering." Mrs. Maynard suddenly stopped and looked at Gwendolyn with a worried expression. "Do these arrangements sound all right?" She began nibbling on her beautifully long fingernails.

"They sound perfect except for, uh," she paused, causing Mrs. Maynard's expression to droop, "how will I be able to pay these people for my keep if I'm not teaching? I have little money."

"Upon my word, Miss Gwendolyn," she scoffed. "You ask the most absurd questions. Especially for one in your condition." The woman continued to laugh. "Surely you don't think we're so inhuman that we'd expect you to pay room and board when it's impossible."

Gwendolyn blushed in embarrassment.

"Now don't go feeling like that," she said, obviously noticing the rising color in Gwendolyn's cheeks. "This is an emergency and you can pay her back later. Besides, Elizabeth has always wanted another daughter and she'll be losing her eldest to another man soon."

Gwendolyn relaxed a bit. The arrangements sounded better than she could have hoped. Already, she wished she'd recover quickly so she could walk bare-footed in the brook, get lost in the numerous paths of the forest, and have a kitten rest beside her on some quilts as she read in the window seat. "I do really appreciate all the extra effort you've gone through on my account. I hope I haven't caused too much trouble."

"Nonsense. I've taken care of just about every detail, I think, so you don't need to worry about a thing. You just need to focus on getting better." Her eyes lit up suddenly. "Oh, I can't wait till you are. I want to show you around the city. We've even got a new library, and I just adore reading."

Once Gwendolyn's clothes were changed, the two women sat and waited for the doctor to return. Mrs. Maynard went over more of the details as Gwendolyn merely sat in awe of everyone's generosity. The Jennys were insisting that she stay with them, free of charge, until she was feeling better and ready to start teaching, and nearly every member on the board had made their own contribution whether it was offered time, meals, or money.

"After the doctor gets here and gives us our instructions," Mrs. Maynard said, interrupting Gwendolyn's thoughts, "my son Peter will be here to carry you to the buggy. And oh," she said with a wink, "don't even think about it. He's already taken."

# Chapter Two

GWENDOLYN SAT IN HER WINDOW SEAT and lazily stroked the brown kitten in her lap. Outside, the snow was falling in a thick blanket of silent flakes and showed no signs of letting up any time soon. It had been nearly a week since the onset of the storm, but still it persisted. How she wished she could spend her days being outside, enjoying the newly fallen snow rather than being trapped in the Jennys' house.

"C'mon, Cinnamon," she cooed. "It's about time I started getting ready for dinner."

She placed the drowsy kitten on her bed before going to the armoire and changing into a gray plaid skirt, white ruffled blouse, and black stockings. Once at her dressing table, she gazed at her reflection in dismay.

"There's got to be something else I can do with this hair," she said to the slumbering kitten behind her. She piled her locks neatly atop her head and added some pins to hold everything in place.

Leaning close to the looking glass, she examined the painfully obvious, pink scar running from her left temple past her hairline and cringed slightly. Doctor O'Reilly had assured her during her visit in October that the scar would fade in time, but Gwendolyn had yet to notice any difference.

She pulled a couple curly strands down, trying to conceal the scar as much as possible, but she knew, as she had known all the other times she'd tried to cover it up, that it really was no use.

With a sigh, she pulled out all the pins and let her rich chocolate curls fall down past her shoulders as always. She'd rather people stare at her for impropriety than gape at her scar and hound her with questions, but the night would be a casual Thanksgiving indoors, after all. She needn't worry.

A timid voice came through the door. "Are you almost ready, Miss Gwendolyn?"

"I'll be right down, Kristine." Gwendolyn stood, then took a few moments to lace up her boots. With a pinch of her cheeks and a weary sigh, she exited the room.

The intoxicating smells of homemade bread and peach cobbler wafted through the air as Gwendolyn carefully made her way down the stairway. The dining room was lined with boughs of dried leaves and perfumed candles and had a very welcome presence. In one corner of the room stood both Mr. and Mrs. Jenny, whispering quietly to one another. Beside the kitchen stood their daughter Samantha with her new husband Peter Maynard, and Mrs. Maynard. Beside the table, stood Kristine and—

Gwendolyn stopped short, instinctively covering her scar with a couple strands of hair. There was a young man—a stranger to her—talking with Kristine.

"Oh, Gwendolyn," Mrs. Jenny beamed, coming toward her in a bustle of skirts and placing a comforting hand upon Gwendolyn's arm. "We're so glad you're able to join us this evening. How are you feeling?"

"My headache has eased a bit," she said, looking warily at the stranger who was grinning at her—rather foolishly, in her opinion.

Sensing Gwendolyn's unease, Mrs. Jenny introduced the young man with haste. "Oh, this is my nephew Robert Jamison, Gwendolyn," Mrs. Jenny said, walking over to the man. "My brother's wife went into labor just a few hours ago, so I decided to invite Robert for the evening."

"Most likely to keep him out of everybody's way," Mrs. Maynard joked. All in the room chuckled while Robert nodded with a good-natured grin.

"Now," Mrs. Jenny said, her voice fading as she made her way to the kitchen. "Everyone take a seat so we can start eating."

Robert immediately went to the table, pulled out a chair and smiled at Gwendolyn in invitation. She returned the smile then seated herself in the offered chair.

He appeared older than her—perhaps in his mid-twenties. He was tall and had curly hair the color of midnight. He took the seat just to the left of hers, and she grew even more nervous. She would just have to remember not to pull her hair behind her ears. Kristine took the seat on her right.

Just as everyone was settled and comfortable, Mrs. Jenny returned carrying a steaming turkey lined with roasted apples and cranberries. She set the platter in the center of the table while everyone cheered and complimented, and she smiled with satisfaction. "Dig in everyone!"

The turkey had been basted with a sweet glaze of apple nectar and cinnamon and was sublimely moist. Other than the main dish, there was sweet corn, Mrs. Maynard's famous chestnut stuffing, light and fluffy rolls drenched in home-churned butter, sweet potatoes with gravy, and steamed vegetables in a rich molasses sauce.

Mrs. Jenny had really outdone herself, but it was no wonder to Gwendolyn since the woman had been working like a madwoman since the beginning of the harvest several weeks earlier. The idea exhausted Gwendolyn.

"How have you been feeling?"

Surprised, Gwendolyn looked up at the sound of Robert's voice. She chewed her food up quickly—awkwardly. "You know of my condition?"

"Unfortunately, news of this nature travels fast, Miss Gwendolyn. But, tell me, how are you feeling…truly?" He leaned toward her, looking at her with obvious concern.

"I uh," she started, momentarily distracted by the intensity of his gaze. She felt an odd prickling sensation at the back of her neck and tried her best to ignore it. "I've had a dreadful headache the last couple of days. I think it's going away, though."

"I hope so." He reached for one of the rolls. "I'm glad I was invited to come tonight so that I could finally meet you. Once it stops snowing, I'll take you for a ride in my father's carriage. I mean, only if you want to. If you're anything like me, you don't like being cooped up for too long."

"That would be wonderful," she said, feeling more at ease.

"And you can tell me all about your hometown. I've always wanted to visit the country."

Or not, she thought. That would be the shortest conversation ever.

Gwendolyn passed the corn at Peter Maynard's request, glad for the interruption. She wasn't sure she liked where her conversation with Robert was headed. Thankfully, Robert had returned to his food, so she turned her attention to Kristine instead.

"How is school going?" she said, leaning toward the young woman. "I haven't heard anything from you these last couple weeks."

Kristine's cheeks turned rosy and she hastily wiped her mouth with her napkin. "I'm sorry, Miss Gwendolyn." She lowered her voice before continuing. "I've sort of met someone. I think I really like him."

"Oh, how exciting," Gwendolyn chirped, clasping her hands together. "How did it happen?" She leaned farther in her chair, ready for the story she knew Kristine would divulge with youthful relish. Her tales and enthusiasm always helped Gwendolyn to feel better.

"I went to the store after school to get some of those chewy caramels," she began, "but Mr. Haversch didn't have any left. So, on my way home…I had just made it to the bridge when Michael, you remember Michael, he pulled out my hand and gave me a bunch of the very same caramels! He said he knew they were my favorite."

"Really? That's just too perfect. But I wonder where he got the caramels if Mr. Haversch was out of them." Gwendolyn smiled mischievously. "He's liked you for a while then?"

Kristine nodded shyly as she played with her nut-brown hair. "He'd better ask me to dance at the Christmas social. I know I'll just die if he doesn't."

"Don't be silly. Of course he will. I promise." Gwendolyn

would make sure of that. She was going to be his teacher, after all. There were plenty of ways. She could think of something. Besides, seeing Kristine at any less than her usual cheerful self just didn't seem right to Gwendolyn.

The room fell silent abruptly and Gwendolyn looked up to see everyone's eyes on her, including Robert Jamison's.

"I'm sorry. What's happening?" She could hear Robert chuckling at her side.

"Not to worry, Miss Gwendolyn," Mr. Jenny said, adjusting his spectacles on the bridge of his nose. "Elizabeth and I were just wondering what your Christmas plans are. Will you be spending the holidays with your family? Grovetown must be quite remarkable this time of year. Oh, I do so love the country."

"My family?" Gwendolyn said, not knowing how to continue. As far as she knew, she didn't have a family. "I'm, uh…not quite sure, to be perfectly honest." She watched their expressions, wondering what they knew that she didn't and hoping they wouldn't press the issue, but everyone at the table seemed completely content, especially Mrs. Maynard who closed her eyes with every savory bite.

"My dear, please don't feel obligated to stay on our account," Mrs. Jenny piped in. "You haven't visited your family at all since you've been here, and I'm sure they're horribly worried about you. If it's the train fare you're worried about, then you don't need to worry any longer, my dear. We'd be happy to help you if we can."

Mrs. Jenny buttered her roll and took a small bite before continuing. "You can go and visit with your family or you can stay here with us. The choice is yours. However," she said, suddenly gaining momentum, "we'd be simply delighted to have you stay and share Christmas with us. Isn't that right, dear?" She looked to her husband then elbowed him in the side just as he dove for another bite of potatoes.

Gwendolyn smiled openly, loving the camaraderie she already felt with the entire family. The Jennys were easy to get along with and had been immeasurably supportive during her recovery. Staying in Hopeton during the Christmas holidays would not be difficult.

And although she felt really nervous at social gatherings, she'd already promised to help Kristine pursue her new friend Michael. There was really no point in leaving. She didn't even know where she would go, anyhow.

"If indeed you all approve of me staying in Hopeton," she started, "I would be happy to do so. You are all so very dear to me and have shown me such kindness these past few months. I'd also like to be settled before I'm supposed to start teaching," she added, "to make the transition a bit easier, you understand."

The whole group exchanged knowing glances and Gwendolyn silently berated herself. It seemed she was forever drawing attention to herself, and oh, how much she despised doing that! She would much rather just sit in the background and observe like one of the family pets.

"Well, we're happy you're staying with us," Mrs. Maynard contributed. The rest in the dining room nodded in agreement. "We've got all sorts of Christmas activities you can participate in, if you're up for them."

"Oh, yes, Miss Gwendolyn," Kristine beamed. "Mother and I can take you to get a new Christmas dress and maybe some of Mrs. Haversch's peppermint taffy, and Mrs. Maynard wanted you to see the new library and…"

Kristine's words spilled forth in a jumble of anticipation, but Gwendolyn couldn't concentrate on them. Her headache was beginning to deepen once again.

She couldn't possibly have a family, could she? For if she did, that would certainly mean they'd been ignoring her for the past several months. She shuddered, refusing to accept the possibility.

Mrs. Maynard had said she'd taken care of every detail that day in the hospital, but Gwendolyn was beginning to suspect that a letter to her family had never actually been written. She hadn't written one, and since Mrs. Maynard had no idea as to the extent of Gwendolyn's memory loss or her circumstances when coming to Hopeton, she couldn't have written one either.

Gwendolyn idly played with the peach cobbler that was placed in front of her and, forgetting all manners, raised her elbow on the table and rested her chin in her palm. She felt dreadfully dejected and confused.

She supposed it likely that her family, if indeed she did have one, wasn't even aware of her accident. After all, the letter she'd found in her traveling bag was addressed to her and had no specific address. Mrs. Maynard would never have known where to send such information. But certainly her family would have written something in the past few months. Did they not love her?

The remainder of the contents in her traveling bag—a couple dirty shirtwaists, a well-read copy of Jane Austen's "Mansfield Park," a clean handkerchief, and a few dollars—hadn't been much help either. She had hoped to find some clues to her identity in her trunks, perhaps some journals or photographs, but the driver from the train station had given them to a man who had claimed to be her brother.

Poor man, she thought, remembering how dreadful and apologetic the driver had been. The stranger had to have been a thief for he had never made any attempts to contact her afterward.

She realized there was no use in pursuing the matter any further. She still had to accomplish two very important tasks before alerting anyone to her unfortunate condition. First, she had to become a teacher. And second, she had to prove herself competent beyond everyone's expectations—including her own.

With renewed determination, she shoved several spoonfuls of the peach confection into her mouth at once, earning herself a couple of curious glances from her companions.

"So, are you enjoying yourself?" Mrs. Maynard asked once she'd reached Gwendolyn's side.

Gwendolyn stood gazing about the spectacular ballroom at all of the well-dressed couples. Surrounding her were silk gloves, stunning beads of pearls, fine cuff links, cigar smoke that made her nostrils burn, gossiping ladies, and beautifully shined shoes. The women's gowns twirled dreamily back and forth with each turn of the song and the men led as if they'd been dancing their entire lives. The candles on the chandeliers gave off an ethereal glow that made Gwendolyn rather sleepy. Along the staircases, walls, and tables were pine boughs, gold ribbons, and berries. The atmosphere was pleasant enough but she desperately wished to be back at the Jennys', warming herself by their cozy fire while planning for school.

"Yes," she lied.

"Uh huh." Mrs. Maynard immediately snatched Gwendolyn's dance card, lifting the young woman's hand in the process. "You've only had one dance…and with *Michael Hamilton?*" Mrs. Maynard looked up at Gwendolyn in sudden dismay, causing Gwendolyn to blush in embarrassment.

"Tsk tsk," she continued, tapping Gwendolyn lightly with her fan. "I hate to break it to you, Miss Gwendolyn, but that young man is a bit too young for you."

"I was aiding a friend, Mrs. Maynard," she said, quick to defend herself. "I promised her that I would. There's nothing between me and Michael." That would definitely be awkward.

"Oh, all right." Mrs. Maynard chuckled. "But where is Mr. Jamison? Didn't he say he'd be here?" She stood on tiptoe, searching above the crowd for the dark-haired fellow.

"Robert said he'd try to make it. He has to stay with the baby until his parents get back from their Christmas party. Why do you ask?"

"Because I want him to dance with you, that's why," she said, clearly agitated. "You've hardly been around the floor, my dear, and I want you to meet some of the young men in town. What good is a dance if you don't get to dance with anyone? That's what they're for," she huffed then pulled up her sleeves dramatically.

"I'm going to go get Peter. Maybe he can take you for a couple turns about the room and show you off. Samantha won't mind. A pretty thing like you shouldn't remain a wallflower, especially with me as your protector. I simply won't have it." Mrs. Maynard marched off, leaving Gwendolyn alone by the refreshment table.

Wonderful, Gwendolyn thought sarcastically. She'd rather stand and watch people be gay and twirl about than make a complete fool of herself on the dance floor. She'd practiced earlier to see if she remembered the steps she assumed she'd learned in her childhood but soon became too frustrated. Perhaps it would be easier once she had a partner, she thought optimistically.

Her back and neck ached from the many long hours she'd spent earlier studying and making lesson plans. She was looking forward to getting back home where she could relax and reflect back on her night…the night she'd danced twice—once with an adolescent and once with a married man.

Gwendolyn stepped out into the fresh spring air and inhaled deeply. The scent of tulips, pine, and the frosty earth made her sigh with contentment. She had opened the school's windows for a bit during the day to let in the light rays of sunshine, but nothing could match the felicity of actually being outside. She took a moment to soak it all in.

Feeling thoroughly refreshed, she locked up the large, wooden schoolhouse for the day then began walking along the dirt path toward home. At least it felt like home to her. True to Mrs. Maynard's word, the Jennys treated her as one of their own. Mr. Jenny had given her free reign in his private library while Mrs. Jenny was attentive and frequently complimented her teaching skills. Kristine felt like a little sister, always coming to her for advice and help with her studies. Even Cinnamon, now almost fully-grown, brought his mousy meals and ate them at her feet while she marked her students' papers. She felt safe, she felt loved, and most of all, she felt wanted. What more could she ask for?

Since Thanksgiving, the subject of her family had come up in conversation quite often. She was almost certain now that they existed, and after months and months of waiting at the post office for a letter, she'd quite given up on ever hearing from them. She had no one to blame but herself. Even if she could write to her family, what would she say?

"Good grief, this is pointless," she muttered to herself. For now, she knew she could do absolutely nothing about it. She was a teacher responsible for eighteen amazing students. Better to wait until the end of the term before doing any real investigating into the matter. She grumbled, feeling so utterly helpless.

She had just reached the small bridge on the outskirts of town when she heard heavy steps rapidly approaching from behind. She spun around in alarm.

"Oh, Robert," she gasped, letting out an enormous puff of air. "You scared me half to death. What's going on?"

"Sorry," he said with boyish enthusiasm. "I was just trying to catch up with you. I was at the ironsmith's." He ran a hand through his thick dark curls and looked off into the distance. "I was just wondering if I could escort you to the concert tonight."

"Is that this evening?" she asked, still catching her breath. At that moment, she wanted nothing more than to wring his thoughtless little neck.

Robert nodded eagerly then started shifting his weight back and forth, apparently impatient with her…or nervous perhaps?

She'd completely forgotten about the concert. If she hadn't spent most of the week writing her science examinations, she might have remembered that a prestigious quartet would be performing that night. The last time there had been an orchestral concert, she'd been confined to her bed and what a terrible disappointment that had been. She couldn't believe she'd forgotten.

Robert leaned toward her, giving her the mischievous smile that always made her feel foolish somehow. "Well?"

"Oh, I uh," she stammered, looking into his dark brown eyes. "W-Why certainly, Robert."

Blast! Why couldn't she remember any etiquette? She curtsied slightly, not enough to be too painfully obvious, but enough for him to notice if he were paying attention. She didn't want to be rude, after all.

He removed his imaginary top hat and bowed magnanimously. "Till half past seven then, Miss Mitchell."

Gwendolyn leaned forward in her seat to get a better look at the instrument. It was made of wood—a rich maple with beautiful curves and four strings running down the middle. She knew it was referred to as a 'violoncello,' but how she knew was a mystery to her. She didn't think she'd ever seen one before, having grown up in the country where such luxuries were most likely expensive and hard to come by. Then again, she wouldn't have been surprised if she had. There was something oddly familiar about it.

She sat back and closed her eyes. Blocking out everyone and everything around her, she focused entirely on the glassy-smooth sounds resonating from the instrument. She imagined a large graceful bird gliding its way through the moon's reflection on a lake, making ripples as it went. With each crescendo, Gwendolyn's heart swelled in anticipation and her skin tingled with an overwhelming sense of peace. She flicked a tear from the corner of her eye and sighed with satisfaction.

If only life were as beautiful as that music, she thought. Its mesmerizing melody was almost enough to make her forget her troubles, her memory loss, her anxieties—but not quite. Despite the splendor of its tone, the violoncello seemed mysterious, almost haunting.

Just as the song began its most sincere melody, a strange sensation washed over her entire body. The feeling wasn't at all pleasant. She felt cold, and tingly, and wondered if she was the only person in the entire concert hall that was being affected as she was. She hoped she wasn't catching a chill.

Attempting to put her mind at ease, she closed her eyes once again and tried to relax her back and neck muscles.

In the very next instant, an unfamiliar image flashed through her mind, making her dizzy and a little nauseated. It had lasted no more than a fraction of a second, but her discovery was startling. She blinked her eyes once or twice and managed, once again, to see the dimly lit hall.

She had seen a strange, wooden room with slanted walls and one small window that let in very little light. There was a man facing her, a man she had never seen before—or had she? He was watching her intensely with light blue eyes, as if he knew her innermost thoughts without even having to ask. His brown hair rested against his shoulders in smooth locks, framing his square face, high cheekbones, and strong jaw line. But the power of his gaze on her—

She blushed, knowing that she couldn't, not even in her most imaginative of dreams, conjure such a man. He was too magnificent, and downright beautiful!

Slumping in her seat, she began to feel light, mystified, and a bit hopeful. Was it a memory trying to resurface? She closed her eyes once more, hoping to see the magnificent man again.

The entire episode had to be a clue, a glorious and delicious clue to her identity and the people she'd known.

Ah, she sighed, enjoying the stringed instruments once again. She loved music and knew that she'd always remember that night, no matter what. She couldn't wait to get home and record the events in her diary.

The slight chill of the outside air finally brought Gwendolyn back to reality as she took Robert's offered hand and stepped into the carriage.

The concert had been absolutely wonderful. It had all seemed unreal somehow, as if it hadn't happened at all. But she knew it had. Her heart could not deny it. She knew she would never be the same. She looked out at the moonlit trees beside the road, feeling a renewed sense of confidence and purpose.

"You enjoyed yourself tonight, Miss Mitchell?" Robert asked with a smile as he adjusted his gloves and urged the horses onward.

"Oh, yes. Immensely."

Despite her elation, she felt an odd jolt all of a sudden. Why did he insist on calling her 'Miss Mitchell'? All the other times they'd spent together, they'd had no trouble calling each other by their given names. Why then? Ever since that very afternoon when he'd caught her at the bridge, she realized, he'd been acting strangely formal.

She squirmed slightly, feeling extremely uneasy, although she couldn't understand why. Robert was an attractive and friendly young man. They enjoyed their time together. They fell easily into conversation and shared the same interests, but why did she feel so dreadful?

They continued along the road, an awkward silence hanging in the air, but Gwendolyn attempted to shove her anxieties about Robert aside, deciding she was just being paranoid. Instead, she focused all her energy on her discovery at the concert, on the image of the man she'd envisioned, the man with long brown hair and intense blue eyes. With his strong build, his bold features, and his intense gaze as he looked upon her—he couldn't possibly be any relation, she decided. He'd looked on her with such joy and admiration…and something else. She couldn't quite put her finger on it.

Robert led the team over the bridge and through the narrow path toward the Jennys'. With the aid of the moonlight, she could see the heads of the tulips—red, yellow, orange, and purple—just sprouting from the ground. The sounds of the carriage's wheels riding over the rocky, dirt path did not interfere with the harmony of the cricket's song. Ah, she loved that time of night.

Once they reached the end of the lane, Gwendolyn realized the Jennys hadn't returned home yet. The house was dark except for a small lantern that was hanging beside the door. Mrs. Jenny did so love to talk and was probably driving her husband completely crazy. With a smile, Gwendolyn imagined Mr. Jenny's bored stare as he often dreamed about returning to his library.

Robert pulled the horses to a stop and, instead of coming around to help Gwendolyn down, he sat motionless, staring off into the trees. He removed his gloves and placed them in his coat pocket before relaxing one of his legs against the front of the carriage. Apparently, he wasn't going to be moving any time soon.

Gwendolyn sat still, growing more nervous by the second. The pulsing sounds of the crickets matched the pounding of her heart and the moist clouds bursting from the horses' mouths reminded her that the air was still a bit chilly.

This is ridiculous, she decided, pulling her cloak more firmly about her small frame. It was growing far too cold and awkward for her taste. The Jennys' front door was only a few steps away. She could escape and be inside within seconds…perhaps minutes, after they'd exchanged the socially accepted pleasantries and bid each other goodnight.

"Thank you for taking me to the concert, Robert," she said finally. She smoothed her hands over her dress then made ready to leave the carriage, with or without his help.

"Gwendolyn, wait."

The pleading tone in his voice unsettled her and she slowly sat back down. Yes, she knew what was coming. She and Robert had been good friends, but he wanted more. She was certain of it. Why else would he be acting so strange?

She felt him place a trembling hand on hers and turned to meet his nervous gaze.

"I too had a wonderful evening. Most especially because you were there with me." Without averting his gaze, he raised his other hand and touched her face ever so gently.

She kept still, feeling timid and full of disbelief. She didn't know what to do and didn't think she'd ever been in a similar situation before.

Robert looked at her longingly, and without willing herself to do so, Gwendolyn thought of the stranger with the mesmerizing eyes and mischievous grin. Why was it that she felt more of a connection with a man she'd imagined for no more than a second than she did with a man she'd spent the past several months with?

Could that man have been in love with her? Or *was* he in love with her? The idea that a man from her past—the man from her vision—could still exist and be waiting for her somewhere brought an unexpected smile of satisfaction to her lips.

The next thing she knew, Robert was kissing her…actually kissing her! It wasn't unpleasant, but it wasn't what she had been expecting either.

She felt so confused and guilty. After all, Robert had been really good to her since they'd met. He'd bought the books and supplies she'd needed for her class, taken her for short carriage rides through town when she was desperate to get out of the house, and had treated her with respect and patience through her long months of recovery. He deserved no less from her. She did enjoy his company.

Desperately trying to get the blue-eyed stranger out of her mind, she closed her eyes and thought about the flesh and blood Robert, of his lips as they brushed lightly over hers.

Sarah Tyler placed two loaves to bake in the oven then clapped the flour from her hands as she sat down at the kitchen table. A letter had arrived that afternoon from her friend Ellen and she eagerly tore it open. It had been nearly an entire year since she'd last heard from the woman. She read its contents then stopped.

She blinked a few times then began the letter a second time.

No, she'd read it right the first time, but she reread it again just to make absolutely sure.

She looked up, her spectacles slightly askew, and stared at nothing in particular.

"It couldn't be," she said to herself. "But that would mean that my—"

Shaking her head, she madly began roaming the house, intent on getting some answers. "Dan? *Gregory?"*

After eight minutes of frantic searching, she turned up at the barn to find both of her eldest sons hitching the horses to the wagon.

"You both knew she was alive," she stated angrily, making Dan jump. Gregory continued his work without pause. "When you went to the station that day, you *knew* she was alive."

"Who?" Gregory asked, casually wiping axle oil on his trousers.

"Oh, don't play stupid with me," she scoffed. "You know perfectly well who I'm referring to."

"What makes you think she's alive?" Gregory asked calmly, being careful not to say Gwendolyn's name.

Sarah watched Dan look nervously at his brother then back at her and grew even more suspicious. "Oh, gee. I dunno," she replied sarcastically before waving Ellen's letter in their faces. "I just got a letter from a friend in Hopeton with Gwendolyn's name mentioned in it…*twice*, no less!"

Gregory pounced on her, grabbing the letter from her fingers. "Hopeton?" he roared. "But Hopeton is hundreds of miles off. What's she doing there?"

"Apparently she's been teaching in their new schoolhouse. Now, if you could please explain to me why you both lied to Marguerite Mathewson—my best friend, may I remind you—not to mention me and everyone else in this town, I'd be very much obliged." She folded her arms and waited, her expression livid.

"She abandoned us, mother!" Gregory bellowed, making Sarah jump. He madly crumpled the letter into a ball and shook it in his fist. "This letter proves my suspicions to be dead on. She abandoned us to dust off some ambition in a bigger and better place. I didn't want Mrs. Mathewson to suffer with that knowledge, to know that Grovetown wasn't enough. It's better for everyone to think Gwendolyn's dead."

"That was *not* your decision to make, young man," she practically yelled. "I can't believe it, all these months you both knew she was alive and you purposely kept that knowledge from us. Gwendolyn is *alive*, Gregory! Do you know what this is going to do to her family? To you?"

"I thought I was doing the right thing," Gregory snarled.

"And what about you?" She glared at her other son.

"Greg made me promise not to reveal what we found out," Dan said, cowering somewhat. "I didn't agree with him at first, but after giving it some thought, I decided to trust his judgment. I now believe it was the right thing to do." Dan stood firm, appearing more confident than before.

Sarah Tyler shook her head in disgust, unable to fathom their reasoning. She did not raise her children to act so irrationally.

"Did Gwendolyn say anything to you before she left?"

"No." Gregory was clenching his fists, causing the veins in his arms to pulse with his apparent rage.

"Then how can you profess to know her reason for leaving, huh?" Sarah came up to her eldest son who towered over her five-foot two-inch frame and spoke several decibels higher than before. "I'm surprised that you would be so quick to assume she left for selfish reasons, Gregory. That girl doesn't have one selfish bone in her body!"

"But why else would she leave without telling anyone," he asked, matching her volume. "She hasn't even had the decency to write for the last eight months. She wants us to think she's dead and gone. So, how can you stand there and deny the truth when all the evidence is pointing in that direction?"

"I don't know," she said, shrugging her shoulders. "But I'm not going to assume anything until I've seen Gwendolyn face-to-face and heard her side of the story. Now, give me my letter," she said, prying Gregory's fist open and grabbing the crumpled ball. "I'm going to write to Ellen right away so maybe I can fix this whole mess. And you two…are both in a hell of a lot of trouble!"

Gwendolyn looked at her class as they waited expectantly for her answer. Mrs. Maynard was sitting on a small bench at the back of the schoolhouse with the kids' lunch pails and recess toys, checking Gwendolyn's progress as she'd done several other times during the term.

"Oh, I don't know, Milly." What *did* she miss most from Grovetown, a place she couldn't remember anything about? She looked at the six-year-old redhead and thought the freckles on her cheeks made her absolutely beautiful, despite all her grumbling. "I do miss my family a great deal. I haven't seen them since I arrived in Hopeton last fall."

"So, will you go visit them during the Easter holiday, Miss Gwendolyn?"

"No, but I might during the summer," she said, stealing a glance at Mrs. Maynard. "I bet they would love to hear about all of you."

The class erupted with excitement and embarrassed disbelief.

"Oh, Miss Gwendolyn. Would they really?"

"Oh, I wish I could go with you."

"Did you ride horses bareback?"

"Did you have any wild pets—like squirrels or chipmunks…or skunks?"

"No way! She would never keep a skunk. They *stink*."

"Miss Gwendolyn isn't afraid of anything."

Gwendolyn hid a smile with her fingers. Her students were so special to her. In the short time she'd spent teaching, she had already come to love each and every one of them. She would miss them over the holidays…more so over the summer, but she would worry about that later.

Mrs. Maynard stood, holding her clipboard, which was Gwendolyn's signal to end the day.

"All right, everyone. Settle down." Gwendolyn came from behind her desk and shushed the class by raising both her arms. "I'm going to let you all go a few minutes early. Uh uh," she said, silencing the children again then smiling. "You may only leave right now if you *promise*…to bring some good stories back for me."

The class laughed then picked up their things and exploded out of the schoolhouse, excited for their Easter holiday to begin.

Mrs. Maynard chuckled as Kristine and her new boyfriend Michael left together. The woman came and sat in the desk directly in front of Gwendolyn. "Those kids absolutely adore you, you know."

Gwendolyn blushed at the compliment then sat in her chair with a grand flop. The children had been especially rowdy the last couple days and she'd had a headache nearly the entire time. For right then, she could relax and maybe it would go away for a few days.

"So," Mrs. Maynard said. "When is your family expecting you? I must say, it's about time you went to see them, you silly girl."

"I haven't talked to them about it yet."

"And why not?"

Gwendolyn sighed. "How do you and the board feel about me? Honestly?"

"Honestly?" Mrs. Maynard smiled. "Well, you're the best teacher we've ever had. Why do you ask?"

"Really?"

"Well, you did ask me to be honest, but to further prove my point and secure your satisfaction, I'll try to explain." She adjusted the sleeves on her shirtwaist and re-crossed her legs. "You are young and vivacious and can relate with the children on a completely different level than any of our other teachers. Your students absolutely love you. Nobody knows their subjects better than you, and you haven't even taught for three full terms. It's quite impressive."

Gwendolyn startled at that last remark. She could only remember teaching for four months—just barely one term. Apparently she'd been a teacher before, in Grovetown perhaps, but that really didn't come as any surprise to her since she'd been able to fall into her role as teacher more easily than she'd ever anticipated.

"You're a talented little thing," Mrs. Maynard continued. "Everybody raves about you, you know."

"All right. I am quite satisfied. There is no need to continue." Gwendolyn was beginning to feel overwhelmed…and warm with embarrassment.

"Oh, please. Just one more," Mrs. Maynard begged then continued at Gwendolyn's reluctant nod. "You're honest, fair, and downright humble, that's what."

"That was more than one, Mrs. Maynard."

The woman smiled mischievously. "Now, don't try to avoid my question. Why haven't you contacted your family about a visit?"

The moment Gwendolyn had been waiting for since her accident last August was upon her. It was finally the perfect time to reveal her secret. She had become a teacher and she had proven herself competent. Oh, how she needed someone to talk to.

"Mrs. Maynard," she started awkwardly.

"Yes," Mrs. Maynard urged. "What is it, dear?"

Gwendolyn swallowed. "When you came to me that day in the hospital…I–I couldn't remember who I was."

"I beg your pardon?" the woman choked.

There was no backing out of it. Her statement was loaded and she was obligated to explain. "I do not remember my accident or anything prior to it. My memory began that day in the hospital. I have no memory of myself, my family, or anything else before that day."

"But what about your teaching? You've excelled, my dear. How in heaven's name have you managed that?"

"I don't know. I was completely petrified at first, but it just seems to be coming naturally. I haven't really had any problems in that regard."

"Have you not contacted your family? Surely they have written."

"No, they have not written. I did not know they existed until Mrs. Jenny's Thanksgiving dinner. Since then I've assumed they abandoned me." She placed her elbows on her desk and sighed. "I assumed they wanted nothing further to do with me. But I cannot assume any longer, Mrs. Maynard," she said, suddenly pounding her fist on the desk. "I must know for myself why they have not contacted me. I know I will never be at peace until I discover the truth. Well, maybe not even then, but I must know."

Mrs. Maynard jumped up.

"I knew something was going on with you, missy. I just didn't expect it to be something so…so *terrible*." She placed a hand on her hip, the way she always did when she was about to reprimand or instruct. "I think I understand why you kept silent. But I still wish you had told me about it, my dear. How hard this must have been for you to bear alone. I cannot even fathom it. You are definitely unlike any other woman I know, Miss Gwendolyn Mitchell."

Gwendolyn had done her best to cope during the past nine

months since her accident, but after finally relieving her burden, she gave up trying to be strong. A flood of tears followed.

"Oh, you poor dear." Mrs. Maynard came around the desk to comfort her as she sobbed. "I've never had much patience for tears, but right now, I've got all the time in the world…so you just keep them comin', you hear me? I want your eyes big and red."

It felt like an entire hour before Gwendolyn stopped for breath, when in reality it had only been about a quarter of an hour. She knew her headache would never go away at the rate she was going, but she didn't care. The relief she felt was immeasurable. Using Mrs. Maynard's handkerchief, she wiped around her stinging eyes then took some deep breaths.

"I've got a solution for you, missy, and I will take absolutely no argument from you. Do you understand?"

Gwendolyn nodded, feeling one quarter skeptical and three quarters uneasy.

Mrs. Maynard returned to her clipboard that was sitting on one of the student's desks. She sat down on the tabletop and dangled her legs over the side.

"Three days after you finish teaching for this glorious term," she started sarcastically, "you will return to your home and figure things out. I have a friend named Sarah Tyler who is co-owner of the general mercantile and president of the town's charity committee," she said, eyeing Gwendolyn before continuing. "She sent word to me a couple weeks ago expressing a need for some external help during the summer. Her son is getting married and she will be replacing some of the members on her committee." She paused. "If I had known about you sooner, my dear, I would've written to her right away."

Gwendolyn tried to swallow all of the information Mrs. Maynard was giving her. She was truly overwhelmed, had a blazing headache, and wished the woman would slow down a little.

"After your confession today, I think you would be perfect to fill that position. As soon as I make sure you get to the Jennys' safely,

I will write to Sarah and tell her that I have found someone to fill the position, although I will keep your name a secret. That way you can return to Grovetown on safer terms with no expectations on either end. Are we agreed?"

Gwendolyn nodded, wondering what she ever did to deserve a friend like Mrs. Maynard. "But what if they reject me?"

"Don't be a fool," Mrs. Maynard said, rolling her eyes. "Why would anybody in their right mind do that? You're absolutely perfect…and gorgeous."

Gwendolyn highly doubted that. No one would think so after seeing the six-inch scar running down her face.

"But I guess in the unlikely event that they do reject you, you could always come back here. I don't know what we'll do without you. I almost hope you don't get things taken care of in Grovetown so that you can stay with us forever, but I know that's horribly selfish of me." Mrs. Maynard planted a kiss on Gwendolyn's forehead.

"Now, you just grab your things and I'll walk you home. You've got a little over a month to prepare yourself. You just better let me know if you need *anything* else."

Gwendolyn could feel more tears coming, tears of complete gratitude.

# *Chapter Three*

THE RIDE FROM HOPETON STATION to Silas River had been especially grueling. Gwendolyn had spent most of those six hours keeping rowdy children from barging into her private compartment but hadn't been very successful. Whomever those children belonged to should have kept a better eye on them and not let them run mad through the train cars. Her students had been much better behaved throughout the entire school term than that tiresome bunch. But she supposed she wouldn't have gotten any sleep even if she'd tried.

At Silas River she'd transferred to a smaller train. About four and a half hours later, she arrived at Poplar Grove and stepped out onto the platform, feeling anxious and weary. She had never imagined Grovetown to be so far away. What had she been thinking? The price for fare alone had been enough to scare her out of coming… almost. If it hadn't been for Mrs. Maynard, she never would have made it.

After nearly a year since her accident she was finally home and ready for some answers. She was thrilled to be there but painfully nervous at the same time.

What would her family be like? she wondered. How would they react once they saw her? Would the man from her vision be there?

She shivered.

The sun was high by that time and the air smelled rich with pine and dirt from the road. Men busily hoisted traveling cases and trunks out of the baggage car as two or three other passengers exited the train. Several yards further down, a pair of young men easily piled large sacks and barrels of goods into a wagon bed. The station was much less crowded than the other two she'd been to that day.

She smiled. Finding the stage driver wouldn't be nearly as much of a problem as she'd thought.

She walked confidently across the platform to the ladies waiting area. Standing within was a large man wearing a brown leather vest and an official-looking cap. She walked directly toward him.

"Are you traveling to Grovetown, sir?"

"Yes, miss. It's my second stop. Just go on inside that first coach and I'll fetch your luggage. We'll be leaving in a few minutes."

That was easy, she thought. She handed the man her luggage ticket.

"Thank you, miss." He touched his hat then walked past her.

Grabbing her skirts, Gwendolyn descended the steps. The road leading to Grovetown was lined with mature poplar trees and brightly colored wildflowers. On one side ran a little trickling stream that was likely housing dozens of grasshoppers and butterflies. The idea made her smile.

She desperately hoped no one was in the coach yet—what an awkward situation that would be. She was just too anxious to make polite chatter with strangers. She opened the coach door and smiled in triumph. It was indeed empty.

She ducked her head inside, keeping a hand atop her new wide-brimmed straw bonnet. Mrs. Maynard had recently ordered it for her despite Gwendolyn's protests. The article was slightly over her price range and she owed the woman so much already. But the good woman had insisted, hoping it would help Gwendolyn feel less nervous when she met her family. It *was* doing a marvelous job of covering up her scar and made her feel like more of a woman somehow. She resented the fact that something as insignificant as a piece of clothing would help her feel that way, but she tried not to worry about it too much.

Gwendolyn sat back and pulled her traveling bag closer to her as another woman entered the coach. The flowery scent that wafted from her gave Gwendolyn an immediate headache. Atop the woman's head sat a dreadful excuse for a hat—a robin's nest, complete with three blue eggs and a stuffed robin sitting smartly in the middle, and the long tail feathers of a pheasant bent against the walls of the coach.

Gwendolyn smiled politely at the woman then dove into her bag for a book. She wouldn't be reading it, of course, but the woman didn't need to know that. What could they possibly have to talk about?

After their luggage was safely stowed away, the driver urged the team forward with a lurch. The ride was terribly bumpy and grew old much too soon. No more than a few minutes had passed before she put her book down in defeat. She pulled the dusty drapery of the coach away to look outside but didn't really absorb anything she saw.

She silently went over her directions for, quite possibly, the sixteenth time—get to Grovetown, stop at the Tyler's General Mercantile, *wait* for the driver's assistance, pay the driver, leave the trunk beside the road and hope there are no thieves about, enter the store, find Mrs. Sarah Tyler, introduce herself? *Oh dear…*

The coach came to a slow stop in a shaded area only a couple miles out from the station. The woman sitting opposite her gathered her few belongings and adjusted her maroon velvet gloves just as the door opened.

"Huntington Square, ma'am," their driver announced, bending over to unfold the stepladder.

Gwendolyn was growing more anxious by the minute. Grovetown was only a few miles away and the next stop was hers. She would be meeting her family and friends as if for the first time and really had no idea how to go about it. It wasn't as if her type of situation came up every day. Oh, what a mess!

She grabbed her book and began fanning herself, hoping to cool her nervousness but jumped as her traveling companion suddenly covered her hand.

"It will be all right, milady." The woman's smile spread like warm honey as their gazes locked for a short moment. "I just know it."

The intensity of the woman's gaze and the passion with which she spoke momentarily struck Gwendolyn dumb. Gwendolyn nodded. Taking the driver's arm, the woman exited the coach with a knowing twinkle.

"Just six more miles, miss," the driver said, popping his head inside the coach as a wagon passed them by.

"Thank you." She smiled dazedly. Just an hour more. She could do it.

By the time the coach stopped again, Gwendolyn's head was pounding from the bumpy drive and she desperately needed fresh air. She thought she might collapse upon exiting, but not quite in the same way as her last ride by coach. She hated feeling so fragile and wondered if she'd ever feel complete again.

"You look quite done for, miss," the driver stated once he opened the door. "Please, let me help you out of this thing."

What a sweet man, she thought. She took his hand and descended the steps without incident. He proceeded to get her trunk and placed it by the side of the road at her instruction.

"Thank you so much, Mr...."

"McCullough."

"Mr. McCullough. You've been most kind." She smiled then dropped a couple extra coins than were probably customary into his palm.

"Many thanks, miss," he grinned. "You get yourself some good rest, you hear?"

She stood at one edge of town as Mr. McCullough urged his team onward. Grovetown was definitely small, much smaller than she had anticipated. There weren't many people about. No more than two-dozen shops and houses stood before her. On one side were a ironsmith's, some boarding stables, the sheriff's office, and a small saloon with an inn on the upper level—all of them quite strange and unfamiliar to her. She would never be permitted to enter most of them, being just a woman, but it didn't matter. She'd never want to anyhow. They were just loud and dirty places, or so she'd heard.

On the other side of town were various specialty shops, a post office, barbershop, general mercantile, lumber store, and a few town houses. Resting at the far end and holding everything together was the town hall. Gwendolyn calculated that it would take no more than ten minutes to walk through it all.

No wonder she didn't get any directions to the mercantile, she thought.

Taking a deep breath and remembering the words of her perfumed traveling companion, she walked across the road and entered the mercantile. The doors were standing wide open so there was no bell to alert everyone of her presence, thank heaven.

The interior was fashioned completely with planks and logs of raw wood and smelled absolutely divine. Every wall was covered with goods—from bridles, tools, and fishing gear to kitchen utensils and school supplies. There were small barrels of potatoes, wheat, barley, and sugar, and wooden boxes of boots and shoes, flannel shirts, trousers, and headwear. Some shelves held books and catalogs, others held bolts of muslin and cotton. The store was impressively stocked and well kept.

Gwendolyn tentatively approached the front counter knowing that her life would be very different in the next moment.

A short woman, maybe in her forties or fifties, came backing out of the storeroom mere feet in front of her, and Gwendolyn held her breath.

"Gregory, could you put three or four sacks of flour in the front this time please? We're completely out." The woman turned around and immediately gasped upon seeing Gwendolyn.

Gwendolyn's heart began beating madly and her entire body was trembling. The woman before her had to be Mrs. Tyler. Gwendolyn was starting to believe that her friend Mrs. Maynard knew more about Gwendolyn's past life than she had been letting on.

"Gwendolyn?" the woman whispered, putting her hand over her heart.

Gwendolyn attempted a smile but it felt awkward and forced. She felt more like crying than smiling at that moment.

The woman came around the counter with surprising energy and grabbed Gwendolyn in a fierce embrace, squeezing the air from her lungs. "It *is* you, isn't it? I thought I was seeing a ghost, for a minute."

"Hello, Mrs. Tyler," she managed.

The woman pulled away and narrowed her beautiful blue eyes at her.

Ah, Gwendolyn decided uneasily, biting her lower lip. Either the woman wasn't Mrs. Tyler or she had very good instincts.

"I must go get Ben. You stay right there," she ordered powerfully.

She was gone in another whirl of skirts, leaving Gwendolyn breathless and confused.

The woman obviously cared for her and was a friend of Mrs. Maynard's. Why hadn't she ever written? She had to have known Gwendolyn was in Hopeton, she reasoned.

Gwendolyn suddenly startled from her thoughts when something slammed onto the table right beside her with a resounding thud. She gasped just as a large cloud of floury dust puffed into the air around her. Coughing deeply, she covered her mouth with one small, gloved hand and tried to wave the rest of the cloud away.

"Sorry, miss," a man mumbled behind her. "Didn't see you there. You all right?"

Gwendolyn turned around and gasped. It was *him*—the man from her vision! He stood before her in more vivid detail than anything she could remember from the night of the concert. He was wearing a wool jacket and trousers caked with dirt and woodchips. But there was something else…something almost soothing about him. Was it lavender? She giggled nervously at the thought of such a man using perfumed soap.

His thick brown hair fell in waves just past his broad shoulders and was a bit longer than she remembered. She watched in fascination as he closed his eyes and vigorously rubbed the flour out of his hair and short beard with one hand. Ah, he was magnificent!

Before she knew it, he had taken hold of her arm and unceremoniously began brushing the offensive dust from her shirtwaist, causing her to frown. She could have done the job very well on her own, but the warmth of his hand over her sleeve…of his body next to hers…was like a piece of hot bread straight out of the oven—delicious and irresistible. She shivered as a wave of unfamiliar tingles erupted over her entire body.

Suddenly, she froze, too shocked to utter a single word as his hands brazenly brushed against her backside. No doubt her face was painfully scarlet by now. Did the man have no manners at all?

"You all right?" he mumbled, drawing her attention to his more-than-captivating sea blue eyes.

She quickly realized she hadn't been breathing and dropped her hand to steady the fluttering in her stomach. But the moment she did, his expression turned hard and his gentle touch of concern became a grip of death.

"*Ow!* Please let go of me," she managed nervously. She stared at him wide-eyed, bemused at his sudden transformation. What happened to the sweet, brazen man who smelled of lavender?

"Gwendolyn," he hissed. "What the devil are you doing here?"

What *was* she doing there? she asked herself sarcastically, feeling his fingers squeezing the soft flesh of her upper arm more acutely. Well, there certainly wasn't any easy way to answer his question, so she kept silent. Besides, she wasn't even sure she wanted the suddenly ill-tempered brute to know.

"She's back, Ben. She's really back!"

Both Mrs. Tyler and a man Gwendolyn assumed to be Mr. Ben Tyler stopped short at the sight of the two of them.

"Gregory! Take your hands off the poor girl," his mother ordered. "Have you gone completely crazy?"

"Crazy? How can you call me crazy when Gwendolyn's the one who deserted us without a word or explanation, never contacted anyone although we've been assuming the worst, and is now standing in our store after nearly a year of absence looking so innocent and confused?" He let out an intimidating growl. "No. I'm not the one who's crazy." Gregory tightened his already painful grip even more and stared down at Gwendolyn as if she were the most detestable of all creatures.

Neither Mr. nor Mrs. Tyler said anything. They didn't even attempt to defend her against their son's accusations, so that could only mean one thing.

"No!" she said, shaking her head in denial and wrenching her arm free. "I would never do that." How could it be true? She would never desert anyone.

"Then what excuse can you give us?" Gregory continued.

"I–I don't know," she replied stupidly. She had come to Grovetown to get some answers but was only coming up with more and more questions. A gorgeous man—the man she'd thought could be the only link in helping her—was accusing her of atrocious things, and the woman who had hugged her just five minutes before wasn't even defending her. Gwendolyn wanted nothing more than to find a dark room where she could weep until her head was ready to explode.

"What do you mean, you 'don't know'? How could you not know? You're the only one who possibly can!"

Gwendolyn looked into Gregory's unfortunately gorgeous face as he mocked her and felt uncomfortably small, like she was merely a child being scolded for ruining her dress or sneaking sweets from the pantry without asking. She didn't like it.

Gathering all her courage, she swiftly slapped him in the face.

He barely flinched, his intense blue eyes staring her down… challenging her.

Oh, how she wanted to pummel him…to wipe that self-righteous smirk off his face. She moved to slap him again, but he stopped her easily with one hand—too easily.

"And here you are dressed in all your finery," he continued, moving his other arm the length of her as she fought his grip defiantly. "Have you now come back to your lowly hometown to rub your success in our faces? When did we suddenly become so unworthy in your eyes?"

"That's quite enough, Gregory," Mrs. Tyler said. "You know her better than that."

Gwendolyn looked down at the beautiful outfit the Jennys had given her for Christmas and immediately decided she hated the man standing before her. Gregory Tyler was a rude and arrogant good-for-nothing!

"I thought I knew her," he corrected his mother then looked back at Gwendolyn. "And why are you wearing a bonnet, Gwendolyn? I've never seen you wear one my entire life." He wrenched the bonnet from her head, pulling out a few strands of her hair in the process. Gwendolyn stared at him in horror as he crumpled the hat carelessly in his fist.

"You blackguard!" she shrieked, slapping him with more power than she realized she possessed. It made a delicious sound.

Mrs. Tyler gasped and Gwendolyn was instantly embarrassed for making such a scene…but Gregory deserved it. He was shocked but clearly pleased as he rewarded her with a smirk once again.

She glared at him. Oh, how she loathed the man. Why on earth was he the only person she remembered from her past? It was incredibly wrong for so many reasons.

Mr. Tyler bounded across the floor and cuffed his son roughly on the back of the head before marching him straight out of the mercantile past a gawking customer.

Gregory Tyler was, without a doubt, the worst possible man on the face of the earth. He had torn her confidence away piece-by-piece, destroyed her pride, and stripped her of all dignity. She had nothing left.

She turned away and fought the tears that were forming. Going to Grovetown was beginning to feel like a big mistake. Not only had an attractive man yelled at and humiliated her in front of his parents—not to mention her future employer—but she was even more dreadfully confused than she had been before. Gregory's words had stung infinitely more so than her hand did. All she wanted was to be accepted, to feel loved, and to have a place she could call home.

Mrs. Tyler's arms came around her, and Gwendolyn allowed herself to feel some comfort in the gesture.

"Let's get you home," the woman said, handing Gwendolyn a handkerchief to wipe away her tears. But Gwendolyn was just getting started.

They went out the back door of the mercantile, walked past a couple townhouses, and came upon a green kitchen door. Mrs. Tyler barged right in without knocking, pulling Gwendolyn right behind her.

"Marguerite? Look who I found at the mercantile," Mrs. Tyler announced.

There were two women—Gwendolyn's mother and sister, perhaps—sitting at a table strewn with ribbons, lace, and white silks. Gwendolyn was immediately disappointed. She didn't recognize either one of them. The older one had soft green eyes and long brown hair, but the younger one had hair the color and texture of fresh honey. They looked up at the intrusion and stared at Gwendolyn in astonishment.

Marguerite, the older woman, stood up slowly then rushed forward to hug Gwendolyn, tears suddenly streaming down her creamy skin. "Oh, my darling! We thought you were dead."

*Dead?* Gwendolyn thought in alarm. How was that even possible? The idea that she'd left a loving family to teach in Hopeton—a large and strange city she knew absolutely nothing about—and only had one connection via correspondence sounded absolutely preposterous! She refused to believe she would ever do something so selfish. She knew she might never know the true reason, judging by everybody's reactions, but she also knew deep within her heart that she hadn't left for the reasons Gregory Tyler had accused her of. No, she would never do that, *could* never do that.

The younger woman came from behind and joined in the embrace. "Gwendolyn, you're back, you're really back. Why did you ever leave us?"

"Yes, I would like to know the same thing," Mrs. Tyler said, taking a seat at the foot of the table. "What happened?"

Just then, a man burst through the kitchen door. It was Ben Tyler, looking breathless and quite severe. He was a very brawny sort of man, more so than his son, and had a commanding presence even though she hadn't heard him speak yet. He nodded a reply to his wife then went to stand behind her, grasping the posts of her chair.

Marguerite didn't seem to notice the interruption, but merely pulled back to get a better look at Gwendolyn. Using both hands, she pushed the girl's hair out of her face and instantly pulled back as if a snake had bitten her. "Merciful heavens, Gwendolyn! How did you get that?"

Frowning, the others leaned closer to get a good look at what Marguerite was referring to. Gasps of shock inevitably followed.

"How on earth did I miss that?" Mrs. Tyler said, softly touching the affected area.

They all stood gaping at it as though she had a huge beetle fused to her head, and it made Gwendolyn unbearably uncomfortable. She pulled back and gestured for everyone to sit down then did her best to cover up the ugly scar. If only Mrs. Tyler's idiot son hadn't destroyed her bonnet!

"I–uh, was in an accident the day I left," she answered warily. "I had just arrived in Hopeton to be a teacher. My skirt caught and I fell trying to exit the coach."

"What?" all the ladies said in unison. Mr. Tyler simply stood expressionless, holding his trunk-like arms across his chest as if in disapproval.

"I was unconscious for about a week before waking up in a hospital. I've had some memory loss, but the doctor assured me it was common among most of his patients." She felt terrible having to tell them such horrible news and could only imagine how devastating her revelation would soon be to them. She bowed her head, afraid to see the pain in their expressions.

"What kind of memory loss?" Marguerite asked.

Gwendolyn hesitated. "Uh, I couldn't remember my name or how I'd gotten hurt."

"You couldn't remember your name?" Mrs. Tyler asked, astonished.

Gwendolyn shook her head, suddenly very much aware of the seriousness of her situation. In Hopeton, she had been the only one affected by her condition because she was the only one who knew anything about it. Mrs. Maynard had kept her secret from everyone else since she'd heard about it the previous month. But since Gwendolyn had come to Grovetown and told her family and the Tylers, she knew it wouldn't be long before the entire town heard of her condition.

"But why did you not write to us, Gwendolyn?"

Gwendolyn looked up to the young woman, feeling terribly guilty. There wasn't anything else she could have done under the circumstances…was there?

"Why did you never write and let us know where you were…that you were alive? The whole town spent days searching for you."

Gwendolyn looked at them in complete shock. They searched for her? Oh, what a dreadful mess she'd made of everything, she thought wearily. How had everything come to that point?

"I–I didn't…I couldn't—"

Gwendolyn couldn't finish before she burst into tears once more. The reality of her predicament was just too much to bear alone. Everyone was silent around her, most likely in a turmoil over unanswered questions, fear, and impatience. She knew exactly what that was like. She was beginning to feel the effects of her restless night and weary hours of traveling. After everything was over, she would lock herself in her bedroom and proceed with making her eyes as red and swollen as possible…just as soon as someone told her where her bedroom was.

"Have out with it, then," Mrs. Tyler urged.

Gwendolyn covered her face, not wanting to see their reactions. She knew the image would haunt her forever. She decided to just plunge on in and get it over with as soon as possible. "I couldn't remember any of you. When I hit my head, it erased every memory I had before the accident—every person I've ever known, every place I've ever been to, the games and foods I liked, everything. I didn't think it was possible that I could forget my family…so I just convinced myself that I didn't have one."

The entire group looked at her with varying combinations of

awe, disbelief, and sorrow, and it made her heart ache.

"The friends whom I've been staying with repeatedly inquired about my family…you," she pointed, including them all. "After some time, I began thinking that I did indeed have a family but that I had been abandoned. You see, I never received any letters, but I understand why now…somewhat." She still couldn't believe she would desert such an obviously loving family.

"If you couldn't remember Grovetown," Mrs. Tyler said. "How did you come to be here?"

"The woman I work for, Mrs. Maynard—with the Hopeton Board of Education—is a friend of yours, I believe." Gwendolyn looked to Mrs. Tyler who suddenly turned a darker shade of pink.

"Ellen."

Gwendolyn nodded.

"Just one blessed minute Sarah," Marguerite interrupted, rubbing her forehead with one shaky finger and looking as if she might break down at any moment. "Can you please explain how you can be friends with a woman who has been working alongside Gwendolyn for nearly a year…and not know about Gwendolyn? You had to have known she would be here today?"

"Honestly, I never expected it," she defended. "Ellen and I met while crossing the Atlantic and have written very infrequently since. The last I heard from her was before Gwendolyn left."

Gwendolyn didn't want them to blame each other, not when it wasn't their fault, so made quick to fix the misunderstanding. "Mrs. Maynard mentioned that you needed a new committee member this summer, Mrs. Tyler. She suggested that I take the position immediately after I told her of my memory loss, which was only a few weeks ago."

"She told me her son's wife would be coming."

Gwendolyn shook her head. "Because of the circumstances, she decided to keep my arrival a secret…not really knowing how I would be received. I think she also thought it would be better for me to explain myself in person."

"So, you don't remember any of us?" the young woman sitting across from her asked slowly. "You don't remember Dan…or Gregory?"

*Ugh*, she shivered in disgust. Of course she had to mention *him*. She felt her pulse begin to quicken, not with excitement but with irritation.

Mrs. Tyler reached over and put a hand on Gwendolyn's arm. "You don't remember Gregory at all…besides what happened in the store just now?" Her eyes searched Gwendolyn's, pleading.

"No," she said. She didn't want to admit she'd had a vision of him months ago. It was too humiliating. The knowledge was sure to come back and haunt her, but she wanted to put it off as long as possible.

"Wait! What happened in the store?" the younger woman asked, horror written in her expression.

"So the only thing you remember about Gregory," Mrs. Tyler began, ignoring the question and closing her eyes in concentration, "is that he yelled at you, accused you of things you can't remember doing, mocked your appearance, and destroyed your bonnet?"

"Yes." She couldn't understand why the woman had to ask her repeatedly about an event she'd witnessed for herself not twenty minutes before. However, she appreciated the woman's silence where her own behavior was concerned.

"Damn." Mr. Tyler finally took a seat next to his wife and rubbed one large hand over his whole face.

It was the first and only word Gwendolyn had heard from the man. The fact that he hadn't said or done anything remotely significant since his arrival in the kitchen until his son's name was mentioned frightened Gwendolyn into complete silence. Across from her, the young woman dropped her forehead to the table with a small thud.

Gwendolyn was starting to get an awful feeling in the pit of her very empty stomach. She wasn't promised to Gregory, was she? It would have been a surprise being his betrothed. Of course, it would explain his reaction. Before he'd recognized her in the store, he'd been quite pleasant…and devilishly handsome. But not anymore, not after the way he'd spoken to her. She wanted nothing to do with him. She wondered then if she'd left Grovetown because of him.

"Gwendolyn?"

She lifted her head to Marguerite, growing weary from answering all their questions, but she knew they had more of a right to know than anyone.

"Do you know who I am then?"

Gwendolyn studied the woman's delicate features. They shared the same long brown hair, although Marguerite's was straight and shiny and Gwendolyn's was a mass of soft curls. The woman's jaw line was the same as Gwendolyn's as well as her small curvaceous build.

"My mother?" she whispered carefully. She felt so wretchedly foolish.

"No," the woman replied, slowly shaking her head. "Your mother was my twin sister. She died giving birth to you. But I would be honored if you would call me mother." She watched Gwendolyn curiously.

"What about my father?"

"He died three months after your mother's death. They loved each other very much, you see. Your Uncle Barrett and I adopted you since your sister wasn't old enough to take care of you."

"I have a sister?"

"You have *two* sisters," the young woman across from her stubbornly corrected. She finally lifted her head from the table and smiled directly at Gwendolyn.

"Your biological sister is Rebecca. She lives in Leadville." Marguerite continued then pointed to the young woman at her side. "This is my daughter Daisy…your other sister, apparently." Marguerite chuckled despite the solemnity of the situation.

"That's right," Daisy affirmed with a lively nod. "And I don't want to hear you calling me any different."

Everyone chuckled in unison.

"Who's Dan?" Gwendolyn asked, remembering the name.

Both Daisy and Mrs. Tyler spoke at the same time, garbling their words into incoherence. Daisy looked down shyly, and Mrs. Tyler took the lead.

"He's our other son," she said, nodding to Ben. "He'll be marrying Daisy in about two weeks."

"Yes," Daisy said, drumming her long fingernails together and grinning mischievously. "At which time he will be forever subject to my endless chatter." She laughed merrily.

Mrs. Tyler stood and cupped the girl's face in her small hands. "It will be good to have you as an official member of our family, my sweet."

Daisy gave the woman a smile that could melt even the crabbiest of hearts.

"And you, mistress Gwendolyn," Mrs. Tyler said, coming to stand before her and lowering her voice almost to a whisper. "I know things have been difficult for you, and they will be difficult still. Just don't forget, from this moment forward, that I cherish you as one of my own daughters and will be more than happy to listen to whatever you have to say…whenever you need to say it. You may have forgotten me, but I haven't forgotten you. I will treat you the same as I always have. I hope that in time we will become as good of friends as we were always meant to be."

Gwendolyn nodded, feeling a single tear fall past her cheek. She no longer had any doubts about the woman's character. For whatever reasons the woman had for keeping silent in the mercantile, they had to be good ones. She watched Mr. and Mrs. Tyler leave and felt a terrible emptiness inside.

She turned back to her family—her very own family—and smiled nervously.

"I'm so happy to have you back, darling." Her aunt hugged her once again. "Are you hungry? I'll put a pot of stew on and go freshen up your room. I haven't touched it since the day you left. I guess I've been hoping you would come back one day, and so you have."

Gwendolyn nodded then sat back in her chair, feeling as if she had just released a tremendous burden. She was exhausted.

"Don't think you're getting away from me so easily."

Startled by the young woman's cryptic words, Gwendolyn looked up to see Daisy organizing the dainty white strips of lace into piles. Daisy continued, not taking her eyes off of her task for a second. "For tonight I will let you sleep, but tomorrow night I shall drill you with questions until your head spins. *And,* you shall answer them with far more detail than you've done today because frankly I shall not let you sleep until I am completely satisfied. Just thought I should warn you." Daisy peered at Gwendolyn beneath a set of beautiful eyelashes, a smile apparent on her face.

"All right." Gwendolyn grinned, instantly liking this cous—sister of hers.

# Chapter Four

GREGORY SAT ON THE FLOOR of the half-constructed house, madly hammering away at a stubborn nail. He'd started his work for the day long before the sun had even risen, purposely leaving his family's house before anyone could bother him with questions he wasn't ready to answer. He just didn't trust himself to talk to anyone, especially not after yelling at Gwendolyn the day before. Despite the fact that she deserved nearly every word he'd thrown at her, he still managed to feel a pang of guilt.

He rose from his seat and angrily strode toward the back entry. Crouching, he grabbed Gwendolyn's bonnet from the pile of floorboards and idly fingered the intricate weave with his thumbs as he remembered her fancy dress, her haughty manner, and her blank expression when he'd rightly accused her.

The woman must have completely lost her senses, he thought incredulously. What else could she have expected? He shrugged his shoulders in reply.

She couldn't have changed that much in only a year. Not the girl he'd grown up with for the past two decades—the one who'd caught tadpoles in Myrtle Pond with him, who'd protected their goose from an angry, stray dog, and had verbally pounced on Jimmy Morrison for teasing Daisy back in their school days.

And boy, could she pack a punch! He laughed despite himself. Never before had she hit him with such obvious vehemence. He hated to admit it, but he'd actually been frightened of her at first. But afterward he'd merely felt it as a challenge…one he would accept with relish since she was back.

He hung his head, still unable to forget that day—the day Gwendolyn had disappeared and left him to grieve to the very core. The past several months had been unendurable. With every minute, every memory, every mention of her name, he grew more anxious, more detached, and more angry. At first there was a part of him that had suspected, and foolishly hoped, that she had some brilliant plan and would be back after a few days. But when those days turned into weeks and those weeks turned into months, he realized he'd been a fool. Gwendolyn was gone and wanted absolutely nothing to do with her former life. She'd made that abundantly clear.

He'd tried hard to convince himself that Gwendolyn meant nothing to him and he'd done a rather good job of it until she'd casually waltzed into the store looking so innocent and confused. He growled. She always did make things difficult.

The shadow of a man suddenly appeared over his shoulder and he knew right away who it was. There was no need to look. "If you've come to cuff and lecture me again," he said gruffly, "then you're wasting your time."

Without pause, Gregory tossed the bonnet back on the pile of beams and moved across the floor to hammer down the loose end of a wooden board.

"Why's that?" Ben Tyler asked.

"I know I shouldn't have been so rough or angry with Gwendolyn, but I wasn't thinking." That was a downright lie, he snorted in disgust. In fact, he'd rehearsed the moment a million times while harvesting his father's crop, picking up supplies at the station, crafting furniture, and building his and Dan's houses. He'd never actually thought the moment would come.

He could never tell his father the real reason for yelling at her, although Gregory knew everybody sensed it for themselves. He wasn't an idiot. It just hurt too much to admit, to say aloud. She had wounded him too deeply. Besides, he was a grown man of twenty-six with a building business, property, and real responsibilities. He didn't have time for emotional disruptions.

"No, you shouldn't have." His father left the doorframe and came to crouch before him, laying one large hand across Gregory's broad shoulder. "Son, I know what she's done has been very hard on you—on all of us—and I don't blame you for being angry, but your mother and I didn't teach you to treat women thus, no matter what the circumstance."

"I know that," he growled. "But how else was I supposed to react?" Gregory dropped his head, immediately regretting his words. He slammed his hammer down on the nail one last time before dropping the tool with a resounding thud.

"You could try talking to her again, Greg…but without the yelling and accusations of course. She's got an amazing story to tell."

"Amazing, huh?" Gregory repeated in disbelief. "So you've spoken with her?" He stood, not waiting for an answer and went to stand before an empty kitchen window to gaze upon his field of wild lavender, dandelions, and thick brush. "Was her explanation for leaving amazing as well?"

He turned around and watched as his father went slowly to the opposite corner of the room, grabbed at a stud board with one hand and shuffled a stray nail about with the toe of his boot.

"Gwendolyn did not offer any explanation for leaving, Greg… nor will she ever, I imagine." The man looked up with only his eyes and watched Gregory, no doubt gauging his reaction.

"Oh, of course not," Gregory suddenly roared, waving his arms for emphasis. "It's not as if we have a right to know. We haven't just been close for the past twenty years or shared everything we've ever known with each other. Why would she tell us?"

"Maybe you should ask her."

"No," Gregory said, shaking his head and balling up his fists. "I will not. After everything that's happened, our friendship can never be the same. Gwendolyn is a completely different person."

Ben Tyler ran a hand through his hair and looked overly taxed, or frustrated.

Gregory watched as his old man took several labored steps toward the main doorframe.

Looking up into the sky, his father mumbled, "God, what a mess," then slowly crossed the threshold.

"Good morning!"

Gwendolyn's eyes shot open just in time to see her cousin Daisy plop herself upon the feather tick, rattling her awake. Daisy's hair was pulled back in a simple French twist, and she was wearing a lovely green dress with a square neckline, white eyelet, and three-quarter sleeves. The colors complemented her features nicely.

"I thought you said you wouldn't interrogate me until later tonight," Gwendolyn groaned as she sat up on her elbows. She blinked several times, trying to adjust to the brilliant morning light.

"Oh, don't be silly," Daisy waved casually. "I'm not here to interrogate you…yet. I was feeling generous, so I allowed you to sleep in an extra couple of hours. No no, don't thank me." Daisy said, silencing Gwendolyn before she'd even had a chance to speak. She rose from the bed and went directly to Gwendolyn's closet, opening the door dramatically. "How many dresses do you have?"

"What? Oh, uh…six. Why?" Gwendolyn removed her bed covers and stood just as Daisy pulled her blue dress from its hanger and held it up for her. Idly, Gwendolyn grabbed it from her.

"Oh, good grief! I have at least a dozen. You definitely need more." Daisy leafed through the remaining dresses and gasped. "Oh, this is absolutely gorgeous! It will be perfect for tomorrow night." She held out Gwendolyn's lavender dress—a piece Gwendolyn had purchased in Hopeton for the Easter Ball—and reverently laid it upon the bed, admiring the fabric and elaborate stitching, the perfect tucks, folds, and hemline. Mrs. Maynard and the Jennys had all insisted she purchase it the moment they saw it, and Gwendolyn reluctantly did so. After some consideration, she decided that she deserved a beautiful dress. Robert had certainly seemed to like it.

He'd been tripping up and stuttering all evening, she remembered with a smile.

"What's happening tomorrow night?" Gwendolyn asked, fastening her corset with some difficulty and then stepping into her simple blue dress with eyelet trim.

"A dance…at the town hall. Oh, I'm so excited! Mr. Morrison is celebrating the success of his lumber business this past season by hosting a dance for the entire town. Oh, I simply can't wait!"

A dance, Gwendolyn thought miserably. Under any other circumstance she would have been pleased as punch, but not anymore, not when she couldn't remember anybody's names or faces and didn't have a clue what to talk about. No doubt she'd be the subject of everyone's gossip, if she weren't already. None of the young men in town would dance with her, surely. Oh, what would she do?

Then again it would probably be a good way to get reacquainted and meet people. It had to be done, so she might as well get it over with. She just had to make sure Mrs. Tyler, her aunt, and Daisy wouldn't leave her alone for a single moment.

Gwendolyn went to her dressing table and picked up a brush that had been left for her over the months. It felt strange using all of her old things, sleeping in her own bed, and being with her family—one she'd thought had abandoned her. Everything was as unfamiliar as if she were merely borrowing a guest room for the summer. She shook her head, feeling awkward and silly.

"Oh!" Daisy said suddenly, making Gwendolyn jump. "You don't know this, but Gregory and Dan have started their very own business."

"What kind of business?" Why did she even care? she wondered with disgust. Gregory was a beast—incapable of sympathy.

"They're builders. They build houses, barns, furniture…you name it. Oh, give me that," she said, suddenly grabbing Gwendolyn's brush. She went through Gwendolyn's smooth curls gently as she continued her explanation. "Last summer, they both bought plots of land right next to each other. That way, after Dan and I are married, we can all share one barn and one plot for growing, but we'll have our own houses of course. It's completely brilliant, I think. It would be too much work for a young couple otherwise… you know, when they're just starting out."

"Are you two almost finished up there?" her aunt Marguerite called from downstairs. "Breakfast is almost ready."

"Just a couple more minutes, Mums," Daisy hollered back. She looked at Gwendolyn with narrowed eyes for a few seconds before continuing. "I'm never late when food is involved."

Gwendolyn giggled. Daisy really was a gem.

"Do you want your hair up or down?"

"Definitely down," Gwendolyn said, rolling her eyes in irritation. "Gregory took my new bonnet yesterday—rather rudely, as a matter of fact—and I don't want people asking questions about my scar."

"Oh, well…he probably just took it so he'd have something to remember you by. Perhaps to keep it under his pillow?" she teased, smiling wickedly when Gwendolyn frowned. "Don't worry. I'll get it back for you. And although this scar is obnoxiously noticeable, it doesn't do anything to draw away from your beautiful face…or your kind heart."

Feeling the emotion building behind her eyes, Gwendolyn stood up and threw her arms around her cousin. "What did I ever do to deserve such a wonderful cous—I mean sister? I can't even begin to tell you how much you've helped me."

Daisy returned the embrace fiercely despite her slender frame. "Oh, Gwendolyn! I'm so glad you're home. Life just hasn't been the same without you. Truly."

After a few minutes they pulled apart, each wiping at their tears and sniffling, then made their way down the stairs.

"I really do hate crying," Gwendolyn said upon reaching the bottom floor. "It gives me such a blasted headache."

"I know. It dries my eyes out like crazy," Daisy grumbled.

She and Daisy entered the kitchen just as Marguerite pulled a batch of fresh cinnamon rolls out of the cast-iron stove. Scrambled eggs were sizzling away on the griddle, bringing the room alive with its gurgling noise.

"Oh, good morning, you two." Marguerite greeted cheerily. She wiped her hands on her apron and embraced them both. "It's so good to have both my girls together again. Did you sleep well, Gwendolyn, darling?" She urged Gwendolyn to sit down and grabbed three small bowls of peaches and cream for the table.

"A little too well, I'm afraid."

"Nonsense, you had such a long day yesterday…and you probably didn't get any rest on the train. Am I right?"

Gwendolyn nodded.

"Would you like some eggs, Gwendolyn? Daisy?"

"Yes, please," they replied in unison.

"But where is Papa?" Daisy said, shock apparent on her face. "Won't he be eating with us?"

"I don't think so, dear. He's really exhausted." Her aunt brought their eggs to the table along with a wooden platter covered with steaming cinnamon rolls and sat down to start eating. "He was up all of last night helping deliver Jenny Clark's baby. She and Warren are so proud…they have a strong, healthy boy. Oh, how wonderful it will be to have children running around this house again." She gazed wistfully at Daisy then shook her head slightly. "Now, eat up you two, before it gets cold."

"But Papa hasn't even seen Gwendolyn yet!" Daisy said, ignoring her mother's tactless suggestion and her food. "Does he even know she's here?"

"No. And don't you go waking him up. He got home about three hours ago, and I thought it best to let him and Gwendolyn both get their rest."

Gwendolyn shifted nervously in her seat and debated whether to grab for a cinnamon roll. They were just oozing with frosting—begging to be eaten. She imagined chewing the moist, warm bread, the somewhat bitter filling, and licking the sugary glaze off her fingers afterwards. Oh, she simply couldn't resist. She grabbed one possessively, and the act seemed to prevent her aunt and Daisy from further argument.

"Don't worry, Daisy. I'll tell him when he wakes up. For now," she said, calmly picking up a fork and dipping it into her eggs, "eat your breakfast so we can get on with our day today. We have a lot to do you know."

Daisy simply rolled her eyes in reply and took a couple bites before blurting, "Gwendolyn's only got half a dozen dresses—mostly plain ones—and I don't know what happened to the rest of them."

Nearly choking, Gwendolyn put a hand to her bosom and looked at Daisy in astonishment. Her cousin was completely ignorant of her distress, but her aunt was just staring right back at Gwendolyn. She gulped, her cheeks turning vermillion.

"My trunks were stolen," Gwendolyn explained quickly. Oh dear. She hoped nothing in them had been too valuable.

"In Hopeton?" her aunt asked in alarm.

"At the station near there."

"Do you know who it was?"

"No," Gwendolyn said, shaking her head. "The driver took them back to the station after my accident. He said a man picked them up…someone claiming to be my brother."

Gwendolyn flinched as she was suddenly sprinkled with a liquid substance. She looked up to find her aunt staring at her—blank-faced and utterly oblivious to the peach wedge she'd just dropped in her cream.

"That's ridiculous!" Daisy scoffed. "You don't even have a brother." She retrieved a kitchen towel and casually tossed it to her mother who seemed somewhat recovered but still looked unusually agitated. "Oh, well. Nothin' can be done about it now. No-good thief. We'll just have to buy her some new ones, right Mums?"

Marguerite nodded and then dropped her head to stare at her bowl of peaches.

The young man watched Gwendolyn as she demurely crossed the road, and he felt his blood boil with unadulterated hatred for her. So, she thought she could fool him, did she?

He'd followed her on the train and disguised himself as an extra coachman all the way to Hopeton where he'd seen her fall out of the coach. Her blood slowly pooled beneath her in the gravel road as the townspeople gawked and screeched about. At the time, there'd been no question in his mind—she was dead. Finally. After all those years, he'd finally gotten his revenge. The deed hadn't even required his help. He'd merely stood by and watched, laughing inside. It was over…*she* was over. He'd left, feeling confident, wanting her to die alone. It was what she deserved after everything she'd done.

But there she was, back in Grovetown, looking well…and *alive.* He didn't think she knew he'd followed her to Hopeton and was willing to bet she hadn't staged the entire thing. She wasn't clever enough. She was just a worthless murdering female.

He crept around the corner of the ironsmith's shop and felt a blaze of heat emanating from the forge, soothing him. He eyed Gwendolyn as a snake would eye its prey and began concocting a new plan. Apparently nature had a different plan for her than he did, but he was going to change that.

With bold determination, he headed toward the town's pathetically small saloon for a drink.

Gwendolyn gaped at Daisy in disbelief. She could barely contain her excitement. "No, no, no. Please," she said. "I don't want you to feel any obligation to me whatsoever just because I'm back. I promise I won't think any less of you if you choose someone else." Feigning disinterest, Gwendolyn bowed her head and smoothed the wrinkles from her skirt. In truth, she could think of no greater honor, especially after everything that had happened in the last year.

"Gwendolyn, you're not just *back*," Daisy said in exasperation, "you're *alive.* You're not dead, you're not a guest for us to fuss over, and you definitely have not inconvenienced us in any way. Perhaps you don't realize how much you are truly loved, my dear elder sister."

She gave Gwendolyn a playful jab in the ribs, making Gwendolyn laugh. "But you're going to be my maid-of-honor whether you think you deserve it or not. Now, let's get your measurements."

Beaming with pleasure, Gwendolyn followed Daisy to the tailor's corner and sat in a chair facing an ancient mahogany desk covered with bolts of fabric, small pieces of paper, and various tailoring aids. After giving orders to Mr. Caldwell about the style of dress, Daisy hastened back to the front of the store to break up the argument between her mother and Mrs. Tyler over her own wedding colors.

The measurement process felt awkward and tedious. Gwendolyn stood behind a woolen screen as Mr. Caldwell ordered her to turn and raise her arms. The short mousy man took her measurements with precision and speed and treated her more like an object than an actual human being, not looking in her eyes for a moment. As he measured her bustline and around her rump, she decided she liked being treated as an object…but only at that particular moment, of course.

He didn't seem to know who she was, or perhaps he simply didn't care. But that was just fine with her. She hadn't realized how difficult it would be to recount her side of the story, or what she remembered of it. Since everyone was saying she'd practically abandoned *them* instead of the other way around, she really wasn't looking forward to relating her story anymore than she absolutely had to. She couldn't remember anything about her life in Grovetown. Therefore, all of the blame rested upon her unfortunate shoulders. It was an appropriate punishment.

Just when she had rejoined her group and began admiring their purchases, a bell jingled above the door of the shop. Gwendolyn turned to see a tall young man about her age with golden brown hair and dark brown eyes coming straight for her, grinning broadly.

"Gwendolyn! Is that really you?"

Without waiting for an answer, the stranger pulled her into his powerful, sweaty arms, effectively deflating her lungs.

She let out a hearty wheeze. Did any of the men in Grovetown have manners? she wondered irritably. The first one she'd met had merely brushed her backside and royally rebuked her just as a mother would rebuke her daughter after destroying a new Sunday dress. And the second one, well, he was just a little too welcoming. Would all of her encounters be so humiliating?

Muttering an embarrassed 'good morning' under her breath, she wriggled free from his grasp. She held her hair over her scar and stood back a good couple feet from him. He didn't seem to notice.

"I heard you were back in town," he said, casually leaning against a shelf laden with bolts of brightly colored quilting fabrics. His voice was silky smooth, giving him a rather surprising air of sophistication based on his grimy appearance. She sniffed, sensing fresh pine and sulfur. "Where was it you ran off to? We all thought you were dead."

Gwendolyn froze, suddenly unable to think of an answer that would sound even remotely intelligent. She grumbled under her breath, not having prepared for people's blunt questions. Perhaps that was just the custom in more rural areas, she decided.

"She's been teaching in Hopeton, Mr. Morrison," Mrs. Tyler said, coming to her rescue. "Now, if you'll excuse the poor girl, I desperately need her help with some quilting projects. The committee has their hands full this summer, I'm afraid." She winked at Gwendolyn, bumped her in her aunt's direction, then turned back around to face the young man. "Good day, Mr. Morrison."

What was going on? Gwendolyn wondered, sensing Mrs. Tyler's cool dismissal toward him, although she couldn't imagine why it was necessary. He was adequately charming, except for his tactlessness of her situation, but how was he to know?

He tipped his hat to Mrs. Tyler but made no move to leave. Ignoring the woman's protests, he touched Gwendolyn's elbow gently. "Are you attending my father's dance in the hall tomorrow evening?"

Daisy whirled around and gawked at him, her eyes as round as saucers.

"Yes," Gwendolyn replied, bursting with hope. If he danced with her, maybe the event wouldn't be so dreadful after all, she decided. At least he wasn't an adolescent or married.

Gwendolyn jerked. Or *was* he married? she thought in sudden alarm. Was that why everyone was acting so odd?

"Will you save the first dance for me then…if I request a reel? I know they're your favorite."

He couldn't possibly be married, she determined as she looked into his eyes. Otherwise he wouldn't have asked for a dance. She did enjoy the liveliness of the reel even though it made her head pound. "Yes, that would be love—"

"Gwendolyn," Mrs. Tyler hastily interrupted, plunking her bolts of fabric into Gwendolyn's arms then steadying her. "Will you do me a favor and take these by the house? I have a mind to purchase some more fabric, and I don't think I can carry everything all by myself." She roughly urged Gwendolyn toward the front door.

Did Daisy just snarl? Gwendolyn looked over her shoulder to see the girl glaring Mr. Morrison down although he was a good few inches taller than her, and Gwendolyn smiled.

Upon reaching the outer porch, her expression hardened once again. Something about the entire situation just didn't seem right.

"Why did you agree to dance with him?" Mrs. Tyler probed.

Feeling only irritation with the woman's interference, Gwendolyn remained silent. Did she have no privacy? Was she not allowed to make her own decisions? What else could she have said? She didn't even know the man. Something had happened in the past, something that vexed everyone a great deal, something she couldn't remember or hadn't been around to hear about. Mrs. Tyler had to know that.

As if reading her thoughts, Mrs. Tyler rolled her eyes and heaved a sigh. "I'll tell you about it later. I don't suppose you remember where my house is." She quickly glanced at the shop's door before continuing in hushed tones. "It's less than half a mile down the lane past your house. There's a white fence leading to it. It shouldn't take you more than twenty minutes. You can stay there and maybe take a look at the new kittens, or you can go back home. But don't come back here under any circumstance," she said strictly, pointing a finger so close that Gwendolyn's eyes crossed. "I don't want you anywhere near James again, you hear me? Now off you go."

"But—"

"Uh, uh, uh," Mrs. Tyler chided. "You. Go. Now." She playfully shoved the girl in the right direction and disappeared through the shop door before Gwendolyn even had a chance to protest.

But what if Gregory was there? she thought, spinning around in alarm. The idea caused the back of her neck to erupt with goose bumps—the bad kind. What would he think when he saw her roaming freely through his father's house? He probably didn't know anything about her condition yet, being the arrogant stubborn man she assumed him to be. No doubt he would chastise her again, throw her from the premise with his large hands, fabric and all, and bid her never come back.

Resting her chin on the bolts of fabric, she realized she couldn't avoid him for long. As with everybody else in town, she would need to face him eventually, no matter how unsavory the situation might turn out. If she didn't face him now, she'd only have to dread it longer or be the subject of another humiliating episode. Who knew? Her humiliation debut could be the following night at the Morrison's dance.

Groaning audibly, she made her way across the porch in weary resolution. She would just have to look into the man's gorgeous face and give him a piece of her mind, that's what. It was a shame that his agreeable physique was being wasted by such a poisonous personality. But she knew she deserved to be treated better and would make certain he understood that important fact even if it killed her.

Gwendolyn stepped into the street and gazed skyward. A blanket of puffy gray clouds hung above her and looked beautiful despite its gloominess. She longed to wait out for the rain, but the cloth could not get wet. What would Mrs. Tyler think if she were so careless?

Shifting the bundle to one arm and grabbing her skirts with the other, she awkwardly trotted down the path.

"Dan, my patience is wearing very thin, so if you have something to say to me have out with it and let me be at peace."

Gregory leaned on the roof of his brother's almost completed home, pounding nearly a dozen nails in their places with each passing minute. It felt good to be hitting things.

He shrugged in near defeat. Dan had already attempted to speak with him earlier, but Gregory had made it very clear he didn't want to hear another word about Gwendolyn. Not a quarter of an hour later, his mother had appeared looking quite piqued. Ignoring his bitter attitude and indignant warnings, she'd managed the words—"It's not what you think! Just go and talk with her." He shook his head at the memory.

"Daisy spoke with me earlier this morning…about Gwendolyn."

"Will wonders never cease," Gregory drawled. Maybe he should just go and have a talk with her, he thought, and then maybe everyone would leave him the hell alone!

A peal of thunder rumbled overhead, echoing throughout the valley. Gwendolyn had always loved storms, and Gregory could never understand why. They were just a bundle of noise that quaked and drenched one to their very core.

"C'mon, Greg." Dan put his tools down and sat with his legs outstretched along the newly placed shingles. "Don't fight me on this."

Gregory sighed wearily, not really feeling the fight in him anymore. He knew he needed to apologize to Gwendolyn for yelling at her, for treating her like she was some spoiled brat to be disciplined, but how else did she expect he would react after she'd disappeared for almost a year? She had to know how he felt about her…had always felt about her. With all of the emotions he'd been burying inside, he wasn't even sure he could ask her the questions he desperately needed answers to without blubbering like a drooling, lovesick pup. Oh, how he dreaded their meeting. He'd made such a fool of himself already.

As Gregory pulled back for another swing, the steel head of his hammer came loose and flew past him, clipping his ear. He spun around and watched in shock as it landed with a muted thud on the ground below.

How did that happen? he wondered in alarm. It could have killed him! He didn't even think he'd used that much force with the blasted thing.

He looked up to see that his brother's wide-eyed expression matched his own. Heaving a relieved groan, he tossed what remained of the hammer over his shoulder.

"Something miraculous but…dreadful has happened to her, Greg."

"Explain." Gregory touched his ear, still recovering from his near-fatal accident.

He watched his younger brother move his left foot back and forth as he gazed blindly into the trees.

"Greg, I am sorry, but—"

"What the hell is going on?" he interrupted, stifling the quiver that rose unexpectedly in his throat. "What's happened to her?" And why was he so bloody weepy all of a sudden?

Dan's gaze lowered slowly, not meeting his own. That was definitely a bad sign. "Just go talk to Gwendolyn about it. She'll be furious with me, of course, but I suddenly don't have the stomach for it." Dan abruptly stood, went to the ladder, and descended the steps wearing a grave expression.

*"What?"* Gregory literally flew after him, his heart hammering in his chest. If anything had happened to her…

# Chapter Five

GREGORY ROARED IN FRUSTRATION. Nobody had been at home when he went by the Mathewson's place, and neither his father nor Dan knew where Gwendolyn was when he stopped by the mercantile. Once he'd finally found his mother, Mrs. Mathewson, and Daisy at the dress shop, they'd told him Gwendolyn was on her way to Orchard Cottage to drop off some bolts of fabric and to, for pity's sake, be nice to her.

Well, there he was standing in the middle of his parent's parlor, dripping wet from the rain and staring at the neat stack of bolts lying on the sofa. Gwendolyn was nowhere in sight.

"Gwendolyn," he barked, pulling the hair from his face and wiping his brow. She had to be close. "Where are you, woman?"

He searched through the house one room at a time and found only Caramel, the family German Shepherd, resting peacefully on the floor near his bed. He bent to scratch behind her ears.

"Do you know where she is, ol' girl?"

Caramel licked his fingers then lowered her head once more.

Apparently not.

Descending the stairs two at a time, he made his way through the kitchen door and out into the pouring rain once again. As long as he was there, he thought he might as well pick up another hammer from the barn. He knew his father would be angry when he found out the other one was broken, but Gregory didn't really care. It wasn't as if it had been his fault.

He trudged through the mud for several yards before a soft voice stopped him. It was Gwendolyn. She was sitting right on the ground just inside the barn only a few feet away and, thank heaven, facing the opposite direction.

Using great stealth, Gregory sidestepped into the nearest cluster of trees and hid behind a boulder.

Ah, she was playing with Sophie's new litter of kittens. Of course. He watched as she carefully lifted one of the furry bundles out of the hay-filled pen and set it in her lap.

"Aren't you the most precious little thing ever," he heard her coo.

He watched in fascination as she delicately stroked the white kitten then brought it up to her face to nuzzle. It reached out with its front limbs and playfully pawed at her pert little nose.

With one long finger, Gwendolyn curiously touched the pads of each paw before the kitten grabbed her finger to study it in return. She laughed, and Gregory's heart skipped a beat.

Now, how could he be angry with that? he grumbled, not taking his eyes off of her for a second. The image of her sitting in the dirt, wearing a beautiful blue dress and talking to the tiny kitten as she tenderly stroked its spotless white fur, made him ache for her, for her touch, and for things to be right between them again.

He began to wonder if she'd really changed at all during the time they'd been apart. Maybe he'd misjudged her in the store, he thought mournfully. But the fact that she had been wearing a nice frilly dress…and a *bonnet* was a complete contradiction to her character.

A sickening thought struck him next. Gwendolyn had left under very poor circumstances and it had been her first day back. Maybe she'd been trying to make an impression. He rolled his eyes before roughly punching himself in the thigh for his stupidity.

"I'm so confused," she said softly, interrupting his thoughts. He leaned forward a bit, wanting to hear every word. "Why has everyone been so kind to me…after everything that's happened… everyone except for Gregory? Why was he so angry?"

She hugged the kitten to her bosom and it squirmed in protest. "And why does he have to be so annoyingly attractive, and yet, such an arrogant fool?"

Arrogant? Well, yes, he had to admit he'd been a bit arrogant. But a fool, absolutely not…at least, not in the way he thought she meant it. But the knowledge that she found him annoyingly attractive was gratifying, indeed. He'd been so afraid that she'd thought of him only as a big brother or a good friend. He smiled to himself. Things were definitely looking up.

What was she doing, he suddenly wondered, squinting his eyes to see a little further. Oh, no. She was crying! Please, no, not that. He put his head in his hands and felt nothing but intense remorse for how he'd treated her. Why couldn't he just have been grateful that she was back, hugged her, and told her how he really felt?

"I can't stand it when people are angry with me." She wiped her eyes quickly as if embarrassed then returned the kitten to its pen. "Thanks for listening to me, little ones. You're really lucky to have such a beautiful home, you know. The Tylers must love you very much."

He watched as she struggled to get up. She seemed weary…and burdened, somehow.

Taking one last look at the occupants of the barn, she gave a hearty sigh and set off into the rain. It didn't seem to bother her—the rain—as it seeped through her clothing and dripped down her smooth porcelain skin. She barely flinched when the wet drops began pounding down on her. It was almost as if she'd spent most of her life in such weather conditions.

Leaning against the boulder and wondering about Gwendolyn's mysteries, he watched her until she left the lane then followed at a discreet distance.

Raising her arms and face to the heavens, Gwendolyn closed her eyes and tried to absorb every drop of rain that poured down on her. Oh, how she loved it! It was so pure, so natural, so comforting. How could anybody not love it? The air in Hopeton hadn't smelled nearly as irresistible and fresh as the air in Grovetown, and she knew her students would just love it if they could be there with her. There was just something about the quaint little country town, something utterly magical that Gwendolyn couldn't quite put her finger on. She felt as if she were experiencing everything for the first time, which she was.

She was so grateful to Mrs. Tyler for suggesting she see the new kittens. They were much smaller than Cinnamon had been the first time she'd seen him, and so adorable! She longed to have one but dared not hope. It would never happen anyhow, especially if Gregory had anything to do with it.

She knew Gregory had treated her differently than anyone else in town had upon first meeting her and that puzzled her. He'd been downright hostile. He felt differently about her than others did, she reasoned. Otherwise he wouldn't have been so angry with her.

A ripple of excitement coursed through her veins but she immediately shoved it aside in disgust. She absolutely refused to be attracted to such an uncouth and horrible man! No, she wasn't going to do it. If she ever did marry, which she sincerely hoped she would some day, her husband would just have to accept her for who she was and treat her with kindness and respect. She wouldn't accept anything less.

Suddenly, a gust of wind blasted against the trees and shrubs at her side with alarming force, and her hair and skirts whipped about her painfully. She didn't mind a little wind now and then, but the kind that sent broken tree limbs flying past her through the torrential air…well, enough said. Lowering her face against the pelting rain and holding her skirts in place, she made a mad dash for the Mathewson house. It wasn't very far off. She would be safe inside and standing next to the cozy fireplace in no time.

"Gwendolyn!"

She spun around mid-dash and gulped involuntarily.

It was Gregory, of course, and he was coming straight for her.

Forgetting all resolve to confront him, she bolted. She knew she couldn't outrun him even though she was a fast runner, but she had to at least try. The thought of another nasty confrontation, combined with the fact that she had been caught alone in the rain, was more than she knew she could handle at the moment.

"No, no wait! Please."

She slowed down to a stop. There was something in his tone that scared her into submission—fear, perhaps desperation? She stood and numbly watched Gregory as he jogged the distance between them, looking ready to pounce on her.

"I've been chasing after you for hours. I just want to apologize… for yesterday, you know." He came and stood before her an arm's-length away, closing one eye to the heavy drops of rain beating against him.

Of course she knew, she thought, rolling her eyes. How could she possibly forget?

"I know I should not have yelled at you," he hollered above the rain and wind, "or treated you as roughly as I did, especially in front of my parents. Well, no…I mean, I shouldn't treat you like that in private, either. That's not what I meant. I meant—"

"I understand," she said, trying to spare him. He was actually babbling and it was unsettlingly delightful. She tried to suppress a grin and felt her muscles slowly relax.

He let out a gust of a laugh then looked directly into her eyes, his expression solemn once again. "I'm sorry for how I treated you, Gwendolyn. It was inappropriate, I know. I accused you in an effort to protect myself, and it was probably really humiliating for you." He gently lifted her hand and rubbed it with his square thumbs. "I hope you can forgive me for my occasional foul temper."

Good grief! That had to be the best apology ever, she thought, fighting to maintain her balance. Her corset certainly wasn't helping the matter. With each passing minute, it grew more and more uncomfortable. She looked down at her hand which was still being held in both of his and briefly understood what real peace could feel like. She closed her eyes to relish the moment.

"So, have you forgiven me then?"

Gwendolyn looked at him, astounded by the desperation in his brilliant blue eyes. She instantly remembered his look of intense admiration in her vision and knew they'd shared some deep bond in the past. They'd probably just judged each other too harshly in the store. Besides, how could she not forgive him after such a sincere apology, especially when she'd been the primary cause for his anger? Feeling a blush rising in her cheeks, she realized she actually wanted to forgive him.

"Yes. Yes, of course."

Gregory swept her into his arms and held her head against his chest. "Thank you! Thank you, Gwendolyn. I really want things to be right between us. I want to understand." He pulled back and placed a lingering kiss on her forehead. "I don't know why you left last August, and I don't know why you never contacted any of us."

Uh oh, Gwendolyn thought, growing warm from the feel of his cheek against her forehead despite the growing chill outside. It was finally happening. Well, she didn't really know what *it* was, but she knew it was coming. And he didn't even know about her condition, which made the whole situation much worse and very awkward. She felt as if he had the wrong person, but it was obvious that he didn't. He knew who she was…or at least, who she had been. Why hadn't anyone told him yet?

"I had guessed that maybe you didn't feel loved enough or in the right way…or that you needed some independence and wanted to teach somewhere else. And," he continued, his voice becoming gravelly, "I hoped and prayed to God you didn't leave because of me."

"Gregory, please. I—"

She stopped herself, realizing that she'd actually called him by his given name. Now, why on earth had she done that? she wondered in horror.

He pulled back to look at her, his eyebrows furrowed in concern.

He seemed like a completely different person than before. Not at all like the intimidating beast that had had his clutches on her in the store the day before. He was actually sympathetic and worried for her. At that moment, she felt an overwhelming desire to reach up and smooth his brow but settled for the feel of his taut shirtsleeves instead.

Going against all reason, she bowed her head and prepared for what was to come. She knew she was being selfish, but she couldn't help herself. She wanted nothing more than to hear his rough voice say what he wanted to without her awful secret getting in the way. Besides, what could she do? Interrupt to tell him she didn't remember him at all? Yeah, that would go over well. Something inside her knew it would break his heart and, like a coward, she didn't want to be the one to do it. What was she supposed to do?

"Gwendolyn. There's something I need to tell you…something I should've told you long ago and maybe you wouldn't have left."

She kept her head down and focused her attention on the rain soaking the front of his wool jacket instead of his beautiful face. The rise and fall of his chest had quickened and was becoming shallower with each passing moment. Feeling a little lightheaded, she commanded herself to keep breathing because if she fainted she'd likely miss the most exciting, but probably confusing, moment of her life.

The storm had eased some and the soft pitter-patter of rain dripping down the baby leaves of the trees echoed through her ears. She closed her eyes and deeply inhaled Gregory's damp lavender smell—a smell that was strangely familiar somehow. A wave of peace enveloped her and, as if possessed by some mysterious force, she felt her body lean closer to his.

"Gwendolyn, I love you."

Her eyes shot open in pleasant surprise then narrowed in fear. She felt both his hands move to the curve of her back as he pulled her against him in a tight embrace, and she didn't pull back.

"I know I should have told you sooner," he said, "but I was waiting for the state to approve my lease. Do you know Dan and I have started our own building company?"

Gwendolyn nodded her head against his arm, remembering what Daisy had told her.

"I wanted to surprise you," he continued, stroking her wet and straggly hair with the balls of his fingers. "With the new business, Dan and I were able to make enough money to buy the portion of land Pa set aside for us in only a few short months."

Gwendolyn shifted uncomfortably in his arms and was grateful that he didn't spend much time looking at her face. What if he noticed the scar? That would ruin everything!

"I was going to ask you to marry me as soon as I got the deed… you know, being the romantic fool that I was. I wanted to make sure I could provide a good home and a good living for both of us." He laughed, the bitterness in his tone apparent. "The deed was approved only a week after you left, Gwendolyn."

After hearing the word 'love,' Gwendolyn knew she was in trouble. But after his last declaration, she knew she was definitely in much worse. The man had basically just proposed to her, and she hadn't even known him for two full days. Oh dear, she thought. Once again, the overwhelming and frustrating reality of her situation came at her with full force, and she did nothing to hide her tears. After all, it was raining. Maybe Gregory wouldn't notice.

She hadn't intentionally tried to hurt him, but she knew what was going to happen. Gregory would find out about her memory loss. Then he would hate her for the rest of her life for allowing him to make a fool of himself—plain and simple. But she didn't want him to hate her. She almost hated herself.

Oh, why couldn't she remember what had happened? Her doctor had told her she'd likely never remember the days just prior to her accident and that fact scared her almost completely out of her boots. Of all the scenarios that had been postulated so far, none of them felt right to her, especially the one concerning Gregory. She couldn't have left because of him and nobody could convince her that she had. She felt something for him, as much as she hated to admit it—a strange and deep connection…inside, somewhere.

In the next instant, she felt the rough edges of his fingers tilting her face upward, but she didn't dare meet his gaze. Her heart was pounding within her breast and her mind started racing out of control. She desperately tried to ignore the effect Gregory was having on her and tried instead to think of the effect her silence was going to have on him. The image wasn't pleasant.

She could feel the heat of his gaze on her as he stroked her worried brow then gently wiped at the tears she thought were invisible. To her mortification, she realized Gregory was as aware of them as he was the whipping wind. He continued to touch her—soothingly, protectively—and she knew she couldn't ignore his blissful attentions for much longer.

Oh, what could she do? She had to tell him…before it was too late! Well, it already was too late.

Feeling the overwhelming and dreadful need to confess her predicament, she opened her mouth but was silenced completely when his mouth closed down over hers in a sudden but smooth caress. She looked up in astonishment then closed her eyes as a wave of unfamiliar emotions rippled through her unexpectedly. The feel of his silky lips moving over hers as the two of them stood clutching one another in the rain was powerful…and strangely painful. An ache just below the surface of her skin emanated from her heart out to her arms. She whimpered, finally giving in to the desire threatening to emerge from her traitorous body.

It really *was* happening, she thought giddily.

Shocked by her own boldness, she returned his kiss with explosive eagerness. Using both hands, she reached up to cradle his freshly-shaven face as she deepened the exchange then stroked the flexed muscles just below his high cheekbones.

"Oh, Doly," Gregory moaned into her mouth, letting his wide jaw slacken. He slid his arms around her petite frame and crushed her against him in a blaze of unbridled passion. Ignoring the rain that was drizzling against them, he moved his mouth over hers with a thirst to match her own.

"No, no. We must stop," he panted, abruptly wrenching his mouth away from hers and groaning in frustration. "For if we don't, I will not be accountable for my actions, Gwendolyn. I tell you, I will not!"

Gwendolyn opened her eyes and looked at him in alarm. Oh, no, she thought. She touched her lips, realizing what she'd just done. She was a mere woman, alone in the woods without a chaperone and without memories. She'd likely broken a couple of the rules set down by the Board as well. And there was no telling what Gregory would think of her after she told him about her memory loss. The thought was too mortifying to even think on.

Gregory grabbed the sides of her face and stared wildly into her round, brown eyes. "I have loved you your entire life, Gwendolyn. Ever since your aunt brought you here as a wee babe, I've felt a powerful bond with you. You've always been the sweetest, spunkiest, and most curious of all the girls in town." He placed a quick kiss on the tip of her nose then chuckled low in his throat.

"Do you remember the time you brought me that disgusting toad and dumped it in my lap just as my family had sat down for supper? You were so proud that you'd finally caught one after all those weeks."

Gwendolyn smiled mischievously. That definitely sounded like her, she thought. Oh, how she wished she could remember the Tylers' reactions. It would have been a fun sight to behold. Imagining her life as a child and hearing other's stories of her as if for the first time gave her a good dose of selfish satisfaction.

"I know this may sound strange," he continued, gazing at her in possessive admiration, "but ever since then, well, I uh…I've felt like we were meant to be together. We've shared so much, you know, you and I? Tell me you've felt it too."

She sensed the uncertainty in his eyes and wished with all her heart to give him an honest answer. It was true that ever since she'd caught a glimpse of him in her vision a few months before, she'd felt a mysterious connection. In the two days she'd known him, he'd been angry, contrite, honest, forgiving, downright passionate, and even had a sense of humor—most of them very admirable qualities. And to her chagrin, she knew there wouldn't be any use in denying her blatant, physical attraction to the man. Darn him.

"Yes, I've felt a connection," she admitted. Heat immediately rose to her cheeks and she tried to look away, but Gregory stubbornly followed her gaze. If the situation weren't so awkward, she would have thought his attention to be somewhat endearing, actually.

"I love you and I want you for my wife, Doly."

She stared at him in stunned disbelief then let out the gust of air she hadn't realized she'd been holding. He'd said it! He'd actually proposed. She rather liked his little nickname for her. It was sweet…and simple. But what was she supposed to do? The man she'd grown up with but didn't remember had just asked her to be his wife.

Lowering his head, Gregory touched his mouth to hers and began weaving his provocative spell over her once again.

Ah, who cared about the stupid rules? She eagerly leaned into one of his very capable arms and tilted her head to the side.

With his other hand he touched the soft and creamy skin of her neck, pulling back bits of her hair as his lips worked their way up with tantalizing leisure. His breath warmed her ear and she shivered with uncontrollable delight.

"What is this?" he said, unexpectedly ending his kisses and staring at her left temple. He wiped the hair from her face then took in a sharp breath. "Is this what everyone's been trying to tell me?"

Oh, no! she panicked. How could she have been such a fool? She couldn't tell him about her scar. Not after what they'd just shared and the things he'd admitted to her. How had she let things get so far?

She attempted to leave but he yanked her back, his grip firm.

"Please, Gwendolyn. Let there be no more secrets between us. I beg you." He fixed his eyes on hers with determination, and she knew he would get the answers out of her by whatever means necessary.

She hung her head in dismay, irritated that she hadn't left the situation when she'd first noticed herself weakening. He'd offered himself to her, pledged his love, and proved too irresistible to ignore. They'd grown up together and he knew her well. She had the feeling that she'd loved him before she left—deeply and irrevocably. She stared into his eyes, which were full of sadness and fear, and resolved to hold still.

"When?" He lightly traced the scar with his fingertips from her temple past her hairline. She started to shiver, feeling uncomfortably exposed, and he pulled her closer, shielding the front of her body from the bulk of the rain.

"The day I left," she said. "I fell from the coach once I arrived in Hopeton." Oh, she prayed he wouldn't ask too many questions.

He showed some surprise but recovered quickly enough. "Does it still hurt?"

"Yes," she hesitated, trying to think of the right words, "but the pain is mostly not physical."

"Have I hurt you? I mean…I know I hurt you emotionally and I'm so sorry for that, but have I hurt you physically as well?"

He was obviously fighting an inward battle, so she tried to be a bit more specific in her reply. "No, not really. I think, more than anything, that you've been kind and generous and have helped me more than anybody else these last couple of days." It was the truth. Since he hadn't learned of her memory loss, he was acting exactly as he would have—without any filters, discomfort, or bias. She loved her aunt and cousin, but it wasn't exactly the same.

She felt his body relax against hers and she sighed in relief, even though she knew the relief could only be temporary.

"Gwendolyn, why did you leave?" he said, looking down at her. "I had no idea when you were coming back…or *if* you were coming back."

It was her turn to stiffen. She hadn't realized just how temporary her relief would be. Guilt washed over her and she wished more than ever before that she could remember why she'd left. That question would be lurking in the back of her mind, plaguing her until the end of time. If she hadn't lost her memory, she could be living happily with her family or be married to the handsome stranger in her arms. Her accident—well, her decision to leave—had ruined her life. She'd lived in total ignorance during her stay in Hopeton but was dreadfully lonely and confused. And after all that, she was back where she belonged and was forced to deal with accusations, misunderstandings, and really awkward reconciliations.

"I don't know why I left." She blinked long and hard as a single tear fell past her cheek. The situation between her and Gregory seemed painfully hopeless. There were over twenty years of memories to make up for. How could Gregory be patient enough to start over?

"You have to know the reason," he said more calmly than in the mercantile. "Please tell me. We've always told each other everything."

Habitually covering her scar, she pushed back from him and this time he let her go. She stood a couple feet away and looked at his drenched and dejected figure, wishing she were not the cause of everyone's pain.

Looking straight into his stormy and confused eyes, she repeated her words just loud enough to be heard through the rain. "I don't know why I left, Gregory. I'm sorry. But what I do know—" she pressed a small fist against her heart—"deep down inside is that I never meant to hurt you…or anyone." She paused. "That is all I can tell you at present."

With tears pouring from her eyes, she let her head drop in shame then turned and ran the rest of the distance to her aunt's house.

Gregory stood paralyzed with shock as Gwendolyn ran away from him. Was that a 'no?' he wondered. She had said he was 'annoyingly attractive' in the barn and had proven extremely receptive when he'd touched her. He smiled in satisfaction, remembering how she'd flinched when his mouth had touched down upon hers. She'd been shy at first then exploded with a passion so fierce he had to fight to control himself. It was the same passion he'd seen her exhibit throughout her life—from the times she completed her schoolwork with curious relish to the times she played music for him, enough to move him to tears.

But why had she looked like she was in pain almost the entire time he'd been talking to her…terrified even?

Perhaps she'd fallen in love with someone else? No, he thought, immediately forcing the idea aside. That was ridiculous! She said she felt a connection with him and hadn't exactly acted like she didn't like his attention. On the contrary, he knew she'd liked it a great deal.

She hadn't given him any clue as to whether she would accept his marriage proposal or not and that petrified him. In fact, she hadn't said much at all. He remembered she'd said he'd been more helpful to her than anyone else since coming back, but he rolled his eyes at the notion. He doubted anybody else in town had shouted at her as he had. How could that have been even remotely helpful? It had just made things worse. But she'd forgiven him as she always had. It was one of the things he loved about her most.

Gregory wiped the rain from his brow, remembering the horrified expression on Gwendolyn's face once he'd discovered the long pink scar. He wondered why she hadn't told him about it herself. It was obvious what his family had been trying to tell him all along, what Dan had meant when he said that she'd been through something 'miraculous but dreadful.' Gregory was just grateful she was alive. How could she have survived an accident that had left such a mark? During her recovery—which had to have been quite traumatic—she obviously hadn't tried to contact any of her family. It would have been the sane and responsible thing to do, in his opinion. Why would she want to be with complete strangers during such a time?

Gregory looked up into the sky and felt a headache coming on. The storm had almost completely disappeared but the rain had soaked through every layer of his clothing, making his bones ache from the cold of late spring. He needed to get dry and warm.

Turning around, he briskly made his way back down the lane to Orchard Cottage.

"You just saw her? Oh, well…what did you say?"

Gregory's mother fluttered about as she tried to get a small fire going. Gregory's lifelong friend Daisy Mathewson was sitting in the floral armchair in the parlor, dangling her legs over one side and trying not to look as vastly interested in the conversation as he knew she truly was.

"I apologized to her for yesterday and asked her why she left," he said, purposely avoiding all subjects that would make the ladies of the room squeal in delight. If Gwendolyn refused his proposal, it would break their hearts. He winced at the thought.

Warily, he glanced at his mother then pulled his wet shirt over his head. The skin on his arms and chest was a pale shade of pink, evidence that he'd been outside for too long. He really didn't have the time to get sick. He needed to help Dan finish building the house and furniture before the wedding, and then there was the clearing and planting of his father's fields, which should have already been done a couple weeks prior.

Accepting the dry flannel shirt his mother held out to him, he donned it quickly and went to stand before the growing warmth of the fireplace.

"And what reason did she give you?"

"She didn't give me one," he growled, vigorously rubbing his hands together and wondering if Gwendolyn was being difficult intentionally. "She doesn't know why she left." He forced himself to relax and attempted to see things from Gwendolyn's perspective. Maybe it was just another misunderstanding, he thought.

"Perhaps she just needs some time to readjust," he continued. "It's been almost a year, after all. And God only knows how she'll be able to handle all the gossip and snide comments this town will have to throw at her."

"So, she hasn't told you about her accident."

"Well, yes. She has. I noticed the scar while we were talking—" he said, pointing to the left side of his head—"and she told me she fell out of the coach once she reached Hopeton. Isn't that correct?"

His mother shifted her weight and, he noticed, snuck a peek at Daisy from narrowed eyes. Daisy dabbed at the corner of her eye with a single fingertip then pretended to be resting it against her temple when she realized he was watching her. She flashed him a phony smile and swung her legs to the ground where she held them in a more ladylike fashion, which was completely unlike her.

"What's going on here? That *is* what happened, is it not?" His gaze moved from his mother to Daisy then back to his mother, who was fidgeting with the folds of her apron as if waiting for the results of a pie contest at the county fair.

"Tell me!" he suddenly boomed, making both women jump. He felt the blood slowly drain from his head in waves of needle-like heat and an ache started to develop in the pit of his stomach.

His mother put a hand to her breast, swallowed, and then sighed as if she were about to scold him. "Oh, I wish I were not the one to have to tell you this." He watched with growing unease as she slowly crumpled into a wingback chair and put a finger to her brow. She invited him to sit beside her, but he remained standing. Whatever it was she was trying to tell him, he knew it couldn't be good.

"Gwendolyn did tell you the truth about her accident, Gregory, but she didn't tell you all of it. There's one more thing."

"So, what are you trying to say? Has she fallen in love with her physician?" he asked sarcastically.

"No, of course not."

"Then what, mother? Please just tell me before I'm forced to shake it from you." He went and stood before her as her eyes filled with tears and her chin trembled.

"When she fell," she started carefully, her lips wrinkling with emotion, "she hit her head very hard. She was in the hospital, unconscious with a fever for several days. When she woke up, she had no memory of what had happened to her."

"Well, it was probably very traumatic. She's better off not knowing, in my opinion," he said, encouraging her to get to the point.

She sat quietly for a moment then slumped her shoulders.

"Oh, I'll tell him!" Daisy said, leaping out of her chair and coming to stand before him in one fluid motion. "I don't have to live with him, after all." He saw his mother nod in relief just before Daisy grabbed his hand and sandwiched it in both of her own. He flinched.

"Gregory," she said, looking him right in the eyes. "Gwendolyn's head injury has caused serious damage."

"She's…not going to die, is she?"

"No, but—" Daisy paused, making his eyes bulge in expectation—"this is just as bad. Well, maybe not. I haven't decided yet."

"You speak in riddles," he said, pulling his hand away.

She took a deep breath. "Gwendolyn has lost all of her memories from before the accident, Gregory. She doesn't remember me, she doesn't remember Grovetown, and she doesn't remember you. That is why she couldn't tell us why she left, and that is why she never contacted us. She forgot who she was and why she went to Hopeton. All these long months, she assumed we didn't even exist or had abandoned her."

"What?" he breathed, suddenly feeling overwhelmed. "That's ridiculous. I've never heard of such a thing." He looked to his mother, but she merely looked back in pity and sorrow, and it bothered him. He felt everything around him come to an abrupt and excruciating halt. He stood stiffly, feeling his heart throb dully within his chest. His body felt a hundred pounds heavier than normal.

In just one agonizing sentence, his mother confirmed Daisy's words, pulling his world out from under his feet. "Gwendolyn has forgotten everything, son…including us. She doesn't remember who you are."

# Chapter Six

THE EVENING AIR FELT COOL AND SOOTHING on Gwendolyn's skin as she walked ahead of her aunt and uncle to the town hall. Nothing, not even the thought of arithmetic or scientific equations, could lessen how nervous she was for what lay ahead. Despite Daisy's role-playing efforts and suggestions the day before, Gwendolyn still wasn't feeling adequately prepared to answer all of the townspeople's questions. Gwendolyn had also had some practice when Mrs. Tyler brought her sixteen-year-old daughter to the house earlier that afternoon, but Susie was not at all intimidating. In fact, she was so friendly and engaging that the entire role-playing felt like a joke.

Gwendolyn watched as people came out of the townhouses—talking and laughing gaily as they made their way toward the hall—and started to regret not going with Daisy and Dan when they'd offered. She envied the groups' excitement and informality, but going with a betrothed couple would have been too strange, wouldn't it? Not to mention, it would be a waste of readying a wagon and horse. The hall was only a few minutes walking distance from the house, for heaven's sake.

Grabbing her lavender skirt and petticoats, she ascended the hall's steps and crossed the threshold where she was immediately directed to a cloakroom. She lay off her things then went to stand at the entrance of the hall with a nervous shiver.

The room was alive with jovial music and conversation. An orchestra sat alone in the upper gallery, playing tunes for the couples engaged in the center of the floor. The rest of the occupants stood in groups surrounding the dancers or sat in chairs along the perimeter of the square-shaped room.

Gwendolyn felt a soft hand at her elbow and flinched. "Oh, I'm sorry, Uncle Barrett. I thought you were somebody else." She stared at the tall, thin man she'd met the night before then hung her head in embarrassment.

He put her arm through his and patted her hand affectionately. "Don't you worry, Pinkie. This is supposed to be a happy night." He leaned over, giving her a sample of his minty smell, and placed a soft kiss just above the hair covering her scar, tickling her with his moustache. "Now, let's go find Daisy, shall we? I'll bet you I know right where she is."

Her aunt Marguerite winked at her then looped an arm through her other arm. Together, the three of them marched through the throngs of people toward the refreshment area. Gwendolyn noticed a couple younger women sitting against the wall peering at her over paper fans and whispering. She couldn't help wondering if they were talking about her then decided it would probably be best to focus her attention elsewhere.

"See, Marguerite," her uncle said upon reaching the refreshment tables. "Our daughter is incredibly predictable."

Gwendolyn chuckled. Daisy stood beside one of the tables talking to Dan Tyler as she chewed excitedly. In one hand, she juggled a plate full of frosting-covered pastries, cookies with icing, chocolate cakes, and a tumbler of red punch.

"I don't know how you can eat so much and still maintain that lovely figure of yours, darling. It isn't exactly fair." Marguerite stroked Daisy's cheek lovingly, and Daisy playfully wrinkled her nose in return.

"You're not so bad looking yourself," her uncle stated, taking his wife by the shoulders and kissing her soundly on the mouth right in front of everyone. Her aunt stood back in shock but, by the rising color in her cheeks, Gwendolyn could tell she was pleased.

With a quick wink in Gwendolyn's direction, her uncle touched the brim of his hat then melted into the crowd.

Gwendolyn and Dan snickered, and Daisy rolled her eyes before taking another bite of her cookie and dabbing at her mouth with a paper doily.

"Well," her aunt said, turning to them and blinking her eyes a couple of times. She delicately patted her hair to make sure it was still in place. "Did you two manage to get him here?"

*Him?* Gwendolyn thought in alarm. Certainly they weren't talking about Gregory right in front of her. She might have lost her memory but she wasn't a fool.

"Yes," Dan said, shoving his hands into his pockets. "And it was no easy task, I can assure you." He snuck a peek at Gwendolyn then lowered his eyes as if embarrassed.

Oh, no! she thought. Gregory knew about her condition, and he hated her! She swiftly scanned the room for any sign of him, feeling her face burn with guilt and suddenly knew what it felt like to be a little mouse in an open field with an owl eyeing her.

Then a thought struck her. If they knew Gregory was angry, then they would have to know *why*…they would have to know that he'd proposed to her and she'd said nothing…nothing at all to preserve his dignity. She groaned, putting her hands over her face. She'd been right all along. There was simply no end to her humiliation and there were no secrets in Grovetown. Why was her family talking about her in such a fashion?

"Gwendolyn, darling…are you unwell?" She felt her aunt's arms come around her protectively. "What's happening? Is it your head?"

"Oh, no. I'm just—I'm uh, battling with a severe case of guilt and humiliation right now. I'm fine."

"Gwendolyn! There you are."

The four of them looked up to see James Morrison—dressed in a crisp black cowboy's hat, white shirt, and trousers—pushing through the crowd toward her.

Gwendolyn had completely forgotten about the dance she'd promised him. She realized that must have been why her aunt had specifically insisted they *not* arrive on time and fidgeted with ribbons and doilies instead.

Hastily, Gwendolyn wiped the tears from her eyes, not wanting James to ask her about it.

He practically crashed right into her and she stepped back a ways. He often felt a little too close.

"I couldn't find you for the first dance," he panted. "So I asked the band to play another reel. Are you ready?" Smirking, he held a hand out in invitation. "Please come. You promised."

"No, Gwendolyn. You mustn't!" her aunt hissed, digging her fingers into Gwendolyn's shoulders.

Gwendolyn looked at her aunt, feeling completely bewildered and uncertain as to what step she should take next. James was inches away, waiting for her. She couldn't very well refuse the man after she'd promised him, and it wasn't as if she even had a chance with Gregory anymore. Besides, what harm could there be in one little dance?

She lifted her hand slightly and James practically yanked her to the middle of the dance floor before she could even react. "You remember the steps, don't you?"

She looked at him through narrowed eyes, wondering if he'd meant to insult her then decided against it. She was definitely being too paranoid.

After making sure her scar was sufficiently covered, she went to stand in line with the other ladies. The young woman directly to her left looked at James then back to Gwendolyn, eyeing her from head to toe with an odd smile on her face. Gwendolyn nodded uneasily in her direction. She didn't enjoy being under scrutiny, especially by haughty looking blondes with tight curls and dangerously revealing necklines. She forced her attention back to James and bowed just as the lively music began.

James was an excellent dance partner, Gwendolyn soon realized. He moved about with enviable ease and was confident through every step and turn. With a strong hand on her back, he guided her each time she missed a step, which happened more often than she cared to admit. It was such a high-spirited dance—the reel—full of twists and turns and partner changes, and she quickly grew fatigued. A handful of times, she crossed paths with the blonde who leered every time they got close enough, and she wondered what it was the girl found so amusing. She wouldn't be nearly so amused were Gwendolyn to stick her foot out and trip her. Gwendolyn smiled at the thought.

At the conclusion of the dance, the room erupted in applause and Gwendolyn closed her eyes to ease the ache of its volume.

"Thank you for the dance, Mr. Morrison," she breathed, bowing low. It seemed ridiculous that one little dance could exhaust her so easily—ridiculous and completely unfair. She patted her warm cheeks with her gloved hands and turned to leave.

"Don't go, Gwen," James said, grabbing the crook of her arm. He looked at her with sympathy. "Join me outside for some fresh air, will you? It's awfully warm in here, is it not?"

"Oh, no. I couldn't possibly." Talking alone with Gregory in the rain was one thing, but leaving the hall with James while a hundred or so townspeople looked on, that was quite another. Did he not understand that it would be improper to leave with him? She had no desire to fuel the fire of gossip that was already spreading around town about her, nor did she want to concern and embarrass her family further. The dance was over and she was free from her obligation.

She took a step toward the refreshment area but James' grip tightened. "Ow," she gasped, looking back at him in surprise. His expression turned hard as he glared at her with dark eyes and Gwendolyn was instantly afraid. "I must return to my aunt and cousin," she said.

"You will join me outside," he growled in her ear.

Gwendolyn felt the blood drain from her face and immediately wished she'd listened to Mrs. Tyler and her aunt—etiquette be hanged! She clawed at him as he virtually dragged her across the hall despite the startled gasps and gossip of the townspeople. Once outside, she was surprised to discover how chilly the air had turned in so little time. James wrenched her toward a dark cluster of trees and Gwendolyn panicked.

"Let go of me!" she screeched.

To her surprise and utter relief, he did let go, and she nearly stumbled backward into the damp earth. Standing erect and glaring at his self-satisfied appearance, she swiped the invisible dirt from her dress. Angry, humiliated, and charged with fear, she slapped him soundly across the cheek.

Her breath caught as James slammed her back against a tree, and she could only stare at him in shock. He advanced with teeth bared and lifted her clean off the ground with both of his large hands around her throat. "You must have really lost your memory if you'd willingly spend time with me," he jeered coldly, rendering her immobile as he crushed her body with his powerful frame.

She tried to yell for help but no sound came out. Desperately, she pounded at him with her fists but he just squeezed tighter, making her throat burn miserably and her head pound until she thought it might explode.

Raising her rapidly weakening limbs, she blindly searched for his eyes and, upon finding them, dug her fingers as forcefully as she could.

He bellowed with rage and abruptly let her go. Slowly, she crumpled to the forest floor in a heap of fabric and gasped for air.

She heard nothing except for the pounding in her own head, and so, was startled when a warm hand touched the side of her throat then stroked her cheek tenderly. Wearily, she opened her eyes to see a pair of legs in well-worn trousers standing between her and James and somehow knew it was Gregory. After all the heartache she'd put him through and all the…words they'd shared, he still cared about her. He was her protector and always watching over her. She clung to his pant leg and cried in weak relief, knowing she was safe with him.

James' voice was weak and uncertain. "Gwendolyn, I'm…sorry. I–I didn't mean to—"

"If you come near her again, I'll kill you! You hear me, James?"

All was silent for a moment. James stood several feet away, appearing to be recovering from a blow to the face or head, then slowly retreated into the shadows like a snake. Gwendolyn closed her eyes once more. She could feel the wet earth beginning to soak through her dress and shivered uncontrollably.

"My dear friend," Gregory said, kneeling down and wrapping his arms around her. "You've endured so much."

Well, she thought mischievously, if that was how all of her unfortunate events would end up, she could have all the endurance in the world! Despite the horror and unimagined fear she'd experienced at the hands of James Morrison, she knew she'd give anything for Gregory's friendship.

She opened her eyes to see him looking at her with thinly veiled concern. Lifting her hand, she rubbed her thumb across his whiskered chin then dared to move up to his thin, smooth lips. "Thank you," she whispered hoarsely before allowing exhaustion to finally take over.

The young man cursed silently as he hid in the darkness some distance from where Gregory and Gwendolyn sat. His little scheme hadn't worked, but then again, he knew he shouldn't be surprised. He was cursed and always had been. Ever since Gwendolyn had been born.

No matter, he thought, smiling in satisfaction. There were plenty of ways of destroying the girl, but the next time he would not fail. The next time he would aim straight for her heart, and he knew exactly how to do it.

Gwendolyn blinked her eyes open. She was lying in her bed with the quilts drawn to her chest, and her head and upper back were slightly propped with pillows. All was dark within her room, but she knew she was alone…and safe.

Awkwardly, she sat up and began unfastening the buttons at the back of her dress as her head throbbed. Once the dress was removed, she draped it over a nearby chair along with her two petticoats and corset.

With both hands, she gingerly touched the skin of her neck and winced. Already she could feel the bruises James had given her. Her eyes narrowed as she remembered their encounter.

What on earth had she done to make him so angry? she wondered. It couldn't possibly have been because she'd refused a second dance with him. That would just be too ridiculous. It had to have been from before, something she couldn't remember.

She eased back into bed and pulled the warm covers up to her chin. She remembered Mrs. Tyler's cool dismissal, Daisy's anger and obvious contempt, and her aunt's fear in regards to the young man.

Could they have been lovers? Gwendolyn mused. Could it be that she had chosen Gregory instead of James? The possibility would certainly explain the women's reactions and James' possessive anger towards her.

Then a thought struck her. Did she leave Grovetown because of James? Was his anger and violence what drove her away? Oh, that had to be it.

She sunk lower under her covers, feeling uneasy and a little nauseated. She'd ventured back into the lion's den not remembering the lion.

"I had no idea James was capable of doing something like this."

Gwendolyn's eyes popped open at the sound of her uncle's voice coming from down the hallway, probably the parlor. Curious, she tilted her head to listen.

"I'm so furious I could punch him clean out of his wool socks! I'm going to march over to the Morrison's right now and give that good-for-nothing a piece of my mind, that's what."

"Begging your pardon, Doc, but it wouldn't do any good."

Gwendolyn's skin erupted with goose bumps. It was Gregory—the man who had yelled at her, proposed marriage, then saved her from James's evil clutches.

He was still in the house, she thought, smiling with sudden pleasure.

"I'm not going to just sit here and let James get away with what he's done. He could have killed her and probably would have if you hadn't showed up to save her!"

"You don't think he actually would have killed her, do you, darling?" her aunt asked quietly. "He's never acted this way before… not in all the years we've known him."

There was a silence.

"What happened to Gwendolyn did not go unnoticed, sir. Her reputation could be at stake. James was a fool to drag her out of the hall, especially in front of his family. They had to have seen. I have a feeling James won't try anything again anytime soon."

"What makes you think that?"

"Just now, in the woods…he didn't even fight back. He's a yellow-bellied coward and always has been. But we must still be cautious."

"Yes. Gwendolyn must be watched at all times. Even in the house. She must never be left alone."

Gwendolyn's heart started to pound in fear. Only three days in Grovetown and already someone wanted to hurt her, maybe even kill her. She shivered. Why was her life so complicated? Certainly, it hadn't always been that way. She'd never imagined that coming back to her hometown and family would cause such a negative stir. Sometimes she wondered if she was meant to suffer, to live out all of her days in fear and uncertainty. It certainly seemed to be the case.

"Is Gwendolyn all right?" she heard Gregory ask quietly.

"Yes, I have already examined her. I reckon she'll be fine… physically, at least. She should awaken soon."

"May I see her?"

Gwendolyn jumped in surprise. What would she say? She couldn't very well tell him she had been listening in on their whole conversation without making it known.

Battling her conscience, she finally decided to lie on her back, slam her eyes shut, and feign unconsciousness.

The floorboards squeaked as Gregory stepped into her bedroom then groaned under his weight as he knelt before her. She felt the heat of his gaze on her and she tingled with embarrassment. What kind of game was she playing? She suddenly remembered the clothes she had deposited on the nearby chair and prayed they were not visible in the low candlelight.

She felt his fingers touch her hand and a ripple of excitement burst within her. She fought to maintain control, to appear insensible, but found it very difficult.

At the sudden feel of his warm hand pressing against her forehead, she nearly leapt out of her skin in surprise. She silently cursed herself for her stupidity. It would have been a miracle if Gregory hadn't noticed. She kept her eyes closed anyhow and steadied her breathing.

Memories of their meeting in the rain, of his gentle caresses and passionate determination, came to her mind. Oh, how wonderful it had been. She smiled inwardly, remembering his excited relief when she'd forgiven him and his struggle to finally admit his love for her after all their years together. The feelings and emotions he was evoking from her, especially after less than a handful of days, were more than a little unsettling.

She felt a warm presence and knew that Gregory's face was hanging mere inches from her own. He was going to kiss her!

Oh dear, she thought with sudden realization. It was going to take a mighty amount of restraint to keep from kissing him back.

"We both know you're awake."

Gwendolyn's eyes shot open in alarm, causing Gregory to jump. She pulled back against her pillows and watched in irritation as he started to chuckle. What a fool she was constantly making of herself!

He cleared his throat then leaned over, looking her directly in the eyes with an expression of deep concern. "Are you all right?"

"Yes," she croaked, feeling a painful pressure in her throat. Raising a hand, she pointed to it and asked, "Do you know how long?"

"Before the pain goes away?"

She nodded.

"I'm not quite sure. No more than a couple of days, I imagine.

I can ask your uncle, if you'd like. He's just down the hall. Then again, I suppose you already know that."

He made ready to leave but Gwendolyn stopped him. She didn't want him to go, not yet. From what she'd heard Dan say at the dance, Gregory had to know her secret, didn't he? Why else would he want to avoid her? Why else would Dan look at her so strangely? But that didn't explain why Gregory was being so sweet and patient with her at that moment. Surely the news would scare him off. It didn't make sense. She pulled her hand away.

Gregory sat beside her on the edge of the bed. "I'm so sorry about James. I only wish I'd gotten to you sooner."

"No. You got there and that's what matters," she whispered.

Gregory smiled then lowered his head. "I should probably go. Your family doesn't know you're awake and you should really get your rest tonight." He kissed her forehead softly, paused for a moment, and then, eyeing her warily, placed lingering kisses on the bruises of her neck.

She loved the feel of his whiskers against her skin and she shivered with delight.

He pulled back and they gazed at each other in silence for a long time. The strange look on his face made her wonder if he really did know about her secret. He certainly didn't seem to. She didn't know what he and her family had discussed before she'd regained consciousness. Did Gregory wonder why she had accepted a dance with James? She wished someone would tell her what was really going on.

Gregory stood once again then bent toward her mouth.

She closed her eyes in anticipation, thinking about the soft feel of his lips and yearning for it so much. But it didn't come.

Opening her eyes, she found that Gregory had stopped midway and appeared to be thinking.

"What is it?" she asked nervously.

He remained still for several seconds then slowly straightened his back. After letting out a big gust of air, he forced a smile. Without meeting her confused gaze, he lowered his head. "I will leave you to your family now."

He stepped out of the room and walked briskly down the hall.

Disappointment flooded through her. She wasn't sure how to react. Was he afraid to kiss her, to give in to his feelings for her as he'd admitted in the rain, or did he not want to kiss her? Was he embarrassed or angry with her? She sunk back under the covers, feeling terribly lonely and idiotic all of a sudden. If only things had been different.

Her aunt, uncle, and Daisy rushed into her room a few seconds later, still wearing their dancing garb. They fussed, asked rhetorical questions, and talked about precautions they should all take in the future. Gwendolyn ignored them all, for she was too disturbed to contribute. Her Uncle Barrett examined her once again as she sat numbly, thinking about how she and Gregory would act the next time they met.

It was quite early the following morning when Gwendolyn awoke. She had another of her lovely headaches.

Moaning, she touched the sore spot on her head and discovered a large bump. James must have slammed her against the tree much harder than she'd thought. Thank heaven it was on the opposite side as her previous injury. She'd really be in trouble then.

Rolling out of bed, she carefully donned her petticoats and a loose-fitting yellow dress. She grabbed her corset and dumped it contemptuously on the floor of her closet. Going without a corset in the city was considered a grand faux pas, indeed, as she'd learned her first week there. But in the country, she'd observed that things weren't nearly so strict. She was determined not to wear the despicable contraption again.

She sat at her dressing table then heaved a groan. The woman staring back at her in the looking glass did not look the way she had expected. Not only was her face as pale and haggard looking as a ghost, but she had unattractive purplish bags beneath her eyes as well. Deep-colored bruises already colored her neck where James's fingers had dug into her, and she grew suddenly angry—with herself more than with that dreadful excuse for a man.

After Gregory had left her bedroom the night before, she'd spent the better part of an hour feeling confused and dejected before finally succumbing to sleep once again. He probably knew about her secret, she decided, and had changed how he felt about her. She grimaced at the thought.

Going to the water basin, she splashed some tepid water on her face, and then dried herself with a cloth that smelled of fresh cinnamon and vanilla bean.

A group of birds began singing their springtime song in the tree outside her window just as she finished brushing out her hair. She pulled the drapes aside and couldn't help smiling as the delightful creatures fluttered about the branches, bathing in the dew droplets and shaking their tail feathers.

Spring was her favorite time of the year. It revived her after the long winter months, and she so loved to see the brightly colored flowers, the animals being born, and the fresh smiles on her student's faces back in Hopeton. Winter had ended sooner there than in Grovetown and she was very pleased to experience the springtime twice.

She could hear a great deal of noise coming from the kitchen as she descended the long wooden staircase, scarf in hand. There were more than the usual three members of her family walking about. That much was certain.

"I'll go see if Gwendolyn is awake."

Gwendolyn ran right into her Uncle Barrett just as he came out of the kitchen.

"Oh," he said, holding her by the shoulders. "You scared me half to death. Ha, I suppose we're even now. How are you feeling, Pinkie?"

"I've a bit of a headache but I'm all right."

He lifted her chin and examined the bruises. "I'll kill that darn James," he roared. "I darn will!" He pulled her into the kitchen. "Look what that scoundrel has done to her!"

Mr. Tyler, Gregory, Dan, and Susie were all sitting at the table, staring back at her with mixed levels of horror. Mrs. Tyler, her Aunt Marguerite, and Daisy all turned from their cooking labors and gasped.

Unraveling the silk in her hand, Gwendolyn wound the scarf about her neck and looked back at everyone nervously.

"As terrible as this situation has been," Daisy started with a shrug of her shoulders, "your bruises have got to be the most impressive ones I've seen in a long time."

"This isn't a game, Daisy."

"Of course not, mums! I was only trying to lighten the mood."

"Yes," Marguerite said in understanding. "Let's all just sit down and have a nice breakfast as a family."

Gwendolyn took a seat at the table and snuck a peek in Gregory's direction. He was staring straight back at her and she quickly looked away, pretending to be interested in the…uh, vase full of flowers she couldn't quite name.

Each person grabbed a portion of food for their plates—hash, fruit, and hotcakes—and chewed in awkward silence.

"Oh," Gwendolyn gasped suddenly, clutching her throat as she swallowed a bite of apple wedge. She breathed hard, feeling her swollen insides worn raw from the peel then looked up to see everyone's questioning gazes. "I'm all right." She poured herself a tumbler of water and drank carefully. Its coolness was soothing.

"Gwendolyn," her uncle said, clearing his throat. He leaned back in his chair and placed a heavy hand on the table. "The Tylers will go with you once you're ready to join the committee today, and you will be escorted back once you're finished. You must never again, under *any* circumstance, be without an escort. Do you understand?"

Gwendolyn paused mid-chew. She did understand, unfortunately. "Yes, of course."

"Now, I know everyone is going to be really busy with preparations for Daisy and Dan, but Gregory will be a shadow for you and watch out for you, at least until the wedding. Are we in agreement?"

Gwendolyn startled as her fork clanked unexpectedly against her plate. She looked at Gregory to see his reaction but his eyes were lowered, his expression unreadable. Trying not to think about the effect Gregory was having on her, she sunk lower in her chair and wondered if her uncle's plan really would be a good idea after all.

# Chapter Seven

GREGORY TROMPED ALONG THE PATH behind his sister and Gwendolyn and wondered how he was going to juggle his time between protecting Gwendolyn, finishing his brother's house, tending the store, and completing a handful of other responsibilities that were weighing down on him. There was no question in his mind which was more important, but he had definitely taken upon himself more responsibilities than was ultimately possible for one man.

"Oh, Gwennie! We missed you so much while you were away. Didn't we Greg?"

Gregory looked up, interrupted from his thoughts. Both Susie and Gwendolyn were looking back at him expectantly. He scratched the side of his head.

"That means 'yes'," Susie whispered in Gwendolyn's ear, loud enough for him to hear, of course. She turned back to scowl at him then pulled Gwendolyn close, laying her head against Gwendolyn's arm.

"Don't worry, Gwennie. He just has a lot on his mind right now."

He saw Gwendolyn stiffen and wondered if she truly had lost her memory. He hated to consider the possibility that she couldn't remember him at all, but he'd given it a lot of thought and realized all the pieces fit.

After talking with Daisy and his mother, he'd locked himself in his room so that he could think without everyone hovering over him like a bunch of vultures. But it wasn't long before he stomped back out and demanded more answers about the whole affair.

Dan and Daisy had hounded him hour after hour, telling him he would only lose Gwendolyn again if he gave up on her. But he couldn't in good conscience force his attentions on her. If what everyone said was true, she thought no more of him than she did of Dan.

The realization that she'd kept silent during his rather pathetic declaration of love was quite damaging to his already wounded pride, but he supposed he could forgive her for it. It really was better for her to know how he felt about her, while he'd had the courage to tell her. If he'd known about her condition beforehand, he wouldn't have told her, and probably never would have.

At present, he could do nothing more than offer his protection and friendship if she desired it. The previous night had been proof of that when he'd very nearly kissed her senseless just down the hall from her family. It had taken everything he had not to do so, and that was, indeed, an amazing feat. Memories of his lips pressing against hers, of Gwendolyn's eager response, of them standing together while the rain and wind whipped about them, lingered still and he craved more.

He wondered about her reaction, though. If she thought no more of him than she would of a stranger, as everyone was assuring him was the case, then why had she been so familiar with him? She hadn't been acting a part, he was certain, and she most definitely was not a tramp.

Perhaps, Gwendolyn *did* remember him. He blushed at the thought.

As if hearing his thoughts, Gwendolyn turned her head to look at him.

He smiled weakly. Perhaps she did remember him.

Several women sat in small groups beneath the trees sewing, chatting, and tying ribbons. The younger and more limber of the group rested on soft quilts on the grass while the others took up the wooden lawn chairs. A couple tables were provided, bearing etched glass pitchers of fresh lemonade and saucers of cakes and breads. The whole scene reminded Gwendolyn of an Impressionist painting she'd seen in an exhibit in April.

A couple heads turned in their direction as her party approached, and she smiled timidly, thinking about all the questions the ladies would have for her. And to make matters worse, Gregory came and stood right beside her. She clasped her hands together to keep them from shaking.

"I'm going to put you over here with the Adamses," Susie whispered in Gwendolyn's ear, pointing to a mother and what appeared to be identical twin daughters. "They're really nice. They have large orchards and provide most of the fruit at harvest."

The Adamses fairly beamed as she and Susie approached.

Gwendolyn took an empty chair and immediately jumped in surprise as the two girls sprung upon her with girlish energy.

"Oh, Gwendolyn! We're so glad you're back."

"We missed you so much while you were away."

"Carrie! Katy! Let the poor girl breathe. Goodness." Mrs. Adams smiled, joining in her daughters' excitement. She greeted Gwendolyn with a warm smile then shooed the girls away.

They flopped down in disappointment. The sight of them was so funny that Gwendolyn couldn't help laughing aloud, and they were soon all laughing with her. The girls had beautiful smiles, gorgeous blue eyes, and brown braids almost long enough to sit on. A splatter of freckles touched each of their cheeks. They didn't look any more than twelve years old.

"If you're settled here," Susie interrupted with a pleased smile, "I must go help Ma gather more material. And you," she said, pointedly jabbing a finger into her elder brother's chest, "try to stay out of trouble, will you."

It was Gregory's turn to scowl at his younger sister. He then bent down to look Gwendolyn directly in the eyes. "I'll return in a couple of hours. Don't you dare leave by yourself."

Gwendolyn shivered. She wasn't sure if it came on because she'd thought of James or because Gregory was so close to her, but she decided she would mull over the thought later. She attempted to hide the shiver with a strategic scratch. "Of course."

Both Susie and Gregory left her, but she didn't mind. She had a feeling she'd get along well with the Adamses.

A soft breeze whistled through the trees and felt tolerably cool on Gwendolyn's skin. She breathed deeply the rich scent of soil and apple blossoms she loved so much, and knew it to be one of the best smells on earth. It was a far cry better than the dusty roads of Hopeton. She sat in silence for several moments while the girls played with the hem of her dress.

"Gwendolyn?" came a small voice.

Gwendolyn looked down at the girl wearing blue. "Yes? Which one are you?"

"Oh, I'm Carrie." She hesitated. "Will you be teaching here again…soon?" Her eyes were full of hope—pleading.

"Perhaps, if all goes well. I'll have to talk to the board in Hopeton and also see if the position needs filling."

"Oh, but it does, Miss Gwendolyn," said the girl in pink—Katy. "Miss Caldwell said she wasn't returning in the fall." Bending closer, she whispered conspiratorially, "You wanna know what I think? She's had eyes for my brother since before I can remember. I think Simon's just finally figured it out, the nincompoop."

Gwendolyn smiled, thinking the girl was a lot like Kristine Jenny. "Well, in that case, I'll see what I can do." She playfully tugged on both girls' braids and watched as they giggled to one another. She knew that Grovetown was her home and, although she didn't quite know the reason for her leaving, thought she would do very well if she stayed. The small country town would, no doubt, provide smaller classes where she could get to know her students better. Her aunt and uncle's house was in town, close to all the shops. It wouldn't be nearly as difficult to meet and get to know others as it had been in Hopeton, and the girls she'd met already were, quite simply, endearing.

A small bundle of quilting squares wrapped with twine was

dropped into her lap, startling her from her thoughts.

"Here you go, Gwennie," Susie said. "You just get started on those. Carrie? Katy? What would you like to work on—we've got squares, ribbons—"

"Oh, please? Can we work on squares, too?"

"Mama taught us some stitches over the winter."

The girls' eyes were wide with desperation. Mrs. Adams smiled but remained stitching.

"Certainly. Take these." Susie plopped another bundle between the two girls. "You can share that and if you need more…you know where to find me."

She flounced off to check on the other groups whilst Carrie and Katy squealed and giggled with delight.

Opening her reticule, Gwendolyn found a needle, spool of thread, and a pair of tiny sewing scissors then got to work.

They sewed for nearly an hour as the birds sang in the trees above their heads and a light wind kept them cool. Mrs. Adams took charge of the conversation, much to Gwendolyn's relief, asking about her teaching experiences, students, and how she found Hopeton in general. The girls sat contentedly working, stitch-by-stitch, only asking their mother for help once or twice. They were quick to learn and got quite a bit finished. Mrs. Adams didn't ask a word about Gwendolyn's accident, and for that Gwendolyn was grateful.

Looking down at her squares, she realized she'd nearly completed three rows. She smiled in triumph. In Hopeton, she hadn't had many opportunities or time to sew and was grateful to see she hadn't lost the skill completely.

"Miss Mitchell?"

Gwendolyn jerked her head up at the tart voice. The tight-curled blonde she'd seen at the dance the night before was coming toward her. Gwendolyn forced a smile, thinking her afternoon in the sun was about to be ruined.

"I imagine you had a good time at my father's dance last night. My brother says you dance like an angel." She giggled—a sound Gwendolyn knew she was beginning to hate above all other sounds.

"Well," she continued, "I suppose he was just being modest."

James' sister…yes, she fit the profile of a Morrison—over-confident, conniving, and a compulsive liar. Gwendolyn fought to control the snarl forming in her sore throat.

James' sister batted her lashes innocently and fidgeted with the beadwork on her reticule. "James said you'd forgotten a lot since your accident but that you made it obvious you hadn't forgotten him." She giggled again. "He says you still taste as sweet as strawberries. Can you imagine that?" she scoffed wickedly.

Gwendolyn stood up, paying no heed to the contents in her lap as they spilled onto the grass. "How dare you?" she said, looking at the young woman in disgust.

"Oh, so you're not denying it? James was always such a tease. I couldn't be sure, but I am now." She smirked then lifted her chin as if daring Gwendolyn to argue with her.

But argue she would.

"Is that so?" Gwendolyn started, feeling remarkably calm. She swallowed, remembering the soreness in her throat. "Well, did he tell you what the sting of my slap felt like…or the pounding of Gregory's fist, maybe…or even the feel of my fingers *digging* into his eye sockets?" She waited for a reaction from the woman but heard only gasps from the ladies and girls that had gathered about them.

"Melissa!" Mrs. Adams hissed from behind Gwendolyn. "You spiteful creature! When are you going to learn to behave like an adult?"

Gwendolyn watched as Mrs. Adams leapt up, angrily tossed her sewing on the chair, and came to stand beside her to act as her guardian. Carrie and Katy joined them. After smiling in appreciation, Gwendolyn returned her fiery gaze on Melissa as Mrs. Adams continued.

"Is it not enough that the girl must relearn everything and everyone without your lies and trickery? Shame on you!"

Melissa Morrison sauntered directly toward Gwendolyn and stopped a nose breadth away. In a cool, almost seductive voice, she said, "I heard tell of what you and Gregory were doing last night."

Gwendolyn raised one eyebrow in confident disbelief, knowing that she hadn't done anything with Gregory—at least, not the night before.

"I heard that you were sitting on the forest floor together… with arms about one another—"

"Enough! That is absolutely enough!" Mrs. Tyler interrupted, marching through the small crowd. Melissa stood back a couple paces, smirking still.

Gwendolyn thought she could breathe fire at that moment and felt her heart pounding with actual hatred for the lying snake standing in front of her. She didn't think it was possible to hate someone so quickly and so thoroughly, but she was grateful to be wrong. What was Melissa doing? What could she possibly gain by setting the townspeople's tongues wagging about her?

Mrs. Tyler stood in front of Melissa and glared with an expression that would have frightened Gwendolyn were she not so angry herself, but Gwendolyn couldn't imagine Mrs. Tyler ever looking so… enraged. One thing was for sure, once their blessed garden meeting was over, she would think back on Mrs. Tyler's expression with a smile and be grateful the woman had stood up for her, as well as the Adamses.

Melissa was smiling and staring directly at Gwendolyn with an evil glint in her eyes.

"Who told you such lies?" Gwendolyn demanded.

"A young man I met in town yesterday. Robert was his name."

Gwendolyn flinched. The man couldn't possibly have been Robert Jamison, could he? Not her friend, Robert. She tensed and looked around at the trees and shrubs. Surely he wouldn't have followed her to Grovetown and immediately started spouting lies about her. Then again, if he was really desperate to see her, she supposed he could be telling lies just to get her back to Hopeton, but the very idea felt like nonsense.

Melissa continued. "He said he was visiting and that he saw the two of you in the woods. Handsome fellow, I daresay. Dark… French, perhaps." She toyed with her curls and smiled devilishly.

French? Was Robert French? She didn't think so, but she really had no idea. The stranger was probably just another man with the same name. She shook the suspicious thought from her head.

But why would a visitor to their town immediately set out to destroy her…a complete stranger? She just couldn't understand it. Unless, of course, Melissa had managed to bewitch the man enough to convince him to join her cause of making Gwendolyn's life miserable. It was more than likely that Melissa was making the entire story up.

Gwendolyn grasped Melissa's wrist suddenly and squeezed as tight as she could in her rage-driven state. Melissa actually looked frightened for one delicious moment.

"You seem to think your brother can do no wrong, Melissa." She chewed on the last word as if it were a gob of rotted pumpkin rinds. "But you're wrong. *This* is actually what your brother did to me last night!"

In a flash, Gwendolyn released the silk scarf from around her neck and revealed the deep bruises James had given her. There were gasps all around, but Melissa stared warily…silently.

She threw Melissa's arm down then made slowly, confidently, for the Tyler's house.

"Ma? *Ma?*"

Gregory stormed through the kitchen door of Orchard Cottage, on the verge of panic. Gwendolyn hadn't been with the Adamses. Neither his mother nor his sister was outside as he'd assumed they would be. When questioned, the women of the committee had pointed toward the house without a word, and he knew something was amiss.

He rounded the corner and immediately stopped, not knowing whether to laugh or cry. The three women in question were sitting companionably in the parlor but his eyes were drawn to Gwendolyn whose eyes were stained with tears.

"What happened? What's wrong?"

He reached Gwendolyn in two strides then slid to his knees.

"Melissa Morrison is what happened," his mother replied bluntly. "I hate to sound unchristian and be a bad example to my children, but…I think I hate that wretched young woman."

"Oh, Ma. Really!" Susie said.

Gregory rolled his eyes. "You'd be a bad example to your children if you weren't truthful and let them know what type of qualities to look for and admire in a person. Now, what has she done?" He pulled a handkerchief from his back pocket and helped wipe away at Gwendolyn's tears.

"Well," Gwendolyn started, staring at him in the oddest fashion, "she began by telling everyone that James and I had some sort of secret rendezvous during the dance last night where I compromised myself or some such nonsense."

Gregory snorted at the thought. Melissa really was clueless. Nobody in town would believe such drivel, especially considering Gwendolyn.

"Then," she continued, "she told me that a man in town had told her he'd seen you and me together…*last night*…doing something that would also compromise ourselves."

"Last night?" He paused, automatically thinking back to their passionate meeting in the rain then shaking it from his mind. "Who? Who told her that?" He looked up to see his mother smiling down at him with suspicion. Was it possible she thought he'd been sparking with Gwendolyn when the girl's life had very nearly been taken? Women. He would never understand them, not as long as he lived.

Ignoring his romantic of a mother, he turned his attention back to Gwendolyn.

"She said he was Frenchman named Robert. That's all the information she gave." She chewed on her bottom lip. "I'm starting to think she made the whole story up just to make me sound loose, or like a…like a tramp or something."

That was certainly possible, although Melissa had always been unpredictable. Nearly everything she did or said seemed to be without any cause except to inflict pain on others. She was just like James in most regards except that she chose words instead of physical violence to punish her victims. Taking care of James the night before had been easy; just one good blow to his pretty face had scared him off, but what to do with his wretched sister? He couldn't very well hit her, as much as he'd like to. But Melissa could not get away with her childish games…ones that could destroy Gwendolyn's life. He would not have it.

Gregory patted Gwendolyn's hand, kissed her forehead, then jumped up with masculine purpose.

"What are you going to do?" Susie asked as he made for the door.

He growled, warning the women to stay out of his business. Melissa Morrison needed to be taught a lesson once and for all, and nobody was going to stop him. He bounded down the steps and walked through the tall grasses littered with dandelions, daisies, and grasshoppers, feeling ready to pounce.

Melissa was sitting serenely in one of the white lawn chairs among some other ladies of the town and looked up as he approached her.

"Oh, Gregory. How nice of you to come and see me. Shall we sit and talk a little?" She motioned to the empty chair beside her with one slender arm and smiled suggestively.

He remained standing and purposely spit in the grass beside her chair, making her jump in disgust. With a look of shear disapproval, he folded his arms and squared his shoulders.

"I missed you at the dance last night," she said, wrinkling her nose. "Why did you not come and find me? I so wanted to dance with you. Father even bought me a new dress for the occasion. If you come by later, I can show it to you."

Gregory stood still, his expression unwavering. How many times would he have to tell her he wasn't interested? It seemed she never gave up. During the past year, Melissa had been relentless—catching him alone in the barn, making suggestive comments in the mercantile, and even sneaking around to catch glimpses of him while he worked. He knew everything she said to Gwendolyn was in pursuit of him, and it angered him near to boiling.

"Who is Robert?" he asked bluntly.

"Oh, just a young man I met in town yesterday," she said, smoothing the folds of her dress. "You have nothing to worry about, darling. He means nothing to me, I assure you."

Gregory looked at the ladies sitting about and saw their questioning gazes on Melissa.

"How does he know Gwendolyn?"

"I'm not sure," she said airily. "He says he's been to town many times over the years. He does trading with the local markets and such. To tell you the absolute truth, Gregory, he seemed a bit boorish. I'd much rather be talking about wood and furniture… and hammers."

Gregory snorted, ignoring the girl's none-too-subtle flirting. She really had a lot of gall to be talking so, especially in front of the other ladies. It disgusted him, and he wanted to rid himself of her as soon as possible.

He took a quick step forward, making her cower backward. He leaned over her, placing each of his hands on the arms of her chair, and got right in her face. "Miss Morrison…I don't want you *ever* talking to Miss Gwendolyn again. Do you understand me?"

Gregory pulled back the instant Melissa puckered up, narrowly missing the touch of her detestable lips. He chuckled then grabbed the girl's chin fiercely. "If you or your filthy brother get anywhere near Gwendolyn again or spread anymore gossip about her, I will gladly hunt you down and make sure that you suffer for her pain."

Melissa's eyes were so wide he wondered if they would pop out of their sockets. He pulled his hand away, instinctively wiping it on his trousers as if she were a stray with all manner of contagious diseases.

"I love that girl and would rather die before seeing her hurt again." He spat at her side again for good measure, just because he enjoyed watching her squirm. With a nod of finality, he turned to go back to the house but stopped dead in his tracks.

Gwendolyn stood only a couple feet ahead him.

"Gwendolyn," he said, blushing a deep crimson at the realization of what she must have overheard…and seen.

"I wondered if you might escort me home now." Gwendolyn carefully looped an arm through his, eyeing him strangely, and urged him through the gaping committee members toward the lane.

Gregory held her arm firmly, admiring her courage after what Melissa had put her through. Gwendolyn had always been afraid of what others thought of her, but at that moment, she didn't seem to have a care in the world as they walked leisurely down the lane together.

The oak trees towered over them, their leaves rustling in the light breeze. They grew along both sides, providing relaxing shade from the noonday sun. It was a blessed relief after the short work he'd done high up on his brother's roof. Just a couple more hours and it would be finished. And once it was, he could get started on the cabinets and complete the work he'd started on the furniture months ago. No doubt the ladies would be happy to hear that bit of news. They had wanted to get the draperies, rugs, and blankets put away before Dan and Daisy were to live there. And if all went well in the city, Dan and Daisy would have found a stove, laundry press, and a feather tick, as well as other odds and ends for their new home.

Gregory envied his brother's happiness and progression in life. Dan was a partner in a growing construction company, was engaged to be married, and would soon have a wife. No doubt, he and Daisy would give birth to many children down through the coming years.

He cast a sideways glance at Gwendolyn, wondering if she remembered him even a little. Just two days before, he had thought that Gwendolyn would accept his marriage proposal and their own wedding plans would ensue. He had been excited for the all the firsts he and Gwendolyn would have—ordering things from the city for their home, planning a wedding, and—he wasn't ashamed to admit—even picking out fabrics for the interior. He wanted to see how Gwendolyn would command others during the preparations, what type of clothes she would have made in town, and see her excitement as she planned meals and decorated their own home. He wanted to see the look on her face after she'd given birth to their first child—

No, he was getting much too far ahead of himself. He knew he must not think about that. What he must think about was starting over, and getting Gwendolyn to fall in love with him all over again. All those lost memories. He heaved a sigh of frustration.

"Is something wrong?"

Gregory looked up, but couldn't look at Gwendolyn. He didn't want her to see the pain in his eyes. "Gwendolyn, do you…remember me at all?" He felt her arm tighten within his and wondered if he shouldn't have asked the question.

Damn it! Of course he should have. For his own sanity he needed to know.

"Yes."

Gregory whirled around to face her and grabbed her by the shoulders, swallowing. "You do? You actually remember me?"

Gwendolyn squirmed slightly. "It isn't much. I only remember you sitting before me in a room somewhere. You were watching me with your arms folded across your chest." She paused. "I'm so sorry it isn't more. You don't know how sorry."

He straightened, feeling a little disappointed.

"You're the only one I have remembered, though. That should count for something, shouldn't it?"

Gregory smiled, appreciating her sensitivity. He held his arm out for her once again and they continued down the path. Once they reached the dusty road leading out of Poplar Grove, they turned down the path and walked toward the Mathewson house.

"What kind of room?" he asked.

"Oh, dark with slanted walls and one little window. I don't know what I was doing. The image lasted only a fraction of a second."

"You must have seen your attic, I imagine. You often go up there to practice your violoncello."

Gwendolyn stopped in the road and stared at him as if he were some ghost that had come back from the dead.

"What's going on, Gwendolyn? You're starting to frighten me." Instinctively, he took a step back from her, feeling uncomfortable by the wild look in her eyes.

"The violoncello? I play the violoncello?" A smile began to creep at one corner of her small mouth and Gregory cherished the thought of kissing it once more.

"Yes, Gwendolyn! You play the violoncello. Your mother bequeathed it to you as part of your inheritance when she died." He watched as the expression on her face changed from happy, to confused, to positively giddy, and couldn't help smiling himself.

The next thing he knew, she flung herself into his arms and wrapped her arms about him, strangling him with her excitement. The sensation wasn't at all unpleasant. He wrapped his arms around her back and hugged her tightly, relishing the feel of her touch.

"I knew it! I just *knew* it, Gregory! Ever since I heard the quartet playing in Hopeton. I just closed my eyes and felt the music. That's when I had the vision. Oh, thank you! Thank you!" she cried, pulling back to smother his face with kisses.

He pulled back suddenly and looked at her, trying to read her thoughts. She looked instantly embarrassed as if realizing the inappropriateness of her position, but he wasn't about to let her get away. In a flash, he grabbed her face with one hand and kissed her ferociously, as if he would die of thirst and she were the only thing that could possibly quench it.

She whimpered, and the sound fueled his passion even more. He felt her fingers as they wove their way through his hair and rested to hold his head in place as she deepened the exchange. He locked his fingers together around her back and, to better support her weight, lowered his arms to rest just below her rump. She gave a squeak of surprise, but he merely swatted her in reply.

Gregory had never imagined that kissing Gwendolyn—his best and dearest friend whom he'd grown up with—could ever taste so sweet. She was like a warm nectar—the purest and sweetest tasting fruit, planted specifically by the gods for his nourishment. He never wanted to let go. But let go he must or else there would be serious trouble.

He kissed her slowly, relishing their last few moments together then pulled away with much regret. Some day soon, he would be able to kiss her properly and thoroughly.

He opened his eyes and saw Gwendolyn staring back at him in shock. She bit her lower lip, and he placed a light kiss on the tip of her nose. He smiled at her blush.

Carefully, he set her back down on the ground and watched in amusement as she hastily straightened her skirts. He gallantly held his arm out for her and she took it, licking her lips absentmindedly. They resumed their walk in silence and at a much slower pace.

They arrived at the Mathewson house a little too quickly.

"Will you come inside?" she asked, almost timidly.

He followed her through the kitchen, smirking.

"Oh, did you have fun your first day with the committee, Gwendolyn?" Mrs. Mathewson asked. The woman was sitting in the parlor, crocheting a doily, most likely for Daisy and her upcoming nuptials.

Gwendolyn looked thoughtful then nodded. "Yes, it was full of surprises." She cast a meaningful glance in Gregory's direction and he tried desperately not to react.

He didn't know what he was feeling—relief, hope, or pathetic love for her. It was probably a combination of all three.

"Those bruises look absolutely dreadful, my dear. How are you feeling?"

"I'm fine," she said, pulling the forgotten scarf from her bodice and replacing it around her neck. "Really, you don't need to worry. I've got an excellent watchman." She looked at Gregory and smiled.

"Good afternoon, Mrs. Mathewson," he said, slamming his hands into his pockets. "I trust you're well?"

"Very well, indeed. Thank you, Gregory. And how are you?"

"Oh, I'll bet you'll be pleased to know that I could have the roof finished by this evening, that is, if your niece can stay put for a couple of hours." He winked at Gwendolyn.

"That's wonderful!" Mrs. Mathewson beamed. "Dear boy. So, does that mean that we can start with our…things?"

He nodded, smiling to himself. "Tomorrow morning, if all goes well."

Mrs. Mathewson clapped her hands merrily then made a show of settling herself to resume her crocheting. "Thank you, dear boy. Now, be off you two! I have work to be about, you know." He saw her wink at Gwendolyn, and the latter chuckled in reply before heading up the stairs.

Gregory watched as Gwendolyn practically skipped through the darkened hallway in front of him, her dark curls bouncing against her back and shoulders. She opened the attic door with a creak then bounded up the small staircase two steps at a time. Same old Gwendolyn, he thought.

She stood silently for a moment, staring at the octagonal window in front of her, then spun around, her eyes wild with anticipation. Chuckling, Gregory swerved out of her way as she dove for the violoncello case resting behind him. He watched in fascination as she knelt in front of the case, reverently tracing her fingers in the dust.

"Well, go on then," he urged her, kneeling by her side.

They had been up there literally hundreds of times before, but he felt as if he were experiencing it for the first time, as she was. It was like finding a long lost treasure after so many years of searching. If he had any doubt about her memory loss before, he certainly didn't at that moment.

She unfastened the latches and lifted the lid, then gasped. "Oh, no. What's happened to it?"

He looked inside and chuckled. "Don't worry, Doly. It's just the strings. These instruments require constant upkeep and you've been gone for some time. Look." He pulled the instrument from its case, being careful not to catch the strings or pegs on anything. "I'll help you fix them. Let's just hope this thing still works."

She held the bridge in place as he realigned the strings starting with the C-string, and, with some difficulty, tightened them with the wooden pegs. They made awful creaking noises as they stretched.

"Looks like all of your strings are adequate, but you'll probably want to replace them soon. Now we need to tune it."

"How do you know how to do all of this?"

"I've seen you do this a million times, Gwendolyn. I'm a master."

He chuckled at her look of awe then proceeded to tune the beast of an instrument. He was always surprised at how difficult it was.

"No, go back a little," Gwendolyn interrupted a minute later. "It's too high."

Gregory looked at her and smirked. "You remember?"

"Yes," she said, excitedly. "It's strange but I feel an overwhelming sense of peace and…confidence whenever I hear music. It's almost as if I'm a different person. Do you think that's strange?"

"Not at all. You used to say that all the time when you were younger and growing into your instrument." He considered her words for a moment then continued. "Did you say you had your vision of me while listening to music?"

She nodded, her cheeks turning slightly rosy.

"Do you think music could possibly help you remember?"

A slow smile crept on her lips. "I've been wondering the same thing."

"Well," he said, jumping up and handing her the violoncello. "Let's get you started. Do you remember how to play?" He grabbed her bow from the case, removed a couple broken strands, tightened it, and then handed it to her.

"I hope so."

After pulling her chair from out of the corner, he dusted it off with his handkerchief and pushed it behind her.

She sat down and shakily assumed the position. "I can't believe I'm doing this. I hardly know what I'm doing."

"You certainly look like you know what you're doing," he argued, pulling up his own chair. Ignoring the dust, he promptly sat down.

She smiled at him then looked down at her instrument. She looked so unsure of herself but very happy to be where she was. The minute she glided the bow across the strings, she paused and stared at what she was doing as if it were a very serious thing, indeed.

Gregory watched her curiously. Her slender form was almost completely hidden by the bulk of the dull mahogany instrument and the contrast of their two bodies was very complementary.

Her slender, creamy arms against the pear-shaped curves of the violoncello and her long and curly hair against its straight neck was a beautiful juxtaposition. He leaned back, watching her legs as they fought the folds of her canary yellow dress and wrapped about the instrument.

"But don't I need music to read from?" She looked lost and confused.

"Nah," he said, shifting in his seat. "You never did spend much time with sheet music, though you could read it exceptionally well." Her face beamed with pleasure at the compliment. "Try playing what you heard in Hopeton," he suggested.

He laid his head back on the chair and rested his eyes as she played different notes and experimented with various fingering positions. He hoped to God she remembered how to play. Her skill was just too precious to lose. But if she had lost it, he could very easily imagine himself tying her up there until she could learn to play once more. Well, perhaps not, he chuckled to himself.

He felt the room darken and knew another storm was brewing. Grovetown had had more rain that season than any other year, which was highly advantageous since he still had his father's planting to get to. If he could only get those darn seeds in the ground! He groaned inwardly, wondering why he was wasting the afternoon away in the Mathewson's attic listening to Gwendolyn rediscover her talent when he had plenty of other things to do.

Gregory paused then realized, with a jolt of surprise, that she was playing an actual melody! He opened his eyes to see Gwendolyn playing her violoncello with deep concentration, opening her eyes now and then to check her fingering. The melody was something he'd never heard before—a simple tune but powerfully soothing. He sat on the edge of his chair with his head in his hands and watched in awe. God, he loved her!

She leaned over her instrument masterfully…passionately, her fingers moving about the neck with ease. Once or twice she fumbled over the fingering but was quick to fix it. The end result was very fine.

He waited a moment after she played the last note in a descending vibrato before speaking. "Gwendolyn, I want you."

She looked up, appearing completely afraid and stunned into silence, and he was instantly embarrassed. He cleared his throat then stood up, wondering what on earth had possessed him to say such a thing. He nervously scratched the sides of his stomach then stepped toward her.

"I want to kiss you," he amended stupidly. "May I?"

She recovered quickly, smiling mischievously up at him. "If you feel you must."

"Yes, I must," he nodded firmly before bending to press his lips to hers. He had meant for it to be a light farewell kiss, nothing too difficult to pull himself away from, but Gwendolyn had other plans. To his surprise, she grabbed his shirt collar with one hand and pulled him toward her, hard.

He laughed as they kissed, wondering what it was—if not for her memories—that drew her to him so quickly. He thought it might be his charm and good looks but hoped it was something that went far deeper…something like destiny, perhaps. He'd never believed in it before and felt quite foolish for even thinking about it, but he couldn't help wondering. There was just something uncanny about the last few days. Something that drew him to her in a way he'd never felt before. He reckoned she must feel the same way.

Gwendolyn pulled away abruptly, lowering her head.

"Confounded, woman! Why must you always be so embarrassed?" He wanted to shove her interfering violoncello aside and hold her close, showing her she had no reason to feel so.

"Because I've only known you for four days, that's why," she whispered.

"That's nothing to be embarrassed about, Doly. Or do you mean you're embarrassed because it's only been four days and you're already throwing yourself at me? I must say I've been awfully curious about that." He smirked.

She slugged him playfully. "Go work on that house of yours, you beast."

He smacked a loud kiss on her cheek then skipped out of the attic before she could stab him with her bow.

# Chapter Eight

THIS IS DEFINITELY NOT A GOOD IDEA, Gwendolyn thought as she watched Gregory leave the attic, laughing mercilessly. She didn't know what had gotten into her. Ever since she'd met Gregory in the mercantile, she'd felt drawn to him as if he were her life force—the very reason her heart kept beating. To her chagrin, she was finding it more and more difficult to stay away from him and she didn't know why. She yearned for his company, his approval, and most of all, his help in rediscovering who she was. He was the only one who really could help her since Dan and Daisy would be getting married in a little over a week. All of their time and attention would be devoted to each other, not that she could blame them. She had the feeling that, were she and Gregory also engaged, they would feel much the same way.

But what to do then—she couldn't very well tell her uncle that she and Gregory needed an extra chaperone or that she needed a different one in general. That would be too embarrassing. She desperately needed someone to talk to and confide in—a person who had spent the most time with her and knew her best.

She hung her head in defeat. There wasn't anything she could do except get a grip on herself and learn to control her physical impulses, no matter how innocent her intentions were. And somewhere, sometime, she would need to beg Gregory to do the same.

What a good laugh that would give him, she thought irritably. He did so love to tease her.

She smiled. It wasn't so bad being teased by Gregory, not really.

She shook the thoughts from her head like a dog straight out of the brook then waited for her dizziness to subside.

She hadn't been surprised to discover she played the violoncello, not since the concert in Hopeton, but she had been overwhelmed with relief and anticipation for what lay ahead of her.

Music was the key.

Another vision was bound to reveal itself and she would keep practicing her violoncello until it happened. Yes, that was what she would do.

When she'd first started playing, a wave of fear crept over her, and her back and neck prickled. Then her goose bumps had turned into giddy curiosity and things had just fallen into place from that point onward. She'd closed her eyes, praying that her intuition would guide her fingers and bow. With a great deal of concentration, she'd focused on the music from the concert…and it had come! It was truly frightening at first, and then it felt like a drug and she had to have more of it. She'd been in a trance, even after the song was over, at least until Gregory had interrupted.

She wasn't completely ignorant of what he'd meant, but she'd been shocked, nonetheless. Despite the fact his comment was completely inappropriate, she'd been more shocked by the fact she'd wanted to smile at him in return.

Never mind him, she thought. The wretched man was trouble and she needed to focus.

Gwendolyn spent the following couple of hours replaying melodies she'd heard over the past year and making up some of her own. They were mostly nonsense, the ones she made up, but they kept her fingers busy.

She watched her left hand as she played vibrato, watched as her wrist rocked back and forth and listened to the sounds it made. She tried different fingering techniques, played notes with multiple fingers, as she plucked and slid along the strings. Her bowing arm seemed to act of its own free will, sliding gracefully, slurring notes together, and even combining strings. The sounds felt so familiar, and yet, strangely new.

By the time her aunt Marguerite called her down to supper, her fingers felt raw and swollen and her back hurt something fierce. She wanted to continue playing but knew that if she did, she might never want to return to the attic to play again.

Out of habit, she loosened the bow, retracted the metal endpin, and returned her instrument to its case. With a groan, she stretched then went to the window. Another townhouse stood right next-door only a couple dozen feet away. Her aunt's garden took up most of the space in between where small plants and herbs had just sprouted from the earth.

After brushing the dust and cobwebs from her dress, Gwendolyn exited the attic and headed down to the kitchen where it was much cooler. Both her aunt and uncle, Gregory, Dan and Daisy were sitting around the table spooning beans into their mouths.

Her aunt immediately stood up to help. "I wasn't sure when you were coming down, darling."

Gwendolyn pointed her back into her chair with a friendly scowl. "I can dish up my own food, Aunt Marguerite," Gwendolyn said, going over to the cast iron stove and ladling a couple spoons of beans into her bowl. It looked like a mixture of kidney, white, and pinto beans with onions, green peppers, and bits of pork. "You just relax and eat your food. It looks delicious." She grabbed a square of cornbread from a tin pan and sat at the end of the table between Daisy and Gregory, trying her best to ignore the latter's blue eyes as they watched her.

"Did you have a good time in the city today?" Gwendolyn asked Daisy. She couldn't help it, but ignoring Gregory seemed to be the best solution to their problem at the moment.

"Oh, yes. Papa Tyler told us right where to go so we found everything fairly quickly. We ordered a stove, a bed, some laundry things, an ice box, and…what else, Dan?"

"Furniture, that sort of thing, and some useless knickknacks."

"They're not useless, you bore," Daisy argued, smacking Dan on the arm.

Dan simply chortled as he took a bite of his cornbread. Gwendolyn thought he resembled his elder brother quite a bit at that moment.

"I heard you've been making a lot of progress on the house, Gregory. Is that right?" Her uncle finished off the water in his glass with one gulp and her aunt jumped up to fetch the pitcher.

"Yes, it was nice of the rain to hold off as long as it did. I finished the roof about an hour ago."

"That's splendid, my boy. I reckon you'll finally be able to plant your father's blasted seeds then."

"I'll get to it one of these days," Gregory chuckled, wiping his mouth with the napkin in his lap. "There's still a bit of work to be done on the house. I also promised Ma I'd help tend the mercantile while Pa goes to Mooresville for supplies next week."

"My appointment in Leadville fell through," Dan said. "So, it looks like I'll be sticking around next week. No doubt you could use the extra hand."

"No doubt."

Gwendolyn watched as Gregory held his bowl and spooned the beans into his mouth as if he hadn't eaten for days. Below his well-worn cowboy hat, she could see the dampness of his temples and his tanned arms glowed with sawdust. She rather liked the sloppy way his sleeves were folded and the tightness of his shirt. Now that she thought about it, he did seem worn out, not really tired, just burdened with responsibility.

Poor man, she thought, feeling guilty all of a sudden. What had he been thinking when he'd agreed to watch out for her? He didn't have time to watch her play the violoncello, let alone escort her everywhere. She knew there wasn't really anyone else who could do it, except for Dan, but the idea of a betrothed man following her around and protecting her just didn't seem right, and as much as she hated to admit it, she liked having Gregory around. She would just have to come up with a way to help him somehow.

A smile spread across her lips. She knew just the person to talk to and it was high time Gwendolyn took charge and did something good for someone else.

Gwendolyn couldn't wait to see the look on Gregory's face once he figured out what they were up to. The ladies had spent the morning livening up the new house. After services, Gregory had taken her back to Orchard Cottage where she'd immediately enlisted the help of Mrs. Tyler, Susie, Daisy, and Dan in her endeavor. If Dan could just keep Gregory busy past sunset for the next few days as he'd promised, Gregory wouldn't have a clue what they were doing until they were finished.

It was high noon. Gwendolyn straightened her aching back and gazed down the sun swept field. Just clearing one row of the Tylers' field had taken the four of them nearly an hour to complete, and there were dozens more. The task was daunting, but Gwendolyn knew it would all be worth it in the end. She simply couldn't wait.

"You always have the most romantic ideas. You know that, Gwendolyn?" Daisy said after a cow mooed loudly from the barn. Rebelliously clad in a pair of Dan's much larger trousers and clunky boots, Daisy knelt in the dirt and pulled the roots of old pumpkin plants from the moistened ground with a grunt. She suddenly shrieked and wrung her arms and hands in the air as a garden spider crawled across her fingers.

"Thank you for doing this," Gwendolyn said, trying not to laugh at her cousin's theatrics.

"Oh, anything for you, dear sister. I just hope you're not inclined to do this every spring. Yuck!" she said after accidentally wiping dirt on her face. "And I can't believe I'm wearing Dan's trousers. Of all the strange things—"

Gwendolyn couldn't believe it either. She was actually wearing a pair of Gregory's herself, which hadn't been part of the original plan. But Mrs. Tyler had insisted by saying, "You'll ruin your beautiful dresses, ladies…it's a really dirty job, you know," and they really didn't have anything else. Gwendolyn knew the woman was secretly giddy with the idea that they were wearing her sons' clothes, but she wouldn't give her the satisfaction of knowing she was secretly pleased with it too.

She wiped the edge of her nose on the collar of Gregory's shirt and the smell of fresh lavender wafted. Gwendolyn immediately erupted with goose bumps. "Oh, good grief!" she howled, making Daisy frown at her in confusion.

Through the next several hours they grew more and more efficient, so by the time the sun started its descent, they had completed fourteen rows. Gwendolyn was so excited that she jumped and clapped and hugged each of her companions making them smile despite their weariness. They made quick with hiding all of the tools and plant disposal, then frantically washed themselves in the barrel outside the kitchen, wearing only their chemises and drawers. Their dog Caramel barked at their heels as they donned their petticoats and dresses. It was completely chaotic, but glorious fun.

"Now, try not to look so worn out, dearies," Mrs. Tyler warned merrily as they tromped along behind her into the kitchen. "The men will be arriving soon."

Each of the girls slumped into a chair and glared at the woman's back. Mrs. Tyler still had so much blessed energy. After nearly a full day's worth of backbreaking work, she looked refreshed and was already preparing a late supper.

With the ache in her back and the soreness in her knees, Gwendolyn wondered how on earth she would be able to continue for the next three days.

She stood and went to the sink. Slowly, she pumped water into the basin and drank straight from the pump, her throat too dry for words. Of course, she immediately started coughing.

"Slow down, missy. Here, try a cup." Mrs. Tyler filled a cup with water then handed it to her. "Is it your throat?"

Gwendolyn nodded.

"Gregory told me it was bothering you. Perhaps you shouldn't be helping us with the planting—"

"No!" Gwendolyn said with vehemence then blushed at her outburst. "I–I want to help."

Mrs. Tyler smiled. "You like my son, don't you?"

"Oh, well…I–uh…" Gwendolyn stammered. She scrunched up her nose and looked at Mrs. Tyler through narrowed eyes, not knowing exactly what to say and feeling dreadful.

"That means 'yes'," Susie interjected.

Daisy exploded with laughter and it wasn't long before Mrs. Tyler and Susie were laughing along with her.

Gwendolyn, on the other hand, was still too confused to do anything but stare at nothing in particular. Of course she liked Gregory. He was an easy person to like and easy to get along with as long as he wasn't angry. So why couldn't she openly admit it, especially to the women in the room whom she trusted?

She knew why, by golly, and it was far too embarrassing for her to admit. After only a handful of days of knowing him, she was beginning to think she might actually be in love with Gregory. Could it be possible? she wondered incredulously.

She thought back on their times together. In the mercantile, he'd gone from being quiet, mysterious, and unabashedly handsome to passionately angry, violent, and vulnerable. In the rain, he'd apologized with confidence then boldly, beautifully, asked her to marry him.

Gwendolyn's heart started beating faster and she couldn't stop the tears that were beginning to form. It was as if she was only just realizing the impact of what he'd done, of how he felt about her. It was strange, but the words she'd overhead him speaking to Melissa the day before meant more to her than any of his private admissions. He'd confessed his love for her in front of all the committee without shame or remorse. Gregory loved her.

She hastily wiped the tear that fell past her cheek, hoping nobody had seen, but she hadn't been discreet enough.

"Gwennie, what's wrong?" Susie asked, her face full of concern. "Oh, Gwennie. We were only teasing."

"It's not that. I just feel…just give me something to do. I need a distraction."

Susie warily placed a couple cans of vegetables and a saucepan in front of her, and Gwendolyn went to the stove to heat them up. She fed three or four small pieces of wood to the stove's inner chamber then proceeded to stir the saucepan's contents.

Oh, where were they? Gwendolyn wondered impatiently, looking out into the darkened landscape for any signs of life.

Just before her corn and green beans began to boil, she saw a shadow move past the house and she nearly cried out with excitement. At last! They were there.

Using as much poise as she could muster, she grabbed a crocheted hot pad and shimmied her way through Daisy and Susie, who were setting the table. On it sat a small platter of sliced ham, a bowl of boiled potatoes, and her vegetables, as well as bread and strawberry preserves from the larder. The meal looked as if it had taken much longer than the three-quarters of an hour they'd actually spent. Gwendolyn smiled in satisfaction, knowing that Gregory couldn't possibly suspect a thing.

Sitting in one of the hand-carved dining chairs, she wondered once again where the men could be. The shadow she'd seen had to have been that of a deer or moose. She had expected someone to show up in the house before she'd finished setting the silverware, but no one had. How long could it possibly take to put the horses away? Dan was certainly holding up his end of the bargain, perhaps a little too well.

The kitchen door slammed open and all the women jumped in fear. Gregory stood at the threshold, his face ashen and full of horror.

"Quick, bring water! The blasted barn's on fire!"

Gwendolyn felt her heart drop to her stomach as she watched him jump down the porch steps and disappear into the darkness.

Without another word, both Susie and Mrs. Tyler brought buckets from the storeroom and the four of them quickly filled them with water using both the kitchen and the outdoor pump. Awkwardly, they ran to the barn—a bucket in each hand—and immediately poured them onto the flames, which engulfed one corner of the structure and rose to the moon like some fiendish creature. Mr. Tyler and Dan were doing their best to smother the smaller flames with saddle blankets, but Gwendolyn couldn't see Gregory anywhere.

"Quick! Before it reaches the loft!" Dan bellowed.

Gwendolyn was full of adrenaline as she tossed one bucket of water and then another up against the barn. To her dismay, she realized it would take many more buckets to keep up with the flames but the pumps were too far away. She gasped in shock as the fire quickly spread over the front of the barn, then coughed violently—the smoke burning her throat and lungs. She gagged, then with a frightened gulp, turned and started for the house.

"Gwendolyn! The water trough," Mrs. Tyler said, leading her around the side of the barn where the horses' water was kept. "Give me your scarf," she ordered. The woman dumped the silk in the trough then tied it around Gwendolyn's face to mask the smoke. After filling their buckets once again, they rejoined the fray.

The animals trapped within the barn roared and kicked at their stalls in fear and the sound was truly terrifying. Gwendolyn tossed another bucket of water as one of the stallions neighed and whinnied for release as if the devil itself had possessed its body.

"Greg! The livestock!" Mr. Tyler bellowed beside her. "Get them outta there, now!"

Oh, no! Gwendolyn thought as the blood drained from her face. She ran toward the entrance, screaming Gregory's name over the crackling flames. Oh, God! He couldn't die.

She rounded the corner and saw, to her alarm, the Tylers' ebony stallion coming straight at her. Bending her knees, she dove toward the hard ground just as the horse charged past her with a mighty whoosh.

"Gwendolyn? Are you all right?" Mr. Tyler asked, rushing to her side and grabbing her arm to steady her. "Damn the beast."

"Yes. Yes, I'm fine."

He hefted her up with one arm, nodded, and then ran back to his previous task.

Taking a deep breath of relief, Gwendolyn ducked under the

flames and rushed inside the smoky interior, grabbing the bucket she'd left behind. Once inside, she sloshed some of it against the wooden wall then stomped and scattered a pile of smoking hay. All of the saddles, bridles, and supplies had been thrown haphazardly against the opposite wall. Against the sounds of screeching animals, she sprinted down the long corridor and, to her relief, found Gregory. He was alive but crouched down on the ground with a hand at his stomach.

"Gregory! What happened…what's wrong?" She knelt down beside him and placed a hand over his. "Are you sick?"

"No," he grunted quietly. He pointed ahead of him with his chin and Gwendolyn turned to see the dangerously splintered remains of one of the stall doors.

"The stallion?" she asked behind the wet scarf.

He nodded once, weakly. "*Your* bloody stallion."

With a huff, she jumped up and grabbed the bucket. "Close your mouth," she said a second before she sloshed the remaining water at him. He coughed and spluttered as she went to help him up.

"What was that for?" he gasped, wiping the mucky soot from his eyes and nose.

"I don't want any of your gorgeous physique getting burned," she replied sarcastically, watching his long locks drip. "Now, let's get you out of here."

"The animals…"

"Fine," she cried in exasperation. "*You* get out of here. *I'll* get the animals. Now, git, you big oaf!"

He laughed—well, it was more of a wheeze—then stumbled his way out of the smoking barn.

Gwendolyn coughed then unlatched all of the stalls, paying no mind to the pounding fear in her chest. The mare bolted without any encouragement, but the smaller animals needed a swat or two on the rump to get going. Once she'd gone through all the stalls, she checked once more just to make sure she'd gotten them all, then headed out.

*Meow!*

At the threshold, she stopped dead in her tracks and spun around. "Heavens, Sophie! What are you all still doing in here?"

Cowering in the corner of a small pen were all of the kittens, heavily guarded by their mewling mother. Grabbing her empty bucket, Gwendolyn reached inside the enclosure and was rewarded with a hiss.

"Sophie, your kittens are going to suffocate in this smoke if we don't get them out of here right now." Cautiously, she reached for them again, and this time Sophie was compliant. Gwendolyn carefully, but quickly, placed the fluffy kittens inside the bucket one-by-one then made a mad dash out of the barn with Sophie hot on her heels.

She didn't stop running until she reached the fence at the other side of the corral where it was safe and cool. She turned around. The lower portion of the barn was still on fire but the majority of the flames had been contained.

Gwendolyn set the kittens beneath an opening in a nearby shrub and watched as Sophie stood on her hind legs and peered into the bucket to check on her little ones. Gwendolyn tipped the bucket carefully to allow better access before running to help the others.

It took several more trips to the water trough to douse the remainder of the flames, and by the time they were finished, everything seemed eerily quiet. The trees glared at them beneath the full moon and Gwendolyn shivered. The group all looked at the charred structure in relief and fatigue.

Mrs. Tyler wearily walked toward her, wiping the back of her hand against her forehead. Her skirts, Gwendolyn noticed, were smeared with sweat and soot and had small holes where bits of fire had burned through.

"Where's Gregory?" Mrs. Tyler asked breathlessly.

Gwendolyn looked around at the group and realized, with a tremor of anxiety, he wasn't with them. That was odd, she thought.

"I guess he must have gone to the house," Gwendolyn said. The idea didn't sound quite right. In fact, it sounded downright idiotic. She knew Gregory wouldn't leave any disaster unless—

They both gasped at the same time as realization struck then ran in the direction of the house, yelling Gregory's name. The rest of the group followed close behind.

Gwendolyn yanked the scarf off her face as she dashed across the lawn and tried to banish all thoughts of dread from her mind, but it was no use. The dread crawled up her spine and across her limbs with agonizing speed. She ran despite her fear that Gregory was lying dead in the house somewhere. She ran so fast that she didn't see the old fallen log until after she'd tripped and landed—hard—against her face in the brush and dirt.

She lay still for several moments and stared into the starry sky, trying her very best not to cry out, but it was impossibly difficult. Her arms and face stung from the impact of her fall and she felt the overwhelming build up of tears behind her eyes. A small whimper escaped her lips, but she coughed it off then slowly stood and limped the remaining sixty feet or so to the house.

There was a great scuffling sound coming from the kitchen and Gwendolyn entered slowly.

"Gregory isn't here," Susie bellowed as she jumped down from the hallway stairs. "Oh, good Lord, Gwennie. What happened to you?"

Everybody spun around and gasped.

"Is it that bad?" Gwendolyn groaned.

"Much worse," Daisy replied, biting her lower lip. "What happened? It's only been…what? Three blessed minutes?"

"I tripped over an old log, but really…don't worry about me. We need to find Gregory. I have a really bad feeling." Gwendolyn felt something drip down her cheekbone and she automatically wiped it with her hand.

It was blood.

"There aren't any old logs in the field," Dan said warily.

Everyone looked at Gwendolyn and she immediately started to hyperventilate, of course.

"Good Lord," she breathed. "It was Gregory." Tears came at full force then, and she wasn't embarrassed to show it. "I–I thought it was the smoke…but the horse…it must have—"

Dan and his father barreled past her, their eyes full of what she dreaded most, and Susie and Daisy both erupted into fits of hysteria. Mrs. Tyler went to comfort them but was soon crying as well.

Gwendolyn couldn't do anything but stand and stare in shock, even as her aunt and uncle rushed in from the front room.

"We saw the fire," her uncle announced. "Is anyone hurt? Oh, good God, Gwendolyn!"

"Gregory," Mrs. Tyler whispered, pointing to the kitchen door. "The horse."

Her uncle pushed past them and grabbed Gwendolyn's head to examine her wounds. "Marguerite, don't start crying. She's all right. Just get her cleaned up." He ran out the door yelling. "Don't move him!"

Gwendolyn felt sick to her stomach. If the stallion had in fact kicked Gregory, he could be—

"No!" she wailed, making the other women jump. He couldn't be...dead, she plead silently. He just couldn't be! Her body started feeling very heavy, too heavy for her to stand up any longer. She reached for a chair to sit in just as the ground rose up to meet her, and all went dark.

# Chapter Nine

GWENDOLYN AWOKE IN AN UNFAMILIAR ROOM of yellows and greens. The light from the sun shone in pillars against her four-poster bed and rested on the hardwood floors, making the room seem celestial and cozy.

She reached up to scratch her face and hit bandages instead of skin. Oh, no, she thought, suddenly remembering the fire…and Gregory. She started to cry, her eyes dry and burning, and if it were even possible, her throat hurt worse than before.

Oh, she'd been so rough and impatient with him in the barn, what with throwing water in his face and practically pushing him out to seek refuge from the smoke. But it hadn't been the smoke at all. It had been that darn horse! *Her* horse. Well, she didn't want the beast anymore. It could run wild in the forest forever for all she cared.

She rolled onto her side and groaned. The effects of the planting were definitely taking their toll on her body. But none of that even mattered. Gregory would never see what they'd done for him. She buried her face against the pillow even though the gauze bandages scratched against her raw flesh and stung fiercely, and cried. She could deal with the physical pain.

The minutes rolled by slowly. Gwendolyn couldn't fall back asleep.

With a weary sigh she heaved herself out of bed, grabbed a wrap to cover her nightgown, and wandered down the hallway. She was still in the Tyler's house but, as far as she could tell, there was nobody in sight.

Near the kitchen door she found only one pair of muddied boots and decided everyone had to be outside. She donned the boots then trudged out the door to investigate, being careful to avoid the area where she'd tripped over Gregory.

She found Mrs. Tyler, Susie, and Daisy in the field clearing away more of the dead plants, just as they'd all done the previous day, and looking far too happy about it. They'd just lost a family member, for goodness' sake!

Or hadn't they?

She approached them warily.

Daisy raised her head and her face immediately lit up. She jumped up and lumbered toward Gwendolyn, the rope hugging the trousers about her waist making her seem impossibly thin.

"You haven't even been here a whole week and already you've fainted twice. What am I going to do with you?" Daisy placed her hands on her hips in much the same fashion as Mrs. Maynard did and Gwendolyn smiled in spite of herself. "Well, I guess it's a good thing you're so clumsy," she smirked jokingly. "Otherwise, we might not have found Gregory until the morning, and by then he would have been in much worse shape, I'm sure."

Something snapped inside Gwendolyn's mind and she snatched Daisy by the shoulders, her arms trembling. "He's not dead?" She couldn't believe it but would do so gladly if it really were true.

"I guess you missed that part, didn't you?" she said, almost to herself. "No, you poor thing. He's not dead. Although, he will be once he wakes up and I get my claws on him." She bared her teeth like a ravenous animal.

Could it be? Gwendolyn wondered enthusiastically. She felt the life flow through her once again, and suddenly she felt some purpose to her existence after all.

Susie and Mrs. Tyler approached. The latter clapped the dirt from her hands then grabbed both of Gwendolyn's hands in her own. Mrs. Tyler looked at her with the same blue eyes as her eldest son and whispered, "I believe you were meant to find him and I don't just mean in the field last night. I mean always." She reached up and wiped a tear from Gwendolyn's cheek.

"All right, enough of this mushy nonsense," Daisy ordered.

"But what about the horse?" Gwendolyn asked, remembering the splintered wood and the way Gregory had been holding his stomach.

"Oh, he got kicked all right," Susie said. "Your uncle says one rib was broken but his lung wasn't punctured, thank goodness."

"He really should be resting," Mrs. Tyler interrupted, looking worried, "but he high-tailed it out of here at first light...after looking in on you, of course. Ben had just gotten on the road." She rubbed Gwendolyn's arms. "Will you go to Gregory, bring him back home so he can rest? He shouldn't be working in his condition and I know he'll listen to you."

"Where is he?" Gwendolyn asked.

Mrs. Tyler smiled with relief. "We'll saddle Red for you and you can go to him. Don't worry," she said, reading Gwendolyn's mind. "Red is the mare. She's quite gentle. You'll be safe with her. Susie," she said, snapping her fingers. "Can you round Red up, please, and Daisy, will you fetch Gwendolyn a larger wrap? We can't have her riding through town dressed like this. What would the townspeople think if they were to see her?"

"This is so exciting," Susie said, skipping off after the mare.

"But don't you think, Mrs. Tyler," Daisy interrupted, "that Gregory would be easier to persuade if Gwendolyn were to go dressed exactly as she is?"

"Oh, git, you little imp!" Mrs. Tyler cried, trying to swat the girl on the rump, but she wasn't quick enough. Daisy took off through the grasses, laughing merrily.

Gwendolyn chuckled then followed Mrs. Tyler for several minutes. Once they approaced the barn, Gwendolyn gasped. The structure looked much worse in the daylight. It looked as if a big bite had been taken out of it.

"We've had much worse, to be sure," Mrs. Tyler said, going inside to grab a saddle. "It happened last summer. We lost half the livestock and had to rebuild the entire barn. Never did figure out how it started, come to think of it."

"What about this one?"

Susie arrived with the mare, pulling her by its bridle.

Mrs. Tyler shrugged her shoulders. "Don't know. I do know I was the last one to put away the tools last night, but I specifically remember hanging the lantern on the hook outside the kitchen."

Mrs. Tyler threw the reins to Susie then placed the blanket atop the horse's back. Mrs. Tyler proceeded with the saddle, slamming her body against the horse's stomach and buckling the straps tight.

Gwendolyn winced.

"It's strange, but the men found the lantern...broken…lying on the ground just there." She pointed to the corner of the barn where the grasses were charred and dusty.

Daisy arrived carrying one of her own wraps, a full-body one made of wool. Gwendolyn wrapped the thick garment about her shoulders and secured it down her front before looking up at Mrs. Tyler.

"Up you go," the older woman said.

After stepping into the stirrups, Gwendolyn hoisted herself up and was immediately surprised by how high she was. She looked down into the women's expectant faces.

"Follow the road behind the post office for about a mile. There's a single large oak where you'll need to turn. My sons' properties are on the left next to the brook."

"But what about the planting? He'll see you working when we return."

"We'll be in the house. Here, take this." Mrs. Tyler handed her a single spur.

Gwendolyn looked down at the vile contraption in confusion. "I can't use this."

"It's not for Red."

Gwendolyn nodded then gulped in understanding. Instinctively, she scanned the Tylers' property for any signs of intruders. She thought about the shadow she'd seen outside the kitchen window and wondered. "Do you think James—"

"Just be careful, dear child. Go quickly and don't stop for anything."

Without further ado, Gwendolyn stuffed the spur down the thin fabric of her bodice then kicked Red's flanks. "Ya!"

The two of them went flying through the pasture gate, past Orchard Cottage, and down the lane toward town. Gwendolyn couldn't believe that Gregory would be fool enough to leave after all that had happened the night before. He was seriously injured and would make it far worse if he didn't stop acting like an idiot.

The cool spur bit against her breast as she galloped. It was a sharp reminder of how much danger she was in, but she tried not to think about that. She held onto the reins tightly as she neared her aunt and uncle's house then guided Red toward the post office. Women and children gasped in alarm as she hurtled past and she realized, with a chuckle, she must be quite a sight. With nothing but a full body wrap to cover her indecency, she galloped through town with it billowing behind her like a highwayman's cape and her face covered in bandages.

As she turned down the road by the post office, she realized she didn't care. In fact, her state of undress might even aid her in the situation as Daisy had insinuated. She smiled, enjoying the thought of enticing Gregory.

The trees grew thicker the further she went, blocking out most of the sunlight. Ahead of her down the road stood a dark-haired man with a horse and cart, and he was watching her. She leaned forward in her mount, urging Red to go faster. As she passed him, she realized he wasn't just watching her but scowling—fiercely. She didn't know what it was, but something inside her told her he wasn't just scowling at her lack of propriety. She gulped in fear and avoided his gaze.

"Whoa," she cried several minutes later, spotting the large oak Mrs. Tyler had mentioned. Tall rose bushes hid the path she needed to turn down, a path which was so narrow she could have passed it right on by and ridden another mile without realizing it.

"C'mon Red."

They maneuvered their way onto the path, that couldn't have been more than eight feet wide, and resumed their previous gait. On their left sat a massive orchard behind a white wood fence, most likely belonging to the Adamses. The blossoms were bright and fragrant and the bees buzzed about happily.

Gwendolyn could hear the gurgling of the brook nearby and thought the place was absolutely beautiful. The area was secluded and the air was cool and clean—an ideal spot of land, in her opinion. She was glad that Daisy and Dan would get to live in such a place. The Adamses were a delightful and friendly sort and would be good neighbors.

She turned left once more and spotted Dan beside a newly constructed house. A beautiful, chestnut-colored mare grazed beneath a cherry tree to her right.

"Gwendolyn…what are you doing here?" Dan said, dropping his tools on an upturned chair before approaching her. His left eye was red and swollen. "You're not supposed to go anywhere without an escort…and you don't even have proper clothes on, for mercy's sake," he blurted, waving his hand in her direction. "Are you purposely baiting your attackers?"

"I'm perfectly decent, and besides, I didn't have time to—"

She paused, realizing what he'd just said. "What do you mean 'attacker*s*'? Is there someone else after me now?"

The color drained from his face and he lunged at her, grabbing the horn of her saddle. "Is somebody hurt?"

"Oh, no! Dear, no!" she said, suddenly feeling guilty. "I came to fetch Gregory. He shouldn't be working in his condition and I'm prepared to bash him in the head if he refuses."

Dan slapped her in the leg, making Red flinch, and Gwendolyn looked at him curiously.

"Hey, you're practically my sister, Gwendolyn. That's what brother's do. Besides, you scared the hell out of me." He took a slow steady breath. "I'm coming with you." He pulled her booted foot out of the stirrup and hoisted himself up behind her. "Perhaps you'll have better luck getting him home than I did."

"*Gregory* hit you?" she asked incredulously, feeling odd with Dan's legs wrapped around her. She had a hard time imagining Gregory hitting his own brother, especially for trying to help. Then again, Gregory did tend to overreact when his pride was being threatened.

"Aye, he did, and I'd like to bash him in the head for you. So, lead the way, fair Lady Gwendolyn."

Gwendolyn smiled in spite of herself, remembering the gauze all over her face, but immediately frowned once they reached Dan's property. Next to an unfinished cabinet laid Gregory—on his back in the dirt.

Gwendolyn threw her leg over Red and was at Gregory's side before Dan even had a chance to dismount. "Gregory?"

No answer.

She thrust two fingers at his neck, the same way he had done after James had attacked her, and found, to her relief, he was still breathing. "He's passed out again."

Dan knelt beside her. "Look's like somebody beat us here. See here," he said, gently twisting Gregory's head to one side. Gregory's brown hair was soaked with blood and Gwendolyn gasped. Upon further inspection, they found a large gash near the back of his crown. Dan looked up and scanned the area warily, whispering, "I was here but fifteen minutes ago."

"He didn't hit his head on the cabinet," Gwendolyn surmised, feeling a little cold all of a sudden.

"Don't think so. Here," Dan said, dragging a wide piece of wood toward her, "put him on this—carefully—while I get the wagon. Will you be all right on your own for a minute or two?"

She swallowed. "Yes, I…have something," she said, remembering the spur.

"Well," he said, scratching beneath his hat, "at least we won't have to fight him back home. And I was so looking forward to it, too."

Gwendolyn glowered at him then rolled her eyes. Men.

"Oh, well, that's not exactly what I had in mind," Mrs. Tyler said, looking first at Gregory lying in the wagon bed and then at Dan's swollen eye as she descended the porch steps. "Did you really have to hit him, Dan?"

"I didn't."

"Then why did you? Certainly he would have come home without a fuss if you'd given Gwendolyn a chance to just talk to him."

Gwendolyn blushed.

"I said I didn't hit him, Ma. Someone else did."

Mrs. Tyler's head turned toward Gwendolyn in confused accusation.

"I didn't hit him either," Gwendolyn said in exasperation. It was truly ridiculous that they were having such a conversation when Gregory was bleeding profusely beneath the cloth she'd wound about his head. "We don't know who hit him, Mrs. Tyler, but we need to get him up to his room right away. He's bleeding. My uncle follows close behind."

As if on cue, her uncle came galloping down the way holding onto his hat for dear life then skidded to a halt beside them.

"Sarah, his room, if you please," was his only greeting before jumping down and helping Dan and Gwendolyn to lift Gregory. "Let's get him inside. The fool never listens to me."

Mrs. Tyler jumped up the steps and ran inside the house saying, "Oh, my goodness," as if the sight of a doctor were the only thing that could prove the direness of the situation in her eyes.

Once they got Gregory's bulky form settled into the bed upstairs, Mrs. Tyler charged in front of everyone, including Susie and Daisy who had just joined them. "Now, what happened?" she said. "Tell me everything."

Gwendolyn's uncle checked Gregory for any additional injuries while Dan relayed the story succinctly.

"And you say you weren't gone for more than twenty minutes?" her uncle asked.

"That's right."

Gwendolyn went and sat on the bed beside Gregory and was careful not to jostle him as her uncle began cleaning and dressing the wound. She ran her fingernails up and down the skin of Gregory's hairy arms and wondered if James Morrison could have been the one to do such an atrocious thing. He'd certainly proven himself capable. Perhaps it wasn't the first time, she thought with a shiver. She remembered all the none-too-subtle hints everyone had passed her way and decided she would get to the bottom of it. She would ask Gregory and he would tell her. That was, if he woke up.

Her uncle sighed, gathering his needle and thread, then spoke rather quietly. "Dan, you must go to Sheriff Jenkins straightaway. Tell him what's happened, everything—James' attack on Gwendolyn, the fire, and now this." He paused. "I think at this point I need to override Gregory's decision for silence where James is concerned. I don't know why I didn't tell the sheriff before. Also, see to it that he questions everybody about the possible stranger in town. Gwendolyn, what was his name?"

"Robert. I heard Melissa Morrison tell Gregory he comes here to trade. And he might be French."

Her uncle nodded. "Gregory was most likely hit from behind and might not have seen his assailant, but we will not know for sure until he regains consciousness. Go now, Dan."

Dan left in a rush while her uncle cleaned his equipment with a cloth and antiseptic. He stowed everything away in his medical case then stood. "Gwendolyn, you should stay and watch over him. I daresay you're the only one he listens to, the brute. Just make sure he doesn't move from that spot for *at least* three days. No excuses this time."

Gwendolyn nodded, feeling reassured that Gregory would awaken. She needed that assurance. However, she wasn't exactly confident she'd be able to keep Gregory in bed once he woke up, especially considering his size and how she felt about him, but she would be happy to try. It would give her an excuse to stare at his beautiful face and wonder about him for hours on end.

"Oh, no you don't."

Gwendolyn looked up at her cousin in surprise. "Why not?"

"Because, dearest Gwendolyn," Daisy whispered, admiring her nails wistfully, "I'm not too fond of getting dirty. Therefore, *I'm* going to stay here and watch over Gregory while *you* and the other ladies play in the dirt with the spiders and worms, and when Gregory wakes up, he'll be too afraid to even think about leaving this room."

"Afraid? Afraid of you?" Uncle Barrett inquired incredulously as both Mrs. Tyler and Susie exited the room, smirking.

"Of course," Daisy said, tapping her fingers together in a scheming way and smiling mischievously. "I've got a bone to pick with him…several, in fact." She paused. "I can be quite frightening when I want to be."

"If you say so, daughter." With an amused chuckle, he grabbed his hat from the nightstand and plopped it firmly on his head. "I'm going to catch up with Dan so I can provide medical testimony. Ladies," he touched the brim of his hat in farewell.

Gwendolyn watched her uncle as he left the room, thinking he didn't look like any doctor she knew. He was of medium build and casually dressed in a white shirt, worn leather jacket, and trousers. The way his clothes stretched against his skin was evidence that he kept himself in good physical shape, even though he was over fifty years of age. He seemed to always have energy and Gwendolyn envied him for it.

She paused for a minute then realized, with some difficulty, she'd had more than enough energy over the last few days. She turned her attention back to the man lying unconscious beside her and wondered if he was partly responsible.

"Can you believe that?" Daisy said, dragging a chair to Gregory's bedside and sitting down in it with a flop. "My own father doesn't believe I can be frightening."

Gwendolyn looked at her cousin and stifled a grin. "You'll just have to prove it to him one of these days, I suppose."

Daisy sat up straighter, appearing to have regained her previous enthusiasm. "Yes, indeed I shall. Now, be off with you. I have a *frightening* lecture to prepare for this lummox."

Gwendolyn stifled a yawn as she hunched over in her chair. It was late Tuesday evening, nearly two full days since Gregory had been attacked, and she wondered if he would ever wake up. She didn't know how much longer she could possibly wait to see those captivating eyes of his. On half a dozen occasions she'd been tempted to hit his cheeks or dump another bucket of water on him just to see him looking back at her, but managed to refrain. It would only make it more difficult to keep him in bed once he was conscious again, that she knew. Besides, he needed the time to heal.

She took a small sip of the peppermint tea Mrs. Tyler had left on a tray for her then leaned over her diary, which she had started not too long after her accident last fall. She found it helped her remember things more easily. She skimmed through several entries, remembering how lost and alone she'd felt while writing them, and discovered she was actually happy despite all of the unfortunate events that had happened recently. In fact, she couldn't remember feeling happier. So much had happened during the past seven days and she was eager to learn more about herself. She wanted to hear Gregory's mumbling voice again, telling her stories of their times together and teasing her until she either blushed or punched him.

Gwendolyn watched the steady rise and fall of Gregory's chest then smiled peacefully. Putting her quill to paper, she began the tedious task of writing about the morning she and Dan had found Gregory then moved on to more exciting topics, like her continued efforts with the planting, listening to stories told by the ladies, and bathing Gregory's face, arms, and legs with a damp cloth during the warmer hours of the day.

"Any changes?"

Gwendolyn looked up to see Daisy at the bedroom door, wearing a long white nightgown and looking unusually agitated. Gwendolyn shook her head.

"Did you hear about James?"

Gwendolyn nodded, suddenly feeling agitated herself. Sheriff Jenkins had come by the house the day before bearing very bad news—James had been dropping off a lumber order in Huntington Square at the time of the attack, and the Frenchman had literally disappeared. Nobody else in town knew anything about the attack on Gregory. She'd really hoped James had been the guilty one. The ten days of jail time he'd been awarded for attacking her were not nearly enough to satisfy her desire for retribution, but James had claimed he'd never meant to hurt her. Gwendolyn had laughed at that, but the Sheriff had decided, based on James' clean history and remorse, that he would be lenient.

"And how are you feeling?" Daisy asked.

Trying not to think about how truly dreadful she must look with her newly formed scabs free from their bandages, she said, "I'm fine."

"Well, of course you're fine," she muttered. "*You* get to sleep right next to your man tonight. I, on the other hand, have to—"

Before Daisy could utter another word to embarrass them both, Gwendolyn snatched the rag from the washbasin and threw it at Daisy's face. Gwendolyn smiled in satisfaction as it hit its mark with a hollow splat then snorted uncontrollably at the thoroughly disgusted look on her target's face.

"I suppose I should have seen that one coming."

The wet rag landed on the floor at Daisy's feet.

Heaving a theatrical sigh and wiping the slime from her face, Daisy turned down the darkened hallway to retire for the night as Gwendolyn laughed mirthfully for a good long time.

Hundreds of miles away, against the rugged terrain of the Rocky Mountains, Robert also laughed, but his was not the laughter of an amused man. His was the laughter of a man who'd had a taste of vengeance and hungered for more. After all his thirty-one years, he could sit back and relax knowing Gwendolyn suffered. How could she not when the man she loved had been dealt such a blow to the head, and all by his hand? But he needed to back off and bide his time for the next attack. He relished the thought.

After taking a seat in his favorite chair, Robert put his feet up over the railing and crossed his ankles. Bitterness welled within him as he looked out over the bustling city. Everybody seemed so ambitious and excited about life as they walked this way and that, mining for silver, purchasing supplies, or selling goods to the local merchants. None of them knew what it was like to be cheated in life and lose everything they had. No one shared his misfortune.

With a flick of his wrist, he struck a match on his boot and lit a cigar, trying not to think about what would happen to him within the end of the month. His sister was soon to be married, which meant he would be homeless. When his parents had died nearly two decades before, they'd left the deed to the property in his sister's name. His father had established a good trading business and left it to him, but no matter how hard Robert had tried to keep the business running once he'd been old enough to run it, his efforts hadn't ever been enough. He just wasn't the trader his father had been.

It had been nearly two years since the night he'd gambled what little was left of his father's company after drinking too much damned whiskey. He'd lost everything he had in that one round of poker. Since then, he'd had to steal and cheat just to remain alive.

He spat in disgust just thinking about Gwendolyn. She'd been dead. He'd destroyed her luggage and immediately had his solicitor draw up the necessary paperwork once he'd reached the city. His future had been set.

But Gwendolyn was alive and he had nothing. She had survived her accident and gone back to Grovetown. It was a deliberate slap in the face. She had not heeded his warnings so he had no choice but to hurt those she loved.

His last stunt had been drastic but necessary. He'd originally planned on attacking Gregory before the dance, but Robert had been spotted…and by a woman, no less. Of course, it was much better than the alternative. Men were, by far, the more powerful and intelligent of the species and would likely have seen clean through his lies. Melissa Morrison, on the other hand, was an ignorant and heartless bit of fluff. Despite her flaunting her deliciously plump breasts, the only thing he found remotely tolerable about her was the evil glint in her eyes once he'd mentioned Gwendolyn's name.

So, he had an ally. They'd struck a bargain—she would help him destroy Gwendolyn and he would help her win Gregory. Of course, he had no intention of fulfilling his end of the deal. He made it a point not to make deals with women, in general. They were impossible to trust. No, he would simply use his charms to get what he wanted before leaving Melissa to her own devices.

He had rather hoped the man named James—who he'd later discovered was Melissa's brother—would be able to help him. After seeing him roughen Gwendolyn up in the woods, Robert knew it would take little coaxing on his part. The next time he traveled to Grovetown, he would seek the man out.

In the meantime, he would just write a few letters—special gifts for Gwendolyn.

# Chapter Ten

"GREGORY DID WHAT?" Gwendolyn halted midway down the row and leaned distractedly against her planting stick, digging it into the ground. She stared at Mrs. Tyler, and with her mouth wide open, no less.

Not missing a beat, the woman continued dropping seeds from the pack strapped about her waist into the holes she made with her own stick.

"Oh, yes," Mrs. Tyler said. "He and Dan went to the station to look for you the day you left."

"Then they both knew I wasn't dead," she realized aloud. A feeling of betrayal swept over her, and she didn't like it. "But why did everyone else think I was? Surely the men wouldn't keep something of such importance to themselves."

Mrs. Tyler heaved a hearty sigh. "My dear, you told Marshall you were on your way to visit Rebecca in Leadville, but by the time we received her letter denying your claim it was too late to try and find you. You must have changed your ticket along the way, I reckon. Leadville is at least two days away. You could have ended up anywhere."

Rolling the information about in her mind, Gwendolyn returned to her task. So, she'd left Grovetown deliberately and disguised her final destination…but why? Had she been hiding or merely trying to escape Grovetown?

No, she couldn't imagine doing the latter.

Mrs. Tyler continued, "You'd said you would be going on a stroll early that morning, but you left no note, no forwarding address, nothing. And you must have taken very little with you to Hopeton because when Marguerite checked your room, most of your belongings were still there." She paused then continued on to the next row in the field. "You can see how that seemed to the boys… how it would have seemed to us had we known you were still alive."

Gwendolyn swallowed, feeling her anger melt away. "They were protecting me?"

"As well as the rest of us. Gregory's a very thoughtful son. Oh, but don't misunderstand me," she said with a bit more animation. "When I found out they had lied to all of us, I was livid. Ben, on the other hand, was frustratingly calm about it. I had hoped he would go barreling out of the house with his rifle like he used to when we lived overseas…you know, give them a good scare and such, but he just had a quiet talk with them instead." Mrs. Tyler smiled mischievously.

"I wish I'd known. I was so alone…and all that wasted time—"

"It wasn't wasted, my dear. Think of all the wonderful things you were able to accomplish."

"But what about this," Gwendolyn said, pointing to her scar. "If I hadn't gone, I would never have lost my memory."

"Well, we can't change the past, now can we? So there's no use going on about it. Who knows? You might get your memory back, but if you don't, the worst that can happen is you'll get to experience everything again for the first time." Mrs. Tyler continued down the row, whistling a merry little tune.

Gwendolyn couldn't help but smile at the woman's optimism. It was quite infectious despite the bleakness of her future.

They worked side-by-side far into the day, sharing stories beneath the sunshine. Gwendolyn told of her experiences as a teacher and the friendship and hospitality of the Jennys and Mrs. Maynard, and Mrs. Tyler told her how much she admired Gwendolyn's curiosity and fascination of all of the forest's creatures as a child. Gwendolyn laughed at the retelling of the toad story—apparently a family favorite—and all the extra descriptive words Mrs. Tyler used. It wasn't until nearly suppertime that Gwendolyn looked up from her work to see Daisy running toward them, her skirts flipping about.

"What's wrong?" Gwendolyn blurted once her cousin reached her side.

"Nothing's wrong," Daisy said, catching her breath. "Gregory's been awake for a couple of hours. Stop," she said, pushing Gwendolyn back, "he's fine. We've been discussing a few things, but now he's threatening to leave his bed. I thought it best to fetch you before he does anything foolish."

Gwendolyn was in the Tylers' kitchen within seconds, desperate to see him. She jumped out of Gregory's boots and stripped off all her soiled clothing. After donning her dress and apron, she turned then immediately gave a squeak of surprise.

Gregory stood before her—out of bed—wearing nothing save a pair of cotton drawers, gauze headgear, and a very pale face.

"Gregory! What are you doing out of—"

Too late, she thought as Gregory's eyes rolled into the back of his head and he slumped to the floor.

"What now?" she breathed, looking at his bulky figure with relief and irritation but knowing she wouldn't be able to lift him. She took a moment to think of more important things rather than the fact he was wearing only his long johns, then realized she was not the only conscious one in the kitchen.

"Hmph!" It was Dan. "Gwendolyn, help me get him back in bed."

It took a great deal of grunting and groaning on both their parts to get Gregory's unconscious form back up the stairs and into his bed. Once they did, Dan let out an exaggerated groan of irritation then swiftly retreated down the stairs.

Gwendolyn turned back to Gregory's half-dressed form and immediately felt the heat rise in her cheeks. Going to the bed, she readjusted his legs and safely pulled the coverlet over him. She wrung her hands nervously as she sat down in her usual chair.

"What were you thinking of, you silly man?" she asked, eyeing the unconscious form on the bed. Exhausted with worry and strain from the past four days, she rested her head and arms against the side of the bed and let out a groan.

"You."

Gwendolyn raised her head in surprise at the sound of Gregory's rough, mumbling voice and looked at his face suspiciously. He appeared to be sleeping, just as soundly as before, and didn't seem to have spoken a word. Had she imagined it?

No, of course not! He was merely doing the same thing she had done the night of James' attack. He was baiting her.

Smiling mischievously, she stood and crept to within an inch of his face then stopped. His lips, surrounded by a week's worth of unruly whiskers, seemed to call to her…to beg her to touch them to her own. Memories of the kisses they'd shared—desperate, hungry ones in the rain, foolish and demanding ones along the road, and playful ones in the attic—made her shiver with anticipation. She licked her lips, aching to just plant a big one on him. If he really was still unconscious, she knew he wouldn't mind the intimate contact. Then again, he likely wouldn't mind it were he awake either, she thought with an amused smirk.

"We both know you're awake," she whispered, testing him.

He didn't move. He didn't even flinch and she tried to shove aside her disappointment. Fool that she was, she wanted to kiss him while he was awake, but when she didn't know he was awake.

She held still, studying his lips for quivers or twitches that would give him away, but observed none. Perhaps he was unconscious, after all.

Swallowing hard, she slowly bent and touched her lips to his. His were warm and slightly dry from the days spent in bed, but no less satisfying. She imagined the warm air being exhaled from his nose blew harder and faster against her jaw as she moved over his sweet lips caressingly. She removed her resting hand and boldly dipped it beneath the coverlet to touch his chest. She knew she shouldn't, but she wanted to finally feel the solidity of his hardworking form without propriety and an annoying shirt getting in her way.

She heard a groan and immediately looked up, keeping her adventurous hand flat and still against his chest. Her heart was pounding, and so was his, as a matter of fact.

Gregory remained still, showing no signs of consciousness, and she instantly felt giddy.

Lowering her head once more, she gave him one last, simple kiss. She pulled her hand from its very comfortable spot on his chest and started to pull away from his mouth when the tip of his tongue touched her lips.

Letting out a yip of surprise, she pushed off the bed and stared at Gregory in astonishment. Despite the low lighting, she knew he was awake. The open eyes and smile of mirth were dead giveaways.

"Hey," he said, putting up both of his hands defensively. "We both knew I was awake, right?"

Gwendolyn scowled at him, wanting him to think she was appalled, though secretly she was downright pleased. Of course, she hadn't been expecting him to touch her with his tongue. The idea seemed incredibly disgusting once she rolled the image around in her mind, but it had felt…well, scandalously glorious, she had to admit.

She shook her head, feeling more and more of a hussy with each scandalous thought. The things she'd been doing, and thinking, over the past week were most improper. But how could anything that gave her goose bumps and made her feel warm all over be anything but good?

"You didn't know I was awake? Oh, please."

"I thought you might have been awake, but you were holding so still," she defended.

He rolled his eyes then paused, seeming deep in concentration for a moment. When his eyes returned to hers, one corner of his upper lip twitched with amusement and she knew his next question would not be an easy one to answer. "You like me, don't you?"

Yes! she wanted to scream but chose something less gratifying for his big head. "Of course not."

She turned in her seat and folded her arms as Gregory chuckled in the background. She enjoyed his teasing manner, even if she was the subject of his teasing, but decided to change the subject. "Now, why were you downstairs just now? You could have seriously injured yourself, you know, fainting dead away."

"I did not faint," he said, chewing on the last word as if it were something to be ashamed of. "I was merely overcome with fatigue and hunger. Plus, the sight of you half naked inside my kitchen—boy, that did me in."

Gwendolyn could feel her entire body blushing, if that were even possible. "You saw that?"

"Oh, it's not every day a man goes down to his kitchen for a bite to eat and finds the very thing he's been wanting to sink his teeth into…and looking so lovely in her undergarments too."

Not knowing whether to run away in embarrassment or scold Gregory senseless for his improper, but flattering words, she settled for an intelligent episode of stuttering instead. Brilliant! she thought, hoping he hadn't seen her wearing his trousers as well.

"I'm going to kill him for leaving his bed!"

Startled, Gwendolyn looked up to see Daisy storm into the bedroom as if she owned the place. Gwendolyn looked at Gregory to see his reaction but found him lying back against his pillows with eyes closed. She covered her mouth with one hand and tried desperately not to laugh.

"The nerve of him!" Daisy said, pacing the room nervously. "I will not let him kill himself over that stupid house. I don't care if the wedding is only a week away. He needs to rest."

Gwendolyn sat, watching helplessly as Daisy continued her rant, and felt her amusement over Gregory's antics burn up with Daisy's rage. Although she knew the real reason for Gregory's trip to the kitchen, she had to admit he would have left to work on the house the moment their backs were turned. The stubbornness of the man.

"I don't care how big his ego is—"

Gwendolyn put her elbow on the bed and rested her head in her hand in exhaustion. She watched the scowl on Gregory's face grow deeper and deeper with each passing moment and wondered how he could hold so still amidst the high volume of her cousin.

"—and he's going to kill himself if we don't do something about it."

Daisy was becoming hysterical. Gwendolyn watched as tears coursed down her cousin's face and thought it was time for Gregory to stop feigning unconsciousness. Enough was enough.

Gwendolyn rubbed Gregory's leg through the coverlet, starting to feel a headache coming on.

"We talked about this. He promised me he wouldn't—"

"Enough!" Gregory suddenly shouted, coughing weakly from the effort and holding his side with a grimace.

Daisy jumped back in alarm then narrowed her eyes in Gregory's direction, realizing she'd been duped. Baring her well-kept claws, she prepared to lunge at Gregory like a feral cat. "You promised me!"

Knowing Daisy meant business, Gwendolyn leapt up and covered Gregory's body with her own in one swift move. Perhaps too swift, she thought, hearing Gregory groan once again. She looked down, realized she'd put some of her weight on his broken rib, and then pushed off of him in alarm. "Oh, I'm sorry!"

He shifted a bit then smiled at her roguishly. "Anytime, love."

Gwendolyn couldn't help smiling back.

"Oh, get off of him, you traitor," Daisy hollered, elbowing Gwendolyn in the ribs and pushing her out of the way. "I want to kill him!"

"Dammit, Daisy. Settle down!" he bellowed, putting up a hand to stop her from hitting Gwendolyn anymore. "I was just foraging for food like a good little rat."

Daisy paused mid-pummel, looking at Gregory then at Gwendolyn. "Is this true?" Daisy's hand, grasped tightly in Gregory's fist, was inches from smashing his face in.

Gwendolyn nodded, afraid to breathe. Her side ached from Daisy's wild determination.

Nobody moved for several seconds as they watched Daisy contemplate her next move. In the next moment, Daisy loosened her brow, then pushed off the bed. "Oh, okay."

Gwendolyn furrowed her brow in confusion as she watched her demon of a cousin saunter over to the bedroom door and wondered how such a small person could inflict such fear in a person. Gwendolyn gulped involuntarily. Daisy truly was frightening.

"Well, Gregory, it's obvious you're awake and wanting nourishment," she said, playing with a broken bit of her fingernail and flicking it to the floor. "Your dear mama is putting a picnic basket together for us…and Dan. I think it's best you find some clothes to cover that ridiculous underwear of yours. And Gwendolyn—"

"What's going on up here?" Dan said, pushing past Daisy into the room, his eyes immediately resting on Gwendolyn and his elder brother…in the bed together.

Gwendolyn laughed nervously, just realizing how inappropriate it must look for her unmarried self to be lying next to an unmarried man, and a half naked one at that. She attempted to roll off but Gregory stopped her with his two large arms. "Stay with me, love."

"But Gregory, it's inapp—"

He shushed her then wrapped his arms around her more securely.

Utterly embarrassed, she could do nothing but bury her face in his neck as Gregory chuckled. Oh, how she wanted to die!

"Looks like we've got another wedding to plan," she heard Daisy say.

"Yeah, it looks that way, doesn't it?" Dan said, chuckling.

Gwendolyn's head shot up in surprise, but Gregory gently guided it back down with one of his large hands.

"Shh," he whispered in her ear as Dan and Daisy left the room and walked down the stairs. "Don't worry. They don't think poorly of us."

Gwendolyn buried her head deeper, wishing to hide herself forever. She was more embarrassed than the time when all of her students thought she was engaged to Robert Jamison. The situation was unendurable. Daisy would never stop scolding her for it.

She and Gregory lay that way for several minutes, and Gwendolyn eventually relaxed…a little. It was difficult to relax completely while lying beside a man—a man who was deadly attractive *and* had a broken rib. Strangely, he didn't seem to mind the latter. She shifted more to her right, knowing he had to be in a great deal of pain.

Gregory finally broke the silence. "Why are you moving away from me, love? I seem to remember you saying I have a gorgeous physique. Have you changed your mind then?"

Gwendolyn moved back to stare at him curiously. She couldn't remember having said any such thing. Of course, she'd been thinking it ever since she'd clapped eyes on him in the mercantile, so she couldn't deny the possibility aloud.

"What happened to your face?" he asked.

Gwendolyn frowned in embarrassment then shoved off of him before he could capture her, moving her face out of his sight. "I fell."

Gregory frowned back. "You...fell?"

"Yes."

"I've never seen you fall in the whole course of my existence, Doly."

"Well, it seems to be happening a lot lately," she said sarcastically, going to his closet. She pulled out a pair of tan trousers and a white shirt then turned around. "And I'm glad I did…this time." She didn't want him to know it had been his fault.

She flung the clothes at his face along with a thin undershirt that was resting at the foot of his bed. "Put these on. I'm starving as well."

He seemed to read her thoughts and didn't ask anymore questions, thank goodness. Lifting the coverlet, he swung his legs out of the bed. He grabbed his trousers then winced audibly.

Feeling guilty and a little selfish for protecting her innocent eyes, she knelt before him and helped him into his trousers. She looked up to see he was looking elsewhere and realized, with a touch of surprise, that he was also embarrassed. The thought made her smile. She helped him to sit before aiding him with his shirt.

"How long have I been out?"

"A couple of days. It's Wednesday…afternoon."

He growled.

"Don't worry, please," she practically begged. "Everything will be taken care of. I promise. You're just…going to have to trust me." She looked into his light blue eyes, trying to share her confidence without giving away her surprise. She covered each of his large, square feet with socks before helping him to stand.

She looked up to find him staring directly into her eyes as if he could see through to the depths of her soul. "I trust you."

With a twinge of guilt, she realized the impact of his words—that he did, in fact, trust her after everything that had happened, but she didn't feel she deserved it. In fact, she couldn't trust herself completely until she figured out what she'd been thinking the year before. She felt like a traitor.

"Gregory?"

"What is it, love?" He put an arm over her shoulders for support as they walked past the bedroom door and into the hallway.

"I know you still may hate me for leaving," she started. Gregory stopped her just before they came to the stairway but kept his body and eyes forward.

"With each passing day," she continued, "I'm more and more convinced that I left for unselfish reasons. I know I may never know the complete truth behind my actions, and that fact scares me to death. But I have a bad feeling," she said, turning to look at Gregory with tears growing in her eyes. "I have a feeling I was running away from something…or somebody…that I was hiding."

Gregory nodded solemnly. "I've had a bad feeling too." He carefully leaned down to plant a lingering kiss on Gwendolyn's forehead. "We'll figure this out together, all right?"

She closed her eyes at the soothing feel of his warm cheek resting against her forehead and knew she could accomplish anything, get through any obstacle, with Gregory at her side.

Bees buzzed and grasshoppers hopped about the meadow as the Tylers' wagon slowly made it's way along the bumpy dirt trail later that afternoon. Gregory lay in the wagon bed along with Gwendolyn, who cradled his head carefully in her lap and held him each time they went over a bump or a dip. He tried not to think about Gwendolyn's long, slender fingers as they touched his shoulders, or the distracting little freckles on her arms, or the way she held onto him so protectively each time he winced. He might have snuck in a fake wince or two, just to feel her arms wrap around him more tightly, but he couldn't be sure.

He thought about the way Gwendolyn had leapt on top of him to save him from the painful clutches of the tigress named Daisy. At the moment Gwendolyn touched him, he knew two things—one, it would take every ounce of concentration to keep his hands to himself, and two, Gwendolyn loved him. She had to, for who else would act so quickly, as if on instinct? After all the times and affection they'd shared over the past week he knew she wasn't just tending to him like her uncle's little assistant or using him for his protection from James. She wasn't even pretending to like him just because everyone else wanted her to. She liked him for herself.

He smiled, remembering the stunned look on Gwendolyn's face after Daisy's comment about another wedding. He had pulled her to him, ignoring the pain in his right side and never wanting to let go. The way their bodies fit together—her tiny, scrunched up frame that smelled of earth molding to his bulky frame—was truly amazing, and comforting.

The wagon lurched to a stop and he took a deep breath, as deep as he could muster. The sweet smells of fresh pine, lavender, and untouched earth livened his senses, and his appetite. Images of a large and juicy chicken breast baked with marmalade just the way he liked it and a whole loaf of honey wheat bread with home made jelly, made his mouth water in anticipation.

"We'll need to walk the remaining distance," Dan said, coming to open the back latch of the wagon, "if we're going to avoid the bumps."

"Fine by me." Gregory watched with admiration as Gwendolyn hopped out of the wagon with girlish enthusiasm. In the broad light of day, her recent injuries were far more obvious than they'd been just an hour before in the darkness of his room. By the looks of her face—bruised and scratched with one large scab just above one eyebrow—he wondered how she could be glad to fall. It seemed a very odd idea, one he would have to ask her about later. He smiled, thinking Gwendolyn an undeniably beautiful bit of mystery.

She turned around, her skirts whirling and her brown eyes radiant. "What?"

He simply watched her—watched the way she nervously covered her scar with a lock of curly hair and the way she literally glowed in the post afternoon sunlight—and felt truly happy she was part of his life.

She blushed, rolled her eyes, and then grabbed the large picnic basket and quilts while Dan and Daisy helped him out of the wagon.

"Try not to faint again," Dan said, getting Gregory to his feet.

"I did not faint!" he roared. Why did everyone keep insisting he had? At the sound of their amused chuckles, he decided he would strangle the next person who mentioned it. Yes, that was what he would do.

The three of them followed Gwendolyn to a flat spot near the creek where she laid the quilts side-by-side then fixed the corners to lay flat. All around them, the emerald grasses grew just past his knees and were alive with all manner of creatures and bugs. He smiled, remembering the time Gwendolyn had come to him holding a jar full of grasshoppers she'd found, upset because Daisy had thought they were disgusting.

The three of them helped Gregory down onto the quilts, being careful not to bend his torso, but he started coughing anyway—hard. Gwendolyn cupped her hand under his mouth.

"If you start coughing up blood, mister," Daisy said, "we'll send you right back to bed…for weeks."

That got his attention. He coughed a bit more then got it under control, feeling thoroughly exhausted. He took Gwendolyn's hand away from his mouth and snuck a kiss into her palm, earning himself a smile.

Daisy sat on her legs then rearranged her dress before asking, "Who's hungry?"

Gregory could hardly wait. He rubbed his hands together vigorously as Gwendolyn carefully laid his head against a soft pillow.

She then, along with Daisy, laid out a loaf of bread wrapped in cloth, a wooden canister of home churned butter, a jar of apricot preserves and another of sliced pear halves, slices of roasted ham wrapped in brown paper, and crackers with cheese. It was a feast.

"And this," Daisy said, eyeing Gregory as she pulled out another jar filled with a murky, yellowish liquid, "is *your* dinner."

Gregory frowned in disgust. "What is it?"

"Chicken broth! Delicious *and* good for you." With a gleeful smirk, she deposited the jar in Gwendolyn's lap then proceeded to devour the real food.

Gregory grumbled, using words he wouldn't usually use in polite conversation, but stopped at the touch of Gwendolyn's hand. He looked up and she winked at him.

They ate their meals with leisure, enjoying each and every bite, except for Gregory, who downed his detestable broth in several quick gulps as Gwendolyn propped him up. Better to get it over with quickly. He grunted, feeling completely unsatisfied then glowered at Daisy as he wiped his mouth with the back of his hand. The solid foods sat quietly, tempting him.

Once Dan and Daisy had had their fill, they stood and walked along the creek's bank, talking about wedding plans and other such nonsense betrothed couples often talked about. Gregory snorted as he watched them walk around the bend and out of sight. He turned to see Gwendolyn holding a slice of ham in his face.

Smiling wickedly, he grabbed both the meat and Gwendolyn's hand. Keeping his eyes on her, he bit and chewed the meat until he came to her fingertips, where he nibbled and kissed them. Gwendolyn trembled, her cheeks blushing crimson, and she snatched her hand away.

"I don't want you to make yourself sick by eating too much," she said, not making eye contact. "You haven't eaten anything for days, you know." He watched her eyes roam the foodstuffs anxiously. "You can have a slice of bread and one pear half, and if you're good—" she stopped, eyeing Gregory mischievously—"you can have one of the cookies your mama baked…but only one."

Gregory chuckled. He was glad she hadn't lost her mischievousness along with her memory. That was one of the things he liked most about her. He watched her prepare his bread for him with preserves instead of butter and marveled. She made it just the way he liked it and even cut it diagonally!

"Have you had any other memories resurface?" he asked hopefully, taking a large bite out of the bread she handed to him.

She shook her head slowly.

"Do you remember your aunt or uncle? Daisy? My family? James?"

"Good grief! Should I remember James?" She looked truly frightened. In fact, she looked as if she'd just seen a ghost.

"Let's just say he's not worth remembering."

Gwendolyn absentmindedly popped a piece of cheese into her mouth, rolled it around a bit, then bit down hard. "Tell me about him…please? I can't get anyone else to."

Gregory hoped she would never remember James and all his hatred. He was grateful for the opportunity to warn her against him, not that she needed additional warning after what James had done to her, but Gregory never wanted to speak of the man again.

He opened his mouth to speak, but Gwendolyn interrupted him.

"I didn't know he was dangerous, Gregory. Honest! Everyone was acting so strangely around him and urged me not to accept a dance with him, but they never told me why…even when I asked." She picked a blade of grass and started splitting it with her nails. "He looked like a decent enough fellow. I saw no harm in one dance, and I didn't want to be rude."

Gregory started feeling sick to his stomach. "Do you…find him attractive?"

"I did," she admitted, "but I definitely don't now." She grabbed several more blades and split them down the middle as well. "I did notice something strange about him the minute I met him in Mr.

Caldwell's shop. He was too attentive—suffocating, really. We weren't ever…together, were we? Me and James?" She scrunched up her nose and looked afraid.

"No, but it wasn't for lack of trying…on his part."

She sat back with legs crossed, nervously splitting grass over the pile already resting in her lap and watching him expectantly.

He smiled. "James was one of our playmates growing up. That is, he was until the summer after you turned thirteen."

"Why? What happened when I was thirteen?"

"You started growing into a woman."

"Oh." She shifted her seat about the quilts then hunched down a bit as she gazed across the meadow. She seemed uncomfortable talking about herself that way and the thought of it made Gregory grin with amusement.

"He became really…attentive, as you put it, but you liked the attention then." He grabbed a cookie out of the picnic basket and watched as Gwendolyn mulled the idea over in her head.

She lifted her head slowly and looked him in the eyes. "I'm sorry."

"Why? You were entitled to like whomever you wanted. I mean, you still are. You know that, don't you, Gwendolyn?"

She nodded, still looking him in the eyes.

In truth, he'd been heartbroken. He'd stood by and watched as the girl he grew up with and loved immediately set her fancy on one of his friends, one who had begun acting strangely competitive and short-tempered. It wasn't until then—when Gwendolyn was thirteen and Gregory was nineteen—he realized he was actually *in* love with her, and for a nineteen year old to declare love to a thirteen year old…no, it was improper, especially if they spent every waking minute together. Gwendolyn's reputation would have been lost at the hands of the gossiping townspeople.

Instead, he had settled on a pact of forever friendship with Gwendolyn in their secret place. They'd carved each of their initials in the old willow tree's bark and buried some of their collected treasures in its hollow base. He would need to take her there sometime soon. It might even help her remember some things.

He moved to grab another cookie but his hand was promptly slapped. He'd forgotten about the one-cookie rule, but he scowled at Gwendolyn anyway.

"What else?" she asked.

"Well, there was a point where he got too attentive," he continued, feeling his anger and hatred swell toward James. "You told him to leave you alone and he wouldn't. He began stalking you, accosting you at the schoolhouse, in town, and even at services. You came to me…told me everything, and I did my best to protect you. I'm afraid he's never gotten over it."

Gwendolyn's brows furrowed. "He didn't…I mean, I haven't lost my…I'm still—"

"Intact?" he offered.

She nodded sheepishly.

"Yes, you're still intact. Well, as far as I know." How could a woman not know? he wondered.

Gwendolyn blushed but seemed to recover quickly. "But why did no one talk to the sheriff about him?"

"He hadn't broken any laws. This last Friday was the first time I've seen him do anything violent." He didn't want to tell her the rest but she had a right to know, after all. "There are also some rumors going around," he continued, "but I know how you hate gossip. I probably shouldn't tell you."

"You will tell me." She dropped her hands in her lap and leaned forward anxiously.

He lay silent for a moment then spoke. "There are rumors that he's married a girl from Clarksville," he said carefully, "and that he's ruined another young woman."

Gwendolyn gasped, putting her hands to her still-bruised throat. "Do you believe it?"

He remained silent. What good would come of his telling her what he suspected? He knew it would only upset her. Besides, there really wasn't anything he could do apart from what he'd already done.

"Do you suspect he was the one who started the fire and…hit you?"

He put his hand on her knee and rubbed it lightly. "I wouldn't have thought so a couple weeks ago, but now, I'm not so certain. He's been reserved and angry of late. And his behavior towards you, well..."

Early Monday morning, Gregory had just finished battling with Dan when he'd been hit from behind with a thick slab of wood. He saw a man's shadow form over him only a second before he'd fallen unconscious to the ground. At first he thought it had been Dan's doing, it being the only way to get Gregory back home and resting when there was so much to be done. He deserved it after hitting Dan. But when he'd awoken days later with an excruciating headache and felt drained of energy, he knew Dan hadn't done it. A blow such as the one he'd received, especially after the fire the night before, could've killed him. His next suspicion had been centered on James, but the sheriff had quickly disproved it. Who else would want to hurt him—an unsatisfied customer? Surely not.

Gregory lay back against his mother's quilts and, shoving his troubles and questions aside, tried to enjoy the beauty and mystery of nature. Overhead, the sky was a delicate blue littered with fluffy, white clouds of all shapes and sizes. The wind rustled through the trees and grasses, carrying feather-light clumps of cotton in its wake as they sat.

A soft rustling sound came from a group of brush a couple feet away. Gregory tensed, then immediately relaxed. Using one of his knuckles, he tapped Gwendolyn's foot then pointed toward the edge of the creek. They watched in fascination as a duck suddenly came out of the brush near them and plopped into the water, followed by five…no, six ducklings. He loved seeing all the newborns in spring and watching them as they took their very first steps.

"Why were you glad you fell?" he asked suddenly. The blades of grass in her lap, he noticed, were starting to actually develop structure and she seemed completely oblivious of the fact.

She groaned low in her throat. "Why do you want to know?"

"Oh, c'mon! Is it truly embarrassing?"

She scowled. "I do not wish to tell you." She stuck her chin up in the air in finality but he wasn't one to give up so easily.

"I know you're trying to hide something from me. Just tell me what it is?" He started toying with the ruffled hem of her sky blue skirt, grinning impishly. She swatted at his hand once more and he chuckled. "Would a kiss wrench the truth from you?"

"Of course not, you—"

"Beast?" he finished for her. She appeared shocked but he knew her tricks. Inside, she had to be scandalously delighted by the very idea. The rosiness of her cheeks gave her away. Then a sickening thought came to his mind. "Was it James? Did he touch you again? Because if he did I'm going to kill—"

"No, nothing like that. It was my own fault. Well, no, it wasn't my fault…but James had nothing to do with it, I–I don't think."

He was confused. "I don't follow you."

Gwendolyn heaved a sigh of profound exasperation. "All right, I'll tell you! I can see you'll never leave me alone if I don't."

He nodded then groaned as the back of his head started to throb.

"I fell over you, all right!"

Gregory looked up in surprise. "How do you mean?" He was almost too afraid to ask. Gwendolyn looked very irritated, indeed.

Then everything came out in a rush.

"The night of the fire, I sent you out of the barn to seek refuge, you remember? You collapsed in the fields close to the house. Once the fire was contained, we noticed you were gone. It was really dark and I'm unfamiliar with your fields. I fell over you," she said, touching the marks on her face, "and landed against a dry shrub before hitting the ground." She paused. "But it did give me the chance to see the stars," she added a bit more positively. "They were lovely that night."

He took a few moments to digest everything she had told him.

"I'm not upset with you, if that's what you're worrying over," she said.

"Why on earth would you be mad at me, Doly? It wasn't as if I passed out in that precise spot so I could purposely try to trip you once you came running by."

"Oh, good grief," she said. "I do realize that. I just didn't want you to feel guilty. After all, I know some of the burdens…er, responsibilities you bear and I don't approve of how you go about them." She looked down at him with her mesmerizing brown eyes and he longed to run his fingers through her silken curls. "You need to take better care of yourself, Gregory," she continued. "Dan and Daisy will survive if they do not have a fancy kitchen cabinet, for example. What would they put in it, anyhow?" She paused, looking thoughtful. "Perhaps you could fashion it for them in a few years, you know, as an anniversary gift."

Gregory knew she was right. Somehow, when Daisy had lectured him about the very same thing earlier that day, it had been much more damaging to his pride. He'd been irritated, to say the very least. He liked it better when Gwendolyn said it.

"What are you smiling at?" she said, eyeing him warily.

"I believe I owe you a kiss…milady."

Gwendolyn gasped, her heart racing as Gregory flashed a crooked smile up at her. He was forever teasing her. In truth, she liked being teased, but only by Gregory, for he did it best.

"A kiss?" she swallowed, trying to ignore the fluttering within her bosom. "For what?" She dropped her head nervously. In her hands, she was startled to find a delicately woven sheaf of grass with beautifully variegated blades. Had she really done that?

"You told me how you fell, and I," he said, touching the heinous scab on her forehead, "promised you a kiss for it."

"You did no such thing." She closed her eyes, reveling in the feel of his touch as it descended to the rub burns on her cheeks and chin. His fingers traced the outline of her mouth ever so softly and she yearned to kiss them. She pursed her lips but his fingers disappeared.

"Oh," she cried in surprise as Gregory grabbed the collar of her shirtwaist and yanked her down to the ground, level with him.

"What?" he asked, the devilish gleam in his eyes making her a little light-headed. "I can't reach to kiss you. My rib ails me a great deal, you understand."

By the pleased look on his face, she highly doubted the latter but decided to oblige him anyway. It wasn't as if it would be a terribly difficult thing for her to do. With a nervous smile, she leaned downward and touched his arm.

In a flash, Gregory moved his hand beneath her hair to the back of her neck and she gasped. But she was not afraid. Oh, no. She was positively on fire! She looked into his eyes and saw all the love he felt for her glowing bright with a passion to match her own. He lay on the brightly colored quilt with his head bound in bandages, looking at her with fierce determination as he ran his fingers through her hair. Oh, he was magnificent!

Using his other hand, he caressed her scar with the edge of his thumb and she instantly grew uncomfortable, more so by the painful reminder of her unsolved desertion than the feel of his glorious touch.

She started to pull away but he yanked her back—ever closer. Growling deeply, he yanked her head to him and latched himself to her temple as if to take a bite out of her. She shivered as the heat of his breath tingled every inch of her blasted scar, and she knew his loving torture had only just begun. In the next moment, his tongue touched her heated skin and she jumped in surprise. She felt her body erupt with goosebumps the size of corn kernels.

A moan escaped her lips and the noise seemed to fuel Gregory's passion ever more. His chest rose and fell rapidly as his tongue danced across her sensitive flesh in a blaze of desire. Grabbing her face with both hands, he fervently kissed every spot his tongue had touched then pulled back to look at her.

Instead of tenderness, she saw only fiery anger in his expression. Had her scar reminded him of her betrayal? She couldn't bear the thought of it and tried to pull back once more, but Gregory's hands were stronger than her fear of rejection.

"You are mine," he growled, squeezing her head a bit tighter than before. "You are mine and I will have you, Gwendolyn. I don't care how long it takes or what I must do, but I will have you."

In the next instant, his mouth met hers with urgent, flaming possession, pulling the very breath from her lungs. As his lips moved over hers, she knew she had never known such rapture, such complete and utter fulfillment! He had cast his spell over her, quickly and thoroughly, and she knew she could never belong to any other man but Gregory Tyler. She loved him and she could no longer deny it. Nor did she want to.

She returned his passion with desperation, not able to comprehend or even begin to describe what she was feeling. There was something unearthly about it all, as if she were being guided by something other than instinct or love or passion. She didn't care. All she did care about was the sweet and teasing friend of her youth that she loved... and that, miraculously, loved her in return. She held his whiskery face in her hands as a single tear fell past her cheek.

As they continued the exchange, Gwendolyn reached across his torso and held onto his shoulder. He exhaled into her mouth in surprise.

"Oh, have I hurt—"

He captured her mouth once more, rendering her speechless. His whiskers scratched her tender flesh and she was surprised at how much it stung. But she ignored it, for what could be better than to have her dearest friend share something so perfect with her?

She wove her fingers through his long brown hair, wishing she could spend every waking moment doing so. From days lying in bed, it had grown coarse and dirty. For a moment, she imagined herself washing his hair over a large porcelain tub, and smiled wistfully.

"What are you two doing?"

Gwendolyn jumped at the sound of Daisy's voice so near and hastily moved away from Gregory. Her entire body burned with mortification at having been caught in the act of something so intimate, and the aftereffects of her and Gregory's kissing didn't help the matter any. She turned, wishing she could sink into the earth unnoticed.

"We leave you two alone for no more than a half an hour," Daisy said, "and you spend the whole of the time, uh—"

"Sparking?" Dan supplied happily.

Daisy shook her head, looking half disgusted and half delighted. "This is the second time today, you two."

Gwendolyn jumped up. "We weren't doing it the entire time, thank you very much. We've been talking."

She heard Gregory growl as Dan came to crouch before his elder brother, wearing a knowing smirk.

"Are you growling, dear brother, because we've interrupted your amorous pursuit of Gwendolyn or is it because you're finding it increasingly difficult to keep your hands off of her?"

Gregory rewarded his younger brother with a dark look that would frighten even the most courageous of men. Dan, however, only chuckled.

"Now, boys," Daisy scolded. "Play nice while Gwendolyn and I pack up our things. We must be getting back. Night is nearly upon us and we have a surprise waiting back home for you, Gregory."

The ride back to Orchard Cottage seemed much longer than it had going in the opposite direction, but she knew it was all because of their surprise. She could barely contain her excitement. Gregory would be so thrilled—so relieved that the planting had finally been finished. And what a delicious yield they would have come harvest time! She had planted some extra carrots and onions, for they were her very favorite, as well as peppers, which were Gregory's favorite.

The wagon turned and Dan led the horses down the lane toward Orchard Cottage. Only a minute more and Gregory would see the straight rows of mounds in the now fertile field. She held her breath and pulled Gregory closer. He sat in-between her legs with his back against her breast—a position he had insisted upon without argument—and Gwendolyn marveled at how natural it felt.

Standing at the top of the steps of their wraparound porch, Gwendolyn saw Susie and Mrs. Tyler waiting, bearing bright smiles.

Gwendolyn held her breath as Dan brought the wagon to a steady halt just beside the field's fence. Simultaneously, Dan and

Daisy turned back on their bench to look at Gregory, fighting the smiles that were so close to surfacing. A chuckle escaped Daisy's throat and Gwendolyn felt Gregory shift.

"What's going on here, Dan? Why have you stopped here rather than the usual spot nearer the house?" His gaze shifted from Dan to Daisy, the latter's face turning a hysterical shade of pink. Not receiving any answers, he looked at Gwendolyn over his shoulder. "What's going on?"

Gwendolyn's heart skipped a beat at the adorably confused expression on his face. She managed a wink then lifted her chin ever so slightly in the direction of the field, which blushed with color beneath the setting sun.

Following her gaze, Gregory turned and looked at what lay before him. Gwendolyn twisted her head to get a better look at his face then glowed with pride and satisfaction at what she saw. Her goal had been met.

With eyes wide and mouth agape, Gregory slid to the back of the wagon unaided, removed the safety latch and board, and stepped down to the ground with only a mild groan of pain. Susie and Mrs. Tyler approached the wagon beside Gwendolyn and leaned over the sideboard with both arms.

"Who's done this?" Gregory said, whirling around to face them.

Gwendolyn frowned. Was he upset? Had they done something wrong? Perhaps the mounds were too big or the spaces between each row were too small.

"We all pitched in," Mrs. Tyler answered casually. "Dan agreed to keep you busy while the rest of us worked on the planting. But," she said, putting her hands on Gwendolyn's shoulders, "it was all Gwendolyn's idea to do this for you, Gregory."

Gregory fastened his gaze on Gwendolyn, eyeing her from the soles of her boots to the top of her head. He looked so serious. Why hadn't Mrs. Tyler just kept her darn mouth shut? Couldn't she see how upset her own son was?

Gwendolyn simply couldn't bear for him to be upset with her. "Gregory, I'm sorry. I was only trying to help. I thought you—"

"So, I wasn't imagining things. You really were wearing my clothes," he interrupted, coming toward her, "earlier this afternoon?"

"I insisted they do so, Gregory," Mrs. Tyler explained. "I didn't want them to ruin their beautiful dresses, you understand."

"Indeed," she heard Dan mumble sarcastically as he jumped down from the wagon. He walked to his mother and was rewarded with a smack upside the head. "Ow!"

Gregory came to stand at the opposite side of the wagon, his eyes daring her to look away with their smoldering intensity. Their gazes locked. He put a hand on the wagon for support and brought the other up to signal her forward.

Bewitched, Gwendolyn crawled toward him and shivered with delight as his hand touched her face. "You're not angry with me?" she asked, beginning to doubt her first assumption.

With a roguish smile, he continued in a hushed voice so only she could hear. "You were wearing my clothes." He licked his lips then growled like an animal about to devour its meal.

Gwendolyn blushed but couldn't keep herself from smiling with delight. She wanted to kiss him—badly. Every time she'd worn his clothes she'd promised herself not to get overexcited about it, but after the first several hours of smelling his lavender scent and knowing the clothes he'd worn were touching her skin, she'd gone crazy with longing.

She leaned forward to kiss him, then remembered they were not alone. Pulling away but still watching him, she cleared her throat and began nervously toying with a lock of her hair.

"Gregory." Dan walked to his brother with a weary sigh and put a hand on his shoulder, diverting his attention. "We've all decided you're working too hard." Gregory scowled but Dan ignored him. "Daisy and I bought some extra things while we were in the city last week so you wouldn't have to worry about the furniture. The ladies have taken care of all the planting. All I want you to worry about is helping me finish the house. There's not much left to do. Oh, and maybe pray for rain…for the crops."

Gwendolyn watched in admiration as Gregory's expression turned from surprise, to loathing, to playful acceptance. He shoved Dan away with one of his big hands before returning his gaze to her once more.

"Although I do greatly appreciate everyone's hard work and forethought on my behalf," he said, smiling at her as he rubbed his whiskery chin, "I think I should thank Gwendolyn properly."

"Now, Gregory," his mother warned.

With eyes unwavering, he lifted Gwendolyn's hand to his mouth and kissed the back of it tenderly. She was no longer surprised when he touched her knuckle with the tip of his tongue, and she burst out laughing. From behind, she heard chuckles but none that gave her more joy than when she heard Gregory's unrestrained laughter.

"Oh, thank you! Thank you, Gwendolyn!" He grabbed her face in his hands and gave her one hard kiss on the mouth.

She blinked when he released her, feeling momentarily stunned.

"This is one of the nicest things you've ever done for me," he said, smiling like a fool. "You have no idea what this means to me."

"I–I think I do."

Gregory's smiled faded. He grabbed the edge of the wagon with both hands and moved his face directly in front of hers.

Gwendolyn fancied she could see through his blue eyes to the very depths of his soul. She hadn't thought she could be happier than when she was in his arms, but she'd been wrong. What she wanted now, more than anything else, was to see Gregory happy.

She held her breath, somehow knowing that in the next moment her life would change forever.

Gregory swallowed as his gaze melted. "Marry me?"

# Chapter Eleven

IT HAD BEEN THREE DAYS SINCE GWENDOLYN had last been at the Mathewson house. She'd forgotten how quickly her little attic room grew unbearably warm. When she'd woken up that morning with the sun just peeking through the pine and aspen trees and the crickets still chirping, she'd finally decided on a gift for Dan and Daisy—a song. Even though it had only been a week since she discovered she could play the violoncello, she knew she'd be able to come up with something.

Before any of the others had gotten out of bed for the day, Gwendolyn had crept up the attic steps, closed the door, and begun practicing. The wedding was less than a week away and she needed to practice every spare moment she could get.

Honestly, she was scared out of her wits by the very idea of performing in front of everyone in town. Well no, that wasn't entirely true. She was mostly afraid of playing in front of Melissa Morrison. She was bound to find some way to humiliate Gwendolyn further. After Gregory's reprimand, Melissa would, no doubt, have something extra special in mind for her. The fact that Melissa's elder brother would be in a small jail cell during that time helped Gwendolyn's confidence a great deal, but she hoped Miss Hoity-Toity wouldn't show up at all.

After nearly four hours, Gwendolyn decided to give her back and fingers a break. She stood up, laid her violoncello aside, and then went to the window. After her first visit to the attic room, she'd cleared away the dust and cobwebs and washed away the year's worth of grime on the windowpane. The view was a great deal better than before and she'd congratulated herself by snitching an extra slice of pecan pie when nobody was looking.

She gazed up at the fluffy white clouds, just as she'd done with Gregory the day before as they lay amongst the emerald grass and sunshine.

She smiled, remembering the almost frightened look on Gregory's face after she'd answered 'yes' to his proposal—the second one. She still couldn't believe it had happened. The word had jumped out of her mouth before she had even realized it, but she no longer cared what other people thought of her. The only thing she cared about was being happy, and she knew Gregory could make her so. If it took all her life, she would endeavor to do the same for him.

After Gregory had seized her with the words, "Now, you really are mine and I will not let you go," Mrs. Tyler had thought it prudent to return her and Daisy back to the Mathewson house. Although Gwendolyn missed Gregory achingly, she could see the wisdom in the woman's decision.

Her and Gregory's last kiss, shared beneath the twinkling stars of twilight after the Tylers had gone inside the house, had been one of the most powerful Gwendolyn had ever experienced. It resembled Gregory in every way—starting with possession and relief and ending in passionate lust. If it weren't for their mysterious attacker lurking about, Gwendolyn would have snuck out of the house during the night and begged for another taste of Gregory's lips. She would have climbed over the wooden porch and gables to be with him, if need be.

Gwendolyn sighed then wearily sat back down. Dan and Daisy were about to start the most important chapter of their lives and were gloriously in love, although Daisy would never publicly admit such a thing. There was only one thing she could think of to inspire her music and to prove her love for her cousin and soon-to-be brother-in-law, and that was Gregory.

Embracing her violoncello once more, she leaned over and played what she'd come up with so far, using all of her heart and trusting her instincts. She imagined rain, a light wind, and two people in love surrounded by a forest glade. It was heavenly!

Several minutes later, a knock sounded on the door and she stopped.

"Gwendolyn?" It was her aunt Marguerite. "A gift was left on the porch for you, dear."

Gwendolyn was out of her chair in a flash. She bounded down the attic steps two at a time, flung the door open, and whizzed past her chuckling aunt in the hallway. She knew the gift was from Gregory and the thought of maybe catching a glimpse of him made her positively giddy.

Daisy stood at the base of the stairs, clapping her hands and jumping with delirious excitement. "Oh, Gwendolyn! Hurry! I want to see what he brought you."

Skipping the last two steps, Gwendolyn landed on the wood floor with a resounding thud and opened the front door.

Before her sat a plain wooden box with a flawless white rosebud resting on top. She smiled then lifted her head to scan the surrounding area for any sign of Gregory.

"Well, come on. Bring it inside!" Daisy shoved past Gwendolyn and lifted the box into her arms before Gwendolyn could protest. "For pity sake, must I do all the work?"

Gwendolyn gaped at her cousin in surprise and tried her very hardest not to be angry. It was her gift, wasn't it? She hoped Daisy would at least let her open it herself.

She followed Daisy into the kitchen where her uncle calmly sat with his breakfast. Her aunt glowered at Daisy.

"What?" Daisy asked innocently. "I thought it might be heavy… and Gwendolyn's not supposed to be lifting heavy things. Isn't that right, Papa?"

"Yes," he said, drawing out the word as he looked at his wife, who was still glowering at Daisy. Gwendolyn noticed him smirking beneath his bushy moustache and smirked herself as he hastily wiped it away with his hand.

"All right, I'm backing away." Daisy took several slow steps back and raised her hands up in surrender until her mother nodded with satisfaction.

"Go on, Pinkie," her uncle said. "Open it up before Daisy dies from impatience."

Gwendolyn carefully picked up the rose and breathed its faint perfume in deeply. It reminded her of the path leading to Gregory's house. No, not Gregory's house—*their* house, the one they would share together. She shivered with delight at the idea of managing her own home with the love of her life working beside her.

"Oh, get on with it," Daisy urged then stepped back as both her parents glowered at her. Mumbling, she added, "I wish Dan were this romantic."

"Here, you can have this." Gwendolyn handed the white rose to a wide-eyed Daisy before rolling the box's lid back on its hinges and grabbing the folded paper that lay on top.

"Bless my soul," her aunt cried, putting a hand to her bosom.

Gwendolyn looked down past her note to see that within the box was a smaller handmade crate bearing a fluffy white kitten. It meowed in greeting.

"Oh," Gwendolyn gasped with glee. Setting the note aside, she lifted the kitten out of the crate and rubbed its soft fur against her cheek. Yes, it was the one she'd played with in the Tylers' barn just before meeting Gregory in the rain, and it was her favorite because it was the most curious of all of Sophie's kittens. Using her middle finger, she stroked the spiky hair on its head and smiled as the kitten tried to trap her finger within its paws.

"Please Mums?"

Daisy greedily snatched the note once she'd gained permission and read it aloud. "Dearest Gwendolyn," she started then immediately muttered an 'oh, please.'

Barrett Mathewson slapped a hand on the table, startling everyone. "Dai-sy!"

"Oh, I was only kidding. Good grief! You're all such spoil sports." She cleared her throat dramatically then started over. "Dearest Gwendolyn…I have given you this little one because I know you'll love her and give her a good home. She is the only survivor of her family and will need lots of…love."

"What?" Gwendolyn instinctively held the kitten tighter and met Daisy's sorrowful expression. "No! That can't be. They were all alive when I carried them out of the barn."

"It was the smoke, Pinkie," her uncle said slowly. "There wasn't anything you could do."

Gwendolyn felt tears build up in her eyes as her aunt placed a comforting hand on her shoulder. Those poor little things, she thought in despair. If only she'd gotten to them sooner they might have all survived.

Her uncle urged Daisy to keep reading and she did so with less enthusiasm.

"Please don't cry," Daisy continued, reading Gregory's words.

Gwendolyn smiled through her tears. Gregory knew her so well. Wiping away a tear, she listened to the remainder of his words carefully.

"She is strong. She is a fighter just like you. Take care of her, love. Always yours, Gregory." Daisy carelessly tossed Gregory's note on the table and pulled a dainty handkerchief from her bodice to wipe her misty eyes. "Well, that was depressing."

Gwendolyn's uncle reached into the box and moved the straw about. "There should be a—ah, yes. Here it is." He produced a small bottle with a rubber feeder on top and put it in his wife's outstretched hand.

"I think some warm milk is just the thing she needs, poor little dear." Her aunt moved past Daisy to stoke the stove fire then went to the icebox for some milk.

"Oh, but is it all right for me to keep her here in the house, Aunt Marguerite? I know you don't keep any pets."

"Of course it's all right, dear," she answered with a wave. "That kitten needs a good home and we're going to give it to her.

Besides, I usually catch the bunnies I find chomping around at my vegetables and let them hop around inside for a while. It seems to distract them, but it drives Barrett crazy." She looked adoringly at her husband, who playfully scowled in return.

"I don't care for swatting them out with a broom," she defended, shuddering. "It just seems like such a horrid idea. They're so sweet even if they are obnoxious." She grabbed the water-filled saucepan from Daisy and set it to heat up on the stove.

Daisy came around the table and carefully scratched underneath the kitten's chin. "What are you going to name her?"

Holding the little bundle several inches in front of her, Gwendolyn examined it. She was perfect—white fur, tiny nose, round eyes looking for mischief, sweet temperament, and feather soft. "She survived the fire…so her name shall be Snow."

"Oh, that is a perfect name," her aunt cried, setting the milk bottle inside the warm water. "Snow can be as soft as a snowflake and as strong as an avalanche. I love it."

It really was a good name, if Gwendolyn did say so herself. She desperately wanted to see Gregory and tell him the name she'd chosen, but with less than a week until the wedding and Dan and Daisy's house to finish, she knew she shouldn't bother him. He would come to the house at the end of the day, and she would just have to sit tight and dream about him until then.

"Oh, it's just too wonderful!" Gwendolyn's aunt cried, stitching the finishing edge on a beautiful pinwheel style quilt. "Both of my daughters…married to their best friends by Thanksgiving. Isn't that right, Gwendolyn? Weren't you and Gregory thinking of doing it in late fall around the harvest?"

Gwendolyn nodded, grabbing her sewing scissors from the parlor table beside her with shaky hands. With all that had happened over the past week, she didn't know if she could get through the next few months without pulling out all her hair. It seemed like an unbearably long time to wait, but wait she would. For what could be better than waiting to marry the man of—literally—her dreams? He was definitely worth it. In the meantime, she would think of the house they would share—a house built solely by Gregory with all the love, and frustration, he had felt for her over the past year. She would think of Gregory building furniture for the people in town, of him working in the fields, of frequent visits between her two families, of the children they would have one day. And there were the meals she would prepare, the animals they would keep, and the clothes that would need washing, ironing, and mending. Well, perhaps that last bit would lose its appeal sooner than the rest, but Gwendolyn was excited for it all anyhow.

Gwendolyn looked over to one corner of the parlor to see Snow resting peacefully in the soft bed she had made for her. Snow was only a few weeks old and didn't roam about the room much, which was good because Gwendolyn knew she would be frantic if Snow ever went missing. She didn't want her to get lost in any cracks or holes or for someone to accidentally step on her. Oh, that would be dreadful.

"How many quilts have we yet to finish, Mrs. Tyler?" Gwendolyn asked, holding the completed front portion of her box quilt. Her own design was nowhere near the complexity of Mrs. Tyler's and she wondered how many years of practice it would take to reach her skill level. Mrs. Tyler's work was known across the entire county, or so Mrs. Adams had told her, so she supposed the answer was… most likely never.

"Let's see," Mrs. Tyler said, raising her head to think. Her hands, Gwendolyn noticed, continued to move of their own accord, as if bewitched. It was very distracting. "Jean Jenkins finished hers Monday evening. Then Emma Clark brought hers and her mother's. Oh, and Martha May—that's Mrs. Adams—she brought hers just this morning. Her stitching is always so precise."

Gwendolyn wondered how the woman could look so wistful over Mrs. Adams' fine stitching when her own was so extraordinary.

"Anyway," Mrs. Tyler continued. "Theirs are all finished. I believe we're just waiting for the three of ours. Oh, and Julie Morrison's, as well." She rolled her eyes and went back to her sewing. "I don't ever expect to see her quilt finished, that much I can tell you."

Her aunt Marguerite nodded in agreement then shook her head in disgust.

"Why not?" Gwendolyn grabbed the material for the back of her quilt and laid it evenly over the floor. The little puff of air it made blew right at Snow who woke with an irritated jerk, licked her lips and looked around, and then rested her head against the bed once more.

"She mostly joined the committee for show," Mrs. Tyler answered. "I think she wants people to think she's contributing. There's also the good amount of gossip our dear committee ladies contribute." She smiled at Gwendolyn. "You'll find that Melissa and her mother are very much alike. That's why I've decided to release them from the committee."

Gwendolyn had a hard time imagining another woman as spiteful as Melissa and prayed she would never find herself so unfortunate as to be alone with the pair of them. What a frightening thought that was.

Her aunt left the room and returned a minute later bearing three cups of iced tea and another of sugar. "I've often wondered how Jenny survived such a family," her aunt said, taking up her seat once more.

"Have I met Jenny?" Gwendolyn asked. She lifted her cup and tasted raspberries.

"I doubt it. She married Mr. Clark's son Warren about two years ago. Isn't that right, Sarah?" Mrs. Tyler nodded and her aunt continued. "Jenny is often sick. She didn't leave the house much growing up. But now she's married and has a baby and is away from her family. So, that's a good thing. And Warren takes such good care of her. He loves her so."

"Well, she deserves it after seventeen years of hardship, the poor girl."

Gwendolyn smiled, enjoying the honesty between the two women. She couldn't help noticing how relaxed her aunt looked and, when in her friend's company, how relaxed her speech was. She liked knowing her aunt could be a little wicked and gossipy now and then.

"Have you seen her baby, Sarah?"

Gwendolyn looked up to see the envy written all over her aunt's face as Mrs. Tyler related the baby's virtues and couldn't help wondering. "Why did you never have more children, Aunt?" Gwendolyn finished pinning her quilt then gathered it into her lap.

Her aunt set her own quilt aside and took a long sip of tea before speaking, looking Gwendolyn directly in the eye. "You've never asked me this before. But I will tell you," she said quickly, seeing the worried look on Gwendolyn's face. "Barrett and I tried for years to have children. I miscarried several times and always got very sick and ad low spirits afterward. This went on for about ten years, and at that time I was so miserable and frustrated that I shut myself in a room for days, not eating or drinking. I nearly died, actually."

"Oh, yes. It was terrible," Mrs. Tyler added solemnly.

"Barrett helped me…fed me…he even made me take short walks with him through town to get my strength back." Her aunt shivered in disgust. "It wasn't easy for either of us, but most especially, for Barrett. Then I got a letter from Leadville saying that my sis—your mother had died in childbirth. Those were not good times, Gwendolyn darling."

Gwendolyn was so shocked she accidentally stuck her finger directly into a pin then yelped in pain. She watched it bleed for a second before sticking it in her mouth and sucking on it.

Near the far wall, a clock chimed the sixth hour of the evening, and Gwendolyn wished it were the eighth hour so she could see Gregory.

Her aunt continued, appearing quite calm. "Three months later, I received another letter saying your father had also died, but by that time I had improved somewhat. Barrett and I traveled to Leadville for the funeral. Your sister Rebecca was sent to live with another family in the city. So, Barrett and I adopted you." She slumped her shoulders and smiled mischievously. "Well, actually, Barrett signed the papers while I ran off with you cradled in my arms. Can you imagine how happy I was to have a baby? To have a daughter…my own beautiful sister's daughter?"

Gwendolyn smiled as a single tear fell past her cheek. "What about Daisy?"

"Oh, that's the best part, my darling," she said, scratching the back of her coiffure with one long fingernail. "We have no idea. I discovered I was with child not long after bringing you home with us. But judging by Daisy's temperament, she most likely just couldn't wait to come into the world and get to know you. You know, she actually came early. There were some complications. Oh, but what joy we've had in raising the both of you." Her cheeks turned rosy and her eyes sparkled. "You were always getting into trouble, Gwendolyn, but it was glorious fun to see how excited you were about everything and how disgusted Daisy was about your daily treasures. You always seemed to be in love with life and I envied you, truly."

"Envied me?" Gwendolyn furrowed her brow, having a hard time believing such a thing. In truth, the very idea made her uncomfortable. However, it was highly likely nobody envied her right then, not a girl without memories of her past. That idea comforted her, somewhat.

"Oh, yes dear. You were always so…I don't know, enraptured by everything. You found everything interesting, even the slimiest and vilest of creatures." Her aunt giggled, putting a hand on her apron just above her stomach. "You used to snitch my bottled goods out of the pantry and come home with live creatures inside instead of peaches. It always made Daisy squirm so. Do you remember, Sarah?"

"Of course. I also remember the time I saw a little brown-eyed girl peaking over my counter at the mercantile," Mrs. Tyler said, peering at Gwendolyn with amusement, "wondering if she could buy a stick of peppermint to give as a special treat to our puppy, Caramel."

Horrified, Gwendolyn asked, "Certainly I wasn't always so much trouble, was I Aunt?"

"For pity sake, Gwendolyn. You weren't *trouble*. You were just… free spirited, 'tis all. But you did seem to mellow out as the years went by. Come to think of it, you grew very quiet just before you left last—"

All of the women jumped as a sharp knock sounded on the front door.

Gwendolyn's heart pounded. Gregory couldn't be finished with his work already, could he? Perhaps his rib was troubling him and he needed to go home early, she thought. Or maybe he just needed to see Gwendolyn as much as she needed to see him. Yes, she liked her last idea best.

Her aunt got up and answered the door.

"Good evening, madam. Is this the residence of Miss Mitchell?"

Gwendolyn jumped in surprise. She recognized the masculine voice but couldn't quite put a face to it. Slowly, she went to the door to see none other than Robert Jamison standing on her porch! "Robert? What are you doing here?"

"Robert?" Her aunt's face grew pale as she looked from Robert to Gwendolyn and back to Robert again. "Robert?" she repeated.

"Well, to answer both of your questions," Robert said, looking unusually confident, "yes, I'm Robert. I hail from Hopeton. And I presume you're Gwendolyn's lovely mother, *Madame* Mitchell."

Gwendolyn's heart stopped. She'd never heard Robert utter a single French word during all the months she'd known him. Not during all of their carriage rides through the snow, not during their walks through the city, and not during any of the times they'd spent eating lunches in the sunshine. She watched in horror as he lifted her aunt's hand and kissed the back of it tenderly. Her aunt was so shocked she didn't even bother to correct him about who she truly was.

Robert wasn't the Frenchman Robert, was he? No, he couldn't be, she decided, feeling sick all of a sudden. She eyed him suspiciously, looking him over from head to toe. Gwendolyn had to admit he was handsome and he was dark, as Melissa had so generously pointed out.

Gwendolyn was almost too afraid to ask her next question but simply had to. "Robert, are you French?" she asked, nearly choking on the last word.

"Ah, yes, *mademoiselle*. I am. Well, only part," he shrugged. "My mother was French."

"Was?" Gwendolyn gulped involuntarily. She noticed her aunt was still staring at the man on the porch as though she were about to be eaten by a grizzly bear, her hands clenching the fabric of her skirts.

"Yes, my mother died several years ago."

"But she just had a baby, did she not?"

"My father remarried. Gwendolyn, are feeling all right? You're growing rather pale." He reached a hand out to steady her. "In fact, you both are. Why don't you invite me in and we can all sit down together. Yes?"

Now there was the Robert she knew. He seemed to be acting his usual impolite self again. Gwendolyn shook her head and tried to banish all of the terrible questions that were rolling around inside. It could just all be a coincidence, couldn't it? Of course, it had to be a coincidence.

With a nod in her aunt's direction, she nervously led him inside to an empty chair in the parlor. He carried a small box under one arm and laid it on the floor beside him before taking his seat.

"And who might this be, Miss Gwendolyn?" Mrs. Tyler asked, looking cheerful and completely ignorant of her and her aunt's discomfort.

"Robert, *madame*." He reached over and shook Mrs. Tyler's hand once. "Pleased to meet you."

Mrs. Tyler removed her spectacles and glared suspiciously at Gwendolyn, who cringed. "Robert…the Frenchman?"

"The very same," Robert answered for her, beaming. "Gwendolyn, I see you've been telling many of the townspeople about me. Why, a couple of gentlemen at the inn even seemed to recognize my name. I must say I'm quite flattered."

Both her aunt and Mrs. Tyler shifted their worried gazes to her, and Gwendolyn felt like screaming.

"I haven't told anyone about you!" That didn't seem to ease the situation. In fact, it made it worse. Instantly, Mrs. Tyler straightened her back and looked at Gwendolyn as if she suspected her of hiding something. Her aunt Marguerite hunched over her sewing, avoiding everyone's gazes.

Gwendolyn supposed it was up to her to start the conversation, awkward as the situation was. She looked back to Robert, who was grinning wildly. "How long have you been in town, Robert?"

"Just a little while."

Gwendolyn grabbed her quilt and took up her seat once more, wondering if he was purposely being vague. 'A little while' was completely relative and didn't mean a thing to her. For instance, it could mean he'd been in Grovetown for only a few minutes or that he was, in fact, present the night of the dance the previous week. Gwendolyn shivered at the thought. It just didn't fit that Robert Jamison was the man in Melissa's story. Gwendolyn had never thought of Robert as being charming, but after his sudden arrival on her doorstep wearing gentleman's attire and speaking perfectly-accented French terms, she was willing to reconsider.

Her aunt and Mrs. Tyler looked very uncomfortable, nearly as uncomfortable as she felt. Even though it wasn't her fault that Robert had shown up, she still managed to feel dreadfully guilty. Attempting to distract herself, Gwendolyn gazed past the lace curtain through the window, wishing their visitor had been Gregory and not Robert. The hour was growing late and it was beginning to grow dark. They would need lanterns soon. She should fetch some.

Gwendolyn began to stand, but the moment she did, Mrs. Tyler spoke. "What brings you to Grovetown, sir?"

Gwendolyn sank back down into her chair, wondering if Mrs. Tyler was purposely avoiding his name. She probably was, for the name only meant mystery, secrets, and danger to the people of the town.

Gwendolyn looked down to see Snow still asleep, snoring softly and unaware of their new guest.

"Oh, forgive me. How rude I must seem to you all."

Listening to Robert's sudden, but obviously practiced, display of etiquette made Gwendolyn want to retch, and she wondered if it had been wise of her to allow him in after all. He seemed like a completely different person than the one she'd gotten to know in

Hopeton. Feeling the rise of goosebumps on her neck, she realized she didn't like his new persona. It seemed…artificial, somehow.

"I would have expected Gwendolyn to have told you by now, but no matter."

Gwendolyn looked up and stared at him warily. What on earth was going on in that man's head?

"I came to see Gwendolyn. You see, we're engaged."

"What?" Gwendolyn shrieked. She looked at her aunt, who was looking about the room as if lost then slumped her shoulders, looking sick.

"I beg your pardon?" Mrs. Tyler spoke each word very slowly as if she were being challenged.

Grinning as if the idea were the most heavenly of all ideas, Robert nodded.

Gwendolyn wanted to punch him in the nose.

Mrs. Tyler turned in her direction with eyes full of fear. "Is this true, Gwendolyn?"

Ignoring Mrs. Tyler, Gwendolyn glared at Robert with sudden realization. "You were the one who told my students, weren't you?"

"Of course," he said innocently. "When I came to share lunch with you that first day, they all inquired about us…and our relationship. So I told them, but with less detail, of course. Have I upset you?"

Gwendolyn shook her head, swallowing the bile that was slowly rising in her throat. She wanted to cry, or scream, or better yet, bash Robert's head in! What business did he have in spreading rumors about their relationship? He'd kissed her once and that was it. She hadn't allowed him to kiss her after that, nor wanted him to, for that matter. The image of Gregory had been on her mind ever since the night of the concert, and it didn't feel proper kissing Robert when she was thinking of another man the entire time.

"Here," he said, grabbing the ornamented box beside his chair. "I brought a gift for you. I just know it will cheer you up." He stood and placed the box in her lap.

Scowling and half dazed, she untied the thick white ribbon and wondered where he'd gotten the money to purchase something so lovely. The box, too, was decorated with strips of shiny colored paper and silvery string.

Cautiously, she lifted the lid and immediately flinched as a young brown cat leapt from it. "Cinnamon?"

The feline went directly to little Snow as if she'd known all along there was another cat in the house and sniffed at her curiously. Awake but with eyes still shut, Snow lifted her nose and poked through Cinnamon's whiskers.

Gwendolyn's heart swelled with joy seeing the two of them together. She'd missed Cinnamon dreadfully since leaving Hopeton and imagined Cinnamon would be a good little companion to her orphaned Snow.

Smiling, she lifted her head and looked at Robert in a new light. He couldn't possibly be the same Robert that Melissa had mentioned. Or he could be and Melissa had lied about where she'd received her information. "But how?"

"My aunt decided you must keep her. Ever since the day you left, Cinnamon's been sleeping on your bed and moping about. She's yours by right, and she'll be happier with you anyhow."

Gwendolyn watched as Cinnamon padded onto the little bed and cuddled up beside the white ball of fluff to rest.

"Thank you, Robert."

"You're most welcome." He smiled and Gwendolyn thought it endearing.

"Well," Mrs. Tyler said, jumping up all at once and grabbing her quilting things. "I must be off. Marguerite…Gwendolyn…sir…I bid you all a good evening."

She hadn't moved more than a couple steps before Gwendolyn stopped her. "Mrs. Tyler? You get back here—now." She couldn't believe she was being so commanding with one of her elders, not to mention her good friend, but she couldn't help herself. She didn't want the woman running home and telling Gregory about Robert before she had a chance to explain the situation. She didn't like the idea of everyone calling her a jilt, and she didn't want to humiliate Robert in front of others. He was just confused.

Mrs. Tyler reluctantly sat back down in her chair, not meeting Gwendolyn's gaze and looking disgruntled.

Robert looked about the ladies of the room and frowned. Finally sensing the change of mood, he stood and put a hand in one of his coat pockets. "I believe, Mrs. Tyler, that you are friends with Mrs. Ellen Maynard." He pulled an envelope out of his pocket and gave it to the woman. "She asked me to give this to you since I was going to be coming here."

Mrs. Tyler turned the letter over and muttered a polite 'thank you' in return.

"I fear I have overstayed my welcome, Gwendolyn. But I hope to see you again soon. Tomorrow, perhaps?"

Knowing she would need to straighten things out between them, Gwendolyn nodded. But oh, how she dreaded it. Robert was in love with her and would be heartbroken after she explained her feelings. But how could he go around telling everyone they were engaged when they most certainly were not? Perhaps, she thought in fear, there was a custom she'd forgotten about.

He retrieved his ebony bowler hat from the table at his side, bowed, and then showed himself out.

The minute the door closed, Mrs. Tyler was on her feet. "Gwendolyn," she whispered harshly. "You will marry my son, and that is final. You have grown up with Gregory and have loved him your entire life and I will not let this Robert person stand in the way of that. I don't care who he is or how much money he's got."

Knowing it might be a while before Mrs. Tyler would let her speak, Gwendolyn sat back, folded her arms across her chest, and waited. Her aunt, Gwendolyn noticed, continued stitching with shaky hands and didn't say a word.

Mrs. Tyler continued, pacing across the five-foot expanse and raising her volume with each sentence. "You must go to Robert first thing tomorrow. Yes, that is what you should do. But why haven't you told us about him before? Is he truly the Frenchman Robert everyone in town has been talking about?"

"I don't know. Do you suspect he is?"

"I think you would know better than anyone else in town, apart from Melissa. Well," she said, coming to stand before her, "what do you have to say for yourself, young lady? I must say I never would have thought you'd do such a thing."

Gwendolyn sighed, relieved that she could finally explain herself. Seeing Mrs. Tyler angry was a very frightening thing indeed.

"I have not done this," she began slowly. "Robert Jamison and I are not engaged and never were."

"Then what was he going on about?"

"I honestly don't know, Mrs. Tyler," she defended. "We've been good friends. Last April, he expressed the desire to be more than friends but I discouraged him. He told my students we were engaged, but at the time I thought they'd only heard a bit of gossip in town and run wild with it. I do not think this can be possible unless I've forgotten something—a custom or tradition?"

Her aunt Marguerite finally looked up from her sewing and spoke. "Did he ever kiss you?"

Gwendolyn was shocked by her aunt's bluntness, especially after such a long period of silence, and then was immediately embarrassed. "Yes," she replied timidly, "but I thought about Gregory the entire time."

Mrs. Tyler spun around. "What do you mean? You said you lost your memory!" She paused then a shadow fell over her face. "You haven't been playing a farce this whole time, have you?"

"Of course not!" Gwendolyn took a steadying breath before continuing. "I might not have told the whole truth that first day when you asked if I remembered anyone, but I was too afraid to admit it…at that time."

"Go on." Mrs. Tyler took up her seat once again and rested her arms on the armrests.

"I attended a concert in Hopeton in April and heard the violoncello for the first time."

Her aunt looked about to say something then decided against it, waving for Gwendolyn to continue.

"It was beautiful—so poetic, so alive. I closed my eyes and saw an image flash through my mind…but only for a second."

"And?" Mrs. Tyler urged.

"It was of Gregory. He was sitting in the attic, watching me. That's all I had to go on—the only vision I had had since my accident. But the memory of his blue eyes and his look of admiration captivated me so. I could concentrate on little else for months afterward. I even dreamt about him." Gwendolyn blushed but continued after seeing the obvious delight in both her aunt and Mrs. Tyler's expressions. "I knew he was important to me but didn't know who he was until the day I arrived in Grovetown. That's why I reacted so poorly in the mercantile. I had expected Gregory to be a savior for me, to help me understand who I was and to treat me with the same admiration as he had in my vision. Instead, he was rough and coarse and angry."

"Oh, you poor thing." Mrs. Tyler wiped her misty eyes with her thumbs. "You didn't react poorly. If it had been me, I would have given him a good, hard kick in the—"

"Sarah!"

Gwendolyn laughed at her aunt's blush of modesty then sighed.

Mrs. Tyler grinned then turned back to Gwendolyn. "You do like my son, don't you?"

"Yes," Gwendolyn said without hesitation. She was no longer afraid to admit it, but she was surprised to feel her eyes fill up with tears. "I love him."

"Why don't you go on over and ask her, boy?"

Gregory considered his father's words as he stood at the entrance of the mercantile watching the obviously rich, young man saunter down the street before entering the inn.

After nearly twelve hours of work, Gregory had decided he'd had enough for the day and needed to see Gwendolyn, hungered for Gwendolyn. On fire with anticipation, he'd left his brother's house only to find a well-dressed stranger standing on the Mathewson's porch with a gift case resting at his feet. He stood there for a couple minutes before being permitted to enter, and Gregory hung back, curious as to the nature of the man's business.

The stranger was handsome and no more than a score and five years. He had to be visiting Gwendolyn, Gregory realized with a surge of jealousy, and the case was for her. Gwendolyn didn't know anybody outside of Grovetown and Hopeton, so there was no doubt in Gregory's mind—the stranger had to be a rich lover or admirer and had traveled far to see her.

"No," Gregory said, going to the front counter. "Papa, did you see how that man was dressed? Even with my business, I wouldn't be able to give Gwendolyn nice things, the things she deserves." He shook his head, wondering how he could've been such a fool. "I don't know how I could've thought she'd want to live out here in the wilderness after living with the luxuries of Hopeton. I'm such a fool!"

"She did say 'yes' to you last night, did she not? She has promised to be yours?"

"Yes, but perhaps she's just confused. I mean, she doesn't even remember me! Maybe what she wants is someone who can take good care of her and give her gifts and take her to concerts every week, and," he said, pointing out the front window, "maybe *he's* the one she wants."

His father came around the counter and put both hands on his son's shoulders. "How do you know until you ask her? I think you're making too much of a fuss over this. You don't even know if he's really a suitor or not."

Gregory couldn't bring himself to ask her. If she preferred the luxuries of Hopeton to the toil of Grovetown, if she wanted that more than she wanted him, then so be it. She deserved so much more than what he could give her—what he'd spent his whole life working for in order to prove himself to her. But even as he thought it, he ached for her and wanted her close by.

# Chapter Twelve

THE SUN WAS ALREADY OUT BY THE TIME Gwendolyn awoke the following morning, and she had to blink several times before her eyes would adjust. Cinnamon lay atop the foot of her bed, curled in ball and twitching the end of her tail, and Gwendolyn thought for a moment she was back with the Jennys. Grateful to be mistaken, she tossed aside her covers and skipped over to the washstand to pour fresh water into a basin.

After Robert had left the night before, she'd stayed up late hoping Gregory would pay her a visit and had sat in the chair closest to the window so she could look out for him, but he never came. When Dan had returned with Daisy around a quarter past eight, he'd claimed Gregory had finished his work for the day hours before and didn't know his current whereabouts. But the fact that he'd said it while avoiding her gaze made Gwendolyn seriously doubt his latter claim.

No matter, Gwendolyn shrugged. There was no doubt in her mind that Gregory loved her. She'd puzzled over the reasons far into the night and finally decided it was Mrs. Tyler's doing. She laughed, imagining Mrs. Tyler being dragged across the kitchen floor in an attempt to restrain her ardent son from rendezvousing with his true love so late in the evening.

With a whimsical sigh, Gwendolyn dressed quickly then floated down to the kitchen where her aunt and cousin were quietly eating breakfast.

Her aunt Marguerite was the first to greet her. "Did you sleep well, darling?"

"Honestly, it's been rather difficult these past couple of nights." Her aunt and Daisy exchanged glances of amusement and Gwendolyn couldn't help giggling herself. "However, I am well rested. Thank you for asking."

"Don't worry, Gwendolyn," her aunt said. "You'll see him before the day is out. I'm certain. Now eat up, darlings. We've got a busy day ahead of us."

With a twirl, Gwendolyn went to the stove and, ignoring the bacon, dished some scrambled eggs and seasoned potatoes onto her plate. It smelled delicious! She took up her usual seat across from her aunt and listened as the woman prattled on about arbors, flowers, cakes, and dresses.

Gwendolyn had just filled her mouth with a forkful of potatoes when Daisy said something to distress her. She chewed quickly then swallowed. "No, no. I don't need another new dress. I can get married in the one we're picking up today. Or perhaps, we can alter it," she added hopefully. For goodness sake! How many dresses could one woman possibly need? She didn't own a fortune.

"What?" Daisy's mouth was hanging wide open and Gwendolyn imagined a bug flying into it. "You can't get married in that boring muslin!"

"For goodness sake, Daisy," her aunt chided. "That 'boring muslin' was good enough for you once. You picked it out for her, didn't you?"

"Well, yes, but this is Gwendolyn and Gregory's wedding, Mums! It's so much more important than mine. Don't you see?" Daisy leaned both elbows on the table beside her forgotten breakfast plate. "Perhaps we could order away for some embroidered organza to disguise the dress or some French silk…oh, yes, wouldn't that be perfect?"

"Silk? Daisy, are you out of your mind? I could never afford—wait. Why French silk?" Gwendolyn asked, feeling a sudden aversion to anything having to do with that specific country.

Daisy looked at her strangely. "Well, you're French, of course. We both are. Well, part French. Our mothers were born in Bordeaux. Isn't that right, Mums?"

Gwendolyn's eyes went wide when her aunt nodded. She'd certainly never considered her heritage.

"Yes. Our mother brought us to America after our father died. I don't remember much. We were still quite young then. The journey took nearly two months but it felt like years. We settled in Missouri. That's where your mother met Douglas," she said, pointing to Gwendolyn, "and I met Barrett." She picked up her fork and stared wistfully at a spot on the table.

Gwendolyn placed a forkful of eggs into her mouth, not giving their cool temperature much thought as she considered her aunt's words. So, she was French. Her family was French. The stranger in town named Robert, whom she hoped wasn't Robert Jamison, was French. Robert Jamison's mother was French, and Robert Jamison was French. Gwendolyn scowled, not liking the suspicions that were running around inside her head. She doubted, once again, that everything could just be a coincidence.

"Aunt," she began. "Do you think Robert is the Frenchman Robert? Is that why you were so quiet last night?"

"Whoa, what did I miss?" Daisy said, coming alive with excitement.

Gingerly, her aunt Marguerite set her fork down and dabbed her mouth with a napkin before speaking. "I suspected he was at first, but I do not think so now."

Daisy looked like she was about to erupt with curiosity, but Gwendolyn ignored her. She was relieved that her aunt agreed with her about Robert, but Gwendolyn wanted to know her reasons, for she was a little shaky about her own. "Why not?"

Her aunt looked down at her plate again, avoiding Gwendolyn's gaze. "Let's just call it a hunch."

"But what happened, Mums?" Daisy practically whined.

Grabbing her plate, Marguerite stood and went to the kitchen's washbasin. "I'll tell you later, dear."

Letting out a grand moan of exasperation, Daisy crossed her arms and flopped back into her chair to sulk.

Mrs. Tyler walked right through the kitchen door as Marguerite was putting the food away and greeted everyone with a cheery grin and rosy cheeks. "Good morning."

"What brings you to our kitchen, Sarah?"

"Oh, I just thought I'd come by and read Gwendolyn some of Ellen's letter."

"Yes, please do," Gwendolyn said. "Tell me how she's doing."

Grinning, Mrs. Tyler melted into the nearest seat and pulled the letter out with both hands. She cleared her throat then began. "I suspect Gwendolyn has made it safely home by now and has reunited with her family and friends. We all miss her so but wish her well. I fear I must apologize for keeping her arrival so mysterious. You see, I wasn't certain how she would be received, nor did I understand why she would choose to teach in a city so far away from her home. But no matter. It's all over and done with. You have to admit it was glorious fun and I do so love surprises."

Gwendolyn smiled. She could picture her friend exactly—writing her letter and tapping her fingers together as she plotted. Mrs. Maynard reminded her of Daisy, in fact.

Mrs. Tyler flipped the letter over and continued reading Mrs. Maynard's words. "Now onto less pleasant topics." Gwendolyn gulped. "I have heard a troubling rumor in town concerning our Miss Gwendolyn and must know if it is true. I heard that she is engaged to be married, and to Elizabeth Jenny's nephew, of all people."

"What?" Daisy blurted, slapping her hands flat on the table. "But you're engaged to Gregory, aren't you, Gwendolyn?"

Gwendolyn nodded then dropped her head on the table as her aunt finally explained everything to Daisy.

Yes, Gwendolyn would definitely wring Robert's neck the next time she saw him. The audacity of the man!

Once Daisy had settled down, Mrs. Tyler continued the letter, chuckling. "Oh, he's a fine man, to be sure. I've always thought so, until he came to my office the day Gwendolyn left for Grovetown and announced their engagement, grinning like a fool and puffing out his chest like a turkey. It seemed rather suspicious, if you ask me. Gwendolyn would have told me herself if it were true, surely."

Gwendolyn banged her head on the table several times, wondering how she was going to set things right between herself and Robert without killing him. It seemed a perfectly sensible thing to do—under the circumstances.

"Have our dear Miss Gwendolyn write to me straightaway, as I do not know her address," Mrs. Tyler read. "I must know for myself whether these rumors are true. If they are not, I will do everything in my power to discredit his claims. Sincerely yours, Ellen Maynard." She set Ellen's letter upon the table, clasped her hands together, and let out a puff of laughter.

Not seeing any humor in the situation, Gwendolyn scowled.

"So, you're not engaged to this Robert then?"

Gwendolyn looked up to Daisy and shook her head wearily. "Not that I'm aware of."

"And he's not our mysterious Frenchman?"

"No, he is not!"

Mrs. Tyler, Daisy, and Gwendolyn all startled at Marguerite's firm and possibly irritated tone and looked at the woman curiously.

"But how can you be certain? Do tell, for I believe you know more than you have been letting on, dear mama."

Goosebumps erupted along the back of Gwendolyn's neck as she watched her aunt gaze into each of their eyes without denial, and she realized Daisy had to be right. Her aunt Marguerite backed against the kitchen basin as a rabbit would cower beneath the steely glare of a fox, and her eyes glistened with unshed tears.

Narrowing her eyes, Gwendolyn wondered if her aunt knew Robert Jamison from previous acquaintance then immediately decided it had to be impossible. Otherwise, Robert would have told her of her family long before her teaching contract had ended. And her aunt couldn't possibly know the Frenchman or she would have said something days ago, surely.

Her aunt's shoulders relaxed and she tossed a wet dishcloth into the basin in resignation. "If my suspicions are proved correct, I fear you may all discover the truth very soon."

A dark cloud of fear penetrated Gwendolyn's heart and she wondered what secrets her aunt was keeping from her—from everybody, including her own daughter and best friend. "What truth, Aunt?"

"Gwendolyn, darling," her aunt said, suddenly snapping out of her melancholy. "Let me get you some paper so you may write to your friend—Ellen, wasn't it? I bet you're anxious to get this little hiccup with Robert straightened out."

Gwendolyn watched as her aunt scurried out of the kitchen and wondered if the woman had heard her question at all. She turned to Mrs. Tyler and Daisy, but they merely shrugged their shoulders with the same confusion.

A sneaking suspicion began to gnaw its way at Gwendolyn's mind and she couldn't rid herself of it. Her aunt had purposely avoided her question, Gwendolyn was certain, and refused to reveal what she knew or thought she knew. Could her aunt really know the Frenchman by name or reputation and not have told her about it?

Her aunt returned a moment later and placed a fresh sheet of paper, a quill, and inkwell in front of her on the table. Gwendolyn watched her suspiciously as she whisked away the last of their breakfast dishes, knowing her aunt wasn't ready to talk about it. She wouldn't press the woman, for the time being.

"There was also a letter on the writing desk addressed to you." Her aunt pulled a small letter from her apron and tossed it to her before going back to her dishes. "I don't know where it came from."

"Oh, that was me," Daisy piped up. "I picked it up at the post office yesterday. Sorry, I forgot to give it to you, Gwendolyn. Well, no, I'm not sorry," she said, suddenly sticking her chin high up into the air and gazing about the ceiling. "It was Dan's fault, after all. He distracted me."

"Of course." Gwendolyn grabbed the letter, wondering who would write to her, and ripped it open. "I know how 'distracting' men can be." Inside she found only a small card, which was folded in half once. She unfolded it and read the first few lines of the masculine script.

Fear gripped her suddenly, and she saw several things at once—a dark figure watching her in the woods and an arm—her arm—stuffing a letter inside a hidden cloth compartment of her violoncello case.

What did it all mean? she wondered. Had those things really happened? And who would write such hateful things to her?

The blood drained from her face and she suddenly felt sick to her stomach. She needed to be alone—she needed to go into her attic room to think.

"Gwendolyn, darling," her aunt said, turning from her work and staring at her with obvious concern. "Whatever is the matter? Who's it from? Is it bad news?"

Mrs. Tyler leaned over to look at Gwendolyn's letter, but Gwendolyn folded it back up and hastily stuffed it into the envelope where it couldn't be seen. "I wonder if you'd all excuse me. I'd like to write my letter to Mrs. Maynard in private."

"As long as you're not planning on spurning my son for this Robert fellow," Mrs. Tyler said casually, "you go right ahead."

Gwendolyn nodded to all the women then sped out of the kitchen and up to the privacy of her attic room, where she bolted the door and immediately started crying. She tried to muffle the sound of her sobbing with her hand as she pulled the letter from the envelope and read it all the way through.

You must think you're smarter than me, don't you? Well, you're wrong. You're a fool, Gwendolyn, as ever you were. I've warned you many times before, but still you returned to Grovetown like the impertinent chit you are.

I hope this letter finds you as heartbroken as I was when I lost two of the people I loved most in the world. A fitting revenge, don't you think? I can just see you now, sobbing over the wooden coffin of that Tyler fellow. He was pathetically easy to kill.

*The next time I see you, if you have not done what I have asked or if you've told anyone about this letter, someone else you love will die.*

Gwendolyn's shoulders were shaking uncontrollably and she knew her world had been pulled out from under her. She closed her eyes and pressed her face to the cool oak door, attempting to draw strength from it as her knees wobbled and her teeth chattered.

Who could have written such a hateful letter? she wondered. Who hated her enough to try to kill Gregory—the one and only man she loved? It had to have been a man, judging by the script and verbiage. Gwendolyn couldn't imagine any woman possessing enough strength to render a man like Gregory unconscious. But whoever the man was, he didn't know Gregory was alive and well. His plan hadn't worked, but Gregory was still in very grave danger, and all because of her. But what had she done? The man had as good as accused her of murder! It was impossible.

A knock sounded on the other side of the door and Gwendolyn wrenched her face back as if she'd been struck.

"Gwendolyn?" Daisy said. "Are you all right? You forgot your writing things."

Brilliant, Gwendolyn thought. She hastily wiped away her tears, took a deep breath, and opened the door a crack. "Thank you, Daisy," she said, accepting the paper and tools with forced dignity. "I–I don't know what came over me."

Daisy eyed her suspiciously. "All right. What's going on? Your eyes are all red and puffy." She started to push against the door but Gwendolyn shoved her booted foot behind it.

Remembering the last few threatening words of the letter, Gwendolyn sighed. "I'm just overwhelmed, Daisy. So much has happened since I've come home."

Daisy looked thoughtful then smiled, withdrawing her hand from the door handle. "Don't worry, Gwendolyn. We'll get this whole mess with Robert taken care of in no time. I'll even go with you, if you like."

Gwendolyn nodded, hoping her cousin wouldn't question her further. She detested lies.

"Do you still want to go with us into town?"

"Of course," she croaked. "But later."

Gwendolyn slowly shut the door in her cousin's face then turned around. Her eyes rested on the violoncello case at the top of the stairs and she immediately remembered the hidden compartment in her vision.

Setting her writing things aside, she hoisted her skirts and took the steps two at a time before sitting beside the case. Her fingers trembled then moved their way across the shaggy blue cloth of the interior. It didn't take long for her to find it, but it wasn't a compartment at all. It was merely a flap of cloth that had fallen loose over the years and was just wide enough for a small hand to fit through.

What would she find? She tentatively dipped her hand deep within the case and produced several small pieces of paper, all written in the same hand as the one she'd just received. She trembled with trepidation as she leafed through them one by one. She just had to find some answers, like why the man wanted her to leave Grovetown and what he could possibly want her to do to save the people she loved.

She frantically searched through the pages for clues—catching words of hatred, warning, and relentless degradation to those of her own gender—and felt the air around her grow unbearably hot as another memory assaulted her. She was standing in front of the Tylers' barn, shielding her eyes from the heat and brilliance of the inferno, and felt her heart charge with fear for the animals screaming within. It had to be the fire Mrs. Tyler had mentioned, the one from the summer before.

Gwendolyn rubbed the prickling sensation off the back of her neck as a realization struck her—a frightening but relieving realization. It was him—the man who had written the letters. He set fire to the Tylers' barn both Sunday and the summer before. She was certain of it. He was trying to hurt those she loved…to hurt her. They were warnings. But why? Had he ever hurt her own family—her aunt or uncle or Daisy?

She shuffled through the offensive pages once more, trying to draw out any additional clues that could help her know what step to take next, but she slumped in defeat. What could she do? She couldn't tell her family about the letters or else the lunatic would find Gregory and finish him off for good. She couldn't tell Gregory because he would just hunt the man down and end up getting himself killed in the process.

The thought of Gregory's skull being crushed repeatedly by a crazed and vengeful lunatic came unbidden and Gwendolyn's stomach churned.

She shoved the morbid thought aside and decided instead to think of more positive things. Despite her fear of things that were surely to come, and soon, she was able to glean one good thing from the letters. She was nearly relieved at the thought, almost. After months of questioning and days of suffering the painful knowledge that she'd left her family without a word, she finally knew the real reason she'd done it.

She'd left out of love. She'd left to protect her families.

Feeling only a touch more confident and a little more than weepy, she stuffed the letters back into the violoncello case and went to stand before the small window. The sky was a mucky gray color and reflected Gwendolyn's mood quite perfectly. She heaved a shaky sigh. The weight that had been lifted upon discovering her innocence had come crashing back down again like a fallen tree in the middle of a silent wood and she lay beneath its crushing weight, praying for deliverance.

She desperately needed someone to talk to—someone to comfort her and say that everything would be all right, that they would take care of everything and she didn't need to worry—but she knew she must keep silent, deathly silent. She felt more lonely than ever.

She couldn't reveal the letters—not to clear her name. If she spoke of them to anyone, there was no telling how many hours, or minutes, would pass before the man discovered it and came to carry out his threats. And why must she leave Grovetown? She couldn't possibly do it, not after everything she'd been through. She had found her family once again and they loved her. She wasn't going to give them up, no matter what the creep claimed she was guilty of. She would fight for them until her dying breath.

The window rattled as thunder rumbled low throughout the valley. Gwendolyn closed her eyes, smiling in spite of everything. Oh, how she loved storms!

The truth would soon be out. She could sense it. In the meantime, she would simply have to keep silent and bear it as best she could.

Gwendolyn and Daisy trotted across the muddy street toward the mercantile, clutching their shared umbrella close as the rain poured down on them in big, fat drops.

Cassandra, Mr. Caldwell's daughter, had had all of their catalog dresses, bonnets, and gloves packaged and ready to go by the time Gwendolyn and Daisy arrived. The young woman's eyes had lit up the moment she'd seen Gwendolyn, and she regaled them with stories of the town's students, talking so fast that neither of them could utter a single word. "Do you plan on staying in Grovetown, Gwendolyn…to teach this next term? Oh, the Adams twins are so sweet. Their enthusiasm is so contagious. And I just love Susan. Did Mrs. Adams tell you she's now top of her class? Now, Molly is just as troublesome as any Morrison could ever be, except for Jenny, of course. Jenny is such a cluster of honey. I had hoped Warren would hold off with his proposal a little longer so that she and I might spend more time together. I really am a selfish creature, aren't I?"

Gwendolyn liked her. She was honest. Her fiery curls were pulled back in a sloppy chignon, screaming to be let loose so they could bounce against her shoulders with abandon. Gwendolyn smiled, thinking of how the women in Hopeton would gossip over the indecency of it.

Gwendolyn and Daisy wiped their boots on the mat outside the mercantile before stepping across the store's threshold. A bell sounded at their heads.

It was pleasantly warm inside, or perhaps it was just Gwendolyn's blood pumping through her body.

She quickly scanned the store for Gregory, but he wasn't there. She swallowed her disappointment.

Mr. Tyler turned from his sweeping in the corner next to the trowels, rakes, and gardening hoes and greeted them with a warm smile. "Mornin' ladies." He set the broom aside then strode toward the back room. "I have your order back here, Daisy."

Gwendolyn lowered her head and watched water drip from her bonnet to land in a pathetic puddle at her feet. Her dress was soaked several inches up the hem, but she didn't care. Of all her dresses it was the one she least favored. It's muddy brown color and cream lace trim screamed school marm and reminded her of the drab, lifelessness of late autumn.

She adjusted the paper-wrapped package under her arm just as Mr. Tyler returned with an armload of goods.

"Let's see what we have here," he mumbled, dropping everything on the counter. He produced a box from below and began stacking things inside. "Flour, sugar, salt…"

Gwendolyn ambled on over to a shelf containing books and magazines. She grabbed a catalog and idly flipped through it, wondering where Gregory was and hoping he wasn't avoiding her. She knew it had only been a little over twenty-four hours, but she ached to see him, to know that he was real and that nobody had hurt him.

"Tell your mother her thread should be in tomorrow, would you, Daisy?"

Mr. Tyler yelled for an absent Susie to look after the store as he hefted the box of goods into his capable arms and made ready to escort them both back home.

Gwendolyn stopped him, unable to remain silent. "Where is Gregory, Mr. Tyler? I was hoping to talk with him today."

"Who's Gregory?"

Gwendolyn, Daisy, and Mr. Tyler simultaneously turned their attention to the main entrance of the store and fell silent.

Oh, for goodness sake, Gwendolyn thought. It was Robert Jamison, clad in a *brown* suit to boot. He came to stand beside Gwendolyn and leaned over her possessively, his stiff cologne smell wafting. She'd never known him to wear cologne. She backed away.

"Who's Gregory?" he repeated, looking at the three of them warily.

As if it were any of his business, Gwendolyn thought irritably.

"I am."

Gwendolyn jumped at the booming voice directly behind her, then smiled with satisfaction. Like a lion, Gregory had crept up behind them all without a sound and was there to champion her. She looked back at Robert with her head held high.

"And who might you be?" Gregory asked.

"Robert Jamison." Robert scooted closer to Gwendolyn and touched her arm. "Why would you want to talk to this man, Gwendolyn?"

Gregory growled. "We're to be married, you weasel. Now, get your paws off of her."

Robert shied as Gregory took a step forward.

Gregory wrapped his arms around Gwendolyn's waist, brazenly resting his hands just below her stomach. She could feel the heat of his body, flush with her own, as he stood behind her. She leaned back into him, relishing the feel of his arms.

Oh dear, Gwendolyn thought. She looked up and, seeing the horrified look on Robert's face, suddenly realized what she was allowing Gregory to do. Things were not going at all how she'd imagined. She needed to talk to Robert alone, not in front of Gregory, who likely wanted to tear the confused man apart with his bare hands.

Robert leaned forward and whispered, "You're not with child, are you?"

"What?" she screeched, pulling herself out of Gregory's comforting embrace. "Are you crazy?"

Robert had the gall to look embarrassed.

"It's not even been two weeks, you buffoon! How could I be with child?" She took a deep, calming breath before continuing. "Robert. We need to talk…privately."

Gregory marched through the storeroom past Susie, who was staring right back at him with her mouth hanging wide open. He would have stopped to talk to her if he hadn't been in such a hurry to eavesdrop on Gwendolyn and that Robert fellow.

He grinned, remembering the shocked look on the whelp's face once he'd announced his and Gwendolyn's engagement. He'd promised himself as he stood in the storeroom, listening in, that he wouldn't interfere in Gwendolyn's business, at least not where men were concerned, but he couldn't help himself. He wasn't going to allow Robert to have the upper hand again.

Gwendolyn's voice stopped him and he immediately plastered himself against the wall.

"What are you doing, Robert? Why have you come here?"

"Gwendolyn, I had to see you. The day you left…I–I've been so miserable."

"It's been eleven days, Robert."

Gregory slid his nose around the corner, anxious to see the look on Gwendolyn's face. The rain poured down upon his head, but he paid it no heed. Gwendolyn was vexed, that much was certain, and Gregory was somewhat comforted. She and Robert were standing in a dry spot beneath a large pine with no more than a foot between them.

"But I thought you'd be pleased to see me. I don't know how I could have misunderstood your letter."

Gwendolyn looked confused. "What letter?"

"The one you sent me just after you got here. And don't tell me you've forgotten about it because I won't believe you."

Gwendolyn hesitated then shook her head.

"You said you loved me," he practically whined. "You said there was no one else on earth who could make you feel so happy, so adored. You said I was the one and only man for you."

"I didn't say that."

He produced a small piece of paper from his jacket pocket and handed it to Gwendolyn. "See for yourself. It's written in your hand."

Gregory couldn't listen anymore, he couldn't breathe. He turned from the spot and felt his legs carry him further and further away from Gwendolyn. He'd lost her, again, but for the final time. She'd gone to Hopeton, lost her memory, and promised herself to a man she barely knew, all before Gregory had managed to ask for her hand. The whelp had snuck in and taken what belonged to him!

The rain felt like small daggers as it pounded against him and he willed his mind to the previous week when he and Gwendolyn had shared their first kiss. Yes, they had *shared* it. He had not forced her. In fact, he'd had to literally push her off of him to preserve both of their virtue.

Was it possible she had already forgotten her beloved Robert—the one and only man she could ever be with? Or perhaps she'd been so mesmerized by Gregory's charm and raw masculinity that her memories of the clean-shaven pretty boy had been squeezed out of her completely. Or, he thought with a jerk of dismay, could she have been trying to tell him all along? Was that why she'd spoken so little and looked so frightened as the storm raged about them? He had thought her reaction was out of fear for revealing her memory loss which, once he'd discovered it, had been a heavy blow indeed. But could it have been for a different reason?

Gwendolyn had appeared shocked, but it didn't matter whether she remembered writing the letter or not. What mattered is that she'd written the letter and professed her love for another man shortly after returning to Grovetown, possibly after her and Gregory's none-too-friendly meeting in the mercantile. She hadn't even waited long enough to rediscover her past or find out what Gregory really was to her.

What had Gwendolyn turned into? he wondered in shocked

disbelief. Could she really be so different after only one year? He shook his head, feeling like an utter fool. Gwendolyn had taken advantage of him but she would not do it again. He would not give her the opportunity.

Gwendolyn shoved the letter back into Robert's hands, thinking she'd had just about enough of *letters*. The script did resemble her own, but the strokes were more bold and the paper's material was smooth and unfamiliar. Plus, the syntax was all wrong.

She hadn't written it, but one guess told her she knew who had—the Frenchman. It made perfect sense. It was just one more attempt at destroying Gwendolyn's life and getting her to leave Grovetown for good. But she'd found happiness—she'd found Gregory. She wouldn't do the Frenchman's bidding anymore. She knew what he wanted, but she wasn't about to give it to him. After the past week, she knew she couldn't live without love. She simply wouldn't.

"Robert," she started, peering about their surroundings warily. "I did not write that letter."

She absolutely hated causing others pain but it couldn't be helped. She refused to bind herself to a man she did not love, no matter how much it would hurt that person.

"Do you understand?"

Robert's forehead wrinkled in confusion. "Are you certain? You have lost your mem—"

"Yes, Robert. I'm certain." She was tired of people reminding her of her memory loss. Of all the things she had managed to forget, she could never forget that miserable bit. She wasn't an idiot.

"Then you don't love me?" He seemed to shrink before her eyes as the truth of her words finally sank in. He frowned.

"No. Not in that way."

He stood silent for several seconds before turning from her. With labored movements, he plopped himself on the ground then leaned against the pine's trunk in dejection. Drawing both of his knees upward, he rested his arms over them and stared vacantly at a cluster of grass. The fact that she could see his hairy legs peeking out from over his crumpled wool stockings made him seem so much more human—and vulnerable.

Gwendolyn felt terrible. "Oh, Robert. Do you really want to marry someone you barely know? Someone who doesn't even know herself? Someone who could never love you the way you deserve to be loved?"

"Who wrote the letter?"

"Oh, I…don't know," she stuttered. With everything that was going on, she decided it would be better to keep her suspicions to herself.

"Who wrote the letter?" he demanded a little more forcefully.

Afraid, she stepped back a pace. He was angry…and Robert never got angry.

"What am I supposed to do now?" he asked nobody in particular. "I've told everyone of our engagement. I've bought your ring. Mr. Clark's even hired me on as an apprentice in his shop for the summer."

Despite how sorry she felt for him, she wasn't too sorry. After all, he hadn't officially confirmed the words written in the letter nor had he bothered to discuss any of the particulars with Gwendolyn. It irked her that he would do anything and everything without her input. Gregory hadn't gone about their engagement that way.

Gathering a good deal of courage, she went to stand before Robert and placed her hands on her hips. "Do you really love me, Robert, or am I an inconvenience to you? Perhaps you don't think I'm worth the effort you've gone through. Is that it?"

# Chapter Thirteen

"WELL, WHAT DID HE SAY, GWENDOLYN?" Susie asked the following Sunday.

Gwendolyn stared down at the carrots and celery she was chopping and paused thoughtfully. Not only were her aunt, Mrs. Tyler, and Susie in attendance, but also Mrs. Emma Clark, the wife of Robert Jamison's future employer. Gwendolyn didn't want to say anything that might jeopardize Robert's credibility or reputation, no matter whether he decided to stay in Grovetown or return to Hopeton. Her aunt had warned her beforehand to be careful of what she said in front of the woman, and after meeting Mrs. Clark, Gwendolyn could see why. The woman's silence and tight bun of a hairdo gave Gwendolyn the feeling Mrs. Clark said little but heard much.

Gwendolyn gathered some of her chopped vegetables and dumped them into a pot of boiling water then resumed her place at the cutting board. "He felt really awful and apologized. I think he understands now."

"So, he's all right with you not wanting to marry him?" Mrs. Tyler said, adding her chopped potatoes to the pot.

"I believe so. I don't think he was ever really *in* love with me… not the way Gregory is." Gwendolyn saw Mrs. Tyler smile then continued. "Robert cares for me a great deal. I know he does. I just think he was excited about the idea of getting married." She wasn't going to mention the fact that Robert had said kissing her felt like kissing a sister. They didn't really need to know that.

Her aunt sprinkled flour onto the table and began kneading a big roll of dough without enthusiasm. "Did you give him any reason to think you might want to marry him? I mean, why would he just go around and tell everyone if it wasn't true? He must have had some reason to believe it was so."

After tossing the rest of her vegetables in the pot, Gwendolyn sat down at the table next to Mrs. Clark, who was mixing up some sort of chocolaty dessert. Gwendolyn had known the question would be asked eventually and, she was ashamed to admit, had mentally prepared her answer during services that morning instead of listening to the sermon.

"He received a letter that was forged to read as my own. We think it could have been a prank from someone in Hopeton." She had to tell most of the truth otherwise the entire town would think Robert Jamison was some crazy lovestruck stalker.

"Can you help me with the spices?"

Gwendolyn stood and followed Mrs. Tyler to the counter and began measuring out ingredients.

Her aunt spoke next. "That's just the meanest—and you don't know who wrote it?"

"No, we don't. It could've been anyone, really. It could've been one of my students for all we know." Or it could have been the evil Frenchman who wanted her dead.

"So, everything is taken care of?" Mrs. Tyler said. "We don't have anything to worry about as far as Robert is concerned?"

"As far as Robert is concerned, yes. I believe."

They worked for another hour, chatting endlessly about Daisy's wedding arrangements, decorations, and foodstuffs, as well as the local gossip. Gwendolyn learned that Susan—Mrs. Adams' eldest daughter—had quite the green thumb, and that Sheriff and Mrs. Jenkins were crazy to be with child again. It would be their ninth.

Mrs. Clark had just pulled a tin of brownies from the stove when the kitchen door opened and Gregory materialized from behind it, looking tired.

"Afternoon," he mumbled in his usual endearing way, quickly glancing about the room. When his sea blue eyes finally met Gwendolyn's in a wave of obvious desire, she beamed with satisfaction. Oh, how she'd missed him!

She took a step forward but stopped in confusion when he broke their gaze to talk to his mother. "Where did Dan and Daisy want the kitchen cabinet to be kept?"

Gwendolyn watched as Mrs. Tyler absently dropped her stirring spoon in the steaming soup and looked at her eldest son as if he'd lost his mind.

"You've finished it?" Mrs. Tyler asked.

"Yes. Where does it go?"

Peering at Gregory beneath her eyelids, Gwendolyn wondered why he seemed so agitated and why he had looked away from her. Had she done something wrong? Had he been expecting her to visit him over the past couple of days?

"Gregory," his mother chided. "You promised you wouldn't worry about that until after the wedding."

"I've had some extra time."

Susie snorted.

"Well, when have you been working on it? You were putting in the doors and windows just yesterday."

Gregory shrugged impatiently. "So, I stayed up all night to finish it. What of it? Just tell me where the cabinet goes, woman!"

Mrs. Tyler glanced in Gwendolyn's direction and, for whatever reason, nodded with a mysterious smile. Was she trying to tell Gwendolyn something?

She placed a hand on her son's arm. "Might I talk with you privately for a moment, Gregory?"

His eyes swept the room, missing Gwendolyn completely.

There. He was avoiding her, but she didn't have a clue why. The only time she'd seen him since he proposed had been Friday in the mercantile, and as far as she knew, Robert hadn't said a word about their supposed engagement. Closing her eyes, she remembered the possessive feel of Gregory's hands on her abdomen and felt her heart skip a beat.

"Forget it," he barked, making everyone jump. He spun on his heel and left faster than he'd come.

Heaving a sigh, Mrs. Tyler went to the soup and fished her spoon out with a wooden spatula. "That boy," she breathed.

"Whatever is the matter with him?" her aunt asked putting her hand over her mouth.

Was she smiling? Gwendolyn wondered.

Susie slumped into a chair opposite Gwendolyn and hung her head. "Oh, he's just in one of his sour moods. It will pass eventually."

"I think he's jealous."

Everyone looked at Mrs. Clark, surprised to hear her voice after nearly an hour of silence.

"What makes you think that, Mrs. Clark?" Gwendolyn asked as both Mrs. Tyler and her aunt turned with their backs to her and began whispering.

Gwendolyn wished the woman's evaluation were true. She remembered Gregory's possessive touch in the mercantile and started feeling anxious and nervous at the same time. Although it went against everything she'd ever believed about the inequality of gender and such, she rather liked the idea of belonging to Gregory, of being his.

"I saw the way he looked at you," Mrs. Clark answered, scratching at the base of her tight hairdo. "Or, *didn't* look at you, that is. No doubt the entire town knows all about Mr. Jamison by now." The woman smiled faintly as she stared at the table and resumed her silence.

Of course! Gwendolyn realized, mentally smacking herself for her stupidity. Gregory had to have heard rumors about her and Robert from the innkeeper or Mr. Clark, at the very least. Robert had arrived four days before and likely announced their engagement as his order of business for coming to Grovetown.

But if Gregory had heard the rumors, he would also have heard them refuted. Surely he didn't still think there was any truth to them. Gwendolyn would just have to have a talk with him as soon as possible and get things straightened out.

"How much further is it?" Gwendolyn whispered to Susie as they approached Dan and Gregory's properties. She was beginning to regret her decision to carry the stew instead of presenting it to Mrs. Clark's son Warren. She was doing her best to keep it from sloshing out of the pot as Mrs. Clark guided the horse over a particularly rough bit of road. That last rock they'd run over had almost been the end of both the stew and her dress.

"It's just past the Adamses'…not far," Susie smiled.

Setting the rest of the food safely aside, Susie suddenly jumped up from her spot in the wagon bed and cupped her hands over her mouth. "Gregory…Dan…Daisy!"

"Susie Tyler!" Mrs. Clark scolded. "You sit down this instant."

Gwendolyn turned to see Gregory and Dan lugging a heavy chest inside Dan's house followed by Daisy, who was carrying an armload of linens. They didn't appear to have heard Susie.

"Susie!" Mrs. Clark hissed.

The young woman rolled her eyes then sat back down on her legs for the remaining few minutes as Mrs. Clark mumbled something about the proper behavior of young ladies. Once she got into the subject of petticoats and corsets, Susie and Gwendolyn looked at each other and burst into a quiet fit of giggles.

The wagon lurched over a small rut just past the Adamses' orchards, and a small field of tall, wavy grass greeted them. Behind an old wooden fence sat Warren and Jenny Clark's charming yellow house, which was lined with an assortment of wildflowers and just small enough to be adorable.

Mrs. Clark pulled the horse to a stop then came around to gather her tin of fudge brownies and a small jar of purple grape juice. After hopping out of the wagon, Susie turned around and took the pot of steaming stew from Gwendolyn's hands then made a face at the mess on Gwendolyn's apron.

"What happened to you?"

"It might have sloshed out a bit," Gwendolyn admitted, wiping the excess stew from between her fingers and trying not to think about how much her burns stung. Why couldn't Mrs. Clark have driven in the middle of the trail and avoided the rain-cemented ruts altogether? she wondered in irritation. The possibility that she might not be able to play for the wedding frightened her and she decided she must ask her uncle for some salve the minute she returned home.

She lifted a small basket of rolls and home-churned butter and followed the women to the front door where a young, blonde-haired man stood beaming at them.

"Mother…ladies…how good of you to stop by. Please, come inside." He led them through a small receiving room to a kitchen decorated in bold blues and faded yellows. Several miniatures of birds and woodland creatures rested on the icebox, cabinet, and round dining table.

Gwendolyn went to the latter and carefully placed her basket on top next to a vase of flowers, securing the cloth to keep the rolls fresh and moist.

"Miss Mitchell, how would you like to see the baby? I've just been dying to show him off."

Gwendolyn started. She didn't know whether to feel more uncomfortable by his calling her 'Miss Mitchell' or by him singling her out of the group. They couldn't have been good friends.

"Oh, I'd love to see him as well, Warren," Susie whined. "Could I, please?"

He looked uncomfortable then immediately relaxed, plastering a smile on his face that Gwendolyn knew to be false. "Ma, why don't you and Miss Tyler set down your things while Gwendolyn and I go get little Jake. We won't be long."

He discreetly tugged at Gwendolyn's elbow and she followed him in silence, staring at his back with curiosity. Warren, she noticed, didn't fit into his clothes as well as Gregory did. They were loose about his thin form and he wore suspenders. Gregory never wore suspenders.

When they reached the end of the hallway, Warren held a door open for her and she stepped inside. It was strangely dark and stuffy in the bedroom and she wondered why they had pulled the drapes over the windows. Perhaps it was easier for the baby to sleep by, she thought.

She took a step forward and ran into something just as Warren closed the door behind them, plunging the room into total darkness. A loud whack sounded on the hardwood floor in front of her and Gwendolyn jumped. She waited for a baby to start crying but heard nothing. What was going on? she wondered, feeling incredibly uncomfortable.

She backed against a wall, which was surprisingly close by, and started shivering as Warren's breathing grew heavier…and closer. She couldn't see him at all. "Mr. Clark…where have you brought me? This isn't the baby's room at all."

"Of course it's not. It's the closet, for heaven's sake." He took a hold of her arm. "Now hush up before someone hears us."

Gwendolyn gulped. "What are you going to do to me?" Surely he wasn't planning on forcing his attentions on her. He was a married man…and a *father!*

Abruptly, he covered her mouth with one of his hands. "I'm going to make sure you don't give us away, for starters."

She struggled against him, disgusted by the idea of being assaulted by a stranger mere feet from his wife, son, and mother. The only man she ever wanted touching her from that point forward was Gregory. Where was he when she needed him?

She struggled harder, knocking another thing to the floor. When Warren didn't let go, she grabbed the hand covering her mouth and bit it—hard.

That did the trick, for he let go with an angry growl. "What'd you do that for? I was only trying to talk to you."

"Then talk," she hissed, "and don't touch me again."

He let out a puff of air. "I–I wasn't *touching* you, Miss Mitchell. I was just…trying to keep you quiet."

Gwendolyn started tapping one foot on the floor, impatient for him to get on with what he wanted to say.

"It's my wife."

Now they were getting somewhere, she thought. "Go on."

"I need you to bring your uncle soon. I think she may have an infection in her…uh," he hesitated, but Gwendolyn had a good idea of what he was talking about. "Well, she can't feed our Jacob, you see."

Gwendolyn relaxed immediately then blindly swung her arm out, hoping it would hit him. It did—in the stomach. He deserved no less for scaring her half to death. And if they were to be caught—

No, she grimaced. She would *not* think about that.

"Then why all this fuss, Mr. Clark? Why go through the charade of pulling me into this dark and stuffy closet?"

"Jenny made me promise not to call for your uncle. She doesn't want anyone finding out about it. But she needs help, Miss Mitchell. I can't just let her suffer. And little Jacob isn't getting the nourishment he needs. I don't want him to get sick too. He's so small."

"What have you been giving him instead? It's been over a week."

There was a short pause. "Jen forbade me from asking anyone for help so I…uh, stole milk from the Adamses' cow during the night while everyone was asleep. I used the last of it just this morning and I don't dare go back. You know me to be an honest man, Miss Mitchell, but I feel terrible. The Adamses' have been so good to us."

Gwendolyn let out a breath of relief. She doubted Martha Adams or her husband would care overmuch that some of their milk had gone missing, especially if they were to discover why. "Don't worry, Mr. Clark. You've done the right thing. Your wife's condition is quite common, I believe, so she has no reason to be embarrassed. Not enough to put lives at risk." She didn't know how she knew that.

"But you can't let your uncle know I told you. Jenny would have a fit if—"

"Mr. Clark?" she interrupted, silencing him. She could just imagine him through the darkness, cowering against the closet door as if he'd said or done something wrong. His wife sounded like a selfish and prideful creature, certainly not the cluster of honey Cassandra Caldwell had described her to be. Gwendolyn knew she would never value her own pride over the health of anyone, let alone a helpless babe.

"I don't want you to worry about a single thing, Mr. Clark. I mean it. I've got a plan…and it won't incriminate you in the least. I don't know the entire story, I'm sure, nor do I know all the hardships your wife has been through in her life, but she has no right to endanger her own life or the life of your son. It's selfish and irresponsible. Do you understand?"

Silence.

"I can't see you. Are you shaking your head or nodding?"

"I understand."

She felt him fumble in the darkness for her hand then erupted with goosebumps when he brought it to his lips and planted a kiss on the back of it.

"Thank you, Miss Mitchell. You are a kind and generous woman, and I know I can trust you."

A married man was kissing her hand…in a closet…in the dark. She shivered. "Let's go see this little boy of yours, shall we? What was his name again?"

After he checked to make sure the hallway was clear, he helped her step out of the closet and they walked into the small baby's room.

"We named him Jacob Warren Clark—Jacob after my father and Warren after me. Jenny didn't want to name him after her own father, you see."

Poor girl, Gwendolyn thought. How would it be to live without any positive male role models in your family?

"I wonder if you might like to play a game with me," Gwendolyn said, casually taking up the chair next to her uncle in the parlor later that afternoon. She'd just returned from the Tyler's barn with a small milking can full of fresh milk. Mrs. Tyler hadn't asked any questions and Gwendolyn hadn't given any explanations. She hoped the woman would think she was gathering it for her two feline friends. The can was currently resting on the floor of her uncle's buggy.

Her uncle set his medical journal and reading glasses down on a small table and looked her squarely in the face, eyes wide with anticipation. "I would love to, Pinkie. Which one should we play?"

"I thought we could play a new…game."

He clasped his hands together and smiled. "All right."

"This is a game where you do exactly as I say without asking any questions."

He repositioned himself in the chair then gazed back at her curiously. "I'm intrigued. Go on."

She smiled. Getting him to cooperate was going to be easy, she thought. What fun they must have had. "I would like you to go and visit Warren and Jenny Clark…just as a friendly sort of gesture."

He paused for several moments before finally speaking. "This isn't a game, I imagine?"

"No."

"Well," he said, smacking his fists on the arms of his chair. "It would appear you've beaten me this round. I must away to hide my shame."

Gwendolyn couldn't help laughing. Her uncle was a very wise and funny man. "But before you go," she said as he stood, "there are some rules."

"No venting my frustration on the walls, I presume?"

"Yes, but you must also take the buggy and your medical case." She looked away, afraid she might give herself away. "You never know what might happen."

"Is something going to happen to me? Will I lose one of my pawns?"

"No, of course not," she giggled. "And you must not mention my name to either of them. Tell them you were just passing by after taking a look at Gregory's rib or head…or something."

"But that's a lie, Pinkie."

Shocked, Gwendolyn looked up. Her uncle wasn't really that prudish, was he?

He smiled mischievously at her before innocently gazing up at the ceiling, and she relaxed. He was only teasing her. "I suppose I could actually go and check up on Gregory, you know, just so I wouldn't have to lie to them."

"Good man." She smiled. "Oh, one more thing. Could you tell me where to find some salve? I burned my fingers earlier today."

"Same old Gwendolyn, I see." He returned to plant a kiss on her forehead then grabbed his coat. "I keep a special tube of it in the cabinet next to the stove. Your aunt likes to burn herself as well."

The following morning, Gwendolyn had awoken exhausted and sweating for the third consecutive morning. Visions of a man dressed in dark, drab colors, his cape billowing in the breeze as he watched her through the forest, began to melt away the minute she sat up in bed. But the fear, the consumable, aching fear lingered for hours. When she'd removed herself from the bed and begun dressing for the day, she had the strangest sense of foreboding. She could feel a dark emptiness surrounding her as if she'd died and was masquerading about in an empty shell of flesh and bone.

In the attic, hours later, the mystery of the dangerous Frenchman loomed over her. Who was he? What did he want? She couldn't possibly have done what he'd accused her of. It was all a big mistake, wasn't it? The idea that she might see him again—well, for the first time—haunted her. She desperately needed someone to talk to. Having always been bound to silence in order to keep her loved ones alive and well—she could understand why she'd left. What a lonely and harrowing life she must have led all those years he'd harassed her.

Giving up, she placed her violoncello back in its case. She couldn't concentrate on her music. Although she'd wrapped each of her stew-scalded fingers with bits of cloth and religiously applied salve every four to six hours as her uncle had instructed, they still stung each time she pressed down on the strings.

And Gregory was still avoiding her, so her soul's inspiration was gone. She'd attempted to speak with him the previous evening but hadn't made any progress. She'd ridden by horse to Gregory's house with the Tylers' spur tucked safely away in her bodice. But once Gregory had found out she'd traveled without an escort and in the dark, he'd lunged at her like an angry grizzly bear, jumped into the saddle behind her, and dutifully deposited her back home, making sure the Mathewsons didn't let her out of their sight again. It had all been rather humiliating.

And to top it all off, her sister Rebecca was due to arrive from Leadville at any moment. Her uncle Barrett had left with the buggy a little over an hour before, so she knew it couldn't be much longer.

Earlier that morning her aunt had informed her of Rebecca's imminent arrival. Secretly, Gwendolyn was grateful her aunt had waited so long to tell her. She knew it was silly but she was scared out of her wits to meet her real sister—a woman who shared her blood ties and whom she didn't know very well. Throughout Gwendolyn's life, Rebecca had only been able to visit once or twice a year and only for a week or two each time. Then there was also the memory loss factor to consider. Would her sister be loving and accepting, or would she just be plain heartbroken? Gwendolyn would find out soon enough, so worrying over it would just be a waste of time.

Gwendolyn sat in a spot of dust on the attic floor, not really caring whether her dress got dirty or not. She needed to wash herself that day anyway, so maybe she would just jump in the warm tub water, dress and all. It would certainly make things easier.

With a sigh, Gwendolyn slumped her head to the floor and fought to control her tears. Life was just really rotten. At that point, she was pretty sure things couldn't get much worse. Nothing seemed to be going right and she didn't have a clue how to go about fixing it.

"Gwendolyn, Papa has returned with Rebecca," Daisy's muffled voice called from behind the attic door. "She's waiting for you in the parlor."

Gwendolyn remained flat on the floor until the sound of Daisy's footsteps faded away completely. She stood up in resignation and, using both hands, smeared the tears from her eyes. It was going to be a long and emotionally exhausting afternoon.

Holding her chin up high, she walked out into the hallway and slowly descended the staircase where an unfamiliar, soft-spoken voice was speaking.

"Oh, it was fair," the feminine voice said. "It was just as long and tiresome as usual. I did, however, decide to splurge and buy myself an Italian soda." She paused before speaking again. "But I'm sure that's all rather fascinating for you to hear."

Splurging on a soda? Gwendolyn thought, laughing in her throat. Was she kidding? They couldn't cost more than a dime. Surely if she had the money to travel to Grovetown for Daisy's wedding she had enough to buy a mere soda.

Or, maybe she was being sarcastic, Gwendolyn mused.

Taking a deep breath, Gwendolyn turned around the corner just as her uncle Barrett was removing the woman's traveling cloak. Her sister was facing the opposite direction, which was nice of her because Gwendolyn wanted to get a good look at her. She had the same dark wavy hair and slender build but was a good couple of inches shorter than Gwendolyn had imagined a much-older sister to be. She was ashamed to admit it but the fact that her older sister was shorter than her helped ease some of her anxiety.

Gwendolyn's aunt, uncle, and Daisy all smiled at Gwendolyn as she approached, but they said nothing, which was rather odd. Their wordless gazes shifted back and forth between each of the Mitchell girls.

As if sensing her presence, Rebecca's back went rigid. She turned slowly, as if in a daze, with eyes bulging and face growing paler by the second. She mouthed Gwendolyn's name then stood gaping at her, her chin falling to the floor.

"Hello," Gwendolyn muttered uncomfortably. She didn't like the odd way her sister was staring at her. "It's good to see you, Rebecca."

Without a word, Rebecca lunged at her with both arms spread wide.

Gwendolyn flinched at the impact then groaned. Rebecca's small stature in no way affected her grip as she embraced her.

With one shaky hand and a nervous smile directed at her family, Gwendolyn patted Rebecca's back soothingly. It felt odd, hugging a sister she couldn't remember, but she decided she could get used to the feeling—in time.

Rebecca pulled away after a long moment and stared at Gwendolyn. Her eyes were a darker brown than Gwendolyn's and glistened with tears. "How?" she breathed.

Confused, Gwendolyn looked to her aunt. "You *did* write to Rebecca when I first got here, did you not?"

A blush crept up her aunt's face as she shifted in her chair. "Well, no I didn't. Now, don't be vexed with me, dears," she said, putting up a hand in defense as Rebecca clenched her own fists to her sides with barely concealed irritation. Her aunt directed her attention back to Gwendolyn. "Rebecca was already coming down for the wedding and couldn't get here any sooner. I didn't think it would do any good to tell her when she couldn't do anything about it. Besides, I thought it would be better for Rebecca to see you in person…like your friend in Hopeton thought when she sent you here."

"Hopeton?" Rebecca cried suddenly. "You were in Hopeton?"

Gwendolyn flinched at the pained look in her sister's eyes.

"But it's not even a day's travel from Leadville," Rebecca continued with a weak voice. "Why did you never visit? Or at least write to me? I've thought you were dead all these months!"

Gwendolyn didn't know what to say. Her aunt hadn't told Rebecca anything, not about her memory loss or even the fact that she was alive.

"And you," Rebecca continued, turning her attention back to their aunt and looking suddenly deflated. "How long have you known?"

Her aunt motioned for Rebecca to come and sit by her, but Rebecca was stubborn and remained still.

Marguerite sighed. "I haven't deceived you, dear. We knew nothing of Gwendolyn until she showed up almost two weeks ago. You wouldn't have gotten my message, if I'd sent one, for several days, and you said yourself that there were no trains to Poplar Grove last week. I thought I was making the right choice."

Rebecca stood motionless for a moment, her back as stiff as a wooden board, before spinning back to look at Gwendolyn with narrowed eyes. "Let me get this straight. Last August, you *weren't* kidnapped or lost in the woods. You intentionally deceived us…led us to believe you were dead. Why would you do that, Gwendolyn? Why?"

"I–I, uh—"

"Don't you know how much we loved you…*love* you? All these months we've been worrying and wondering and—"

"I was trying to protect you," Gwendolyn blurted in reply to her elder sister's accusatory tone. Appalled, she covered her mouth with her hands. How could she have given her secret away after only three days when she'd managed to keep it for years before? What was wrong with her? Had she, after all her silence and sacrifice to protect the ones she loved, actually put them in danger because her pride had been pricked?

Taking a step back, Rebecca stared at Gwendolyn in shock. "What on earth do you mean by that, Gwendolyn?"

Both Gwendolyn's uncle and Daisy looked at her with equal amounts of shock, but her aunt stepped forward, narrowing one of her eyebrows. It was obvious by the woman's posture that she wanted to hear more of an explanation, but Gwendolyn didn't dare. She'd already said far too much.

"I'm sorry," Gwendolyn said lamely. "I didn't mean to say that. What I meant to say was that I had a good reason. I left because I…love you all dearly." And she prayed they wouldn't question her further.

She had no such luck.

Her aunt Marguerite sidled up next to her and gently rubbed her thumb across Gwendolyn's cheek, bringing up some dust she'd missed when wiping away her tears. "You remember why you left."

It was more a statement than a question but Gwendolyn nodded anyway.

Confused, Rebecca looked up at their aunt. "Um, *what?*"

Cradling Gwendolyn's face in her palm, her aunt flashed her a bittersweet smile, nodded, and then turned to Rebecca. "It's a very long story, my darling. Let's talk…in the other room."

After shooing the rest of the family away, her aunt guided Rebecca down the hallway leading to the laundry room. Gwendolyn stared after them for a long moment, wondering why her aunt had taken Rebecca away to talk to her in private. Perhaps, she felt Gwendolyn had had enough emotional strain and wanted to help by telling Rebecca herself. Yes, that was it.

In the next moment, Daisy bounced in front of her. "You have your memory back," she cried, strangling Gwendolyn with affection. Uncle Barrett, she noticed, was shaking his head in amusement. "When did it happen? How did it happen?"

Gwendolyn eased out of the girl's embrace, feeling terrible for what she was about to say. "I don't have all of my memory back, Daisy."

Daisy's shoulders slumped and she frowned.

"It was just a couple memories," Gwendolyn added.

"But you remember why you left. That's wonderful news, is it not?"

Gwendolyn hesitated. "More or less." Daisy tilted her head to the side in confusion, and Gwendolyn continued. "Every memory I have helps me feel more confident in myself…helps me feel less afraid for my future, but it's also very frightening, you know. I don't always know what do to with the information." Or who to talk to about it, she added silently.

Daisy looked thoughtful for a moment then perked back up again. "Perhaps you could keep a diary of what you remember."

"That's a good idea," Gwendolyn's uncle said, chewing on his bottom lip as he came toward her. "I once went to a conference where several delegates mentioned that everyday objects could and did trigger memories in their patients. So maybe it's just a matter of exposing you to more of the things you surrounded yourself with or loved while growing up." He casually hooked his thumbs in the waist of his jeans. "Why don't you try recording what you were doing each time you had one of these memories…and how you felt afterward?"

Gwendolyn nodded. She looked up and smiled at the man before her, realizing she always loved him more than she had the moment before.

"Oh, and by the way," he added, whispering close to her ear. "Your little closet friend sends his best regards and sincere thanks, as do I, Pinkie."

Gwendolyn's eyes popped wide open as blood rushed into her cheeks. That beast Warren Clark! He'd told her uncle about the darned closet after he'd bound her to silence!

Uncle Barrett smiled down at her, obviously enjoying how uncomfortable the story made her. She scowled back at him in good humor for she knew he was only teasing her, but her competitive spirit vowed she would get that Warren Clark back one day.

Evening had begun casting its shadow almost half an hour past, dimming Gwendolyn's room at an unnoticeable pace. After a long pause, she looked down at her diary and realized the words were no longer visible. She'd written about all she could remember and decided she needed to stretch.

Heaving a hearty yawn, she searched her writing desk drawer for a match then lit a small candle. She grabbed the light and the empty plate that had once held a delicious slice of toasted cheese bread her uncle had brought up an hour before, and made her way down the hallway with Cinnamon at her heels.

It had been a little over an hour since Gwendolyn had seen her sister. She admired the woman, in a way. Rebecca had seemed exhausted at first, wholly passionate the next, and youthfully feisty in the end when she'd thought she'd been deceived. Rebecca did have a lot of information to deal with at once, but Gwendolyn hoped after the woman had a long talk with their aunt, that Rebecca wouldn't still be upset with her. She just couldn't bear that.

After setting her dish in the sink with several others, she crept into the pantry to search for something sweet to snack on. She still felt strange snooping around a house she could only remember being in for two weeks, but it was her home after all. Besides, her aunt had assured her it was all right to do so.

Dozens of bottled fruits and vegetables lined the shelves as well as sealed tins of baking goods, small sacks of grain, and miscellaneous tin canisters scattered throughout. When her eyes met with a nondescript orange canister partially hidden behind a wooden beam, she felt inexplicably drawn to it.

Swiftly, she set her candle on a metal dish behind her then spun around to grab the canister. It was much lighter than she had anticipated—almost weightless, as if there was nothing in it at all. With difficulty, she removed the lid and immediately gasped.

It was money—paper notes of varying monetary value. Why on earth would she remember where her aunt and uncle kept their money?

With a surge of panic, she replaced the lid and fumbled getting the canister back to its place on the shelf, safely behind the wooden beam. She pushed it a little further back, just for good measure, then her eyes caught something else.

Ah yes, she thought with satisfaction as a blue ceramic jar came into view—the cookie jar. She remembered the cookie jar!

She greedily reached inside and grabbed two cookies. They were oatmeal chocolate chunk—her absolute favorite. But they hadn't always been her favorite, she remembered. They'd only become her favorite when she'd discovered they were Gregory's favorite.

For the next several minutes, she stood in the flickering candlelight as she munched contentedly on her two cookies and listened to the creaking noises of the house. Well, perhaps she'd had more than just a couple cookies. She'd lost count.

It was while she was daydreaming about milk and cookie picnics she'd taken with Gregory years before that she heard muffled voices coming from the back of the pantry. Using great stealth, she tiptoed to the back and, with one ear, followed the sounds to a small knot in the wood wall.

"You think he's behind all of this—the fires, the attacks, everything? Surely, Aunt, you jest. He's as quiet as a mouse and keeps mostly to himself."

Fear prickled up the back of Gwendolyn's neck and over her entire scalp as she listened to Rebecca's quiet words. Her sister was still in the washroom with her aunt, and they'd been talking for what seemed hours.

With a quivery voice, her aunt Marguerite spoke next. "I'm almost certain of it. Some really odd things have been happening lately, Rebecca dear. Unexplained things—accidents and letters, and Gwendolyn has been acting unusually morose these past few days. Of course, that might just be because Gregory seems to be avoiding her for some reason. But from the clues I've picked up on, mostly from Gwendolyn, I truly believe he is the only one who could be doing this. I think it's been going on for years."

*What?* Had they really just said Gregory was behind everything? Gwendolyn tried to imagine Gregory hitting himself on the head, enough to nearly kill himself, then she hit herself instead, trying to knock some sense into her stupid skull. They weren't talking about Gregory. They were talking about someone else, but who?

A long pause followed. Gwendolyn hissed through her teeth, impatient for the conversation to continue.

"Have you talked with him lately?" her aunt continued. "Is he still angry with her?"

That's it, Gwendolyn decided with finality, not bothering to listen for the answer. She jumped up and grabbed her candle before marching out of the pantry around to the washroom. She knew from the moment she'd opened her eyes that morning that the day boded ill for her. Everyone's quiet acceptance of her moodiness, their strange behavior since Robert Jamison had shown up on their front step, her aunt's strange comments and uncharacteristic shyness—it all boiled down to one thing. Her family was keeping secrets from her—secrets she had a feeling would change everything once they were finally revealed to her. She would simply demand to know what they were. It was her life, after all, and she had a right to know.

Angry, and a little bit nervous, Gwendolyn pushed the washroom door open to reveal her uncle, who was sitting on a wooden stool with one ankle resting casually upon his other knee, and her aunt and sister, who stood beside a large laundry bucket full of murky water. The look on Gwendolyn's face must have shocked them into silence because they all just gaped at her, waiting.

Gwendolyn took the opportunity to speak first. "Who were you just talking about?" she demanded. "And don't tell me it was Gregory because I won't have you thinking such absurd things about the man I love. He is a good man of sound character."

She caught Rebecca smiling but didn't think what she'd said was humorous in the least.

"Gwendolyn, dear," her aunt said carefully. "Were you listening in on our private conversation?"

"Yes, but it wasn't my fault. I was in the pantry looking for some cookies and heard you through a knot in the wall."

Her uncle busted out laughing then looked at Gwendolyn with what she could only describe as admiration. "Oh, Pinkie," he said, wiping the mirth from his eyes. "It's a good thing you're such a curious creature or problems would never get solved in this family." He smacked a large hand upon one knee. "Marguerite, darling. Why don't you tell our little Pinkie what it is we've been keeping from her for her whole life, hmm?"

*"Barrett!"*

"What?" he said in defense. "I think it's about time Gwendolyn knew the truth, don't you?"

"*I* do," Rebecca added confidently.

Aunt Marguerite looked terrified at the very thought.

"I think I have a right to know, Aunt," Gwendolyn assured her with the friendliest expression she could muster.

"Then will you tell us what you meant earlier when you said you were protecting us by leaving?" her aunt countered.

Gwendolyn flinched. She should have seen that one coming. She closed her eyes and began to speak. "I know it may seem completely illogical and hypocritical of me to say this, but I won't know whether I can tell you the truth of it until after you tell me what you have to say. Actually," she amended, opening her eyes, "perhaps not even then. But please believe me when I say I'm aching to tell you everything."

The three of them each raised an eyebrow at her and she suddenly felt very foolish. What reason did they have to trust her?

"Pinkie, come and sit by me."

Gwendolyn walked over to her uncle and sat upon the crate he fashioned as a chair for her. The other two women settled and Gwendolyn prepared herself for the worst.

"We have a brother," Rebecca blurted.

Gwendolyn sucked in a gulp of air then sat motionless, staring at the woman she felt she barely knew.

Aunt Marguerite scowled at Rebecca.

"What? I was only trying to move things along. Besides," Rebecca said, examining her cuticles, "you looked like you didn't know how to start."

Uncle Barrett chuckled beside Gwendolyn. "You've had twenty years to prepare for this, Marguerite. Let's get on with it."

"You hush up!"

"Is it true, do I really have a brother?" Gwendolyn held absolutely still, afraid she would awaken from the awful, yet earth-shattering, nightmare she was currently living.

Her aunt nodded slowly.

She had a brother. It didn't come as nearly so great a shock as she thought it should, and she couldn't fathom why. Then another thought struck her. "He's the Frenchman Melissa was babbling about, isn't he? Robert?"

"What! He's been here?" Rebecca's head bobbed back and forth between the three of them like a dog watching kids bounce a ball in a dirt road. "I don't believe it!"

"But we have another Frenchman in town named Robert," her

uncle said.

Rebecca scowled. "There are two Frenchmen named Robert in this little town? Could they be the same person, by chance?"

Gwendolyn didn't think it was possible. Robert Jamison wasn't a violent man. On the contrary, he was quiet and reserved.

Oh, no, she thought, realizing she'd repeated almost exactly Rebecca's description of the man her aunt suspected of all the attacks. "Aunt, you said they couldn't be the same person, didn't you…the morning after Robert visited?"

Rebecca turned up her nose. "Robert came by and *visited* you?"

"I don't think they're the same person," her aunt answered, putting up a hand to stop the oncoming female hysteria. "Although I'll admit it is a frightening coincidence. But I suppose we won't know for sure until Rebecca sees him. Your uncle and I have only seen Robert twice since he was born, and only during his childhood. So, we wouldn't recognize him. He could very well be Robert Jamison, but I'm almost certain he is not."

Gwendolyn swallowed, repulsed by the idea that Robert Jamison could actually be her brother. Certainly he wasn't so mad as to pursue a relationship with her and kiss her. Ick!

She looked down in her lap and realized she still had a cookie clutched in her left hand. She'd completely forgotten about it. Hoping to get the awful taste of Robert Jamison—who could be her brother Robert Mitchell—from her mouth, she stuffed the confection in and rolled it around awkwardly until it became small enough to actually chew.

Her aunt looked at her pityingly and Gwendolyn swallowed.

Once she finished the last of the not-quite-as-delicious-as-she-remembered cookie, she spoke again. "But why have you kept him a secret all these years?" Based on all the events she could remember or had record of, she had a good idea as to the answer but didn't like to make presumptions. They usually got her into a good deal of trouble.

Both her aunt and sister glanced at each other, silently communicating with their eyes.

"Gwendolyn, dear," her aunt started, as she so often did. "Marie—your mother—died shortly after giving birth to you. We Bellamont sisters have always had complications with childbirth, you see." She heaved a sigh then continued. "After the funeral, your father shut down. He was so heartbroken he stopped taking care of himself, as well as the three of you. When we traveled back for your father's funeral, your uncle and I made arrangements for Rebecca and Robert to stay with some friends in the city. We didn't have a lot of money, you see, and our friends had children closer to their age. We thought it best to keep them there where they could stay in school and be around those they were familiar with."

Here aunt hesitated a moment before continuing. "Your mother wrote to me often before she died and expressed her concern for Robert. She'd said he'd grown quiet and aloof upon hearing of her pregnancy and that he became more angry as the time for your birth drew near. It wasn't until your father's funeral—when we realized the extent of your brother's bitterness—that your uncle and I decided it would be best to take you home with us."

Gwendolyn looked at her uncle Barrett, who was staring at his hands and smiling, and melted with gratitude. How hard it must have been for both of them, for her aunt to have so many miscarriages, and then lose both her sister and her sister's husband. She was grateful to have been born, at least for her aunt and uncle's sake.

Rebecca picked up on the story next. "Robert took our parents' deaths too hard. He turned quiet and angry, and a few years later he started drinking with his friends. He was much too young to be doing such a thing, in my opinion. But once he was old enough to live on his own, he declared everlasting hatred for you—don't ask me why—then moved back to our parents' house. I lost track of him after that. I had heard in town that he'd developed quite a reputation for gambling."

"Do you see now why we've kept him a secret from you, dear?" her aunt asked.

Gwendolyn shook her head, not thinking the knowledge of a brother's hatred for her enough to keep his existence a secret. In fact, she would have given a great deal to know.

"At first, we didn't tell you because you weren't old enough to understand, you see. You were such a free-spirited girl, always happy and spreading your sunshine on others. Once you grew up and became a fine young lady, we were—"

Her uncle cleared his throat suddenly and her aunt scowled.

"All right, *I* was too afraid to tell you," her aunt corrected herself. "You were such a sweet thing. I–I didn't want it to destroy you, Gwendolyn."

"But you said I'd mellowed out over the years," Gwendolyn said, "that I grew very quiet just before I left Grovetown. Why didn't you tell me then? I might not have left had I known."

Her aunt looked at her strangely then hung her head. "I'm not a brave person, Gwendolyn. I never have been. I have many regrets, and my not telling you about your brother is one of the biggest ones." The woman started sniffling then and Gwendolyn felt terribly guilty. She knew her aunt had made the wrong decision by not telling her, but she couldn't fault the woman for it. Had the roles been reversed, she understood how difficult it would have been to reveal.

"My brother hates me because I caused the death of both our parents," Gwendolyn thought aloud.

Rebecca shifted uncomfortably. "That may have been his original reason, but surely he's adult enough to realize it was no fault of yours. You were an innocent and beautiful child. And he's thirty-one years old, for goodness sake!" she scoffed. "I certainly don't blame you for it. He can't possibly still be mad at you for that."

Taking a deep, calming breath, Gwendolyn stood and faced her family with resignation. Yes, she had to tell them what she knew. But she would have to keep them quiet about it. "I assure you he still blames me and I think I can prove it to you."

"How can you possibly know that for sure, Gwendolyn?" Rebecca asked incredulously. "You didn't even know he existed ten minutes ago. And what about your memory loss?"

Gwendolyn seethed inwardly, fighting to maintain control of her emotions. Could her sister be any less understanding? It was obvious Rebecca knew she was the older sister, but Gwendolyn didn't worry about it overmuch. In a few moments, her sister would realize she was wrong.

Gwendolyn's breath caught suddenly but she managed to whisper, "Come with me."

Her aunt, uncle, and Rebecca followed her out of the washroom, up the staircase, and down the darkened hallway in silence. Gwendolyn was trembling beyond control. She knew in her heart that she was doing the right thing, but that knowledge didn't make it any less terrifying.

She stopped before the attic door and spun around.

"Good grief, Gwendolyn," her uncle said, taking a soft hold of her arm. "You look as if you're about to faint. Breathe."

Ignoring her uncle's concern was the only way she knew she would be able to finish what she'd started. She needed to tell them what she'd planned to tell them, and she needed to tell them fast.

After taking several shallow breaths, she plunged on. "Can I put my full trust in you to not tell *anyone* about what you see or hear unless it's absolutely necessary?"

Uncle Barrett frowned. "Of course, Pinkie."

Her aunt and sister nodded as well, looking concerned.

But Gwendolyn needed them to know how important their agreement was. "From what I've been able to discern, I've kept this secret for years…and I've done it to protect you." She paused, taking a moment to rid herself of her lightheadedness. "You'll understand what I mean once I show you."

With her uncle's support, she opened the attic door and ascended the steps as if in a daze. After lifting the lid of her mother's violoncello case, she dipped her hand behind the ripped velvet and produced a handful of cards and letters.

"Last Friday," she began, directing her attention to her aunt, "when Mrs. Tyler came over to read Mrs. Maynard's letter, you gave me this letter which came for me by post." She handed the topmost page over and listened as her aunt read it aloud to the rest of the group. The moment she was finished, the three of them simultaneously stared at Gwendolyn with varying levels of shock, disbelief, and horror. The powerful intensity of their gazes frightened Gwendolyn more than the letter had and she fought to keep the tears away.

"I had another vision after reading that letter. I saw a man with dark hair and sinister eyes watching me through the trees and I saw this hiding place in mother's violoncello case. That's how I found the rest of the letters. Read them."

The three of them shuffled through the letters one by one, taking turns making various sounds of shock and disbelief.

"It really is Robert, isn't it?" Rebecca uttered to no one in particular.

Gwendolyn's eyes met with her sister's as dreadful understanding swept over her. "My own brother."

# Chapter Fourteen

IT WAS THE DAY BEFORE Dan and Daisy's wedding and the two families were alive with preparation. At the Mathewson house, Gwendolyn and Rebecca had first prepared the chicken salad sandwiches and lime sorbet before moving on to the cakes, cookies, and pudding. In a copse of trees outside Orchard Cottage, the Tylers were busy setting up chairs for the ceremony, as well as the decorations provided by the committee—sky blue bows, lace ribbons, and arbors woven with delicate cream rosebuds and ivy.

Screwing up her nose in concentration, Rebecca carefully poured hot chocolate pudding into several glass dishes. "I heard that you've gotten yourself engaged to Gregory," she said, pouring the last of the confection with a satisfied flourish. "Is it true?"

Gwendolyn placed spoonfuls of cookie dough on a baking sheet while she waited for the other sheet to finish baking. "Yes, it's true," she said, blushing slightly. "At least, I think it's true. I haven't seen Gregory since last Friday." She hesitated slightly, afraid to voice her concerns to a woman she'd only just met but needing someone to talk to. "Do you think something could be wrong, Rebecca, that he could be angry with me for some reason?"

Although Rebecca was eight years older than Gwendolyn and had lived hundreds of miles away, the two of them were very much alike. Among their physical attributes, they shared the same temperament and were not afraid to speak their minds. Gwendolyn knew her sister was stronger and more confident than she was and hoped she could ease her own mind about Gregory. She really needed someone to talk to since Daisy was busy upstairs with Aunt Marguerite altering her wedding dress and would be gone and married in less than a day.

"Have you done anything to anger him?"

"No! Well, at least I don't think I have. He seems to be avoiding me but I cannot think why."

Rebecca smiled then came around the table to give Gwendolyn a hug. "I don't think he's mad at you, dear sister. He's just jealous, is all."

"Jealous?" she said, realizing Rebecca was the second person to say that. "How have you come to that conclusion? You haven't even been here a whole day."

"Daisy told me everything…last night, while you were resting. You know how she loves a good story, Gwendolyn, and you've got some of the best, you have to admit."

Gwendolyn rolled her eyes. As much as she loved her cousin, she was glad her family hadn't told Daisy of Robert Mitchell. She might have told Dan, and Dan might have told Gregory, and that just wouldn't do. She wanted everyone to stay as safe as possible. She feared she had already revealed far too much.

"She told me how Gregory reacted when he saw Robert in the mercantile," Rebecca continued, carefully putting the tray of pudding in the icebox. "It sounds like jealousy to me. Are you keeping track of those cookies?"

Gwendolyn spun around to open the stove. "Oh, good," she said with a sigh. "They're not burned."

Grabbing the dishtowel, she pulled the sugar cookies out and rested them atop the stove next to a bowl of blue icing, then put in the next batch. "But why would Gregory be jealous? He has no reason to be. He doesn't even know why Robert is in town."

"My dear baby sister," Rebecca said, sitting in the nearest chair and beckoning Gwendolyn to sit beside her. "I've been around men a bit longer than you have and believe me…he doesn't need a reason. But just think on this a moment…how would you have felt if a rich, beautiful stranger showed up one day and started pawing all over your man?"

"Robert wasn't *pawing* at me."

"All right," Rebecca drawled. "Perhaps Daisy exaggerated. But how would you have felt Gwendolyn, truly, if a gorgeous young woman tried to stake her claim on him with her body…sidled up next to him and brushed her glove against his strong tanned arm?"

Gwendolyn immediately pictured Melissa Morrison with her tight blond curls, conniving flirtation, and overflowing cleavage and knew her answer. "Yes, I see what you mean."

A knock sounded on the front door and Gwendolyn's heart immediately started pounding. "You answer it," she prodded.

"Why don't you?" Rebecca said, teasingly. "It could be Gregory."

Gwendolyn growled. "That's why I want *you* to answer it."

Rebecca stood and, with a wave of encouragement from Gwendolyn, walked to the front room to do her bidding.

Gwendolyn sat with her back flawlessly straight then nervously began playing with her nails as she waited. It had been six excruciatingly long days since Gregory had last spoken to her—a fact that didn't seem to puzzle Gwendolyn nearly as much as it had a few minutes ago. She had to admit both Mrs. Clark and Rebecca's estimations of Gregory's behavior sounded more than plausible. In fact, Gwendolyn was disgusted with herself for not having discovered it first. Why else would he have touched her with such familiarity? He wanted Robert to suspect she was with child and *with* Gregory in every way.

"Gwendolyn?" Rebecca popped her head into the kitchen and whispered, "It's Robert Jamison. He wants to speak with you. I put him in the parlor."

Gwendolyn slumped her shoulders in disappointment. What on earth did Robert Jamison want with her this time? She thought they had settled everything. He should have been halfway to Hopeton already.

"By the way," Rebecca continued and Gwendolyn looked up to see her sister's poorly concealed amusement at the situation. "He's not our brother, in case you were wondering."

"All right," Gwendolyn said more to herself than anyone else. She'd known all along that Robert Jamison couldn't be her brother. She just couldn't picture him with a cape tied about his neck, watching her in the woods as if he were a dark lion about to pounce and devour her. He was too sweet, too simple of a man to plot or, really, be angry with anyone.

Moaning, for she loathed having to talk with the man she'd hoped was Gregory, for the second time, she stood and walked to the parlor without bothering to touch up her hair or straighten her skirts.

Robert stood upon seeing her and immediately started fidgeting with the bowler hat he held. "G–Gwendolyn," he stammered.

"Robert."

Silence followed for what seemed an eternity. Robert stood looking in every direction but hers and she wiggled her ankle impatiently beneath her skirts. Heaving a sigh of impatience, she finally asked, "What is it you would like to say to me, Robert?"

He jumped.

Rolling her eyes at his theatrics, she calmly said, "You don't need to be afraid of me. I think you know me well enough by now for you to know I'm not mad at you, don't you think?"

Robert's tension melted away to reveal a familiar, friendly smile. "Oh. So you're not angry with me then?"

"No," she stated flatly. "Although I will be if you don't tell me what it is you've come to tell me…and soon." She was losing her patience. Dan and Daisy were getting married the following day, and there were still a dozen things that needed to be done. And besides all that, she still wasn't satisfied with her song and was antsy to practice.

Robert hesitated nervously then grew serious once more. "Is there a more private place we can talk?"

Turning in the direction his eyes were pointing, she saw Rebecca walking to and fro about the kitchen and decided it would probably be a good time to visit the Tylers.

"Would you care to walk with me?" Gwendolyn suggested. "There are some wedding things I need to get from the Tylers. Their place is just down the road a little ways."

"Wedding things?" he asked, looking startled. "Surely you're not marrying so soon."

"No. It's my cousin Daisy."

Robert relaxed, then beamed in approval.

After grabbing the bonnet Daisy had retrieved for her and giving instructions to Rebecca, she preceded Robert out the front door to the cool spring air of Grovetown. A strange knot formed in the pit of her stomach but she tried to ignore it.

They walked side by side for several minutes and silently enjoyed the sounds of chirping birds, clicking grasshoppers, and water trickling in the nearby stream. Being outside and enjoying the beauties of nature always helped Gwendolyn feel better. Everything just seemed simpler outside of town away from the noisy shops and the gossipy townspeople, certainly simpler than in Hopeton.

With a sigh, she spread a hand out and fanned it through the tall grasses. The noonday sun was hot and did nothing to ease the soreness in her back. She couldn't wait until she could remove her tightly laced boots and slip into bed for the night.

"I imagined you'd be on the train to Hopeton by now," she started carefully. "Have you changed your mind?"

"I haven't made a decision yet."

Gwendolyn hesitated, hoping his feelings weren't contrary to what he'd admitted to her before. "What reason do you have to stay? Your entire life is in Hopeton."

"I'm beginning to think that my future life is here."

Gwendolyn stopped in the road then looked up at Robert, gulping involuntarily. "What do you mean?"

He turned and stared at her in confusion. "I am not here to cause you grief, Gwendolyn. If I do decide to stay here in Grovetown, it will not be because of you. But if it's possible, I'd like to remain friends. Do you think we can?"

She stared at him warily, wondering if he was just up to some of his usual mischief. When she couldn't discern any, she resumed her place at his side but remained cautious. "All right," she said, walking with him down the dirt path once more.

"My grandfather...died recently," he said suddenly.

"Oh, I had no idea! I'm so sorry." How could she not have known Robert's grandfather had died? He always told her everything. His grandfather had to have died quite recently, possibly right after she'd left Hopeton. She placed a comforting hand on Robert's shirtsleeve, not knowing what else she could do to help ease the pain he had to be feeling. She would need to remember to write the Jennys a letter. "Were you close?"

"I spent many of my childhood summers with him at his estate in Belpointe. He was the president in some publishing company. He taught me to read."

Gwendolyn listened quietly and wondered why he was telling her such a story.

"Neither of his children expressed a great interest in his company," he continued. "A few months ago, my grandfather sold the entire thing. We didn't know anything about it until he died." He paused. "He must have known he was on his way out, I reckon."

"That's terrible," Gwendolyn said absently.

"I thought so too."

With her hand, she gestured for them to turn down the trail to their right that was lined on both sides with a charming white picket fence. The air was sweet with apple blossoms hanging overhead, but somehow, it wasn't nearly as sweet as it was the day before.

They walked beneath a canopy of blossoming trees that provided some shade. It was a blessed reprieve from being out in the open with the sun glaring down on them. In fact, it wasn't long before the shade and news of Robert's deceased grandfather chilled her. She lifted her shawl and wrapped it more securely about her neck and shoulders.

"I'm sorry if I've caused you discomfort," Robert said, looking at Gwendolyn with concern. "The reason I tell you these things is so you understand my situation better. My family met with my grandfather's lawyers last week. It would seem that he…well—" Robert slammed his hands into his coat pockets—"he left me a good deal of money, you see."

That would certainly explain his sudden change in dress, Gwendolyn mused, and his wearing cologne. She had always known Robert to be indifferent to city life, satisfied to walk about wearing his leather apron as well as the soot and sweat from working many hours near the ironsmith's forge. But just because he inherited money from his grandfather didn't mean that he had become a different person. Well, she admitted to herself, money did do strange things to people.

"Please say something, Gwendolyn," Robert said, interrupting her thoughts. "What are you thinking?"

Honestly, she couldn't really think of what to say since she didn't know why he was telling her such things. From the very first moment she saw him that morning, she felt a nagging in the back of her mind and had a good idea of what it could be, but she desperately hoped she was wrong.

"I'm very sorry your grandfather has died," she said carefully, "but I'm glad your relationship with him has ensured that you can support your life's ambition. I'm sure you're overwhelmed with gratitude, despite your loss."

Robert nodded. "Yes, indeed. A great burden has been lifted from my shoulders. He was a great man, my grandfather."

"What do you plan to do?"

"I was considering staying and working with Mr. Clark. It would really be the perfect opportunity for me, you know? I can't get that in Hopeton…not with Mr. Cunningham and his six sons. They own every shop in Hopeton and are well established. There's no opportunity for me there."

Gwendolyn was silent. She was happy for Robert and his success, really she was, but she was having mixed feelings about him staying in Grovetown, especially after everything that had happened of late. No doubt Gregory would be furious once he found out.

"Where will you stay? You can't live in the inn all summer, surely."

They approached the outer gate of Orchard Cottage, and before she had the chance, Robert jumped ahead and swung the gate open for her. "After you, milady."

Frowning, she stepped across the threshold. She hated his awkward little bouts of etiquette. During the winter, when she'd finally recovered enough to get out of bed each morning, Robert would take her for gentle sleigh rides through town. She liked him better then when he would allow her to enter the carriage on her own and sometimes drive the team.

Robert merely smiled at her, then continued. "Mr. Clark's going to clean out the old room in his shop. I don't think his wife was too keen about the idea, but I assured them both that they would not regret hiring me on for the summer."

"I hope the gossip about our false engagement hasn't hampered their opinion of you, Robert."

"Oh, I think it will be all right. Of course, you could just marry me and put an end to all the gossip."

Gwendolyn stopped dead in her tracks and glared at Robert as he turned around to face her a few seconds later. Could he be teasing?

"Please tell me you're joking."

He took slow steps back to her then removed his hat. "No, I'm not joking."

Something inside her knew he wasn't joking even before he'd said it, and she mentally kicked herself for being so foolish. That was why he'd looked so nervous in the parlor earlier, fidgeting with his hat as he was doing once again. That was why he wanted to speak with her privately. Everything began to suddenly fall into place—the clothes, the cologne, Cinnamon, his oddly formal behavior, his job with Mr. Clark, his mention of the inheritance his grandfather had left him—everything was for her. She thought she would have learned a lesson after her less than pleasant experiences with both James Morrison and her brother.

She stepped back a couple feet. "Robert, you told me that if you stayed in Grovetown it wouldn't be for me. You said you wanted to remain friends. I can't do this, Robert. I'm going to marry another man. I'm in love with Gregory, Robert, not you!" She lifted a hand to her heart and tried to steady her breathing. She thought she'd already explained that to Robert, already explained that she admired him and enjoyed his company but had no romantic or long-term inclinations toward him whatsoever. What was he thinking springing such a thing on her?

"I was hoping you would change your mind."

"I'm not go—"

Suddenly, Robert's finger was on her lips, silencing her. She stared up at him, wanting very much to unclench her jaws and bite him.

"I have money, Gwendolyn, enough to care for us both throughout the whole of our lives. You won't have to teach ever again if you don't want to. We can buy a nice big house out in the country somewhere and you can have all the fine dresses you want. You won't ever have to worry about a thing." He pulled her close, burying her face against his stiff white collar that reeked of cologne. "I'll take care of you."

Gwendolyn sighed, more out of impatience than comfort. "Are you quite finished?"

He pulled back then released her with a groan.

"Thank you," she said, brushing the feel of him from her sleeves then standing squarely in front of him. "First, if you think all I care about is money, you're seriously mistaken."

"But I can care for you better than Gregory—"

"Second," she interrupted, raising her volume a notch. "You can't know me very well if you'd think I'd stop teaching. I love teaching and I love my students. I love helping them, feeling like I really can make a difference in their lives, seeing the looks on their faces when they've discovered something new or figured out a puzzle. I love their curiosity and cherish their youth. You know that."

Robert's hopeful expression slowly melted away to reveal emotions she couldn't quite decipher. Understanding, perhaps?

"Third, why on earth would I want a big house? It would take all my time to maintain, to keep clean…and what would we put in it, for heaven's sake? I do not care for expensive or frivolous things…and if we lived in the country, what use would fine dresses be to me?"

He frowned. "It doesn't have to be dresses. I could buy you anything you ev—"

"And last," she said, calmly but surely, "you are not in love with me, Robert, and I am not in love with you."

"You could grow to love me."

"I *do* love you, Robert, as a friend. But I am not *in* love with you."

"What's the difference?" he shouted with exasperation. He put his hands on his hips and glared at her as he waited for an explanation.

"If you do not understand the difference, then you are most surely not the one for me." With that, she walked the remaining hundred feet to Orchard Cottage, leaving Robert in the road with only his thoughts for company.

"You didn't happen to see Gregory outside, by chance, did you?"

Gwendolyn joined Mrs. Tyler at the table in the kitchen and looked about at the wide array of flowers, leaves, and materials. The lace Gwendolyn had brought by the night before had been transformed into a beautiful veil with roses weaved into the crown and delicate blue ribbon streaming from it.

"No," Gwendolyn said. In fact, she'd been so distracted by Robert that she'd completely forgotten Gregory was helping Dan and his father set things up outside. She desperately hoped he hadn't seen her with Robert. Or at least, hoped he'd only seen the part where they were arguing.

"Oh. Good. I was afraid my plan had been ruined."

Gwendolyn screwed up her face in confusion. "What plan is that, Mrs. Tyler?"

"Don't you think it's about time you called me Sarah? I mean, we're basically family, are we not? And you'll be marrying my son in a few months."

Gwendolyn watched as the woman expertly arranged the leaves, rosebuds, and ribbons into bouquets for the bride as well as for two bridesmaids and the mothers. "I'm not so sure that's going to happen anymore."

Mrs. Tyler stopped what she was doing and stared at Gwendolyn in awe. "What on earth do you mean, child?"

"I haven't seen Gregory for days. I think something must be wrong."

"But you still love him."

Gwendolyn nodded.

Lifting herself from her chair, Mrs. Tyler went to the breadbox and pulled out a small, half-eaten chocolate cake. "Now, this is a special cake that I only eat when I'm feeling low. I call it my 'emergency chocolate.'" She grabbed two plates and two forks from the cupboard and sat back down. With a wave of her arm, the bouquets and veil were pushed aside. "Would you care for a piece, my dear?"

A slow grin spread across Gwendolyn's face. "I am quite sure I will adopt this 'emergency chocolate' idea of yours…Sarah."

"That's my girl. Now," she said, placing a generous slice on each plate then handing Gwendolyn a fork, "let me tell you about my plan."

"What do you plan to do?"

Robert Mitchell tilted his head down at the woman who was turning out to be quite an asset, more so than he had anticipated. The lethal beauty had managed to separate Gwendolyn from her lover—a lover who was supposed to be dead. But, Robert mused, better not to have the man's blood on his hands. The attack had done the trick and Gwendolyn was too petrified to even get close to Gregory.

Robert chuckled at the thought.

His plan was going even better than he had originally thought out. He could have done everything on his own, of course, but having Melissa, and possibly James, at his continued disposal had its advantages. If everything went according to plan, the Morrison twins would get all the blame and he could finally ride west to start his life over. Of course, James had been in jail during the attack. That had been more bad luck, but Robert would be well on his way out of Grovetown before he could be caught.

"How is your brother?" he said, flashing Melissa his best smile.

# Chapter Fifteen

GWENDOLYN RAN THROUGH THE FOREST, her boots crunching the frost-covered leaves into the earth. She had to get away from him—the man clothed in the dark, tattered cape and crumpled hat. He never seemed to move but was always behind her no matter how fast she ran.

Ahead, there were only trees—stark and naked, their limbs reaching out to tear at her clothes and skin—but she kept running. She had to get away, far away.

Her chest began to burn and her legs ached as she charged through the forest. Her aunt and uncle had warned her about leaving the house alone. She knew she should have listened but she'd been cooped up for so long. She needed the fresh air. She'd known there wouldn't be many more days like it before the winter storms would hit.

The house was only a little further, just beyond the trees. She should have reached it by then.

She looked back. He was still there—only yards away and getting closer.

The trees grew smaller and smaller with every step and it seemed only seconds before she was swallowed up in the darkness of the approaching night.

Frantic to find someone who could help her, she cried out.

Suddenly, the man was right behind her. She tried to scream but his hand stopped her. She shivered as his moist breath touched her ear in a whisper.

She wriggled out of his grasp easily—too easily—but she didn't wait around to question it. His cold, hard touch seemed to give her the extra energy she needed to get away. With more power than she realized she had, she flung herself over the dead branches, leaves, and unforgiving earth and was able to put some distance between them.

Where on earth was the house? She couldn't possibly have passed it, could she?

A wolf howled in the distance. The cold of night began to seep through her clothes and chill her to her very marrow.

She looked back, then froze. The man was gone!

Quickly, she scanned the forest for any sign of him.

Nothing.

She strained her ears but heard no crunching leaves. Her teeth began to chatter and she turned back to head home.

"Oof!"

She looked up to see what she'd run into and screamed as her gaze met with the man's blood-red eyes. "Let me go!"

His unforgiving hands grasped her shoulders and held her firm. The voice that spoke next was low and raspy and made her stomach churn. "I told you not to tell anyone, Gwendolyn. So now I have no choice but to kill you."

She struggled in his arms—using her teeth, her fists, her knee—but nothing seemed to work. He took each blow as if she were no more than an irritating fly buzzing about. Her tactics were no match for him. That was it—she was going to die.

"No," she screamed. "No!"

"Gwendolyn? Darling, wake up!"

"Let me go!"

Gwendolyn suddenly felt herself being shaken and shot her eyes open. Her aunt Marguerite was sitting on the bed beside her, looking dreadfully worried. "Aunt Marguerite?"

"Were you having another nightmare, dear?"

After finally realizing where she lay and what day it was, she sat up and pushed herself back against the headboard. With one hand, she rubbed her eyes then yawned mightily. "Ugh, yes," she mumbled. "What's the time?"

"Eight o'clock. Just like you asked. Are you going to be all right?"

"I'm fine." She gave her aunt the best smile she could muster then pushed herself out of bed. "I'll be downstairs in about an hour to help. Will that be all right?"

"Of course, dear. I think just about everything has been taken care of." Her aunt flicked a tear from her cheek. "It's hard to imagine that both of my girls will be leaving so soon."

"Oh, Aunt. We'll all be living close by. It won't be that different." In fact, she thought as she went to her dressing table, she'd still be living in her aunt and uncle's house if Gregory kept avoiding her.

Gwendolyn brushed through her hair quickly as her aunt watched. She tried putting it up in several different styles before finally deciding on a simple French twist like the one she'd seen Daisy wearing almost two weeks before. She preferred her hair down usually, enough to cover up her scar, but pulled back just enough so as not to interfere with her violoncello performance. She realized then that she hadn't thought much of her scar for several days.

"Oh," Gwendolyn chirped. "I think I forgot to mention that I'm going to be playing a song for Dan and Daisy. It was supposed to be a surprise. Do you think someone could set aside some time for me after the ceremony…or, perhaps announce when I might do it?"

"What a wonderful idea!" her aunt said, clapping her hands gleefully. "That will be absolutely perfect. But are you sure you feel comfortable doing that? What about your memory loss?"

In all actuality, Gwendolyn was petrified. She had tried so many times not to think about playing in front of nearly every member of the town nor the thoughts that Mrs. Tyler had told her were going on in Gregory's mind about her. No, she would not think about that. Daisy was her cousin and Gwendolyn loved her like a sister. Besides, what was the point of having such an instrument, and knowing how to play it, without performing now and then? "I want to do this for them, so it will be fine."

Her aunt smiled and her eyes shimmered. "Bless you, darling. Bless you." She wrapped her arms around Gwendolyn and squeezed her gently. "I love you. I hope you know that."

"Of course I do." How could she not? Her aunt and uncle had provided and cared for her all her life and she loved them dearly for it. She squeezed her aunt tighter, relishing the feel of having a real family and feeling like she belonged somewhere.

"I know I don't say it enough, but I do love you, Gwendolyn, just like a real daughter. I don't ever want you to forget that."

Gregory stomped to his place beside Dan in front of the wedding gathering and growled angrily. He'd spent the last twenty minutes avoiding a very persistent Melissa and trying to find Gwendolyn, but the latter was nowhere to be found. He supposed she was with her aunt and sister, helping Daisy with her dress and other such nonsense women did, and hoped she wasn't off in the woods sparking with that Jamison fellow.

He felt terribly empty as he remembered the previous day. He'd just finished having yet another argument with his father when he'd looked up to see Robert Jamison embracing Gwendolyn in an obviously passion-driven state. His heart felt as if it had been cut in two.

The fact that Mr. Jamison was a wealthy man and could obviously provide for Gwendolyn better than he ever could, didn't sit well with him. In the past, Gwendolyn had never cared a wit about money, but she was a different person. She'd proved it to him during the past several days. She'd lost her memory and cared for different things than before her accident. She'd spent nearly a year in the city and understood what it had to offer.

"What's wrong with you, old man?"

Gregory scowled at Dan who was, indeed, looking quite a bit younger than he in his freshly pressed shirt and ebony waistcoat.

Feeling ridiculous, he looked down at the creases in his own tailcoat but decided he didn't really care how he looked. He just wanted to get through the ceremony as quickly as possible so he could talk to Gwendolyn and set things straight.

"Lighten up, Greg," Dan said, slugging him in the shoulder and ignoring Gregory as he winced. "I'm marrying the love of my life in just a few minutes."

Gregory let out an impatient groan and forced himself to stand still, but in the next moment, he nearly leapt from his place. Gwendolyn was no more than thirty feet ahead of him. He was about to go to her when he saw a man trailing behind her.

Feeling his heart fall to his stomach, he watched as Robert Jamison took a seat right next to Gwendolyn. Gregory expected her to turn her attention to the man but she looked up instead. Their eyes met.

Come to me, Gregory plead inwardly. *Come to me!*

She flashed him a smile then moved her attention to Robert.

Gregory groaned. "The love of my life will soon be in the hands of that man."

"Sorry, brother. What did you say?" Dan asked.

Gregory scowled at Robert as his heart burned and his knuckles ached to pound something. "Nothing."

The soprano began her aria and the ceremony commenced. Gwendolyn excused herself from Robert's side to join the bridal procession at the back but paused when a hand reached out and touched her arm. It was Warren Clark. Gwendolyn watched as he mouthed a "thank you" to her then winked, then squeezed his hand in understanding.

At the back, she gathered her lady's bouquet then slowly followed Carrie and Katy Adams down the aisle as they tossed cream-colored rose petals to the ground. They looked so adorable in their matching dresses and braided crowns.

After what felt like an eternity, Gwendolyn reached the front of the procession and took her place opposite Gregory just outside the arbor. They were a bit further apart than she would have liked. She snuck a glance in his direction but he remained ramrod straight as he watched the rest of the wedding line. Dan, however, was beaming.

Gwendolyn followed his gaze and watched with pride as Daisy glided down the aisle to join Dan, the man she loved with all her heart. Her dress was a magnificent white with a tight bodice and puffy, elbow-length sleeves, accentuating her small frame. Her honey-colored hair was pulled back into an elegant coiffure with flowers and her veil, and her smile made her shine like the sun, as always.

The preacher began to share a few words about the couple then proceeded with the ceremony. Gwendolyn couldn't help watching Gregory's face. He looked angry. She knew she shouldn't be surprised. His mother had warned her about how he felt, but that didn't explain why he was avoiding her gaze at that moment. She'd wanted to talk to him before but hadn't had a chance. Right then, he didn't seem to want to have anything to do with her.

"I now pronounce you husband and wife."

Feeling a little melancholy, she watched as Dan and Daisy shared their first kiss as a married couple beneath the rose-covered arbor. She was happy for her cousin but she wanted to throw herself into Gregory's arms, force his face to meet hers, and kiss him soundly on his delicious lips.

The guests erupted with congratulations, clapping in their shared excitement. Gregory, Dan, and Daisy moved to sit with the rest of the guests and Gwendolyn looked to find her seat. Susie Tyler seemed to be sitting in it, talking excitedly with Robert. Gwendolyn didn't mind. She would be getting back up in only a few moments and she didn't want to give the town any more wrong impressions about her and Robert. In her opinion, he should have sat with the Clarks. They were, after all, going to be his family as the Jennys had been her family all those long months.

After Mr. Tyler thanked everyone for coming and officially offered his congratulations to the married couple, he announced Gwendolyn's part in the ceremony.

Trying desperately not to shake and give her nervousness away, she grabbed her violoncello and bow and sat in a chair Mr. Tyler had provided for her. She adjusted her skirts and got her instrument situated then looked out at her audience. For a second, her eyes met with Gregory's before he stubbornly looked away. She would have to give him more time.

Instead, she turned to look at the obvious joy in Dan and Daisy's faces and smiled. It was their time.

Taking a deep breath, she positioned her bow against one string, closed her eyes, and began. In her mind, she saw what she always saw when she played her song. It was raining all around her. Not too far off in the distance she could see Gregory walking toward her with determination, wearing the scowl she was beginning to love.

Instantly, he pulled her into his arms the way she often dreamed of. She breathed his soapy lavender scent in and reveled in the powerful feel of his masculine form.

But then, as never before, she saw herself in a small boat. She was rowing down a gentle creek through a curtain of willow branches. The crickets were chirping and a gentle wind rustled through the brush. Off to her left was a small bit of ground next to a large willow tree. She rowed to the side and stopped next to a fallen log, using it as her anchor as she exited the boat. The base of the tree was somewhat hollowed out and provided a perfect niche to sit against.

Gwendolyn marveled at the memory.

As the song swelled to its peak, Gwendolyn tried not to think about the painful welts in her fingers. Instead, she thought of Gregory's possessive energy as he'd kissed her, the male-driven hunger he'd exuded as their bodies touched. She leaned into her instrument as Gregory had leaned into her and rocked it ever so slightly. Remembering the dreadful ache he'd left in her heart after pulling away, she couldn't stop the tears from flowing down her cheeks.

As her song began its decrescendo, a lovely breeze made its way through her hair and she moved her face to embrace it.

She held the last note for several seconds then waited in silence for a moment before opening her eyes once more. The moment she did, her eyes caught sight of a dark form in the trees past all the guests, but only for a second before it disappeared. Had she imagined it?

She didn't have long to think about it before all in attendance erupted in applause.

Wiping the tears from her eyes, she stood and bowed her head nervously. Her aunt Marguerite, Rebecca, Mrs. Tyler, and Daisy all joined her at the front and embraced her.

"Oh, my darling!" her aunt said through her own tears. "I have never heard you play with such feeling. To be sure, your own mother never learned to play so well. And you arranged that yourself?"

Gwendolyn nodded, rubbing the sting out of her burned fingers.

Daisy embraced her tightly. "Gwendolyn! That was absolutely the most perfect gift you could have given us. How did you do it?"

Gwendolyn blushed then watched in astonishment as Daisy shared a few tears of her own. The fact that Daisy rarely showed any serious emotion made moments like this one extra meaningful.

"I know how hard this was for you, but I am so grateful you shared this with us."

After hugging her once more, Gwendolyn spoke her next words with fervent conviction. "I'm so glad to have you as a sister."

The minute she pulled away, Mr. Tyler grabbed Daisy's hand in his right and Dan's hand in his left and hoisted their arms up. "To the bride and groom!"

During the entire performance, Gregory had held his breath. He'd watched the obvious passion in Gwendolyn's face as she played through the piece and knew she had to be an angel or a wooded nymph. The fact that she could play with such mastery, depth, and feeling after such a traumatic accident and after so little time, proved she was as baffling and mysterious as he'd always known her to be. He knew at that moment that even if he couldn't have her as his companion, he would love her and yearn for her long after the day he died.

He sat for a moment in stunned silence as everyone around him stood and clapped. Gwendolyn had an amazing gift. There was no doubt about it. It was unearthly. He felt like jumping up and shouting it to the world.

He waited until most of the guests had offered their compliments and gone to the refreshment table before standing. Gwendolyn was still surrounded by admirers—mostly male, he noticed—including Warren Clark, Simon Adams, and Jesse Jenkins. When his eyes passed over Robert Jamison's frame, he spun around and stomped toward the house.

He and Dan's construction business was quite successful. They had more business than they could keep up with and made enough money to keep themselves and a small family. Perhaps not as well as a rich city suitor could, but definitely enough to provide for all the essentials. Being the wife of a Tyler would be much harder work, he knew, but he and Gwendolyn's love would be enough to sustain them, surely.

"Leaving the festivities so soon?"

Gregory came to an abrupt halt but did not look up. He didn't need to. The high-pitched syrupy voice gave her completely away—Melissa. Why she insisted on following his every move when he'd made it impossibly clear he despised her was beyond him. He shoved past her and took the four back steps in one leap before entering the house.

"Why didn't you tell me you wanted to be alone, darling?" she said, stepping over the threshold behind him. "From the way you were behaving earlier, I thought you were avoiding me."

"I was avoiding you, Miss Morrison," he growled, "and I'm avoiding you now."

There was really no point in being civil with the girl. Any hint of it might send her crumbling to her knees begging for his love.

He knew he couldn't stomach the sight of it, especially not after witnessing Gwendolyn in the arms of Robert.

"Darling, don't you think it's about time you called me 'Melissa?'" She followed him into the sitting room, the hoops of her skirt swishing with every step.

He watched in idle fascination as the ridiculous arrangement of bows and ribbons on her bustle fluffed up as she sat on the edge of a chair. "I did not invite you into my father's house, and I am not your darling."

She giggled. "Perhaps there's another name you wish me to call you?"

Her sticky flirtation was getting on his very last nerve. Ignoring the snake, he walked past her again and entered the kitchen.

"Oh, but where are you going?"

"As far away from you as possible." He hastily removed his wedding coat and, before he could also remove his tie, he jumped back in surprise.

"You can't leave now!" Melissa whined, clinging to him with what felt like more than just two arms. "I need you!"

Turning up his nose, he stared down at her. Her cheeks were rosy but she looked scared out of her mind. She didn't love him. What an actress she was, he thought. He grabbed both of her twig-like arms and thrust them from his shoulders with a disgusted growl.

At the window, Gregory replaced his more comfortable leather jacket and hat then paused. He moved the draperies aside and stared past the glass to the fields. He could have sworn he'd seen the shadow of a figure moving past. No one in their right mind would dress in such a color for a wedding. It was unlucky.

"Please stay with me," Melissa crooned. "I've really missed you these past weeks."

Slowly, he turned back to glare at her for several seconds then whisked himself safely outside, out of the woman's reach.

Melissa was a menace, a conniving seductress that refused to understand, no, practice proper customs because of her selfishness and plotting. She deserved to be locked up somewhere without any mirrors.

With a sigh, he gazed about his father's fields. He still couldn't believe the effort everyone had gone to in order to get the fields finished, and it had been Gwendolyn's idea to surprise him. He'd promised his father he would get the planting done, but he'd gotten so many unexpected orders just before Gwendolyn had arrived, he'd been overwhelmed and didn't want to let his father down.

The Tyler farm provided the bulk of the crops for the town, and if they weren't ready to harvest it in the fall, they'd get behind on their shipments and storage and the food would go bad. They'd lose a third of their profits for the year. He was more relieved than he was willing to admit that the work had been done. He would have never gotten it done in time.

But with Gwendolyn no longer his, he knew that working in the fields would be a constant reminder of his loss.

He looked up to see his sister coming towards him at an awkward pace. Figuring the girl was just trying to pull him into the crowd of Gwendolyn's admirers, he dropped his head and pretended to look busy.

"Gregory," Susie breathed heavily. "I've just heard the most alarming news."

"Oh?" He scratched the back of his neck then fiddled with the knife he kept in his pocket. It would be typical of Susie to come up with some fantastic story in order to get him to do what she wanted, but he wasn't in the mood. He waited patiently.

"I was just talking with Jillian and she said that her father let James out of jail today." She paused then frowned. "Well, aren't you worried?"

He shrugged his shoulders. "The sheriff said he wouldn't let him out until tomorrow evening. Jillian is just telling you stories."

Scowling, Susie thrust her hands on her hips quite like their mother did when she was about to give them a lecture. "She is not telling stories. I just saw him for myself."

Gregory jumped. "Who? Who did you see?"

"James, of course! Who else? I saw him walking that way." She pointed across the fields toward the barn.

Gregory felt all the blood drain from his head. Although he

knew James couldn't have been the one to set their barn on fire or attack him in the woods, he had tried to kill Gwendolyn. Gregory needed to find her. "Where is she?"

"Gwennie? I don't know. I thought she was with you."

They both looked at each other and their eyes went wide with realization.

"Get Pa…and Dan…quietly. Go now!"

Sucking in her apprehension, Susie gathered her skirts and went back to the tents as Gregory ran toward the barn. Something wasn't quite right. Melissa's persistent flirtation, her strange insistence he stay in the house, the attacks, the dark figure that ran past the window, James' early release from jail—everything pointed to danger, everything pointed to Gwendolyn.

Gregory ran as fast as his broken rib would allow and prayed his suspicions weren't correct.

"Oh, Gwendolyn," Rebecca gasped. "You were simply amazing! You must play for me every time I come to Grovetown. Will you?"

"I suppose I could. It would certainly give me good reason to practice."

As promised, Gwendolyn led her sister toward the Tylers' barn. After she'd related the story about the fire, Rebecca had insisted on seeing the stallion for herself. She couldn't blame her. Living in such a big city as Leadville, away from the trees, wild animals, and beautiful flowing streams, had to be very tiresome. Once Gwendolyn had made it to Grovetown and smelled the fresh pine, moist earth, and apple blossoms, she knew she couldn't be happier anywhere else.

The structure still smelled of charred wood. The Tylers had replaced a couple of the main supporting beams but the majority of the reconstruction had yet to be completed.

They walked down the corridor and had almost made it to the last stall when a man stepped in front of them. James.

Gwendolyn screamed but was immediately silenced by one of his large hands.

"You let go of her!" Rebecca screamed, pummeling him with her small fists. "Let go of her this instant!"

"Be quiet!" he ordered.

Since James' arms were occupied with keeping Gwendolyn from yelling or escaping, Rebecca was able to deliver a particularly painful blow—without too much effort—right in his rear. Immediately, his hands dropped Gwendolyn in a heap on the straw covered ground then rubbed the offended area with a growl of pain.

Rebecca rushed to Gwendolyn's aid and carefully helped her up. "Are you all right?"

As Gwendolyn struggled amongst her skirts to stand, she heard James mutter, "You're both in grave danger."

"He's right about that."

Both women spun around to see the figure of a man holding a pistol silhouetted at the barn's entrance.

Gwendolyn felt all her nerves squeeze in fear as she finally beheld the demonic man from her dreams with her very own eyes. He was smaller than she remembered but no less frightening. She turned her head slightly toward Rebecca. "It's him," she choked. "He's come to kill me."

Rebecca slowly moved in front of Gwendolyn, shielding her from their brother. "Why, Robert?" she said carefully. "Why have you been torturing her all these years?"

He took several steps forward but Rebecca remained straight without flinching. Gwendolyn, on the other hand, was breathing faster and faster the closer he came. Was that really it? she wondered, shaking painfully. Was he really going to kill her—his own sister? She clutched the back of Rebecca's dress to keep from crumbling to the ground.

"Why?" he asked with a hint of mockery that made Gwendolyn sick. "Why else? She murdered both our parents!"

Gwendolyn cringed. Her brother was mad! She may have been the cause of her mother's death but it certainly hadn't been her choice to be conceived. She was just an infant!

She felt Rebecca's arms come around and touch her sides protectively. "Robert, you and I both know that Mother was a high risk pregnancy, so don't you go blaming this on Gwendolyn. The doctors warned them."

"But why did she live when it killed Mother? If she had been the one to die," he said, pointing the gun at Gwendolyn, "both of our parents would still be alive."

"You can't assume that," Rebecca retorted. "Mother could have developed an infection or died from blood loss…or from the loss of her child. And Father could have died any number of ways. He could have gotten robbed in the street, shot, or run over by a team of horses."

Robert took several steps closer and stopped only a couple feet away from them. "Move aside, or I shall have to kill you both."

"Killing Gwendolyn isn't going to take the pain away," Rebecca said softly but confidently.

The next moment, he grabbed Rebecca by the collar and shook her roughly. The fire in his eyes blazed with anger as he pressed his gun to Rebecca's throat. "How would you know, woman? I watched Mother suffering all those months she was carrying and knew she was going to die. You were only seven. You couldn't possibly understand the hell I went through."

With his last words, a speck of spittle hit Rebecca's cheek. She didn't flinch.

"If you loved Mother so much," she said coolly, "then why did you leave her to go drinking in town with your idiotic friends? Why were you gone when she needed us most?"

Gwendolyn gaped at Rebecca, astonished that her sister would intentionally provoke a madman who was holding a gun against her throat. She admired her sister's courage but she would be darned if she'd allow Robert to kill her.

"You lie!"

"That's it, isn't it?" Rebecca continued, ignoring Robert's increasing anger. "All these years you've been blaming Gwendolyn for your own failings. You couldn't have saved Mother. There was nothing any of us could have done."

When Gwendolyn saw her brother's face droop slightly, she decided to take advantage of the situation. With fear pounding in her chest, she quickly pushed Rebecca aside before recklessly ramming her knee into Robert's groin.

In the next instant, she heard a whooshing sound and turned to find James drop from the rafters above, followed by a rain of dust and straw. He stood with his back to them. Was he trying to help them?

"Get back," he shouted over his shoulder.

Too confused to object, Gwendolyn turned back around and pushed Rebecca into the adjacent stall. Surely there would be a window they could escape through.

Just before she joined her sister, she heard an earsplitting shot and spun around. Both James and Robert stood still, staring at each other as if they were about to start a duel. But when James listed to one side and eventually slumped to the ground, Gwendolyn understood what had happened. Rebecca's gasp from behind added to the horrific reality.

Too afraid to move, she looked over to find Robert's pistol still smoking from the shot he had fired. Lifting her gaze, she watched his mouth curve into an evil sneer of satisfaction.

Before she knew it, he had snatched her by the arm and thrown her into the opposite stall. She landed painfully against her elbow and hip, but she quickly forgot the pain as she looked up to see the barrel of his gun staring straight down at her.

Rebecca screamed in protest and beat against her brother's back.

"Touch me one more time," he warned in a low growl, "and I'll shoot you in the stomach." Once convinced he had Rebecca where he wanted her, he glared down at Gwendolyn with his hateful eyes. "Any last words?"

At first, Gwendolyn wanted to shout for him to go to hell, but then she noticed the slump of his shoulders, the creases between his eyebrows, and the darkened color beneath his eyes and felt only pity for the pathetic creature. "I'm sorry for all you've suffered, Robert."

She closed her eyes then lowered her head on her bent knees.

The lives of those she loved and cared for were worth far more than her own miserable existence. She would welcome death if only it meant they could all live.

"I love you, Gregory," she whispered, praying he could hear her.

As she waited for Robert to deliver his deathly shot, she heard Rebecca's voice pleading for her life. Gwendolyn tensed. Soon it would all be over.

A sound so unexpected came from deep within Robert's throat rather than from the pistol, and Gwendolyn had to look up. Confused, she watched him walk away from the stall without firing a single shot, as if giving up entirely on his pursuit of twenty years. Had help come for her and Rebecca? she wondered with a sudden burst of hope.

However, his next utterance extinguished all hope. "To hell with the both of you!"

He fired three shots in quick succession at the partition of the stall next to hers—the stall holding her monster of a stallion. She watched in horror as the horse kicked a hole through the partition, and she immediately ducked as splinters of wood came raining down upon her. What on earth had possessed Gregory to purchase such a beast? she wondered. She backed up against the far wall and tried to drown out the sound of the horse's wild neighing and grunting as it echoed through her ears.

"Robert, no!" she heard Rebecca scream just before the horse broke through the wall and came bucking toward her, its hoofs rumbling the ground she sat upon.

The second that Gregory heard the shots coming from inside the barn, he felt his heart drop to the pit of his stomach. Nothing, not the pain he felt or the danger he knew he was running into, mattered at that moment except for Gwendolyn. He had to get to her.

With a rifle in one hand, he vaulted over the corral fence and headed for the barn. Just before he reached the entrance, he heard a woman scream.

"Robert, no!"

Robert? he thought, feeling ill. Was it possible? But where was James?

Gregory threw the leather strap of his rifle over one shoulder, sidestepped to the front entrance, and took aim. "Robert!"

"Look out!"

Gregory instantly dropped to one knee, narrowly missing the shot fired at him. Reflexively, he fired a shot of his own at the dark shadow inside then remained poised and ready for another.

"Gwendolyn?" he said shakily. He listened carefully but heard only the sounds of that blasted stallion, most likely frightened by the gunshots.

Cautiously, he took a couple steps forward—enough to see inside the darkened barn—and was shocked to find not one man on the ground but two, as well as a woman. It was Rebecca Mitchell. She'd been the one to warn him.

"Gwendolyn?" he repeated more loudly.

"Gregory, help! The stallion—"

"Put the gun down, Mr. Mitchell, or I'll put it down for you."

Knowing his father stood behind him, Gregory looked at the man he'd shot lying before him. Mitchell? he thought in confusion.

The man's eyes were on Gregory's as he pointed a gun at his chest.

But Gregory still had his much larger weapon aimed at the man's head. He held completely still then jumped in alarm as a shot rang out. He watched in amazement as the man's gun flew from his hand and hit the back wall of the barn with a loud thud.

Gregory slowly turned around and stared at his father in astonishment.

"What?" his father said nonchalantly as he walked past his son. "You've seen your old man shoot before, haven't ya'? Now, go save Miss Gwendolyn from that stupid horse of yours."

Gregory was shocked to discover Gwendolyn hanging from the

rafters by her hands and boots as the stallion roared and pounced mere inches from the hem of her skirts.

"I don't want to hear any jokes about the indecent state of my skirts, Gregory. Just help me down."

He chuckled with relief before climbing the cross boards outside the stall. Once at the top, he used one arm to pull Gwendolyn safely from the rafters and, despite her squeals of protest, threw her over his shoulder.

Safely on the ground once more, Gwendolyn immediately embraced him. "It's over, Gregory. It's all finally over." She kissed his cheeks as he stared at her in bewilderment then ran to her sister's side. Gregory scratched his head, more bewildered than he'd been in years.

"Are you the bastard who's been tormenting Miss Gwendolyn all these years, Mr. Mitchell?" Gregory heard his father say to the wounded maggot bleeding all over their barn floor from a wound in his leg.

He went to stand beside his old man, feeling immensely proud of him and grateful he'd reached the barn when he did.

His father continued. "And are you the bastard, Mr. Mitchell, who's been setting fire to our barn, killing our livestock, sabotaging our shipments, and stealing our supplies?"

Gregory looked down at the man, seeing only pure hatred reflected in his eyes. He squatted down. "Are you the bastard, Mr. Mitchell," he said, mimicking his father, "who tried to kill me?"

Just as he stood, the man spit a mouthful of tobacco-colored saliva on Gregory's boots. Gregory heard Rebecca, who was conscious once again and bleeding from a blow to the head, gasp at the vile display.

Gregory looked to his father who nodded with firm approval. "Go ahead, son."

After Gwendolyn urged her sister to look away, Gregory's boot met violently with Mr. Mitchell's face, knocking him unconscious.

"These men tried to kill you, Gwendolyn, and I'll be darned if I try to help them!"

Gwendolyn sighed as she watched her uncle clean and dress Rebecca's wound with great care. She understood her uncle's position and couldn't blame him really. She was angry too, from all the years her brother had harassed her and for the position he had put her in before she'd left for Hopeton. Her life was forever changed because of him and his hatred. But something inside her told her that showing kindness towards him was the right thing to do.

"James tried to warn us, Uncle," she reasoned. "The reason he got shot is because he tried to help us."

"From the little I've heard of him," Rebecca offered, "he sounds messed up in the head. But he did try to save us, Uncle. He stood up to Robert unarmed."

Uncle Barrett shook his head in defeat. "All right, you two. I'll help James. But I draw the line at helping Robert. I don't care if he is your brother. He is a good for nothing. Let him rot."

Gwendolyn heaved another sigh. "Then, Uncle, I will need your instruction and guidance when I go to help him. I'll be going to the jailhouse in a quarter of an hour."

"There's no convincing you out of this, is there?" her uncle asked with a rueful expression. "I will only help you if you allow Gregory to be there…for your own protection."

Gwendolyn nodded. She knew Gregory would be livid about the idea, more so than her uncle, but she knew she had to do it. No matter what her feelings were for her brother, she would help him.

Her Uncle Barrett stood by her next to the kitchen table and laid a big hand on her shoulder. "You're a good woman, Gwendolyn, too good for the likes of me."

# Chapter Sixteen

GWENDOLYN PAUSED MID-STEP as she approached James' bedside holding a bowl of fresh water and a compress. He had been feverish for nearly an entire day, thrashing about his bed sheets and muttering unintelligible phrases until Gwendolyn thought she'd go mad.

But this time was different. This time she understood what he was saying.

Quickly, she deposited her bowl on the nightstand then bent over him, gently putting her hand against his fevered brow.

"Rachel," he moaned groggily. "Rachel."

She stood up in confusion. She couldn't recall having met anyone by that name in Grovetown. Perhaps the woman, or girl, was deceased and no one spoke of her.

Or, Gwendolyn mused, perhaps the woman was someone else her family had decided not to tell her about—another sibling or cousin?

But that didn't explain how James Morrison knew about her.

Her memory focused on the discussion she'd had with Gregory by the river and she suddenly remembered his words—"There are rumors that he's married a girl from Clarksville, and that he's ruined another young woman."

Could Rachel be one of them?

With a shrug, she doused the clean cloth in water and expertly wrung it out before replacing it on James' forehead.

An hour earlier, her uncle Barrett had come in to check the wound and found, to his dismay, that the area had become infected. He had pushed her out of the room then so he could remove as much of the infected area as possible without her fainting dead away. But he'd needed her help afterward. Gwendolyn had had to hold her nose as he applied a foul smelling poultice of vinegar and some type of herb before covering it once again with several layers of gauze.

She watched James' chest move up and down as he lay calmly atop the bed once again and shook her head. How could something so foul smelling possibly help one to feel better? she wondered in disgust. Well, that and the laudanum.

She slumped back down in her chair and resumed writing about the events just after the wedding. As she did so, she couldn't help thinking back to just a few days before when she'd sat watching over Gregory. How awful it had been, wondering if he would ever wake up and look at her with those eyes again.

A blush crept up her neck and cheeks as she remembered the feel of his lean body next hers, warm and welcoming.

No, she thought, shaking her head. She must not think about such things. She must not think about his wavy unkempt hair, or the confident way he walked, or the look in his face when he teased her—

"I didn't mean to hurt you."

Gwendolyn's head snapped up and she fastened her gaze on James. Awkwardly, she stood over him. "James?"

"My dove. I didn't mean to hurt you."

She stared at the man in front of her with eyes bulging. Was he talking to her?

Instinctively, she looked up at the bedroom door to make sure no one else was listening before leaning over to whisper to him. "James, are you talking to me? It's Gwendolyn."

He remained silent and she scrunched up her forehead in confusion. Gregory had told her James had had feelings for her in the past, and could possibly still, but for heaven's sake, were they enough to call her by such an endearment? Dove, she scoffed.

"James?" she said cautiously.

"I'm so sorry I hurt you."

Gwendolyn started to assure him he'd been forgiven, especially after defending her and Rebecca from their deranged brother in the barn, when James interrupted her.

"I didn't mean to kill you."

Gwendolyn was just starting to realize how warm she felt and how small the room actually was. She jumped up to open the window a crack, hoping to alleviate some of her nervousness.

She was being ridiculous. The man likely had no idea what he was saying or who he was talking to. Gwendolyn hadn't been killed—she was most definitely alive! But she pinched herself just to make sure.

Ignoring the nagging feeling in the back of her mind, she sat back down. Forgetting all propriety, she raised her feet to rest against the nightstand as she madly scribbled words into her diary.

"What the devil are you doing in here?"

Gwendolyn flinched as she crossed the jailhouse's threshold, her uncle and sister in tow. It had taken a great deal of persuasion to get him to accompany them even though Gregory had not shown up at the Mathewson house as originally planned.

Sheriff Jenkins stood, pulling his trousers high over his portly stomach. "This ain't no place for nice ladies such as yourselves."

Ignoring the sheriff, Gwendolyn walked past the only other cell in the jailhouse, which was empty, and sat in the chair next to her brother's. "Robert. I was hoping we could talk."

"About what?" he growled.

She gulped involuntarily, and the moment she did, Robert burst out laughing. It was the sort of laugh that made a person boil with rage, or want to punch somebody right in the nose.

She remained still, however, her face impassive as she patiently waited for him to finish with his immature display.

"Out with it, then!" he roared with a mocking tone. "Or are you too afraid to speak to me?"

"How dare you talk to my—"

"Uncle," Gwendolyn said, putting a steady hand on her uncle's arm as he took a step toward Robert. "It's all right."

The man was silent but kept a furious gaze on his belligerent nephew, as if he would pound the young man into the ground with his stare alone.

Gwendolyn turned back to look at her brother who was sneering at her through the cell bars. She noticed him clutching his bandaged leg as he lay on his cot. "How are you feeling, Robert? Does your leg pain you still?"

"I don't recall ever confiding in you about the condition that idiot of yours, Gregory, put me in."

Rebecca leapt at him. "You put yourself in this condition, you loathsome creature!" she shrieked as she pounded on the bars with her fists. "You don't think of anybody but yourself."

Turning her gaze to the sheriff, Gwendolyn asked carefully, "Has he not taken what we left for him yesterday?"

The sheriff shook his head wearily.

Gwendolyn looked up to her uncle and sighed. "You're right, Uncle. It was a bad idea to come here. I'm sorry."

Just before Gwendolyn followed her uncle and sister out of the jailhouse, she heard Robert mutter, "What does she mean 'we'?"

The sheriff replied, not bothering to hide his amusement. "Gwendolyn and Doc Mathewson were in here yesterday. Yes, they were, you sorry lout. Gwendolyn—your sister, *and* the one you've been trying to murder all these years, I might add—was tending to your wounds all by herself." He pulled his hat off and scratched at his scalp. "Only God knows why she would care after what you've put her through."

Gwendolyn scowled at the sheriff, not appreciating his last comment. He could have done without it, surely.

"This ungrateful bastard should know about it, Miss Gwendolyn," he said, raising his hands in defense. "He'll be eating humble pie in no time, you mark my words. He and I are going to become the best of friends."

Even though it was just past sunrise, Gwendolyn felt exhausted by the time the three of them returned home. She simply couldn't understand Robert's intolerable hatred for her. Rebecca seemed to think he had been smothering a secret hatred for himself since their parents' deaths by blaming everybody else. Her aunt and uncle believed he enjoyed blaming others for his own failings and hurting others to cover up the pain he felt inside. Gwendolyn didn't know what to think and doubted she would ever know.

In the kitchen, she wrapped a blue apron about her shoulders and waist and proceeded to make a plate of toasted bread with strawberry preserves. After her meeting with Robert, she'd lost most of her appetite.

Several minutes later, she found her aunt at James' bedside. "How is he?"

The woman looked up and smiled as Gwendolyn handed her a plate of toast. "His fever broke earlier this morning. He should be waking soon, I reckon."

The woman nibbled at her toast for several minutes before finally setting it in her lap. The minute her eyes began to droop, Gwendolyn ordered her to go to bed.

"Someone should be in here with you," her aunt said, covering up a grand yawn, "in case he wakes up."

"You don't need to worry about me. Just get yourself in bed. You've been up all night."

Her aunt must have been more tired than she'd thought because she didn't argue at all.

It wasn't until Gwendolyn heard the sounds of children running about the town and carriages passing the house that she noticed James' breathing had changed. She jumped up and pressed her hand against his chest. "James?"

James' eyes rolled about beneath his closed lids before he blinked them open and looked at her.

"Of all the people I thought I'd see in Hell, I never thought the first one I'd see would be you, Gwendolyn."

"You haven't died, James Morrison."

She stroked a lock of bronze hair from his brow then pointed to the dressings on his shoulder. "Uncle has been caring for you. It appears you'll live after all."

"Have you been watching over me all night?" he asked, rubbing his eyes.

"You've been unconscious for nearly two days, James." Gwendolyn busied herself with adjusting the sheets then picked up the cloth resting in the bowl of water, letting it drip dramatically. "Your shoulder became infected and you had a terrible fever. We were afraid you wouldn't make it."

James screwed up his face and looked at her with concern. "You're teasing me?"

"A little," she said casually. "Does it bother you?"

He appeared thoughtful for a moment before slumping back against his pillow. "I suppose I deserve it. Is your sister all right?"

"Robert gave her a good bump on the head, but she'll be fine in a few days."

James grimaced. "Does my father know what happened?"

"He came by earlier yesterday to see how you were doing."

"I don't suppose he was in the best of moods."

"No," Gwendolyn replied, finally breaking a smile. "He wasn't. As I understand it, he gave Uncle a hard time about keeping you here."

"Is it necessary that I stay in this house?"

"It was," she said, sitting at the foot of his bed. "Uncle needed to be close by. He gave you a poultice." She pointed to his shoulder dressings and flinched. "It smelled something awful but it appears to have done the trick."

"It would seem I owe you and Doc Mathewson my deepest gratitude."

"It was the least we could do. You did try to protect me and Rebecca, did you not?"

James turned his head away from her and she wondered if he did it on purpose. "Yes, I did."

Gwendolyn pushed herself from the bed. "James," she said, adopting a more serious tone, "I want to be frank with you."

"Please do."

"I can't figure you out, Mr. Morrison. First, you're smothering me with attention and compliments. Then you're trying to strangle me to death. Then to my utter surprise, you're trying to save my life." She paused to stare at him, thoroughly perplexed but overwhelmingly intrigued. "Please explain to me what is going on. Am I even safe in your company?"

He chuckled, but Gwendolyn could tell it was more out of embarrassment than amusement. "For now you are."

Feeling a good deal braver than she should, she decided to question him further. "Who is Rachel?"

His embarrassment immediately turned to anger and he glowered at her. "How do you know about her? Nobody should know about her!" He heaved his left side up then grimaced.

Gwendolyn jumped up in alarm. "You shouldn't try to move. You'll start bleeding again." After she settled him against the bed once again, she peeled his dressings away just enough to make sure his wound was as it should be.

"Well?"

Deciding honesty was the best way to go about things in their current situation, Gwendolyn replaced his dressings and immediately blushed. "James, I don't remember you at all. The only things I do know about you are that you're persistent, violent, easy to anger, and have rumors going around about you."

"What kind of rumors?"

She looked at him warily, wondering if she should tell him the full extent of what Gregory had told her. Everyone else in town seemed wary about him and had warned her against him. So, assuming it wasn't just Gregory's prejudice, she continued carefully. "I've heard that you've married and that you've ruined another girl's reputation." She dropped her gaze to her lap, feeling incredibly uncomfortable talking about such things in a room alone with a virile but bedridden man. But she had to know. Her curiosity would not let her stay silent while James lay in a bed in her house, completely dependent upon others.

He stayed silent for a long moment, long enough that Gwendolyn thought he wouldn't answer her. Just before she stood to go and fetch some broth for him, he spoke softly.

"I was married," he admitted in a whisper. He turned his head from her once again and let out a deep groan. "I *was* married… once…to Rachel."

Gwendolyn gulped and took up her chair once again. "What happened?"

"What have you heard?"

"I only heard your mumblings when your fever was at its worst," she admitted. "I had assumed you were talking to me before you mentioned having killed someone. Obviously you did not succeed."

James winced and Gwendolyn suddenly regretted having said what she did. "I'm sorry," she said hastily. "I should not have spoken so openly."

"No," he said, sounding as if he'd just heard something utterly painful. With a burst of surprise, she noticed a single tear fall down his cheek and land in his ear. "You have every right to speak so to me. I deserve every word."

"But why did you do it? Why did you strangle me outside the Hall? Gregory told me about our past, but I don't see how—"

"Gwendolyn," he interrupted slowly. "It wasn't your fault. In fact, it had nothing to do with you, I don't think."

"You almost killed me, James!"

"I am not a whole man, Gwendolyn." His eyes stared upward at the ceiling, unfocused as if seeing images through his mind instead. "The woman who lost her reputation became my wife and I loved her more than life itself."

Gwendolyn fiddled with a lock of her hair, not exactly sure how to reply to such an exclamation. She knew he was telling the truth.

"When I found out she was carrying my child, we married right away."

"But why haven't you told anyone? I mean, surely your family would understand."

"She was promised to a man from Clarksville, an arrogant and abusive man she did not love but who had much to offer her and her family. I was delivering a shipment when she approached and asked for my help."

James stopped but Gwendolyn urged him to continue. "What did you do?"

He let out a heavy breath. "I stole her away and hid her in the abandoned cottage up the lane a couple miles out of Grovetown. She thought if she lost her reputation, as you so delicately put it, old Mr. Danby wouldn't want her any longer."

James shifted uncomfortably in the bed and Gwendolyn stood up to help. After getting him settled once again, James continued.

"Gwendolyn, I know I can trust you with the following information. You've always been the kindest and least judgmental person I've ever known. Just talking about it seems to help some."

Gwendolyn blushed at the compliment then steeled herself for what was about to be revealed.

"I went back to the cottage one night after a hard day at work and found Mr. Danby beating on my beautiful Rachel."

Gwendolyn gasped. "How did he find her?"

"He'd been searching all of the neighboring cities and towns for several months and had just happened to come upon her outside of the cottage coming back from the outhouse. When he'd discovered she was with child, his pride would not allow her to go unpunished. She died in my arms that very night."

"No," she groaned in disbelief. What kind of man would beat upon a woman like that, especially one in her condition?

"And what of the baby?"

"Rachel wasn't far enough along. Our baby died too."

"My God," Gwendolyn breathed, turning from James. Her throat burned as she imagined how James must have felt coming home to find his wife beaten to a bloody pulp by the very man she thought she'd escaped from. Gwendolyn would have been overwhelmed with a mixture of emotions—guilt, anger, and emptiness. If she possessed the muscular power of a man like

James and loved Rachel as deeply as he obviously did, there would have been no stopping her from what she wanted to do, which was tear the pompous man to shreds.

"I killed him, Gwendolyn. Left him by the side of the road to rot."

A single tear fell past Gwendolyn's cheek. She could imagine James' heartbreak, the need for vengeance after what Mr. Danby had done. She didn't blame James for his actions. Any man with a heart and mind likely would have done the same thing.

"You do not think badly of me then?"

Her mind wandered to the death of her mother and father and she felt only sympathy for her brother. What was it like to lose those closest to you and never feel completely whole again? Never feel that retribution that came from striking down on those who actually were the cause of your pain?

"No," she said, shaking her head. "I might have done the same thing were I in your position, as frightening as that sounds for me to say it."

James let out a long, steady breath as he closed his eyes. Eventually, he let out a small gust of laughter.

When Gwendolyn felt something brush up against her foot, she started slightly then smiled. Bending over, she picked up Cinnamon and snuggled her close to her neck.

"Her family does not know?" She watched him slowly shake his head then sighed. "I do not think it wise to tell her family yourself since you did go against their orders and basically kidnap their daughter, but you must tell the sheriff. I believe Daniel Jenkins to be a kind and understanding man. You might serve some time in order to appease Mr. Danby's family and the state, but what is that compared to defending your wife and unborn child?" Gwendolyn didn't think he would object to serving more time since he'd obviously survived the last nine days in jail. "You cannot go through life with such anger and bitterness, never having anyone to talk to about your loss."

"But what of my family? They will be devastated once they find out what I've done. I do not wish to disgrace them."

"James, I do not wish to trouble you, but these rumors I mentioned have already been circulated. I'm surprised your family hasn't confronted you about them. How long has it been…since Rachel was killed?"

"Only a few days before you returned."

Gwendolyn nodded in understanding, running her fingers over Cinnamon's soft fur.

"I love you, Gwendolyn. I've always loved you but never the way I loved Rachel. It confuses me sometimes. I want you to know I'm sorry for how I treated you…before. I know I need help."

Gwendolyn leaned over and planted a soft kiss on his forehead. "I will fetch my uncle and something for you to eat."

"When will they be back from their wedding journey?"

Sarah looked up from the dime novel she was reading and smiled mischievously at Marguerite, who was crocheting what looked like a baby blanket. "I haven't heard from Dan either."

She wanted grandchildren every bit as much as Marguerite but had an easier time of hiding it, apparently. To think of it, both girls married by winter. Sarah sighed, grateful their children would be living close by. Their houses would be alive with noise and energy once again.

An impatient knock sounded on the front door and Marguerite went to answer it. The minute she opened the door, Gregory pushed past her to stand in the entry. "Where's Gwendolyn?"

Sarah smiled knowingly. "She left over half an hour ago, Gregory. Why do you ask?"

"I know what you're doing," he said, pointing an accusatory finger at her.

"And just what is that?" she replied casually, warning a troubled-looking Marguerite to keep silent with her eyes.

"You didn't raise me to be an idiot, Mama."

Sarah let out a chuckle. "I should hope not."

"I know you've been secretly laughing behind my back these many days. Susie told me as much. Now, where is she?"

Sarah removed her spectacles and calmly set them upon the lamp table. "She went to the train station in a carriage with that Jamison fellow, I believe."

"What? You just let her go away with him?" he roared.

She shook her head. "Gwendolyn's old enough to make her own decisions, son. I couldn't very well keep her here. Nor could Marguerite. But you'd better hurry. I doubt you'll catch her before they reach the station."

"No, no, no!" Gregory charged out the door and, a second later, could be heard galloping away at a mad pace.

Marguerite closed the door carefully before turning back to Sarah. "Did you have to break it to him quite like that?"

"Of course," Sarah said, returning her spectacles with a smile. "My son has a lesson to learn, my dear Mrs. Mathewson."

Gwendolyn and Robert arrived at the station in Poplar Grove only a few minutes before the stationmaster announced the approximate departure of the train heading to Silas River.

At the platform, Gwendolyn gazed up at Robert uneasily.

"Gwendolyn, you have nothing to worry about," he assured. "I'll make certain of it."

"I'm just afraid of what Mrs. Jenny will think. And what will Mrs. Maynard say?"

"You have the right to make your own decisions. It will be fine." Robert grabbed his bags and boarded the train, handing a man his ticket.

The sound of heavy footsteps quickly approached from behind and Gwendolyn spun around in alarm.

"Gregory!"

Without pause Gregory knelt before her and, to her surprise, lifted her up and hauled her over one hard shoulder.

"You put me down this instant, Gregory Tyler!" she shrieked, kicking her legs and pounding her fists against his sweaty back. "Where on earth are you taking me?"

"Back where you belong."

Ignoring the shouts of the ticket master, as well as those of Mr. Marshall, Gregory hefted her more firmly on his shoulder, knocking all the breath out of her and giving the heavens a clearer view of her rump.

By the time he had descended the platform stairs, her abdomen was sorer than a mule's backside. She couldn't believe the ridiculousness of her situation. Gregory must have thought she was returning to Hopeton with Robert. Honestly, did he really think she would after the promises they had made to each other, after how much she had pledged she loved him?

She stopped fighting against him. There really wasn't a point in her doing so. She wanted to go back to Grovetown. It was her home, after all, and Gregory was much too strong to allow her to do anything but return with him to Grovetown.

She let out a startled gasp as Gregory's hands grabbed her by the stomach. In one quick movement he lifted her from his shoulder and dropped her roughly into the saddle of her wild stallion. "Don't you dare move," he ordered loudly.

Of course, she had no intention of following Gregory's orders. The moment that Gregory left her side to untie the horse, she slid from the saddle and firmly landed on the ground with both feet.

"I told you not to move," he roared, leaping at her. He grabbed her roughly by the shoulders. "I love you, Gwendolyn, and I will not let you go again. Ever."

Before Gwendolyn could utter a single word of explanation, his mouth had fastened upon hers with ravenous energy, sucking all the breath from her lungs. Gwendolyn hung helplessly in his arms as he kissed her, and as romantic as the situation was, Gwendolyn still couldn't breathe. She pushed against his chest—hard.

Gregory pulled back, looking at her as if she'd literally stabbed him through the heart. "Would you dare deny your love for me?"

"Of course not, you fool. You didn't even give me a chance to explain myself." She brushed at her skirts with mock offense.

"Then what is your explanation for leaving with that young man," he said, pointing to the train, "unaccompanied and…and without telling me?"

Gwendolyn rolled her eyes at his last statement. As if he had even been around for her to tell him. After she'd tended to her brother's unconscious and apparently ungrateful self, Gregory had stormed out of the jail in a fit of temper. He'd been missing ever since.

Putting her hands on her hips, she gave her explanation with a good dose of sarcasm. "I was 'accompanying' Mr. Jamison on *his* ride back to the station because I needed him to do me a favor."

"What kind of favor?" Gregory growled.

"Oh, for heaven's sake, Gregory! You don't need to be suspicious of me. I love you and will love you long after the day you die. Why do you still not trust me?"

Gregory ducked his head downward and scowled at her. "Why did you never tell me you had a brother?"

Gwendolyn was surprised by the vehemence in his tone. "Is that why you've been avoiding me these past couple of days?"

Gregory threw his hands up in the air. "Gwendolyn, I can hardly believe our friendship over the years was true when you never bothered to tell me you had a brother…a brother who's been trying to kill you! He nearly succeeded in killing me! And after all he's done, you go to the jailhouse and care for him as if you love him despite everything."

"My aunt and uncle kept his existence from me until two days before the wedding. I didn't tell you about him then because I knew you'd run after him and you were in no shape to do so. You still aren't." Gwendolyn took a step closer to him, putting a hand over her heart to steady her breathing.

"I found some letters from him hidden away in my violoncello case. He threatened me, Gregory. He threatened to kill those I loved if I said anything about him."

Gwendolyn watched as Gregory's shoulders seemed to relax and his eyes turned soft. Thinking it safe to do so, she took another step toward him.

"That's why you left," he said, understanding written over his face and features, "to get away from him?"

Gwendolyn fought her tears at the memory of her brother's hatred. "He blames me for the deaths of our parents, Gregory. Rebecca told me that he gambled away the fortune that was left in our father's business and has been seeking a way to destroy me since the day I was born. He's a sick man, Gregory. Showing kindness was the only thing I could think to do to help him. I didn't know what else to do." She didn't want to tell him about the fortune she stood to inherit once she turned twenty-one. A simple life was all she wanted, away from the loud and smelly cities. She wanted to be with the ones she loved most, to live in a house built by the man she loved, and to understand what it meant to work for a living, even if she didn't have to. "In one way I'm grateful for my accident and memory loss, otherwise I doubt I would have ever returned to Grovetown."

"Oh, Doly," Gregory said, coming toward her slowly. "How much you truly have suffered…and none of us knew a thing about it. You are a strong and infinitely kind woman." He slid his arms around her and she felt safer than she could ever remember.

She buried her face against his chest, breathing deeply of his sweaty lavender smell. "I was only giving Robert directions for the return of my luggage and such."

Gregory pulled back suddenly, looking alarmed. "He's not coming back, is he?"

"You have nothing to worry about, my love." Gwendolyn looked deep into his mysterious blue eyes as he stroked the side of her face.

"You are not in love with him?"

She shook her head, fighting the delirious smile that was about to surface.

"Never be ashamed of this, Doly," he said, wrapping her in his arms and stroking her scar. "Never again, because it's brought you back to me."

Tenderly, Gwendolyn touched both sides of his face and pulled his mouth down to meet hers.

# Epilogue

"GET BACK, YOU BEAST," Gwendolyn said, slapping Gregory's greedy fingers as they rode to a concert. "Can you not wait two hours?"

"No, I cannot," he replied with a chuckle as he thrust his hand against her belly once more. "Right now is the perfect time to feel it kicking since you're so jittery."

Both Dan and Daisy chuckled in unison, gazing at each other with as much love as she'd seen in them the day they were married.

"Go ahead and laugh, Daisy," Gwendolyn teased. "Your little bundle of joy would be kicking too if you were the one playing in front of hundreds of people you didn't know."

"Oh, Gwendolyn," Daisy said, slapping Gwendolyn's knee playfully. "You worry too much. The people of Huntington Square will think you're an angel."

"I second that."

"Oh, you do, do you?" Gwendolyn planted a quick kiss on her husband's mouth before resuming her previously nervous state and posture.

"I thought the exact same thing the day you played for my brother and Daisy. I sat back in complete awe, knowing you to be an angel sent from heaven."

"Oh, you did not."

Gregory nodded. "Oh, yes. I did. Just think what you were thinking when you played this song for Grovetown, whatever that was. Or you can think of your devilishly handsome husband, completely naked and—"

"Gregory!" she shouted in horror.

Gregory and Dan laughed mirthfully while their wives glared at them with equal amounts of disapproval and amusement.

Gwendolyn stood as the concert hall broke out in rapturous applause. There were so many people, she thought in alarm. Before her solo performance, she had ordered herself, with great discipline, not to look out at the audience because she knew she would never be able to get through it without going into labor.

She blushed as Gregory whistled at her from the audience, then stepped out from behind her violoncello as he motioned for her to do so. She would have much rather stayed hidden behind the instrument than show off her pregnant belly. She felt utterly ridiculous, looking like a watermelon in such a beautiful dress. She ruined it completely.

Once the audience settled down, the announcer returned to the podium and Gwendolyn gratefully took her seat on stage.

"We are very pleased to announce, once again, the debut performance of Mrs. Gwendolyn Tyler."

Gwendolyn watched with embarrassed joy as all her loved ones applauded her—the Tylers, the Mathewsons, Rebecca and her fiancé, as well as Robert Jamison, James Morrison, the Jennys, Mrs. Maynard, and even her little redheaded student from Hopeton, Milly Johnson.

"Please come up and say a few words, Mrs. Tyler."

Gwendolyn reluctantly stood and waddled over to the podium.

"Good evening," she said, swallowing the lump that suddenly formed in her throat. Her decision to skip supper had, indeed, been a wise one.

"I would like to thank you all so much for coming. I had not anticipated such a large audience." She laughed nervously. When the audience joined in, she felt her uneasiness subside somewhat.

"I composed this song as a wedding gift to my beloved sister Daisy and her husband Dan, but I had no idea that today I would be here playing it before so many."

She pulled a stray lock of hair from the corner of her mouth before continuing. "My inspiration for this song has been kept a secret…until today." She saw her family lean forward in their seats in anticipation.

"My inspiration came from my husband, Gregory," she said, looking down at him with all the love she possessed. To her utter humiliation, she started crying. "A man who I've loved my entire life but had only just found…a man who came to me in my dreams and saved me from my nightmares…a man who I found through the beauty that is music. Gregory," she said, smiling down at him and wrapping her arms around their unborn child, "you gave me back my song."

She closed her eyes and pulled back from the podium as those in the concert hall applauded her once again.

"Gwendolyn, darling, these peppers are absolutely exquisite," her aunt exclaimed. "And these strawberries," she said, pointing to the dish full of cream, "they are to die for."

Still not entirely used to her family's compliments, Gwendolyn blushed.

Gregory put his hand atop Gwendolyn's thigh beneath the supper table. "Just think, Marguerite, if I hadn't given Gwendolyn her own spot of soil, you might have had to put up with my own pathetic crop for yet another year."

The entire table erupted with laughter.

Gwendolyn thought back to the Jennys' Thanksgiving dinner two years prior and was amazed at how much things had changed.

She and Daisy were both happily married and pregnant, delighted to be in charge of their own homes, and surrounded by friends and family they loved. Mrs. Maynard had recently written to announce the arrival of her first and second grandchild—twin girls born to Samantha and Peter—and oh, what a handful they were. Robert Jamison, who was turning out to be quite the ironsmith, had married Susie Tyler after a long interrogation by Gregory on her behalf. Gwendolyn smiled at the memory.

"Oh, Ma," Susie said, touching her mother's arm. "Have you heard that Simon has taken Cassandra's dresses to Clarksville for an exhibition?"

"That's wonderful. She has such talent, you know. I wouldn't be surprised if Simon came back completely empty-handed."

"What are these?" Daisy asked incredulously, holding a cone made of brown paper with yellow, orange, and red flowers glued inside it.

Gwendolyn snatched it from her cousin's fingers. "Don't laugh. Joscelyn Jenkins made it in class yesterday especially for our table. It's a cornucopia." Joscelyn was only five years old and Gwendolyn absolutely adored her. "And the Adams twins made these doilies."

"They're lovely," her aunt said.

Just as Gwendolyn went to replace the cone in its place on the table, she felt a tremendous pain in her abdomen. She cried, putting a hand on her stomach, and doubled over. A hand immediately touched her shoulder.

"Gwendolyn! Is it the baby? Is it time?"

She nodded, reaching out blindly for Gregory, but he lifted her into his arms and carried her up the Tylers' staircase. "Stay with me, love."

Closing her eyes to the pain, she listened as her uncle hollered out orders for his medical case and other various things.

What seemed only seconds later, she was laid gently upon a bed. "Get James," she said frantically. "I think it may help him."

"But—"

"Please, Gregory," she whined as a small burst of liquid sprang from between her legs.

Gregory scowled at her. "All right. But just remember you're having this baby in my bed," he growled possessively.

Several hours later, Gregory sat on the stairs with his father, James, and Robert Jamison, trying to get the image of his beautiful wife's face contorted in pain from his mind. Not wanting Daisy to go into early labor, Dan had escorted his wife home.

"What have I done to her?" Gregory said, putting his head in his hands. "I've killed her."

He felt a hand on his back and looked up to see James frowning at him with sympathy. He couldn't lose Gwendolyn. She was everything in the world to him.

A minute later, they all jumped as Gwendolyn's screams rent the air. All the blood drained completely from his face.

His bedroom door suddenly opened and Susie spilled out of it.

Gregory stood, grabbing her roughly by the arm as she tried to hop over the men. Her face was frighteningly pale. "Is she all right?" he demanded.

"I don't know."

She ran down the stairs and immediately returned holding a pan of steaming water and a bundle of clean linen.

The minutes rolled by slowly. Gregory listened to Gwendolyn's screams as they grew louder and louder until he knew he could take no more. He needed to be with her.

Jumping up, he stumbled to his bedroom and burst through the door.

"One more, Pinkie," Barrett laughed through his tears as he held his arms out to receive the baby. "We're almost there. Push!"

Gregory teetered back as he saw his child, his very own child, spill out of his wife's body in a bundle of blood and fluid. Barrett swatted the baby's rump and a good strong cry burst from its lungs.

"There's a good boy," Barrett said, cradling the baby in his arms as the women cleaned him.

He had a son! Gregory gasped in astonished relief then went to his wife, holding his breath. "Gwendolyn?" he said, taking her limp hand in his. "Love, it's me."

Her head rolled toward him and her eyes opened slowly to meet his. The look on her face was full of exhaustion but one of pure joy.

Gregory let out a puff of air. "Oh, you're all right."

"Yes, my love. Were you expecting me to die?"

"How can you tease me at a time like this? I've been listening to your screams and not been able to do anything except pace for the last twelve hours! I've never felt so helpless."

"Gregory?" she said, smiling.

He squeezed her hand gently then looked into her eyes. "Yes, Doly?"

"I didn't think it was possible, but I love you more with every passing day."

Gwendolyn unwrapped her infant son from his warm blanket, smiling as he stuck his tongue out at her.

"I named him Douglas," she said, looking at her brother. "After our father. One day, he's going to be just as strong and handsome as his own father."

Robert tentatively reached through his cell bars and touched little Douglas's toes curiously. "Why did you give me some of your money, Gwendolyn?" he asked quietly.

"Why did you take it?" she teased. Their eyes met and she smiled. "I know what it's like to feel all alone in the world, Robert, with no family to love or care for me. When I lost my memory, I was so scared." She looked down at her little boy and laughed. "Now that I've found my family, I couldn't be happier. They are all that matter to me in the world."

"I admire you, Gwendolyn."

"Why ever for?"

Robert turned away from her. "You're such a beautiful person and in love with life. You care for everyone no matter what they've done to you."

"Well, I'm not too fond of Melissa Morrison, actually."

Robert let out a single puff of laughter then tossed a piece of straw from his mattress to the ground.

Gwendolyn smiled at her brother, feeling grateful at last. They had finally made their peace. Her care for him after being shot helped Robert to finally let go of his anger and begin to face his past. And during the months he and James had shared time, they'd shared stories of the loved ones they'd lost and been able to help each other heal. Robert still wasn't a whole man, as James had put it, but he was definitely headed in the right direction.

Holding Douglas close to her bosom, she entered the mercantile to find her husband stocking bags of flour, as he'd done that first day after she'd returned to Grovetown.

Feeling mischievous, she ran her finger through some flour dust. "Gregory?"

He turned around and smiled.

She immediately smeared flour on his nose. "That's for leaving me this morning without kissing me goodbye."

"Oh, you want a goodbye kiss, do you?" he said, looking down at her with a devilish grin. He wrapped his family in his arms and nuzzled Gwendolyn's neck, wiping flour all over her as she squealed with delight.

## Look for Ashley's future titles:

Another novel in the *Western Romance Series*

Marie and Marguerite Bellamont are as different as any twin sisters could possibly be. But when their father dies and their mother's land manager cheats them out of their home and heritage in France, they must use their differences to stay together and stay alive.

With only a few dollars to their name, the Bellamont family travels west in search of new opportunity and land they can call their own. But in only a short time, they realize America is not the land of dreams and hopes they'd imagined. After six years, Marie and Marguerite are destitute and working in a textile factory in Missouri to keep from starving and freezing to death.

But one day, Marie meets a lonely trader named Douglas Mitchell and wonders if he could be the means of their salvation. Will Marie sacrifice her life's happiness to save her family—and herself—from poverty?

Another novel in the *Western Romance Series*

Sixteen-year-old Eloise MacKenna dreams of someday meeting a handsome cowboy who will take her away from her drunkard of a father and the corrupt town in which she lives, and help her build a homestead out west. But all her dreams are suddenly dashed away when her Pa stumbles through the front door in a drunken stupor, saying he's gambled her away to a stranger while playing cards.

And so, to save her Pa from threats of death, Eloise marries Mr. William LeRoy—a man whom she comes to find is an uncouth gunslinger and reputed outlaw. But late that night, when Mr. LeRoy barges into her quarters demanding his husbandly rights, Eloise suddenly realizes she cannot fulfill her father's wishes, no matter the consequences.

Disguising herself as a boy, she escapes to Grovetown—a small farming community—where a handsome farmer named Douglas Tyler offers her work in return for room and board.

But as the months pass by and an attraction to Douglas and the beautiful town escalates, Eloise finds it harder and harder to keep her identity a secret.

# Second Chances

When Alexandra and her best friend Colleen graduate from UCLA, they are sure life can't get any better. Both with good job offers, prospective husbands, and a cruise through the Pacific islands planned, they eagerly plunge into their new lives.

But thousands of miles away from their home, in the heart of Polynesia, an unexpected storm rages, and Allie and Colleen find themselves washed ashore...and miles apart.

Peter Michaels, a marine biologist studying on the small island of Nu'utele, Samoa, has shut himself away from the world after a tragic accident claims the lives of those closest to him. Never had he felt more alone and helpless, until the morning he came upon a woman's body, broken and battered and appearing to have fallen from the sky.

Will Allie be the one to heal his aching heart? And will he be able to let her go?

# Ashley ShaRee HATHAWAY

---

Ashley has been writing novels in her spare time since she was sixteen and absolutely loves it. She feels that there is so much more power and effect in writing a story versus reading it. When she's not writing she enjoys reading, taking pictures, watching good movies, painting, and cooking.

She works full-time as a graphic designer illustrating logos and retouching photos. She also does freelance graphic design and photography on the side. Professionally, her least favorite color is black, as you will notice the word has been completely erased from her literary vocabulary.

Ashley currently lives in Orem, Utah with her supportive and loving husband, Mark Olson.

Ashley would love to hear from you, so send her a message!

**ashareebooks@gmail.com**